LITANIES OF THE LOST STAR

The SOUL OF Chaos

GREGORY WUNDERLIN

Black Rose Writing | Texas

The author grants the final approval for this literary material.

First printing

This is a work of fiction. Names, characters, businesses, places, events, and incidents are either the products of the author's imagination or used in a fictitious manner. Any resemblance to actual persons, living or dead, or actual events is purely coincidental.

ISBN: 978-1-68513-301-6
PUBLISHED BY BLACK ROSE WRITING
www.blackrosewriting.com

Printed in the United States of America
Suggested Retail Price (SRP) $25.95

The Soul of Chaos is printed in Minion Pro

*As a planet-friendly publisher, Black Rose Writing does its best to eliminate unnecessary waste to reduce paper usage and energy costs, while never compromising the reading experience. As a result, the final word count vs. page count may not meet common expectations.

to A
To whom it's not worth it without.

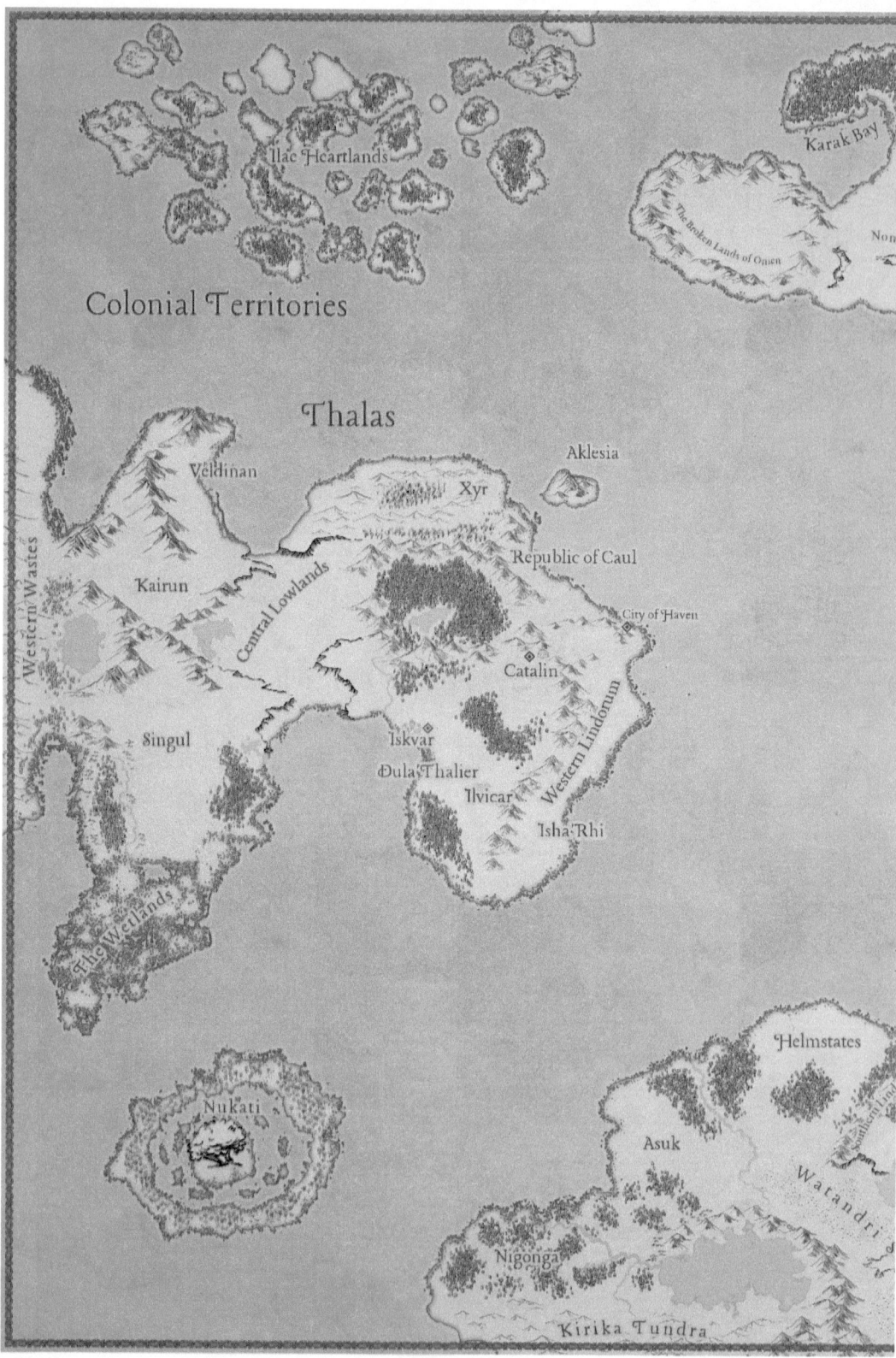

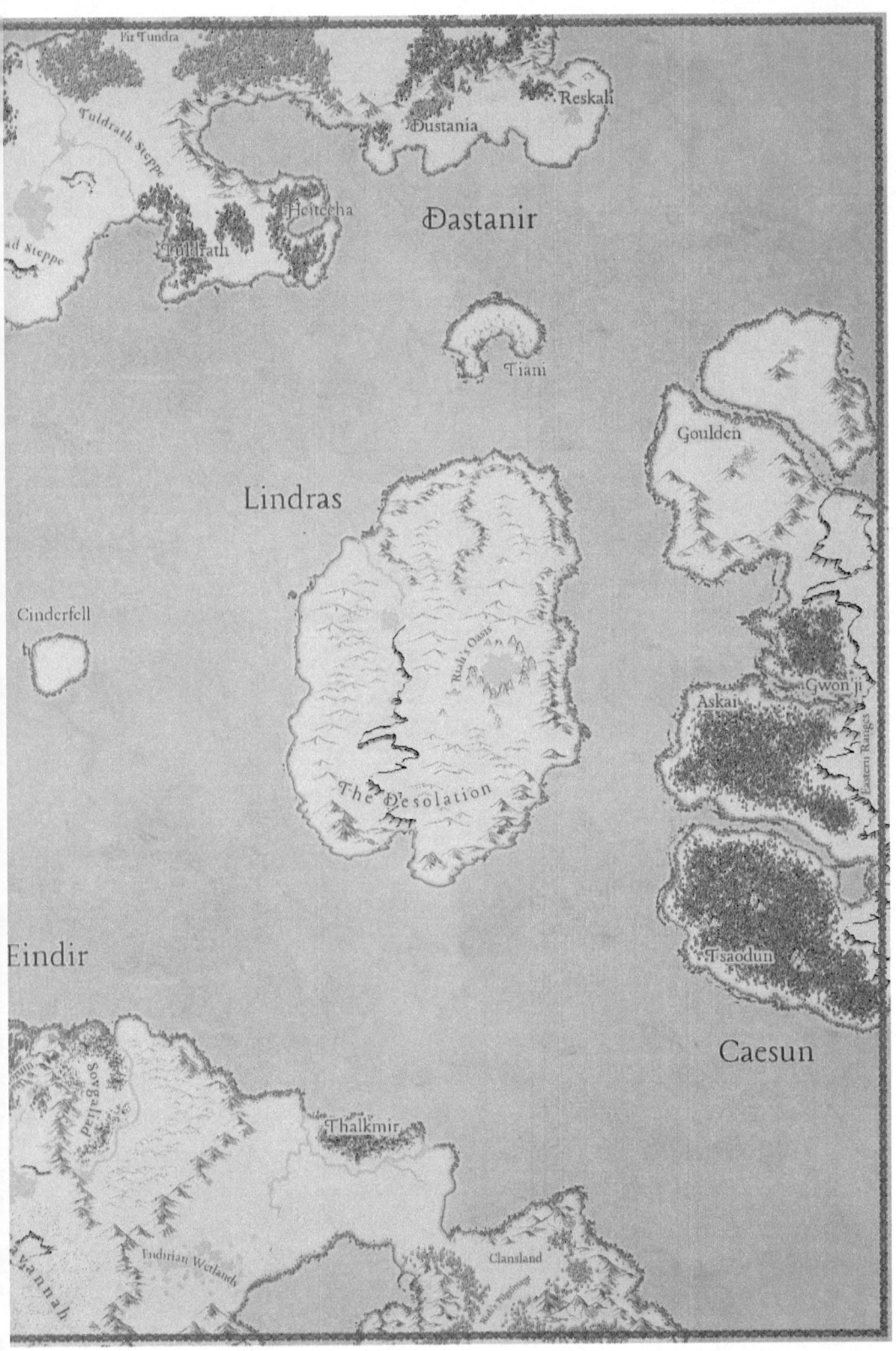

Fir Tundra

Reskali

Ðustania

Tuldrath Steppe

Heitceha

Ðastanir

ad Steppe

Tuldrath

Tiani

Goulden

Lindras

Cinderfell

t

Ruad Oasis

Askai

Gwon'ji

Eastern Ranges

The Desolation

Eindir

Tsaodun

Caesun

Sowgalin

Dengalin

Thalkmir

Clansland

vannah

Endrian Wetlands

The SOUL OF CHAOS

Excerpt from the High Loremaster's Journal

LET US CONSIDER what we know of the Desolation. A thousand years ago, it wiped most of civilization from existence. Turned to ash. Lamentably, our sources are secondhand. Religious texts, interpretations, translations. We must, as scholars, approach our "facts" with skepticism. It is no coincidence that the powers to survive this event are those responsible for its record, and those who police such authenticity to this very day. Can one imagine the implications should even a single thread prove erroneous? We rebuilt this civilization upon the principle of infallibility. Of order.

Woe to the faith, then, that Dula'Thalier was unearthed within the confines of Ilvicar. The dukes will see to its exploitation. And after? What happens to ancient artifacts of power when bestowed on those that value themselves above all others? I fear our grasp of control is more tenuous than we care to admit. Perhaps, then, we could use a little chaos.

Chapter 1
The Breakers

R URIK CURSED as the head of his sledge split down the middle. A solid sheet of rock clattered to his feet from the impact and added to the pile of debris that shaped around decrepit boots; worn leathers coated in black dust. He raised the tool and squinted at the construction, the thin twilight that lit his world a poor illumination. Fantastic. Four candle marks and he found himself at the mercy of a wall. Its obsidian sheen taunted him, a clear, pristine reflection mirrored by the accursed material. In it he glimpsed a sour countenance.

He looked like death.

Rurik lilted back and eyed his companions: a dozen miners clad in black that lost themselves in the persistent beat of metal on stone.

"Sunlord take me," he muttered and brushed his calloused fingers over the band that kept his unruly mop of hair in check. It was cold, drenched in sweat from half a day's labor. He shivered and attempted to wipe the sensation off his bare chest, a mistake that only served to worsen the grime that coated his skin. Rurik sniffed. His eye twitched and he twisted his heel into the ground with a stone scrape. Time for a break.

He separated himself from the line and stalked a short distance off. Behind him, a murmur grew in his absence, whispers of gossip and the occasional laugh beneath the din and disarray of an unyielding symphony of hammers.

"Ya givin' up?" a bald man asked as Rurik approached, his face more beard than skin, scalp wrinkled with age. He sat beside a pile of misshapen hafts, discarded metal implements that Rurik tossed his own sledge into with an unceremonious clatter.

"Tired of getting my ass kicked by a wall." Rurik balked at his own voice; a hoarse tenor weighted with fatigue.

"Aye, ya'd be an expert on tha' by now."

"Oh hah, jackass." Rurik matched a smirk with his own and grabbed a nearby bucket. He dumped the contents over his head: warm, still water that washed that dirt and dust from his hair and face. "We can't all be important enough to sit out the hard part."

"Oi!" the older man, Rust, spat. He grabbed Rurik's discarded sledge and set it on his lap, a flicker of pale green energy emitting from his fingers as he traced the fracture. With his gesture, the wound sealed itself and erased any trace of its existence, though the head seemed smaller now, diminished. "Maybe if any'a ya were as useful as me ya wouldn't need be so jealous."

Rurik shook his head with a snort. He scanned the circular courtyard, its surface the same obsidian sheen of the offending wall, and frowned at the series of empty buckets.

"Where's the rest of the water?"

"Eh?" Rust quirked a thick, bushy brow. "Ya used the last fer yer bath just now."

"Shit."

"Aye."

"I'll ah–yeah. I'll get more. Make sure these idiots stay focused."

The solid-sole beat of Rurik's shuffle accompanied him out into the urban corridor where sheer, black structures lay on the flanks, separated from the sunken road by lipped walkways. A series of metal wire posts lined those sidewalks, each bearing a crystalline sphere at their zenith, all alight with a soft shimmer stolen from what served as a sky in this forsaken place.

Runes danced upon that sky, an intricate web of arcane patterns that pulsed upon a cavernous ceiling of rock. It formed a dome-like half sphere that carved itself from the crust of the world in perfect uniformity. At the center, a single tower ascended to the cavern's height as a shadow upon the horizon. One that soared above a city silhouetted in darkness.

Rurik's green stare lingered too long on that tower. It whispered in the back of his mind. *Try me*, it said, *I am what you seek.*

It was the song that broke his reverie. A haunting dirge spun from a lithe tone. Feminine, it filled the still air of the street, its melody punctuated by the occasional cough or groan. The source, a woman in white robes, her hands and face wrapped in layered bandages, massaged the shoulders of a black clad miner in the last moments of his life. Rurik maneuvered his way through a motley collection of men and women in similar states, some absent the occasional limb while others nursed wounds and rested against one another. They offered nods and grunts of acknowledgement at his passing.

"Six," the woman said as Rurik halted beside her. The accent was thick, attacking vowels with extra emphasis, as if she feared stumbling over their pronunciation. She glanced up, one blue eyed speckled with golden flakes peering out from behind the mess of bandages. "Now, it is. The rest survives. To complaint, but–they live." She swept her hand over the dull glare of the dead man's eyes, closing them for good.

"Six? That's better than I hoped. You sunsingers are worth a hundred surgeons." Rurik took a knee and hoisted the corpse up and over his shoulder. "Could've used you months ago."

"I am no longer a servant of the church," she said.

The two of them rose together. Rurik stood two heads above the woman, her slight frame a stark contrast to the thick, muscular build he cultivated from a one year-too many of beating rocks with hammers.

"And?"

"I." She paused. "I no longer hold such titles."

"Titles tend to stick," Rurik said. "With or without your permission."

With the sunsinger on his heels, Rurik carried the body to a cart laden with its fellows. Two men in long leather coats stood guard nearby; a quiet, ignoble resting place presided over by a pair of malcontents. One stood at attention and brought his fist to his chest, a halberd clanking against the paved street. The other spat.

"At ease, Hal. Save it." Rurik exchanged the corpse for a cask that sloshed in his grip.

"Sorry, Lord."

"See?" Rurik glimpsed the sunsinger who blinked at the sudden attention. "Titles, can't shed the damn things if you try."

"Soldier boy's stuck at Ilduan." The spitting man snickered. Rurik pegged his accent for a lowborn local.

"Better than being stuck with you, Slackjaw." Rurik quipped as the guard spat again. "Charming, soldier. As you were. Come on, Leylia, grab a barrel. The others need you more than the dead."

The trek back seemed longer than his initial approach. They reached the oval-shaped building of the excavation, its massive structure large enough to fill an entire block on its own. It stood separate from the city rows, roads widening to encompass its presence. Paths from every direction fed into its grandiose center where a gilded staircase ascended to a sealed archway, its summit crested by murals and statues of armored warriors in lifelike renders. The figures bore heraldry that matched Leylia's robes: golden sunbursts. A church, maybe? Or a theater. Whatever its use, the builders bragged of riches, and Rurik heard the call of treasure within.

Jovial chatter replaced the relative silence of the line since his departure, a chorus that overcame the ringing assaults as the miners beat fractures into blackened glass.

"It ain't speed that wins." A short, lean woman lectured the men beside her. She picked at her leather gloves and gripped her sledge, lifted it up over her shoulder and brought it down with a resounding force. A small crack split from the impact. "Form! See? Form and precision, can't beat it."

"Su-hure," a nasal-pitched voice quipped in response. Its source, a bronze skinned man, leaned out of formation, his black mop of curly hair bouncing along with his tilted head. "Tell this to Feral. Her strength is of legends. This beats your form, yes?"

A guttural grunt shadowed the sentiment. In the center of the line, a woman stood above the rest. Her arms bristled with thick muscles revealed by a sleeveless tunic too small for her towering form. Elegant dreadlocks fell to her knees; they scurried behind her with each strike, her sledge bigger than the rest by a full length.

"Shut it!" Rust bellowed. He glared at the others, his eyes narrow. "Stop yappin with Sweets, your highness, unless ya like missin' an arm or two."

"That's what we've got you for, Rust! Can't have you miss out on all the fun, sittin' all safe and whatnot." The short woman snorted and set her sledge against the ground. She leaned against the haft and turned, dark curls bobbing with her movement. She opened her mouth to continue the taunt, only to choke as Rurik set both water casks down opposite the metal pile.

"Boss! You're back. With the ah–the leper. Hi!" She waved, smiling, untouched by the momentary embarrassment. Rust sniffed. He stroked his grizzled beard and offered Rurik a curt nod.

"Oh no, don't mind me, Princess," Rurik snarked. "I love making Lanatir pay out death salaries."

"Ah, yeah." Princess shifted and scratched at her temple. "How many we lose?"

"Six."

"Really? Only?"

"You can thank the leper."

Leylia stood impassive beside Rurik, her hands folded in front of her waist. She emitted a strange, infectious aura of peace, one that drew more than a few uneasy stares from the crew.

Sweets chimed in, unconcerned with the reprimand. "Leper is no good. She needs a new name, yes? Melody is best choice, so says Shari, Sentinel of Wisdom."

"Obvious. Stupid," Feral grunted. Some of the others in the line laughed at the primal sting from her broken speech.

"You wound me, sweet one," Sweets lamented.

Another bout of laughter echoed from the crew, followed by a tirade of insults. Rurik cracked a grin and folded his arms up under his chest, watching.

"Why do they give me a new name?" Leylia canted her chin up with a whisper. "Is my language offensive?"

"Nothing like that. It's easier for breakers to not know each other."

"Easier?"

"Easier to forget a nickname than the real thing."

Leylia nodded, somber, though her next words fell flat on Rurik's ears. Something shifted his attention to the breakers, the hair on the back of his standing on edge. Sweets and Princess bantered back and forth, eliciting the occasional chuckle as the others lost themselves in the rhythm of the line. Lift, swing, crash. Lower, repeat. There, in the center of the wall, Feral hit another fracture. A pebble fell from the impact.

She broke through.

Rurik's eyes widened. He grabbed Leylia's collar and hurled her at Rust who scrambled to catch her.

"Break!" Rurik screamed.

Time slowed.

The laughter died and the crew scattered. From the minuscule hole, a violent, red energy sprung to life. A series of jagged runes appeared as snaking arcane projections across the wall's exterior. Men and women bolted. They clawed over one another and fought to the front of the exodus as the energy expanded behind them into a shimmering orb of unstable energy. It stabilized as a coherent half-sphere, holding its shape for a few blissful seconds before it retracted, disappearing into a silent void.

And then, nothing. The air itself died as all sound succumbed to a breathless vacuum.

Rurik leapt forward. He wrapped his arms around whoever he could and dragged them onto the ground, his body offered in place of theirs.

A geyser of flame erupted in a flash. It lapped at the crew's backs and engulfed half their number in a raging firestorm, their muffled cries lost to a chaotic ruckus. The shockwave sent others flying. Breakers leapt aside. Some landed with sickening snaps and others collided with chunks of debris, pieces of jagged glass impaling stone and flesh alike. The violent roar howled into the cavernous night, its harrowing cry a thunderous force that caught a section of runes from the ceiling. They burst at the disturbance, small pockets of frantic energy that tossed sparks of insult onto the scene, wafting fireflies of orange and blue that ashed as they fell.

Moans of agony rose in a wailing echo. Rurik opened his eyes to a haze of cinders mixed with a thick cloud of dust. Black soot stained his vision as he locked gazes with Princess, her green stare alight with fear. He rolled over and felt up the legs of his baggy pants to his crotch. Still there.

"You okay?" he asked.

"Yeah. I think." Princess felt herself up in a similar fashion. Her blouse held some frayed edges, but otherwise showed little wear. "Better than him." Rurik followed her gesture to where a black husk of a corpse lay with its arms and legs curled into itself. Wonderful.

"Sound off." Rurik rose to a knee and wiped the stinging soot from his eyes with a bare arm.

"Princess." She offered a thumbs up and coughed, sitting with her head between her legs. Feral stomped twice.

"Rust."

"Sweets," the nasal voice spoke into a hack.

"Jerk." Another voice, this one annoyed and haughty despite the situation.

Rurik waited. No one else joined the routine. He hoisted himself up, brushed his shoulders off and tousled his hair, the edges now frayed and burnt.

"Leylia? You with us?"

"She's fine, Rik, just shocked." Rust chuckled. "First breakin', eh?"

"Get her up and working. When she's ready, get the others moving, we'll need them to haul. The rest of you grab your supplies and fall in on me. The Diviners will see the break."

•   •   •

The pale emanation of a glowlamp illuminated the structure's interior; an immense foyer supported by a series of decorated columns. Rurik held the metal stick aloft, its lantern left to dangle from a short chain as its light flickered off crystal-mirror surfaces lining the walls. They reflected the glow in an intricate system of recycled energy.

He stepped onto a floor of smooth marble and inched inside, his head on a swivel, eyes wide, caught between a state of alert and awe. Though their inglorious entry marred the splendor of the endless gold and silver motifs, little of the debris made it inward, dedicated to the harm of his crew more so than risking further property damage.

A whistle echoed within the vast interior. Rurik glanced at Princess. She shrugged. The ragged group piled into the opening, Rurik in front, all armed with a sole lamp. From the rear, Feral sniffed and swatted at the air.

"Bad smell. Dark," she snarled.

"Aye, sweet one, this place sleeps for a thousand solstices. Piqua knows." Sweets smoothed out his black tunic, ill at ease.

"No," Feral whispered. "Dark. Violent."

Rurik held up a fist. The group halted. To the far sides of the hall two arches swept deeper into the building and flanked a raised landing of white stone. Before it stood a massive statue; a towering figure of obsidian, its arm raised in protest, a shield held off its side as if erected in defense.

"We need to split up," Rurik said.

"Sayeth the dead men." Jerk pinched the bridge of his hawkish nose and sighed through his nostrils.

"We've got too many wounded, Jerk, and no time. Feral, Princess, you take the left corridor."

"What's a corr-eh-dohr?" Princess asked.

"Hallway."

"Yep." She kicked at the tile.

"Sweets, Jerk, the right." Rurik pointed at Jerk. "Don't." The dark-skinned man bit his tongue with his mouth open. "I'll check out the landing."

"Alone, boss?" Princess skipped backward. Her thick brow lifted, the edges singed from the explosion. She looked well otherwise, shoulders straight and somehow peppy, though Rurik's gaze lingered on the gold-inked tattoos that spiraled down her forehead to her neck and disappeared into her blouse. "Boss?"

"Yes." Rurik itched at the stubble on his chin and blushed. He extended a thumbs up. "Faster that way."

Princess opened her mouth to speak, but paused at a grunt from her savage partner. A shrug followed, and she twirled away in a quiet scamper. Once the others grew scant, his shoulders slouched. A sharp inhale filled the empty hall as he pressed a palm to his forehead and bit back a scream.

"You're fine, Rik," he mumbled and adjusted the collar of his leather coat. "Easy now." Another breath. Easy.

A cloud of dust wafted up from the first stair at his ascent. Dust was good, no runes or other arcane monstrosity. He mimed a silent prayer by holding his palm to his face, fingers spread apart before closing to a fist, though he doubted a sunburst would be of much use this deep below the surface.

Rurik topped the landing to find a set of stone doors that blocked his passage. Lines of diamonds were woven into the gilded surface with regal, robed figures engraved around them. A dull clink followed as he struck a gem with a steel dagger removed from his belt. No dice. He licked his lips and, enticed by the challenge of wealth, he placed the tip around the back of the diamond and tapped a fist to the pommel and it popped off the door into his hand. Hah! One of these could feed his crew for a week. And all of them?

The ground shook. The landing rumbled and Rurik spun on a heel to find the statue's lifelike face canted in his direction. He stared. The statue stared. Neither moved. Rurik raised a hand and waved. Nothing. Okay. Rurik sheathed his dagger.

Forward, then. He grasped a hold of a golden handle–meant for far larger hands than his own–and peered over a shoulder. Nothing. Good. Rurik tugged to no result. He rolled his eyes and placed a hand under the other and pulled again. Nothing.

Rurik shoved his boots into the floor and strained, his teeth clenched as his muscles bulged. He exhaled and set foot on the opposing door, stretched out his fingers and gripped the handle once again. Another heave. A vein bulged from his neck and his face grew pale.

"Voided door. Open!"

The landing rattled and Rurik groaned. The cumbersome hunk of obsidian statue moved of its own volition, its body facing him as it extended an arm. Something akin to a curse escaped his lips as he leapt aside, crashing to the solid floor with a skirting thud. Its motion passed over him and it grasped the handle, pulling once to a shutter and a cloud of dust. A second pull elicited a whining creek from rusted joints as the door popped open. Without further fanfare, the statue receded its hold and returned to its original poise, still and stiff.

Rurik watched, rapt with awe. He stumbled to his feet and brushed out the tail of his coat, bemused and bruised. Stone did not mix well with bones.

"Thanks?"

The statue did not respond.

Crisp air assailed him as he slipped through the threshold, ajar enough for at least three abreast. He wrinkled his nose and advanced, cautious, a nearby splashing encouraging curiosity. The same crystalline strip filled the expanse with ambient lighting and parted only for more grand architecture, an interior waterfall, one of clear water that fell from a ledge into a pool raised from the ground, its edges surrounded by a lush garden.

Rurik's eyebrows lifted. He swung his lamp ahead and wandered marble-hewn paths amidst a host of creeping, wild foliage. Crystal glass adorned the ceiling where once blessed light poured in from a clear sky. Only rock lay above now. Rock and cursed runes. His shoulders tightened, his calm harshed by the reminder of his predicament.

The path brought him through figs and apples and plums that hung from short trees, with squash and tomatoes growing in carefully constructed sections of soil somehow intermingled with the floor. Red and purple roses sweetened the air, even, arranged with lilies and white blossoms that infused the hall with color. All this underground. And alive.

The realization darkened his countenance. Thousands of years of lost knowledge manifested in a simple garden. The depth of power contained here sent his thoughts spiraling. Growhouses, he knew, but without caretakers? Never mind the autonomous statue. His stomach churned at the potential. All this wonder and they spent their time seeking tools and trinkets.

Rurik found himself at the back of the waterfall, where a large obsidian arch lay at the end of his trek, two passages obscured beyond. Etched with foreign script, it rendered complex symbols; layered and jagged lines that crossed one another in sharp patterns. More foul magic. Rurik fished out a silver coin from a belt pouch and tilted his head. He stood six, seven spans away. He backed up. One, two, four steps, then set his lamp on the ground.

What a terrible idea. Rurik inhaled and whipped the coin at the arch. Without delay he threw his hands over his head and dove into the fountain where a sudden wet chill forced the air from his lungs, eyes opening in shock. His entire body submerged into the pool, its depths without a visible end. He thanked his luck and tread below for a moment too long until his lungs begged for release. He broke the surface with a gasp and searched for the assumed devastation.

Or not.

No explosion. No debris or terrible ruins. His coin sat under the arch, unblemished.

Rurik grunted and climbed out from the pool, his shame dripping from his sopping clothes with a staccato pitter. He collected his lamp and slopped his way over to the archway, wet footprints in his wake. He dipped low and scooped up his coin, kissed the front, then examined the runes one last time. They held their own glow, one of a gentle make, the light akin to his lamp. No heat, no obvious demise.

Distracted by the wonder of the room, Rurik failed to notice the inky blackness within the arch. He shivered. Whether from the cold or stray magic, he didn't know. Curious, he dipped the end of his lamp into the darkness, wiggled it, then pulled it back to no effect. A veil, maybe an illusion? Everything here pointed to voidwork. Vile, terrible power from a realm beyond his own.

That matched the tales. Why he spent his days toiling in some cursed, eternal night. To recover what the Void stole. Though more than his sacred duty as a worshiper of the sun, Rurik's loyalty lay with his crew. If a diamond could feed his people for a week, then whatever lay ahead may be what paid the price of their freedom. His freedom.

"May the Sunlord guide me."

Rurik disappeared into the darkness.

Personal Log, 1.02.0275 CE

T HE PRISON IS BRUTAL. Primitive. Barbaric? But it works. The others aren't happy with the inelegant design, but Kal and I agree that "elegant" won't matter much if the cell isn't strong enough. Theory is simple enough. Any kinetic force acts as a trigger that mimics a rapid, exothermic chemical reaction. I've enhanced the velocity formula to use any excess energy and funnel that into the resulting shockwave. In short? You touch, you explode. With a proper battery, the runes will regenerate, though they'll have less effect over a wider area. They're picky. Steel and stone work best. That limits where we can build the cage. I can solve that with the right projection equations.

Chapter 2
Gamble

S HADOWS DANCED within a field of fog. Some sprouted countless limbs, others held their shape for only moments while bodies merged and split. The haze bristled with illumination, soft and ambient as its form shifted from mountains to forests to lakes, its scents morphing with each whim. A sweet sea breeze carried the salt from the ocean to his nostrils only to sweep back on itself and transform into the chilled air of a tundra.

Amidst the chaos, a dull tactile thrum buzzed and overpowered his senses. It expanded, hummed louder, then retracted to silence. All at once, the shadows turned their attention above.

A tendril of darkness pierced the veil.

Rurik opened his eyes as a bead of sweat ran down his wrinkled forehead to his stubbled cheeks. A vision? He grasped at the imagery as it fled from his consciousness. He saw–no. Rurik's brow narrowed. He remembered. He pressed a thumb to his temple and a sigh escaped his lips. The memory faded to a dull memento, then to nothing.

Rurik ran his fingers through his mess of black hair. Why was he so upset? Portal. Right. From a mystical garden to another place entirely, before him lay an octagonal room with another crystalline strip. Shelves lined the walls, filled to the brim with thick, leather-bound tomes. Hundreds, if not thousands, stretched to the tapered ceiling.

"Hello?" Rurik spoke to nothing. He stepped out from under another arch to the doorless, windowless room.

The Loremasters would pay a baron's ransom for a single shelf from this place. This library? Either way, the silver he'd reap could bribe a way out of this forsaken ruin. He leaned in closer to read. Gibberish.

What did he expect? Cavari bore connected lettering with fluid script, and these were singular, separate notations. Lines that ran perpendicular and parallel to each other to form layered shapes, some crossed, others not, recognizable patterns that just as quickly violated their own rules. Same as the runes.

Rurik paced in a circle. He glanced at tomes in passing, unable to read a single word. Did it matter? Nobles paid for privilege and status. A treatise on felines and their types of mewling impressed as much as a tome of arcane proficiency.

His meandering led to the stout mahogany desk in the center of the room. As if practiced, he pulled out a lacquered chair and sat with a scuffle. Comfortable. Familiar? Ashes and dust lay upon the surface among a collection of open tomes, their lettering illegible. Maybe the Loremasters knew enough Thalian to sort out the important bits.

Excited, he slammed a fist into the wood with a hollow thunk, into an existing indentation. Hollow? Rurik pushed the chair back with a scrape. His fingers found a drawer with little effort and slid it free. From within, he liberated a thin obsidian slate and a silver ring with an embedded sapphire. He licked his lips and held the jewelry up to his eyes. Expensive. He pocketed the ring and palmed the slate, wiping the surface clean with a fingerless-gloved hand.

Symbols appeared on its surface. Blue lines raced across the glass-like display as three distinct and simplistic runes pulsed, the background jet black, with a burst of occasional static that interrupted its smooth interface.

The word popped into his mind. Interface. Foreign, odd. He reached for its definition. Nothing. First the portal, now this thing. Yet. This thing is what he sought. A powered artifact. Forget the books. An army would fork over their combined arsenal for something like this. He grinned, wide, and tapped the surface in his reverie.

The display shuttered. Lines scattered and more complex script flashed across the top in full sentences. Rurik glanced at the slate's side. No pages, no bindings. Did it respond to his touch? He pressed a finger against one of the text strings.

> Lindorum pushed our forces back from the coast. Reinforcements from Lindras? The Consul is upset that we stole the entity, as she should be. It looks more human every day, and I swore it spoke to me. Or tried to. I've finished calibrating the lance to its unique signature. It should be more than enough to beat the new casters back, but I've begun to doubt this plan. Are we responsible enough for this kind of power? Am I?

Rurik's eyes widened. He read the script as it appeared on the slate. He scanned the page again, and a third time. The symbols made no sense, but the meaning appeared in his mind nonetheless. Perhaps it translated itself? Thalian technology did stranger things. He tapped the last string.

> We did it. We crossed the line. Sunmother, Mithiren. An entire country burnt to ashes. I could see the pillars of light from atop the Beacon. Power like that is reserved for the mother alone, but we stole it. The entity, the lance. All of it is beyond us. Adirian hailed it as a victory. A victory against what? One Emissary gone for how many thousands? Salivar and Lynesse backed his play. Mother, forgive me. I cannot let them do it again.

Rurik leaned back in the chair. His fingers drummed against the table while he examined the passage. He stared at the thousand-year-old slate, his lips pursed to the side and one eye narrow. The author used ancestral heroes as individuals. People Cavari traced their lineages from, heroes. Do what again? What was Mithiren? Rurik exhaled then swiped his fingers over the surface, wiping it clear. He snatched the slate and slipped around the desk, crossing under the arch without a second thought.

●   ●   ●

The cold damp of his clothes met the chilled air of the gardens in a reminder of his idiocy as he stepped out from the arch.

"Boss!" Sweets popped his head around the fountain. "Vari's luck! You live!" The shorter, wiry man jogged over, his lamp jostling with the excess motion.

"Is Vari that impatient?" Rurik met the anxiety with a raised brow. "I've been gone, what? Twenty ticks? Thirty at most."

"Ticks? We wait for almost a candle to nothing."

"A what?" Rurik interrupted, gesturing toward the arch. "Shit, you won't believe what's back there I–" he paused. The runes dulled and the portal vanished, leaving a gap that only led deeper into the hall.

"You feel well? And ah, why are you wet?"

"No." Rurik's boots sloshed against the marble tile. "I am definitely not well. Let's go."

"Wait!" Sweets grabbed his shoulder. "There are many soldiers. Rust speaks with excuses, but Shari says this will not last."

Rurik rubbed his forehead between his thumb and forefinger. A whole candle? Even with the time lapse they covered their tracks. It took two candles to cross the city outskirts.

"What heraldry?"

"Eh?"

"Their pins, who are they with?"

"Adirian. This is bad, yes?"

Rurik cursed. "You may want to ask Vari for more help."

●   ●   ●

Outside, the remains of the crew gathered around their break. Rubble and debris lay strewn about the courtyard, large blocks of stone blackened by the intrusion. Rust stood opposite a tall woman in a red and black belted tunic, saber belted to her waist with half a golden cape slung over a shoulder.

Across from the leathery-skinned shaper she glistened like royalty. Two lines of ten guardsmen stood nearby, their red leather frock coats hiding a suit of brigandine. They wielded halberds and four in the rear carried long barreled firearms. Arquebuses.

While Rust staved off the inquiries Feral shielded most of the crew, a sledge in each hand while Princess kept a palm on the much larger woman's thigh, her own hammer braced on her shoulder. The other three men able to stand formed a protective circle around Leylia; Jerk, Hal, and Slackjaw, their shoulders tensed.

"Found him!" Sweets waved, an anxious smile plastered on his bronzed face. Rust's shoulders rolled with a relieved sigh.

"What the shit is this?!" Rurik adopted his best foreman's tone with an irritable roar. He pushed his way in, and Sweets absconded to Feral, lamp in hand. Rust turned and Rurik shoved the slate into the shaper's arms and pushed him back. "Who in the void brought armed men to my site?"

The woman lifted her chin. Shorter than Rurik, she fit a northern appearance: blonde hair and pale skin, an utter contrast to his darker features. She flicked her gaze over him with a scoff and adjusted the heraldry pin on her breast, calling attention to the house: An -A curved to the left with two diagonal slashes at the stems within a ring of fire. House Adirian.

"Calm, foreman." She sneered. "The Diviners sent us. They scryed an unauthorized break." She spoke with a highborn accent.

"Unauthorized?" Rurik threw his hands into the air. "Unauthorized my left testicle! Baron Lanatir cleared this section for a crew three rotations ago!"

The guardsmen shifted. Rurik looked to the motion beyond them. His wounded breakers peered from down the street, those without life-changing wounds clutching their worn sledgehammers tighter at the exchange. The gunners would have their way before the lot of them became a problem.

The woman canted her head. "Baron Lanatir? That would make you Foreman Iskarion." Her lips curled into a sardonic smile and Rurik straightened his back. "You know how this goes, *my lord*. I'm honor bound to leave you alive, but your crew is in violation of Cavari Law. And, as I imagine none are citizens?" She surveyed the defensive crew. Feral bared her teeth and growled in the back of her throat.

"Enough, Captain. We can't fight you, so what do you want?" Rurik conceded.

"Your man stalled for you well. I imagine it's because you found something. Such a venture should bring quite the haul for my lady."

Rurik bit back a curse. Her lady. Memories of screams plagued the edge of his mind, terrified wailing, and shrill, tormenting laughter. He offered the woman a tight-lipped smile and glimpsed over his shoulder. Leylia bowed her head in prayer while Slackjaw and Hal, their halberds brought to bear, matched the enthusiasm of the guards.

The rest held sledges aloft and ready. Brave, but against trained killers? Rust gave the man a curt nod and pressed the slate to his side. They were ready to die. For him.

"You got me." Rurik lowered his lamp and produced the pilfered diamond. He tossed it to the captain, and she snatched it out of the air, squinting. "There's a host of them inside. And more. Whole voided building is a treasure trove, but there's some peripheral runes in the deeper halls. You let us finish our job and you take half, deal?"

"Three to every four." The captain lingered on the gem. She licked her lips.

"Half."

"What makes you think you can negotiate?"

"You going to risk a break? I'm sure your men wouldn't mind. If the Diviners know about us, how long before the rest of the foremen show up? You can't kill us without losing. . ." He pointed at the diamond. ". . .all those."

"Fair point. Two-to-three, and consider my patience, *lord*."

"If you think–" Rurik paused and put on his best scowl. "Fine, but we'll need your men to help us haul. Most of my crew is wounded."

The captain smiled. She held her arm up in a sunburst then bowed, her arm extended toward the breach. Rurik surveyed the crew. Most of them slouched now with their sledges lowered. Rust bowed his head. Princess rolled her shoulders, her chest heaving with the motion. Leylia, upright, searched for his gaze. Rurik winked.

"You heard it," he rumbled in that cumbersome, commanding tone. "In you go, you louts. Or do you think you can take a guard line with hammers?"

Together the crew and guardsmen filed into the grandiose hall with Rurik in the lead. Somehow, the crystalline illumination persisted from the original break, guiding the ragtag mix to the base of the statue. As the soldiers distracted themselves with awestruck examinations Rurik split his people into two groups.

"Rik, there's nothing left to break, what're we gonna do when they realize they don't need us?" Princess whispered. Rurik made a fuss of random gestures of mock shorthand.

"I have an idea." He nodded at Rust and pointed to Leylia. The shaper wrapped his arm around the sunsinger's shoulders. "No, I don't know if it will work, but we get one shot to take them down. Now." He raised his voice for the woman and guardsmen to hear. "Get a move on! Send a runner once you breach."

Princess pursed her lips. She fluffed up her black curls and started toward the western exit without so much as a fuss. Sweets, Feral, and Hal followed her while the others took the eastern corridor. The captain, finished with her inspection, raised her hand into the air and snapped.

"And what's up there?"

"Your dreams," Rurik snarked and climbed the stairs. The two of them, escorted by four guardsmen, ascended. He gestured at the massive set of closed double doors. Closed? Of course they were.

"The diamonds pop right out. You can use a pike to get the top few," he said with a shrug. "Your knife."

"You think I'm a fool?" The captain waved him forward. One of the guardsmen prodded him in the back, the light tip of his halberd pinching his skin beneath his coat.

"No, just an ass." Rurik unsheathed his dagger and stepped up to the doors. He inhaled and slid the tip of the blade behind a gem, coaxing it out with a deft hand. He snatched it mid-drop then tossed it to the captain.

"You know," she started. "Two to three seems generous." She turned the gem over in her hand, eyes alight. "Perhaps I should make–"

The landing shook. The armored statue reared its head. Below someone shouted an alarm. The Adirians turned to stare. The statue stared. Rurik pointed at the captain.

"She took it!"

The statue's joints groaned as the colossal stonework lowered its fist and faced the ledge. A clarion ring of steel left the sheath at the captain's side, but she stood stiff as the arm of the colossus swung across the landing and grabbed her by the leg, plucking her into the air. The captain screamed and dangled, her saber waved to little effect as her escort thrust at solid stone, their weapons deflected aside, useless. A sickening, wet thud resounded outward as the statue flung the captain against its shield.

Satisfied, the colossus tossed the now limp body of the woman away. Rurik blinked. The soldiers backed away, faces contorted in horror. Now.

Rurik lunged at one of the guards and thrust his long knife through the back of his neck. The man dropped his weapon and grasped at his throat, choking on his own blood. He fell.

One.

Another soldier cursed and rounded on the foreman, her halberd brought to bear. Rurik twisted. The blade pierced his coat but missed anything vital as he responded by grasping the haft and yanked, liberating the weapon for himself. A sick crack sent the soldier into a spiral as the blunt end found the side of her head.

Two.

Rurik spun and squared up to face the others as the statue swept across the landing. The sheer force sent the remaining guards sailing skyward, their bodies breaking against the walls.

A set of jagged runes appeared at their impact. Rurik's eyes widened. Volatile, red energy sparked from the symbols. They sputtered into tendrils that interlocked with one another until they formed a half sphere that contracted to the surface of the stone. In an instant the runes faded.

Sledges held a precise point of contact. Focused. The force mimicked that, Rurik knew, and returned fire as a mirror. Torsos were not precise.

The runes exploded.

Flames surged from the wall. The force collided with several columns, and they burst outward, expelling debris as shrapnel. Guards screamed; others dove for cover. Rurik's eyes widened as loose stones sailed into the opposing walls.

More runes formed at impact in one-too-many places. A voice called for retreat but did little against the detonations. They ignited in sequence. Fire enveloped the room as another column erupted. More debris. More impacts. Rurik's jaw dropped. He spun and ran to the door, weaving his pilfered halberd through the handle where he gripped both ends. He pulled to no effect.

A stone fell from the ceiling where a column once held the roof intact. Rurik groaned and strained his muscles. He pulled with whitened knuckles, sweat running down his cheeks. Still, nothing. *The statue.* Rurik opened his mouth to speak and watched a jet of flame wash over the construct. Another explosion followed and blew half of the obsidian body to pieces. Clever too late. Another stone fell, this one covered in tile. A small rune formed where it broke apart and spouted a gout of flame.

"What did you do?!"

An irritated soprano pierced the stream of chaos. Rurik glanced over his shoulder as Feral and Princess ran up the stairs.

"Not now! Help me open this!"

"We need to go, Rik!"

"Shut up, Princess! Help me!"

A thicker, calloused hand grabbed the haft next to Rurik's. Feral grunted. She stomped. They pulled. The door opened to a crack. They pulled again. A groan of rusted joints gave way to an opening wide enough to squeeze through. Princess ducked in first then he pushed Feral after. She turned sideways and scurried through the passage.

Rurik paused at the devastation. The columns near their breach collapsed, breaking as the roof fell. Red runes formed over the mass of debris as it collided with the floor.

"Run!" he bellowed.

Rurik pulled himself into the opening and took off after the other two. Feral and Princess hightailed it beyond the pool with Rurik on their trail. He prayed to the Sunlord that the doors held. To all of his incarnations. To the Mother.

The Mother? Rurik stiffened. An armored figure appeared in his vision, a woman clad in the robust designs in the city's motifs. Golden plates hugged the entity's form, and a silken red cape draped from a collar of black fur about her shoulders. She wore an angular helmet with a solid plate where the face should be, her arms held out toward the doors, flashes of sapphire fire flaring from an extended ring.

The ring!

Rurik ripped his pouch off his belt and retrieved the silver band. In a flurry he slipped it onto a finger and thrust his hands out. His ears popped to deafening silence. No rushing water, no thunderous explosions. The gilded doors flew from their hinges and into the garden followed by the maw of a wicked flame. His body rose off the ground and raced backward with a resounding splash.

The world went black.

Excerpt from the high Loremaster's Journal

WHILE THE DUKES and Duchesses of Ilvicar consider themselves to be representative in a feudal sort of way, they tend toward monarchist overtones. The hierarchy is simplistic. Knights pledge to barons, barons pledge to dukes (dukes keep knights of their own, often regaling them with fancier titles to impress their higher station), and anyone of the equivalent rank participates on a noble's council. Within their realm of influence, of course.

Such begins my fascination with ducal heirs. Above any station other than their parentage, nothing is quite expected of an heir except for their eventual succession of power. The first born, of course, inherits all, while the siblings are assumed to support the house in some way. With this lack of direction and excess of resources it creates a unique scenario of study. Motivation. What does one become should they want for nothing?

Chapter 3
Boots

A RAY OF SUNLIGHT crept through a glass screen. Within its path a woman stood with her arms crossed over her chest, her long, auburn hair groomed to the whims of sleep; a mess of bangs set above tired eyes. The chill of the stone floor crept up her bare feet with a shiver.

She threw open the paired set of glass doors and stepped onto a balcony to meet the emerging sun–a sliver of yellow visible upon a sphere wreathed in shadow–chasing away the black of night with a red hewn sky. Her gaze fell westward where the dawn caught the water, glints of color shifted by easy morning zephyrs.

From the courtyard below squeaking cartwheels tumbled over cobbled pathways while a persistent clank of iron echoed against the sloped walls of the castle compound. Vibrant greenery caught the sounds and muffled them for the late sleepers. Trimmed hedges and floral gardens encompassed a glistening glade in the center of the grounds, filled with grand oaks that rustled in the gentle winds.

Those guardsmen that patrolled wore red coats and spent more time looking inward than out, a case no more obvious than the two that gawked at the woman's naked body. She stared back, jaw set, and one man punched the other. They resumed their lazy patrol.

Enough light peeked from the darkness now to inspire more locals to leave the safety of the keep. Kali lingered until whispers buzzed in her ears. She sighed and swatted the sound away, retreating to her chambers.

An idle lump in her bed snored softly. He cuddled an empty bottle of wine against his bare chest with another, or three, scattered about. Kali tilted her head to get a better view. Boyish, and clean shaven with broad shoulders. She grimaced and slapped her forehead with her palm, muttering some kind of curse.

Silk garments lay scattered in no particular order from the night previous, some draped over the fine couch and chairs, others splayed out over an ancient wardrobe. Her gaze swept over her own body. Thick arms, legs, and hips, an ancestral "gift" of her house, though she paid more mind to the fresh bruises on her biceps. Her memory of the previous night ended at dusk. That explained the dull ache in her head.

A wooden knock filled the spacious suite.

"Not decent!" Kali's tired alto followed. The man in her bed stirred with a startled snore-snort.

The door flung open as a man in a more-gray-than-white robe strolled in. His ensemble bore a number of golden sun motifs, all rendered with a lidless eye. The specimen himself looked worse for wear. An age weathered countenance scored with endless wrinkles on dark skin and a short crop of wispy gray hair bespoke a sort of presence to him, albeit clean shaven he deserved less respect than a bearded elder. Men often hid their lack of character behind a mantle of facial hair.

He set a silver tray arrayed with fruits and cheese on a desk and in his spare hand he held a dress. How did he open the damn door? Kali glanced at the sliding chain. She should lock up one of these days.

"Awake at such an hour? What a glorious surprise." Disappointment poisoned a tone that rattled heavy with age.

"Surprise isn't part of the diviner lexicon," Kali scoffed as she liberated a tight white undergarment from the floor and pulled it up her legs. "What's got you so foul?"

"Mayhap such brazen disrespect? Or the craven fool hiding under these covers?" The man waved a hand, dismissive. "He is of station? I ask, foolishly, knowing no such visitor exists."

"Oh–I," Kali followed the man's stare under the canopy of her bed. "Hey, what's your name?"

The man glanced at her, unamused. She shrugged.

"Sorry, Father Dinkira. It's ah–Cerric, my lady, son of Wessen."

"Shaper's son." Kali retrieved a black pair of hosen from the floor which she pulled up over her hips.

"Aye, lady. You uh–you snuck me through the halls."

"Sounds right. Satisfied, Din?"

"Hardly. Cerric, then, remove yourself from these chambers. Make it known you slept your drunkenness off with a servant. Do not make me threaten you."

Cerric mumbled some kind of apology as he fumbled for his clothing. Din aided the event by throwing a wine-stained vest at him and urged him on with a dogged glare. Kali watched with amusement. She blew the young smith a kiss as he hurriedly dressed and admired his backside. Din shooed him out of the room and pushed him into the hall, slamming the door shut. Kali issued a melodramatic sigh.

"Must you always run my lovers out? I enjoy a morning frolic, you know."

"I hoped you would wear something in fashion for today." Dinkira laid the dress over the back of a chair. Blue, trimmed in gold, with sapphires woven into the collar. Kali admired the effort. She responded by slipping a sleeveless blouse over her torso. She did not clasp the collar before she laced a bodice halfway up her chest.

"Sorry to disappoint. It's a little too privileged." Kali winked and clumped a fistful of hair and turned her attention to a nearby mirror. She fussed about and failed at any progress in grooming.

"Then it fits you perfectly. Sit." He pointed at the desk. "You're a mess. Eat."

"Yes, High Sovereign." Kali bowed with an arched back, her form smooth. She snorted and sat in a leather-bound chair and popped a cube of white cheese into her mouth. Dinkira's ancient, weathered fingers wove her hair into a thick braid that pulled at the center of her scalp and trailed down her neck.

"I suggest," Dinkira stressed. "You bathe before the delegation arrives. You smell of copulation."

"Oh?" The cheese disappeared much too quick, and Kali glowered at the larger fruit portion. She dipped an apple slice into some honey, unamused. "I thought men agreed with the scent of sex. It speaks of promise."

"Clever." He yanked her hair back. Kali grunted. "Let's hope the Adirian lordling enjoys your humor."

Kali pursed her lips to the side. She tapped her fingers against the top of the desk in sequence and eyed the remainder of the food with revulsion. House Adirian turned her tastes to bile.

"I don't care much what he enjoys. He's what? The fourth son of a second wife? Please. They wouldn't even waste a hound on him if he disappeared tomorrow."

"Do not be dense, girl. Until that boy is bound to you, he's worth a dukedom. The Red Bastard won't risk control of Dula'Thalier."

"Shit." Kali rolled her eyes and snapped at another apple slice. "Can I not go a single day without hearing about that void-forsaken cesspit?"

"When another fabled, ancient city reveals itself on your father's lands I'm certain the nobility will be happy to divert their attention. Until then it may behoove you to at least feign an interest in the greatest archaeological find of the age. Your brother would–" Dinkira paused, his fingers stiffening.

Kali snatched the braid away from Dinkira and laid it over her shoulder, finishing the weave with a quick series of twists and tucks. She stood and maneuvered around the desk to grab a leather sword belt which she fastened to her waist, the scabbard of a long blade hanging at her thigh and a dagger beside.

"Any word? From him?" Her voice lacked the usual snark.

"Arkalis, I am sorry."

"That'd be a no?"

"There is no news."

"Then, master Dinkira, as the acting steward your responsibilities must keep you busy. Which must make me quite the nuisance." She punctuated her intent by opening the weighted door and gesturing to the exit. "Unless we've more to discuss?"

With a beleaguered huff the steward bowed his head.

"The delegation is due this afternoon. Take care not to stray too far, my lady." He said and took his leave, hidden sandals clopping against stone. Kali watched him go.

Sunshine poured into the hall's grand window from the east, the morning rays illuminating the blue gray tapestries that clung to the walls. Golden stitching of two -I's—one intersecting the other through the center against a rendered eagle–flooded with light. She followed the line of house sigils to the double doors at the opposite end where two red coated guardsmen stood with halberds. Kali suppressed a sneer and ducked into her room. She shivered and glanced at the floor. Where were her boots?

•   •   •

Kali skipped down a flight of steps, barefoot, allowing the warmth of the cobbles to sink into her skin. She wiggled her toes and surveyed the morning's events.

Servants and craftsmen zipped about the compound, disappearing in the twisted paths that wove amidst scattered gardens. From her reverie, Kali scanned the two roads that circled the glade; large enough to fit several riders abreast, they provided a quick navigation to the otherwise complicated trails of the courtyard.

The manor proper scaled over the fortifications. She inspected her balcony and mused at the view. Perhaps she should don a robe in the future. Flying buttresses and exterior pillars bored her by now, but stained-glass windows never lost their grandeur as they caught and amplified the dawning sun. Despite the abundance of rampant vines over cracked stone her ancestral home sang with gravitas.

Warm now, Kali set about the castle. Cramped longhouses flaunted more pedestrian architecture for the servants and flowed into a series of rectangular, glass structures with runic symbols carved into the exterior. They bathed the grounds with a soft white light, sectioned off and cared for by dirty, musk-ridden gardeners that paid Kali no mind as she passed.

Her nose twitched at the sudden scent of excrement. Perfect. One of the few wooden enclosures in the compound, the stable held a full menagerie, three dozen horse-sized mounts and even a second level for a pair of ruhks. Not that she ever witnessed such a creature. Dinkira insisted they lived closer to the wastes.

The lazing stablemaster scrambled up at her approach and fumbled a salute by grabbing the collar of his shirt. Young, with messy dark hair and a dirt-smudged face, the man chewed half a straw stalk.

"It's a fist, Balen," Kali spoke with a brow perked.

"Wot?" He clenched his fingers, but only succeeded in bunching up the stained white linen over his torso.

"Sweet Sunlord. Never mind. You seen a pair of black riding boots?"

"Lost yer fancy footwear, m'lord?"

"M'lady, Balen. I'm a woman. Who taught you to speak to the nobility?"

"Wait a'tick, lord, wassan't ya tha'one that slapped me up good for feigning pretty?" Kali stared at him with her jaw slack. He chewed at her. "Now'n, ya said 'Hoi Balen,'" the yokel accent morphed to Kali's high speech. "'Never degrade yourself for those above your station, your natural self holds its own diginity.' Ah-huh, now'n I'll be 'appy to oblige, m'lady, all'm askin' fer is a bit'a consistency is all."

"No boots then?"

"Oh, nah. Sorry lord."

"Lady. And it's not your fault."

"I know, I'm bein' all empathetic-like, apologizin' on behalf'a the misfortune."

Kali exhaled. She waved a farewell to Balen who promptly returned to his morning slack and crossed the roadway where two more red clad guardsmen stood at ease, their halberds resting on their shoulders.

One perked up at her presence, his fingers tightening around the haft. They locked eyes and he shifted toward a raised portcullis to block an ill-advised trip. She sized up the armor; brigandine with leather gauntlets and greaves with a sallet that obscured their faces. She tapped her fingers on the hilt of her blade then smiled and bowed.

Her trek brought her by the smithy where the persistent clash of metals did little to drown out the yelling but distracted her long enough for a look. Cerric, right?

Kali peered through the open wall to a myriad of apprentices in various stages of work. Forges burned with an intense flame amongst scattered bits of metal complete with sets of runic carvings. The center set glowed with an orange intensity while the two flanking it remained dull. None of the apprentices were true shapers–one used a hammer to mend a cracked breastplate–but in time they may learn the talent.

Wessen, the short, fat master of the forge faced his much taller son, the former waving a hammer in the air, his beady eyes mirroring the flames. Cerric's shoulders slouched, wavy blonde bangs covering those ice-blue eyes of his. Kali grinned. The image stirred a memory of the previous evening's decisions. She waved. The gesture caught the young smith and he looked anxiously between his father and lady.

Have you seen my boots? She mouthed.

Cerric rolled his shoulders and tilted his head to the side, his attention held by his father's scolding. Kali lifted a foot up over her knee and pointed at her bare feet.

Boots. She enunciated the vowels and bit off the "T."

Cerric's brow lifted in recognition. He shook his head and mouthed an apology back. A thick forearm slapped the man across the cheek. Kali snorted into a palm and dipped away, leaving the sorry scene in her egress.

Her quest sallied forth to a drill square of packed earth outside the barracks built into the walled foundations. A mixture of men and women stood at ease in cloth gambesons.

She paused beside their instructor: six feet of pure muscle and salt, he wore a black eyepatch, his face ridden with scars, and sported a long leather coat with a hand-and-a-half sword belted to his waist. He saluted, a haphazard bump to his somewhat exposed hairy chest with a fist short two fingers.

"Lady." At a civil volume, his voice took to a stony rasp.

"Captain. Solara approved drills? I didn't expect we'd have new guards so soon."

"Aye. A pittance." He spat. "All useless, but quick learners. Most of 'em are from the docks. Workers I think, moored sailors, they came precallused."

"At least she caved. You falling in line then?"

"Pah." The captain flinched and raised an arm, a tirade of curses and accusations spewing from his lips at the recruits. More than one of them recoiled in fear. After several moments–when Kali was sure the man held no intention of beheading his trainee–he answered her question. "I've served your father for thirty years. Fished his ass out of more fires than I can count, I'm not about to take orders from some piffy flounce."

"I'll take that as a no."

"Close as it gets." He folded his arms over one another. Kali recognized the posture and shifted her stance, hooking her thumbs into her belt. "I won't abandon you either, someone needs to keep the last Iskarion alive long enough for babes."

"Not the last."

"Right. But I doubt you came to watch idiots fail at basic void-fucking formations!" He shouted that last bit. "Here for training?"

"You wish. You seen a pair of riding boots?"

"Don't remember, eh?"

"I may have had too much to drink."

A smirk crossed the man's lips, hidden by the bush of a beard he grew to hide his ugliness.

"As I recall, lady, you threw them at a serving girl in the feast hall."

"Shit." Kali winced. No wonder Dinkira intruded so early. Revenge. "Doing the Iskarion name proud, huh?"

"Pity the old man wasn't there. You could drink him under the table, even in his glory days. You visit him lately?"

Kali frowned as one of the soldiers turned too fast and slapped the man in front of her upside the head. He crumpled in a heap and Gariant tossed his hands into the air. Even for recruits this crop lacked a little too much sense. The soldiers took a wide berth from the two as the captain advanced. Kali offered a silent prayer for well-timed distractions and set off again to the western wing of the castle. She bypassed the Basilica. Three stories itself, the bulbous roof ended in a steeple that surpassed the castle walls, gaudy in design and intent. Gold, double doors barred entrance, flanked by illuminated stained glass.

One side rendered the Sunlord in full detail: a blazing, bright crown and empty palms extended outward as he sat upon a throne of pure light. Voices poured out from inside, lifted to the morning in dreadful, sanctimonious song. Sunsingers taking ceremony. One day she would make it to ceremony. Or not. Despite the infatuation of the Cavari lowborn, Kali preferred to spend her days outside the eye of holy fervor.

She skipped up a wide stairway from the courtyard into the feast hall and ducked under an open set of heavy wooden doors onto chilled slate tile. Vaulted ceilings greeted her. Multiple long tables filled the hall with a sparse few filling the bench seats, most engaged with leftover scraps, or the fresh, watery gruel reserved for those without noble blood.

At the far end was a table perpendicular to the rest upon a raised stage with cushioned chairs arrayed on a side. A lone woman sat one position off center, her attention set on a stack of parchment. Kali smoothed her countenance and dug her nails into her belt. Her boots lay next to the woman.

The servants ignored Kali's passing. She didn't recognize them in turn, focused as she was on what seemed like an hour's trek to the duke's table. Her footfalls fell silent beside the seated woman.

Solara's pristine gold cape draped over the back of her chair. Kali suppressed her jealousy of that angular face that somehow expressed feminine softness while chiseled from an artist's hammer. Often, she compared it to her own squarish jaw. After a few minutes, the woman set her parchment down, along with an inked quill.

"Lady Arkalis." Her voice was cold and quiet, yet it carried as far as it needed.

"Solara." Kali matched detached authority. Sort of. She came close.

"I am told your behavior last night was less than becoming. I expect this is the last I hear of drunken cavorting."

Kali ground her teeth and moved a hand to the hilt of her blade. The marshal carried no weapons. One stroke and her head would roll. Easy, with little mess. Instead, Kali snagged her boots. Solara followed the motion by grasping Kali's wrist, her iron grip holding steady. The two locked stares; those narrow, yellow-flaked eyes catching Kali by surprise. Goosebumps crept up her arm as her cheeks flushed red.

"Remember your place, Arkalis. Grand Duke Adirian demands respect from his wed relations."

"Yes, Marshal," Kali spoke through clenched teeth. Grand Duke. What a crock. "Is that all?"

"No. Seer Dinkira provided you with proper dress for my Lord's arrival I believe. It is more. . ." Solara sneered at Kali's attire. The marshal wore a fine red surcoat trimmed in black, finery for the position. ". . .appropriate." Solara released her hold and Kali snapped her arm back. "That is all."

"As you will." Kali made for the closest door and tore it open, stepped inside then slammed it closed. She rested against the coarse wood and sank to the floor, her chest heaving and face hot. A servant poked his head up from over an oven. The kitchens kept a skeleton crew for the morning, but today an abundance of servants stuck around to catch a glimpse of her melodrama. Kali grumbled a few choice curses and blinked back her tears. With one leg in the air, she slid the first boot onto an exposed foot.

"Nothing to see here," she forced a grin. "Found 'em."

She did the Iskarion name proud.

From the Litany of the Void: 4th Chorus, 1st Canting

From Voided Depths they emerge, horrors unspoken. Born of deceit and of toil, denizens of chaos converge in darkness to despoil all the Sun's domain.

They shall appear as wights; pale and thin, sickly white, yellow eyes and blood of fire, you will know them by silent whispers, deathly shadows borne of cinders.

Walk with grace in Their splendors. Corruption seeks they who urge; they who coax, they who meddle. Fear not the Sun, fear not the dark, for Riah's wrath burns unbroken.

Chapter 4
Please Don't Be Ugly

K ali snuggled into a woolen cloak draped about her shoulders. Loose tresses of auburn blew free from her braid as she set her elbows on the tower's ramparts and listened to the cry of gulls, their songs intermixed with the crash of the sea against the earthen barricades; the cliffs of which her home stood. From up here, the highest tower of Iskvar, the world felt calm. In the shadow of the castle a bustling harbor buzzed with life. Hundreds of subjects, her subjects, appeared no larger than ants, caught within the throes of daily life. She pitied and envied them. Their simplistic routine, that purity of labor. Not that she knew anything beyond the wiles of nobility.

Such pleasant ruckus stirred an uneasiness in her mind.

The seated man beside her heaved his shoulders in labored breaths. Quaffed hair framed a weathered, wrinkled face, full gray beard waxed beneath tired and listless eyes. He wore his regal blue cloak with the heraldry of his house and an embroidered tunic with gems embedded into the trim. Denrik Iskarion, Duke of Iskvar, stared out into the horizon without intent, placid.

"It's easier to face west, you know," the aged man's regal baritone rumbled. Kali rolled her eyes with a smile and tilted her head toward her father.

"Why's that?"

"No blasted sun in your eyes, girl. Even the horses know that." His ever-so-grim expression lightened for a brief flicker.

"Oh wise lord, how does the rest of the world carry on without your great knowledge?"

"With the sun in their eyes I imagine."

Kali snorted and Denrik chortled. A chilled gust stirred the air of their joviality and Denrik adjusted his cloak and steepled his fingers in his lap. The glint of a sapphire studded ring caught the light, its band imprinted with a small rendering of a dove. Her mother's personal sigil.

"How are your lessons with the sword? Gariant is a rough man, but few know blades better than that ugly bastard."

"Well enough. He says I'm liable to die in a proper fight, but I swatted his rear just this morning. I'll go down knowing my enemy can't sit comfortably for the rest of his life," she lied. Kali rarely took lessons anymore.

"Hah!" The duke bobbed his head in amusement. "If you can't beat them, give 'em something to remember you by, is that it? I recall the battle of Isha Pass. You know that one, yes?" Kali nodded and stretched out, her shoulders straight. "The Ishite rebels led a whole damn legion through the southern passes right into Kalthier's hold. Poor bastard barely had time to raise a militia, and of course there I am, drunk after that idiot's wedding. Couldn't just let those Lindrisi jackasses run amok so we–"

Denrik paused. His face contorted in confusion, his eyes darting from side to side as if looking for something. "So we–I think we–"

"Took a ransom's worth of gunpowder, the shittiest garrison in Ilvicar, and blew the whole side of a mountain clear into the void!" Kali finished the tale. She placed a hand on her father's shoulder and squeezed.

"Not much of a battle." He picked up the cue, regaining a semblance of composure. "Damn Ishites moved like a swarm once the lines broke. Either way, I've yet to hear of a Lindorum incursion since. Sometimes a painful memory is more effective than a quick end, you see."

"No Consul dare cross the border while the Knight of Cinder yet lives."

"Mm. True enough, girl. A lifetime of battles to earn that title. Blood and ash, in spades. Only fools challenge the Iskarion name."

Only fools. Kali closed her eyes and exhaled through her nostrils. Adirian, Kalthiar, Salivar, Lynesse. The house names burned in her mind. With her lineage the five dukes of Ilvicar ruled since after the Desolation, and now? Now she presided over the end of a dynasty.

"The delegation is due. Would you prefer to wear your armor or something comfortable? I'm sure Gwin will pick an outfit for you." She glanced over her shoulder at the thin, wisp of a man that served as her father's attendant. He stood aside, next to the runic tower that acted as a coastal lighthouse and winked. Or tried too anyway. With one wandering eye Kali could never read him.

"Delegation? Why was I not told of this?"

"Forgive me, your Grace, the messenger must've failed his duty. I'll see him punished forthwith."

"Hmph. Good. An outfit only runs as efficiently as its worst member," Denrik grumbled. He licked his chapped lips and rocked for a moment, shifting in his chair. His gaze settled outward onto the horizon, and he became quiet. Kali waited. The old lord said nothing else. He sat without intent, oblivious.

"Father?" Kali moved her hand to his arm and squeezed again. Denrik jumped, startled. He flicked his head to each side before he settled on Kali. His eyebrows furrowed and he unfolded his hands, one grasping for a nonexistent scabbard.

"Who are you? Unhand your duke, girl," he spoke with a regal glower. Kali's eyes softened and she tightened her hold.

"It's Arkalis. Your daughter."

Denrik scanned her face. A brief recognition flickered in his countenance then disappeared in an instant. He scowled and ripped his arm from her grasp, stronger than her even at his age.

"What game is this? My children are but ten solstices, what are you? Near thirty I imagine. Thank your luck I don't throw you into the dungeons, whoever you are. Leave me, before I change my mind."

Kali's brow twitched She tightened a fist against her hip and bit back any further comment, parting ways from the man. Gwin shuffled over to take her place, the aged servant citing a charade of semi-official reports to distract the duke. Kali took her leave. She wrapped her cloak tighter about her shoulders and drew her arms close to her chest.

She always worried at her father's fate in battles decades past. Maybe an arrow took him, a warcaster's spell, or a craven dagger to the back. It never occurred to her that his mind could fall as easily.

A scattered cloud of dust caught her attention from the eastern road. A procession of knights, twenty strong, flanked a golden carriage with bundles of luggage tied to the top. From the outer gate a deep horn signaled the arrival of an important guest. The castle took to a flurry of activity at the warning. Servants burst from all sides of the castle, a multitude of staff that Kali failed to recognize. Dinkira doubled the household, no doubt to pamper their new guest.

Her gaze strayed to the sun, it's fixed station in the east still colored by a crescent shade with most of the sphere exposed. An hour yet before midday. When did a lord ever arrive early?

• • •

Kali adjusted her bust. She fidgeted and pulled at the bottom of the tight and gaudy dress that clung to her body. She wore the damn thing well enough despite the constant glints and flashes of the laced gems, though she flinched whenever she looked down. Not that she could. Beneath the garment a tight corset forced her posture upright and pronounced her chest for all to gawk at, a crude reminder of her importance as a royal chess piece.

Dinkira waited beside her, a new series of wrinkles creasing his forehead. He grew older by the minute.

They took their place at the keep's entryway, atop the grandiose stone landing with the reception hall's doors cast wide. Solara stood ahead of four armored guardsmen, clad in a full suit of black plate with a cavalry saber at her hip. Kali imagined the scowl the woman wore, sour that Kali belted her own weapon to her waist. Baby steps.

Servants and staff filled the courtyard otherwise, arrayed for a king, with Gariant's recruits outfitted with old, battered arquebuses for show. Unloaded of course. They formed a column nearby, guns on their shoulders, with the weathered knight captain in a long coat boasting Iskarion heraldry. A velvet carpet awaited the arrival, flanked by servants at attention. They waited in silence.

Someone coughed, drawing the ire of Solara's intense gaze. That someone earned themselves a trip to the dungeons.

Kali tapped her foot against the stone. She looked about the yard, countenance flat and bored. The doors to the feast hall were open. Odd, but Solara required consistency in her direction. Strange then that she noted a lack of any watch on the walls nor sentries in the towers. The usual din of castle life disappeared altogether, replaced by a distant susurrus in her ears. Kali swatted at what she assumed was a fly. Or a mosquito. Beasts sent from the Void itself.

"Riveting." Kali elbowed Din in the ribs. The old man coughed and scowled at her. "If a fight breaks out, you know I'm dead. I can't breathe in this accursed thing."

"I hoped a lack of breath would still your tongue." A bead of sweat dripped from his brow. "We are at Iskvar, girl. What fight are you expecting?"

"The one where my gallant savior flies in on their ruhk and whisks me away to Nukati to live in paradise."

"Quiet," the Marshal hissed. "Cease your chittering." Kali glared at the back of the woman's head and imagined her as-of-yet unnamed champion landing their mount on Solara's face.

Hoofbeats interrupted her daydream. Stillness broke to a grand procession of riders. Seated upon massive destriers, the riders sported intricate, layered plate and mail with red cloaks over curved pauldrons, their heads covered by narrow visored frog-mouthed helmets. They split into two groups and rode down each side of the courtyard, slowing their pace as they reached the reception. The knights fell into line and the pristine metal shimmered in the sunlight, baring no blemishes or misaligned seams. Gariant would call them combat virgins. Kali was impressed.

Moments later the carriage she glimpsed from the road pulled around the glade. Propelled by four draft horses the vehicle clattered over the cobble until the driver came to a halt at the edge of the velvet walkway.

Kali held her breath. The driver hopped from his seat and jogged to the carriage door, his tailed coat fluttering. She met Duke Adirian once at a diplomatic council ten solstices past. The Red Bastard held no magnificent physique or keen blade skill like her father, yet all it took was a look and any scarred veteran found himself weak with fear. So too, it stood to reason that his son would bear a similar manner. Kali shifted her weight onto one foot and folded her hands at her waist and picked at the sleeve of her dress. That carriage held her future.

"Please don't be ugly," Kali muttered under her breath.

The door opened. No one emerged. A few servants turned their heads. One of the knights adjusted his saddle. Keeping that posture in full armor did terrible things to one's back. No one moved. Kali pursed her lips together and leaned forward to peer inside.

"Oh!" A surprised tenor spoke from inside the carriage. "I ah–hah. Sorry, sorry! Didn't realize we'd stopped. Yes, well." The driver offered a hand. Thin, pale fingers grasped the aid, and the lordling popped his head out. First impressions? Kali scratched the bridge of her nose to hide her grin. Sunken cheeks, wide eyes, with a wispy brow and a blond goatee that adorned only his chin. Soft. The man stumbled as he hit the ground and wobbled to an awkward poise. Kali could no longer contain her snort.

Short. The word tumbled in her mind. While she preferred lean, short did little for her taste in men. Women, yes, but this? She gave him a quick once over: wide cuffed pants tucked into pointed shoes, a tan, single-breasted jacket that ended at a red sash tied around his waist. Over his eyes he wore a pair of queer lenses that clung to his ears to stay upright. And here she felt a fool in her dress.

"Lord Lesandre," Solara began. "Welcome to Castle Iskvar, the ancient seat of Iskarion. May we–" The marshal paused. The lord stuck his head into the carriage and struggled with his height as his arm flailed about inside. After a song-worthy struggle Lesandre withdrew a leather-bound tome from the carriage.

"Solara! Hello! Why are you wearing armor?" Lesandre adjusted his lenses by tapping the sides, his countenance bright and naïve.

"It is customary, lord." Solara bit into the words with a snarl. "May we wish you good fortune, and it is my pleasure to present to you the daughter of Duke Iskarion, the Lady Arkalis." Solara glared at Kali who dropped her hand and cleared her throat. Dinkira pushed her. She clopped forward with a decided lack of grace to the edge of the landing and offered a haphazard wave.

"Hey."

From the column of soldiers Gariant barked a laugh. Lesandre half smiled at Kali and rubbed the back of his head. He stepped closer, tentative, and clutched his book under an arm.

"Yes. Ah, Lady Arkalis, I'm–well. I'm delighted to bask in your beauty, I've heard tales of your–ah."

"I can chug an entire bottle of wine in one breath. Not what you had in mind, though." Lesandre stared at her and she snarked back. Once he regained his composure, the lord launched into a well-rehearsed speech, full of niceties and apologies, but something drew Kali's attention to the captain. Focused as he was on the meeting, he failed to notice his recruits. They stood at perfect attention, their formation tight and precise. Kali raised a brow. The captain knew his stuff, but one morning of rampant military screaming didn't teach military grade discipline. The recruits kept their fingers off the triggers of their weapons.

Until they moved.

The column turned on a heel. The front line took a knee and set the stocks of their weapons against their shoulders as Lesandre spoke.

"We're done!" Kali descended the stairs in a single bound. She bent her knees at impact and tackled Lesandre as a series of loud pops echoed throughout the yard. From no more than twenty paces the accuracy tore into the line of mounted knights. Bullets riddled their shining armor and several of their number dropped from the volley. Some screamed. Servants scattered.

The castle erupted into chaos. From every open corridor men and women streamed out armed with an assortment of weaponry: pikes and blades, yet most carried bludgeons, makeshift flails, even cudgels or staves. They surrounded the procession and charged.

Lesandre coughed and squirmed beneath Kali. She rolled off and hoisted herself to a knee, standing with breaths that came in heavy gasps. Blasted corset. At least she could rub this in Dinkira's face. Kali brandished her blade, the ring of steel on leather singing the clarion call of battle. She ripped the neckline of her dress into the bust then repeated the motion with the garment beneath.

"Get up!" Kali grabbed Lesandre by the collar and lifted him off the ground. The remaining knights set about dispersing the recruits, or whatever they were, reduced to half their strength. Still, the cavalry served, brandishing steel tipped lances that crashed into the gunline. Cries rose as men and women fell, crushed beneath hooves while they skewered others.

The marshal and her guardsmen rushed to meet Kali and their lord.

"Wh—what is going on?" Lesandre panicked.

"How would I know? Come on!" Kali grabbed the lord's arm and threw him at the stairs as the mob approached. She placed herself in front of the hapless Adirian and engaged. A woman, scared in the face, eyes narrow, rushed Kali, flail arcing from her side. Quickly, Kali thrust her sword into the woman's exposed stomach and out her back, skirting the blow with raw confidence. Something akin to a hacking gurgle escaped the aggressor's lips. No time for pity. Kali reared back and took the now limp body with her. She used the corpse to catch a hatchet then withdrew her blade from its human sheath and kicked at the body. It flew at the second attacker who crashed into a heap.

Kali backed up. The knights managed to turn and charge into the mob of combatants, their lances replaced with sabers. Kali retreated to the stairs and joined a short line of halberdiers as several of the peasants impaled themselves on the spear of the pole arms. She fell in next to the marshal who, with her saber brandished, kept one hand on Lesandre's shoulder.

"Care to explain, Arkalis?" Even in the face of battle Solara's voice was icy calm.

"Well," Kali lanced a foot out and caught a man in the groin with a satisfying crunch. She followed with a slash at his throat, drawing an arterial spray that splattered over her dress and skin. Lovely. "From what I can tell someone snuck mercenaries into my home to kill your bastard of a lord."

Within the mob they forced a knight from his mount and beat him to death while flat on his back. Meanwhile, their formation made a slow withdrawal up the steps, the halberds fending off the less skilled skirmishers. Solara caught a blade with her saber and twisted her weapon, sliding the edge down the opposing sword and deftly removing a man's hand from his wrist.

"Someone? Not you?"

"I just saved his void forsaken life!"

Another pop. The guardsmen beside Kali fell with a bullet lodged in his eye.

"Take Lesandre and get inside! He is too important to fall here."

"Agreed!" Kali pulled the lordling's arm after her. "You have no idea how tempting it is to leave you here."

"Please don't!"

Lesandre clutched his book and followed, his knuckles white with fear.

Kali made a break for the door. More pops preceded two bullets as they splintered against the stonework in front of her. Damn good shots. With Lesandre in tow she crossed the threshold and ran through the keep's foyer; a grandiose hall, supported by stone pillars draped with blue gray banners. The hall bore a large, lacquered throne upon a raised dais. Balconies ran the edges with but otherwise the room boasted a cavernous emptiness, lit only from skylights cut from the ceiling, its light caught by mirrors that gave the dull gray some semblance of life.

Dinkira knelt in front of three of the ambushers, poised by the throne, his arms out and his face bloodied. Her footfalls drew the attackers. Kali released Lesandre and he ducked behind her.

With her free hand Kali withdrew a dagger.

"Lady Iskarion. Drop the sword." The one in the center spoke first. A northern accent with as nondescript a face one could hope for. Not strong, not weak, the perfect forgettable face.

"Or you could drop yours."

"You're outnumbered lady, make this easy on yours–"

Her dagger flew into the air and the blade sunk into the speaker's chest. He exhaled mid-sentence and collapsed.

"I can take two." Kali charged.

The remaining ambushers balked at the aggression, the first managing to raise her sword as Kali closed, two blades meeting with a metal ring. Kali shifted to her target's side, away from the second combatant and sidestepped a cudgel. She drew her sword back and met another strike mid swing, flowing in as she kept pressure on the opposing blade. She twisted the steel aside and she sent a fist into the woman's face. The ambusher recoiled and Kali's body heaved from an unwelcome cudgel to her back.

Kali spun and brought her sword with her. The tip drew blood from an aggressor who yelped and countered, his weapon whipping at her face. Kali caught his wrist mid swing. He blinked and she jabbed her sword into his neck.

"Behind you!" Lesandre shouted.

Kali swung about. She stood face-to-face with the mercenary, her blade raised, unmoving. Blood poured from the assailant's mouth as she fell to her knees, to reveal Dinkira who held Kali's blood-stained dagger. He muttered a prayer to the Sunlord and Kali exhaled with relief. What was that Gariant taught her? Better lucky than good.

"Oh Din, you've never been so beautiful."

The diviner groaned and swayed. Kali wrapped an arm around his shoulder to steady him and Lesandre jogged up next to the two with a weary gaze.

"Your father." Dinkira spoke with labored breaths. "They wanted to know where he was."

"What? Who are these people? How did they get into the castle?"

"I don't know. What seeks him evades my sight. Kali, As does a great deal, it seems. He is in his chambers. You must go to him."

"Din, you can barely stand, I can't leave you."

"You must." Dinkira coughed.

"I've got him." Lesandre spoke up. "I'm no fighter, but I can tend his wound. Solara won't let anyone through the front. We're quite safe."

Kali watched Lesandre. She met those dark green eyes with her own, hazel stare. For a moment she considered the opportunity. Dinkira would say nothing. So what if one of the attackers got in a lucky strike? She could end this farce of a marriage here. Something whispered in her ear. It urged her to strike.

"Fine. Here, take him." Lesandre took charge of the diviner. "Don't you die on me, old man."

"As you will, lady."

Kali retrieved her weapons with a grunt. She shared a glance with the old diviner then took off. Her path brought her to one of the small doors along the back wall, up a narrow, stone staircase meant for the servants and out into the main hall of the royal chambers. She emerged next to the lone window at the edge of the corridor. A collection of sellswords crowded the thick wooden double doors of her father's chamber across the hall, two handy with axes.

Three cloaked and hooded figures stood taller than the others, gangly and thin. They carried uniform weapons; black swords with white, runic lettering engraved up the blade and stood without the slightest motion. Five on one. Great odds. Kali tapped her fingers against the hilt of her blade and bounced in place, ready.

The clatter of boots on stone drew the attention of the three. They looked in unison. Creepy. Kali flicked her wrist outward, her dagger intercepted by a sword mid-flight. Oh, shit. She came to a sudden halt and raised her weapon as beneath the hoods sickly, yellow eyes peered out at her, purple veins visible over pale white flesh. She stumbled backward. Voidtouched?

The one in the center raised a too-thin, too-long arm, a gloved finger with too many joints extended in her direction. She heard a distant, unintelligible whisper as clear as a voice in her ear.

"What in the holy high sun are you?" What a time to be brave. Kali brought her spare hand to the hilt of her blade and wrapped her fingers around the leather, her eyes narrow, focused.

The creatures moved as one. They did not run so much as bound, each leap crossing the same distance as a man twice her height. Shit. Kali's legs tremored. They closed and one thrust its blade at her chest sooner than she expected, its long limb giving it reach beyond her experience. Contrails of purple energy followed the strikes. Kali swiped the weapon off course only to find a second assault at her shoulder. She met that one as well and backed up, her eyes drawn to a scoring on the flat of her weapon. The surprise wore off as the foray continued. Another slash, Kali placed her sword in its way to another mark that marred her blade. She ducked beneath a slice and drew back, angling her sword upward, eyes wide.

The creatures pushed and Kali retreated halfway into the hall, farther now from her father's chambers. Her weapon flailed with her defense, desperate to prevent contact, her arms tiring with every move. The creatures made no mistakes. They provided no openings and moved in sync with one another. Something needed to change. Kali deflected another attack and ran. She crashed into the door to her room and leapt inside. One came after. She sidestepped it and slammed the door shut, scrambling to slide the chain in place.

Today was that day, it seemed.

The lone spawn screeched.

Kali advanced on the creature. It parried her blow while its second threw its weight against the door. She spun to catch a counter then drew in close and brought her weapon in a tight circle, the flat beating away the other strike. Undeterred, the spawn snatched her braid and Kali yelped. Its blade came next. She dipped her torso as the weapon sliced through her hair. Now, free, she thrust her sword up as the tip caught the thing in the chin. It screeched. She pushed until the steel erupted out the back of its head, covered in a white puss.

The monster writhed and fell to the floor. It twitched, its limbs fighting for too long. Relief flooded her mind as it stilled. Until she looked at her blade. Whatever was inside the creature dissolved the metal to nothing. Kali dropped the literal half sword and glanced at the door where the other one continued to pound. The chain rattled. She rolled her shoulders, then picked up the now ownerless black blade. It lifted easily, almost weightless, and the runes flashed at her touch. What? Voices flooded her mind. Distant, yet clear. Whispers she recognized. They chanted something incomprehensible

No going back now. Kali placed the pommel in her palm and set her fingers around the crossguard.

The door swung inward. The black cloaked thing rushed inside and lowered its neck, its lidless eyes locking onto Kali. It screeched that inhuman, terrifying howl and she hurled the sword. Distracted by its own intimidation the weapon embedded itself into its chest. A fire erupted from the wound and engulfed the cloak in a burst of white flame.

"Holy shit!" Kali fell to her backside and covered her head. The creature burnt to a husk of char. Huh. In a heave, Kali stood, fetched the unscathed black blade, and faced the last of the creatures.

The axe men finished their work and kicked the set of doors inward only to retreat, taken by surprise. Denrik emerged from his bedchamber clad in a furred robe and a battered breast plate. He donned a golden circlet and stood with one hand on the hilt of an icy blue greatsword, the blade resting with the tip on the tile floor. The duke wielded the weapon in one hand and swung it wide. It sliced a man in halves. The second man roared and swung his axe over his head, or tried to as Denrik wrung the mercenary by the neck and lifted him into the air, squeezing until something popped.

The last creature hissed. It rushed the duke and found its blade against his. As they clashed, the swords sparked in small bursts of arcing energy, the icy finish of her father's weapon resisting the scorch of the black blade. The creature lashed out to no avail with Denrik matching the speed with ease. He kicked a booted heel into the monster's shin and sent it buckling to a knee, his weapon brought to bare as he plunged it into the spawn's neck

"Arkalis?" Her father wiped his undamaged sword off on the creature's cloak and kicked its twitching body. "Are you alright, girl? What in the Sky Father's realm are those things?"

"Couldn't have done that earlier?!" Kali dropped the black blade. She sank low, catching her breath as Denrik made his way to her side.

Personal Log, 7.07.0268 CE

h AH! Shaper's College told me it couldn't be done. Suck on it you old bastards! The trick isn't in the forging process, it's in the metal. I was able to decipher some of the elemental compositions from the lance—compositions, I will add, that do not occur naturally anywhere in creation. From this we'll be able to synthesize a new alloy, one almost entirely immune to the oxidation process. Better? It holds runes without upkeep and can cut just about anything that isn't runecasted. I've already made a few prototypes for the forum.

Kal's calling it Thalian Steel. I suggested Sharpy-Shiney-Bashy-Metal, but he seemed to think the College would be upset. Losers.

Chapter 5
Do Not Pity the Dead

RURIK'S EYES snapped open within an endless void of ocean. He floated, without intent or motion, the armored woman from his vision before him. She laid a gauntleted hand on his forehead, its touch cool and smooth. Gingerly, she pushed him away, up toward freedom. A regret filled his mind. Loss, sorrow.

Find me.

He broke the surface with a gasp. Feral pulled Rurik free and set him onto the marble floor where she huffed and sat, her legs crossed as she busied herself by pruning split ends from her locks with a short blade. Rurik rolled onto his side and promptly hacked up a lung full of water. Feral patted his back with a few wet slops.

"Thanks," he managed, his voice hoarse. "How'd we survive?"

Feral pointed. Debris piled up against a shimmering blue aura, a shield of energy that held the rubble at bay. It spread over the gaping hole where ornate doors once stood. Fire flashed in his mind. He remembered the destruction, the doors blowing toward him, the flame. He felt the heat. Or the chill. He shivered and folded his arms over his chest.

"Some trick there, boss. Didn't take you for a sorcerer." Princess sat on the edge of the pool. She ran her fingers through the water, her burnt gloves resting on her lap.

"I'm not." Rurik tapped on his ear. His torso lurched, wobbling. "That wasn't me. I found this ring." He lifted his hand up to display the sapphire band. "Up here. Earlier. Felt right."

Feral narrowed her eyes at the gem and sniffed. A shrug followed. Princess scrutinized him, suspect. Rurik groaned, stretched, and stood. Most of the water dripped out already, but a few drops took to gravity.

"Felt right?" Princess hopped up.

"Yes. You two see where the others went? We need to find them."

"Hal and Sweets stayed back in the cor-eh-door. We didn't see anyone else in the hall, but Rik, you weren't awake for the quakes. Felt like the whole damn building fell."

"I saw the ceiling come down." Rurik rubbed his temple. "If they got far enough away maybe they survived. Maybe."

Princess smoothed out her blouse and beckoned Feral who stood, sheathing her knife in a belt at her thigh. She cracked her knuckles, her neck, then her back with a grunt.

"I think that's her way of saying 'let's go'," Princess said.

Rurik rolled his shoulder and grimaced. "I was up here earlier, there's more I didn't get to." His wet boots slurped with his labored gait as they advanced. No one carried a glowlamp, but the light from the shield caught the crystal stripping and lit the way through the gardens. Feral snagged a yellow gourd and munched, her chews the only conversation any of them cared for.

Rurik, weary, crossed beneath the archway absent its inky portal and the others followed. The sound of crashing water grew distant as they left the garden and the darkness returned in wisps and shadows. Rurik snapped his fingers. That felt right. Along the hallway a line of braziers lit with a bright, blue flame. The reflection caught from the crystal and revealed another white marble finish and an opening.

"For the record, you're freaking me out a bit, Rik."

"Me too." Rurik glanced at Princess. Her eyes softened and she ran her fingers through her hair, tugging at a knot of curls.

"You don't think it's Voidcas–"

"No." He cut her off. She huffed. "No, it's not willful? It's like the ring is telling me what to do. Like I'm experiencing someone else's memories."

"Willful?" Princess scoffed. "You might want to lay off the reminiscin', Voidwork is crafty, and who knows what all this is for."

"Yes, your highness."

Winged obsidian statues, smaller than the foyer behemoth, lined a red carpet that followed the hall into an open expanse where tapered pews declined to a raised stage. A series of open hallways led deeper into the building, but Rurik's gaze lingered on another archway, this one behind that platform, its edges alight with blue runes.

"Folks didn't do nothin' without style, huh?" Princess frowned at the amphitheater. "Or excess. How many kids you think went hungry to build one of these statues?"

"Enough for you to start a rebellion over." Rurik chuckled and made his way down the incline.

"Oh hah, laugh it up *Lord* Iskarion. You ever have sleep for supper?"

"One eats sleep?" Feral stared at the shorter woman, her eyebrows raised.

Rurik snorted and hopped onto the stage. While Princess failed to translate colloquialisms, he poked at the arch. The same inky blackness held to the surface and the runes mirrored the set from before, flowing, and gentle. As mysterious as his ancient hosts were, they at least bothered to color code their expertise. Red, instantaneous fiery death. Blue, good. Easy.

On a whim, Rurik pressed his palm against a rune. The script flashed and Rurik pulled his hand away and dropped to the floor. No explosion. He peeked open one eye. Blue, good. Right. Rurik sat up and studied the arch. The rune he touched gave off a stronger glow than the others now and the portal had dissipated.

"Thought I told you to lay off the sorcerery!" Feral grunted her agreement as the two approached him.

"It's not voidcasting." Rurik rubbed his chin. He poked another rune and it flashed. Princess yelped. No explosion. Ahah. Rurik repeated the gesture.

The air stiffened. A fresh, morning breeze blew from the archway and the black portal sprung to life. He heard the telltale thuds and stifled a laugh. He craned his neck around and grinned at the others, the two of them on the ground to either side with their hands over their heads.

"They're directions," he said. "You set the runes and they open the portal. This is fantastic. Do you know what this means?"

"Warn us first!" Princess scrambled up to her feet. "And hold up. What are you goin' on about? First the shield thing, the fire, now a magic portal! It'd take a dozen shapers to create somethin' like that, anythin' like that! This stuff is dangerous, Rik, this whole place is."

Rurik clenched his teeth. "Of course it's dangerous! Why do you think those bastards send in people like us? We collapsed a whole void's damned building and killed how many? As far as we know the others are dead. What saved us? This." Rurik flashed the band on his hand. His countenance grew hard, but his lips twitched downward, betraying his anger. "I don't know what I'm doing, Sahira! I'm trying to keep everyone alive. And I'm failing. We need every advantage we can get. So enough with the warnings. I know, I just don't care."

Sahira unfolded her arms. She opened her mouth, then stopped and clasped her hands together. They shared a quiet stare.

"Okay." She shrugged. "Okay. Just be careful, Rik, we need you alive too." Rurik turned to the portal. "What's next?"

"We need to find the others. What did you find in the wings?"

"Didn't get too far. We waited and came back when we heard the screamin'."

"Let's go then. We'll take the west wing, Feral?" The woman perked her head up, chewing the remainder of her impromptu meal. "You stay here in case anyone shows up, tell them to hold steady."

"Wait wait, why does she get to stay?"

"Honestly? I like her more than you."

Feral grunted and brandished her blade. She handed it, hilt first, to Sahira.

"Take. Protect fool chief-man."

•   •   •

A blood-curdling scream hastened them to a run. Rurik and Sahira rounded a corner at a full sprint into a vast room split down the middle by a series of transparent cases. Undisturbed oil paintings and decorative canvases clung to the walls beneath that crystal strip which hummed with light, illuminating debris scattered through the hall, with stone and mortar spilling out from what was once a corridor. Hal and Sweets, blackened with soot, stood off against a group of soldiers, the former carrying his halberd. The weapon shook from an unsteady hand.

The Adirian guardsmen, their flesh marred and hair patchy with charred coats, took up an almost unnatural poise. Their shoulders slouched, their necks craned upward, and heads hung as if too heavy to lift. Neither carried a weapon. Before them another guard lay on the ground. Or a corpse rather, bereft too many limbs. Sweet's hands moved from his protector's back to his side, unsure of how to defend himself.

Rurik halted. He snapped and a set of braziers ignited in the corners of the gallery. Sweets yelped. The guardsmen screamed, an ear piercing, pain ridden wail, and lifted their heads with a bobbing lilt, their eyes alight with a yellow glow.

"What in the holy fuckin' godfather are those?" Sahira exclaimed, both unsheathing their knives. Sweets looked back and his face contorted from abject horror to utter relief.

"Sweets, get your ass over here no–"

The creatures screeched. In tandem, they swept up on each other's flanks, their arms hanging at their sides as they sprinted past Hal. The young man stiffened and the runed creatures ignored him. Sweets ducked.

Rurik pivoted and placed one leg in front of the other. They were on him in seconds. Metal flashed in his peripheral and the creature rammed its body into his torso. Fast bastard. Rurik exhaled on contact, the wind knocked from his chest. It took him to the ground, frothing at the mouth, the scent of its burnt flesh creeping into his nostrils. Rurik, wide eyed, shoved a hand into the dead man's face. Its skin slipped off in char. Something wet crashed nearby.

Sahira?

Rurik stabbed at the creature's back, his blade useless against the charred flesh. His assailant flailed. It hugged him and squeezed. The pain seared down Rurik's spine as his joints cracked from the sheer strength, and the air left his lungs. He stabbed again, his strike clattering against brigandine plates. Those yellow, orb-like eyes stared out from a hideous, ruined face. Rurik gasped for air. It smiled.

A spearhead erupted through the creature's head and the pressure abated. Blood splattered onto Rurik's face. Sweets hovered over him, halberd in hand, his chest heaving. Short and wiry, the man nonetheless took to a warrior's form in those moments. At least to Rurik. He stood up for what felt like the hundredth time. Sahira leaned over the other one and ripped her knife out of its face.

"Nice shot." Rurik said and placed a hand on Sweet's shoulder. He offered the other man a grateful look, one returned with a mixture of fear and anxiety. Sweets gripped the halberd for dear life and Rurik wrapped his fingers over his hands, gently taking hold of the weapon. "It's alright, Sweets, it's dead, yeah?"

Sweets nodded shakily and ceded his hold.

Between the paintings a rendered mural spanned most of the wall, deep reds and oranges resplendent within a haunting blue light. It portrayed columns of men and women in thin plate, plumed helmets and ice blue weapons, all rendered in militaristic tribute. If not for the somehow still smoldering corpses and scent of decay, Rurik imagined himself whiling away the hours immersed in the grandiose exhibit. He stretched his shoulder with a suppressed moan, ignoring a new bruise that spanned his chest. Good day.

"Hal?" Rurik gave a wide berth to the burnt corpse and made his way to the younger fellow. He passed Sahira as she studied her kill, prodding at the horrid exterior.

Hal quivered with his head buried into his knees, his hands dug into his messy mop of blond. He whispered to himself with an almost rabid ferocity.

"Hal?" Rurik spoke gently and took a knee. The whispering ceased and Hal lifted his head, wide, blue eyes staring up at Rurik. The slight hint of a beard caught his chin, the patchy stubble of youth. "You good?"

"I'm sorry, lord. I froze." Hal's voice quivered. "They were guardsmen, I-I couldn't," his words trailed off. Rurik's lips tightened and he squeezed Hal's arm.

"You're not at the front anymore, Hal, and I'm not a lord." Rurik rose and brought the veteran with him. He brushed off Hal's worn leather coat and grasped the flaps, straightening them. "Put it out of your mind, Princess is the only one of us with real balls anyway." Hal cracked a short-lived grin. Good enough.

Three of them convened around the mutilated corpse of the creature Sahira skewered. Rurik poked it with the edge of its boot. Hal wandered off about the room, his boots scuffing with a drag-step.

"What happened?" Sahira nudged Sweets with an elbow.

"A soldier runs into the hall." Sweets started. "No threat, no weapon, yes? He begs us to help so Saiqua's mercy guides us. We grab his friends then the blast. It knocks us to sleep. When we wake the others are dead. Dead as any man. Then they–they rise and tear apart that one. That's when you show up, to Vari's own luck."

"This is some serious shit." Sahira clasped her hands behind her head. "How long we been here? Year and a half? Explodin' walls, yah, neat artefacts, but this? The dead walkin'? That only happens in Xyr, and only then in blight storms."

"Unless you've got a loremaster hidden somewhere, we're not getting any answers here," Rurik said.

"Lord Rurik? You may want to see this."

Rurik rolled his eyes. How many times did it take to get a message through? Lord Rurik Iskarion was a name descended from heroes and warriors of legend. He preferred Foreman Rik.

"It's just Rik, Hal." He struggled to hide the irritation in his voice.

"Yes lord." Rurik dug his fingers into his thigh. "But." Hal pointed at a display case. The icy finish of the glass reflected the eerie blue light of the braziers, creating a mirror that Rurik gazed into. A scar ran down the side of his face from any number of assaults and half of his left eyebrow was gone. His hair slicked to one side with his headband discarded to reveal a wrinkled, lined forehead.

Rurik saw past his vanity to the weapons on display. Ancient blades, bereft rust or decay, attached to stands and suspended delicately for the pleasure of viewing.

He flashed a genuine smile. Everyone paid for weapons. Quartermasters broke out a year's treasury for Thalian Steel, and here he stood with a small armory. A longsword hovered in his vision with dull, unlit runes carved into its base. The handle lacked any decorative fanfare for a weapon on display, but a red, silken scarf graced the pommel where a sapphire lay in silver wire.

"Everyone grab something, we're not leaving this blasted pit empty handed."

·   ·   ·

The weapon laden breakers returned to the amphitheater to cries of joy. Rust and Leylia rushed over while Jerk leaned against the arch, a sledge on his shoulder. Feral slept on the floor. Her snores filled the room with a guttural, savage peace. One that brought a much-needed levity to the battered crew. Rurik searched for another face and did what he could to suppress his dismay at its absence.

"Rik!" Rust waved, the slate still tucked under an arm. Burns scared half the shaper's face and carried down to his neck and shoulder. One eye drooped and when he smiled, it only came from the left side. "Fer sure thought'ya were dead. Buildin' explodin'n all." Leylia stood by

Rust, her white robes blackened from soot and dust. The bandages that hid her hands and face were stained red.

"Figured we'd have to scour the whole damn place to find you." Rurik grinned despite the sorry state of his people. "You look like shit, Rust."

The shaper barked a laugh. "Blasted sunsinger saved m'life, Rik, ne'er seen anythin' like it. Thought I was done fer."

"I did what I was able." Leylia bowed. She rubbed her hands together, her tone low and dark. "I could not save the other. Slackjaw? I am sorry, Foreman. My abilities are limited." Rust rolled his eyes and grasped the sunsinger's shoulder. She flinched but retained her calm demeanor.

"We'd be in worse shape without you." Rurik started as he walked to the center of the room. He nodded to Jerk who returned the silent greeting. "And now we only have to look at half of Rust's face. Did us a favor."

A few of the crew chuckled. Leylia balked. Once she realized the shaper took to the humor, she issued a nervous laugh. Sahira snorted in the back. Upon reaching the archway Rurik stalled and tapped Feral in the ribs with his boot. The woman grumbled and swatted at his leg. He repeated the motion until she opened one eye and grudgingly left the floor.

"Feral find you?"

"Hardly," Jerk scoffed. "We fumbled our way through this dark. Then? Blue torches light our way from nothing and voilà, we find the savage asleep on the floor." Jerk's voice dripped with disdain when he spoke of Feral. Otherwise, it tended to mild annoyance.

"You'd be the only savage here, slaver." Sahira stared daggers at Jerk.

"I believe the Isha'Rhi value Singuli service, no? Without us your people are, how do you say? Garbage."

Sahira lowered her pilfered spear, its black haft lined with gold. A wicked hook curved down the staff from the point, bestowing the weapon a slashing edge.

"That's enough." Rurik's command broke the tension. Both parties silenced and Jerk returned to a posture of nonchalance. "We have bigger problems than each other."

"Shari asks, how do we escape?" Sweet's asked, his tone dramatic, recovered from his fear stupor.

"Yes, that. We've got one sledge? And it'll last what ten ticks, maybe."

"If'n that." Rust sighed.

"Uplifting as always." Jerk pinched the bridge of his nose.

"If we wait for the other foremen to break through, which they will, we're as good as dead. A missing Adirian detachment condemns us all. And these are all Thalian Steel." Rurik flourished the axe in his hand and patted the blade on his side. The axe's haft took the same design as the spear: jet black with golden lines woven into the handle. A ruby affixed itself to the pommel, the size enough to pay for an estate all its own. "We'll be dead before we reach the camp."

The crew looked on with darkened expressions. Their reality of desperation hung in the air with a thickness that choked any vestiges of humor from their souls.

"Lord above." Leylia placed a wrapped palm over her chest then flipped her hand over, her fingers spread out and angled upward. "They would do such a thing?"

"Withou' hesitation." Rust slapped his scalp. "It's as much'a payday fer 'em as us an' we're short a crew."

"So we wait for Saiqua's mercy to reap us?" Sweets asked.

"We have a way out," Rurik said. Feral grunted and stomped her boot against the stage.

"Rik, no." Sahira stood a full head below Rurik, her simple garb of tight breeches and blouse paled to his regal, if frayed, long coat and trimmed tunic, but her demeanor contained all the confidence of royalty as she approached him. "We've got no idea where that leads."

"And?" Rurik held her gaze. "We die if we stay, I'll take a chance at the unknown."

"What do we discuss? *Merde.*" Jerk cursed in his native tongue.

"The portal you're leaning against." Rurik grinned and Jerk jumped, covering his backside beneath his red-trimmed tailed jacket. "Our choices are simple. Potential death or certain death. Which do you prefer?"

The crew exchanged glances, none making any sort of movement toward the other. A dull hum emanated from the portal, one Rurik failed to notice until then. The wafting darkness prodded at the outskirts of his memory, something that railed against his conscious mind. He twisted the sapphire band.

"I'll go." Hal perked up. Rurik startled, surprised. No one noticed his sudden lack of presence. "Lord Iskarion is right, why fight to just to give up now?"

"Found yer balls, boy?" Rust snarked. "If'n he's goin' I sure as the void cannae say no. Not like any of ya idiots can shape steel."

"This logic is sound." Half the crew sneered at Jerk's comment. Sweets went so far as to boo him.

"Your highness?" Rurik raised his brow and glanced at the woman.

"Shit." Sahira huffed. "Like punchin' a boulder arguin' with you is."

"I'll go first." Rurik tossed the axe to Jerk and waltzed into the portal.

Excerpt From the high Loremaster's Journal

ACCORDING TO THE MASTER SHAPERS of Thalas there are several, immutable rules (hah) that govern their art. As any "rule," I am assured these are suggestions to keep morons out of trouble, but I've catalogued them from my own reference. Or, more importantly, so that I might break them and record the effects.

- Material cannot be destroyed, only changed.
- To Shape a thing, one must know that thing. (Crude, but true enough. The best shapers are also metallurgists and amateur scholars.)
- Under no circumstances should an object be shaped with the intention of adding to or replacing its mass without spare material to merge.

Now that I find peculiar. Should? I will need to request additional funding for volunteers.

Chapter 6
It's What We do

A BLUE SKY held the afternoon in its splendor–the sun full, a fixed star high above the center of the world, bereft shadow. Fresh, salty air streamed down the coastline, moving with the crash of the clear waves from an endless ocean. Rurik sat with his rump in the sand, his fingers wiggling in the loose earth.

A bored sigh escaped his lips, and he laid back, letting the warmth of the day sink deep into his bones. He listened to the cries of gulls and reminisced of summer outings, lazy days of golden wines and careless merrymaking.

Time is short.

The voice cut through his reverie. Rurik bolted upright and scanned the horizon. The armored woman appeared beside him. She took the same posture, knees bent, hands in the sand with the helmet tilted back and cast toward the light of day. He followed her gaze. Somehow, he knew she watched not the source itself, but the Sunlord, the deity all the realms knew, if in their own way.

The sun waned. Ever present in its vigil its vast glow dimmed. Around it shadowed figures danced, too far to make clear, a tendril of darkness draining the light into nothing. The gold, slanted helmet inclined to him, where a thin rectangle of blue light replaced a visor.

Remember what you did.

"Boss?" Sweets' face popped into view. The shorter man snapped his fingers in front of Rurik's eyes. "You here?"

Rurik blinked away his hallucination. Reality shifted into focus with its bleak darkness and stagnant air. An ever-present damp sent a chill down his spine. The memory of warmth faded from his mind.

They stood outside–as much underground one considered out– surrounded on all sides by buildings Rurik did not recognize. Taller than those on the outskirts, these reached as high as five stories, though they retained the same black, sheer stone. Their roofs rose to a pyramidic end. Flat, paved obsidian layered a crossing of streets that formed a square of silent emptiness. At the center, an archway hummed to its own tune, alight with a glossy energy, other arches of the same construction nearby in a nexus of portals.

"I'm fine." Rurik waved Sweets off and surveyed his crew. All seven of them. Short thirty. A pang of guilt stuck a lump in his throat. Who else would die before they reached the encampment?

Leylia fussed over Rust, inspecting his burns while the others spread out and took in the cityscape's silhouette. Shadows crept farther now that the runic ceiling grew distant, its muted ambience casting an eternal twilight. Feral, of course, napped nearby, her arms wrapped about their last sledge. Hal tapped the butt of his halberd into the road. The clatter of the chipped and glossy finish echoed out into the street. Rurik winced.

"Sorry," Hal said.

"Too far for anyone to hear, don't fret it."

"Yes, Lord." Hal saluted the foreman.

"Not a lord, Hal."

"Of course. Sorry, Lord."

Rurik resumed his exploration to distract his frustration. He paced about the open square, his ponderous steps clacking in a bouncing echo. Gold script labeled door frames and windowsills. None he could read; shops, he knew. Somehow. A market square. Once, thousands flooded from the portals to partake in exuberant consumerism. An aroma of fresh baked bread reached his nostrils. The loud buzzing of crowded chatter, laughter, and music from corner-side minstrels. The picture grew vivid in his mind. Peaceful days in the southern market. His eyes wandered to an open-air bar top, stools left in place where he remembered them. Remembered?

He rubbed his eyes and braced against the side of an archway. Sahira had a point. These thoughts did not belong to him. No more than the ring. He twisted the jewelry on his finger.

"We're in the inner tier," he mumbled.

Sahira, pruning her nails, perked up at the absent comment. "You mean inside the outer wall?"

"Mhm. The webway has a city-wide network."

"My Cavari must be shit. What?"

"It." Rurik quirked a brow. Webway? "I–the arch, I think it has connections all over the city."

Sahira narrowed her eyes. "Maybe you should take that ring off, Rik."

"Maybe, But I think it brought us here," he said and patted the archway. "With it we can jump wherever we want. All we have to do is figure out the combinations."

"Is that wise, Foreman?" Leylia approached the two "Akleasn law teaches restraint in excess technology, lest we court the Void."

"You're a sunsinger. Do you sense voidcasting here?"

Leylia flicked her gaze to him. Thin and frail, he worried she would crumple at any moment. Instead, she cupped Rurik's cheeks. Sahira gagged. Leylia closed her eyes and a gentle hum rose from her throat. A thin golden light enveloped her hands and warmth flowed into his skin. On instinct he laid a palm over her grasp. The sapphire band flashed and the sunsinger's hallowed aura grew. It expanded and filled the square, a chime ringing out in its effervescence.

The humming ceased. Leylia's eyes snapped open, and she staggered backward, the light gone. The rest of the crew stared, their eyes wide and mouths agape.

"That," Leylia spoke between gasps. "I am not enough to summon so much. How did you?" She trailed off, bemused.

"It wasn't me. It was–" Silence.

Rurik's vision flew over the city, out of his body. It passed by and over towering buildings, speeding to the heart of the city itself. A tower loomed above the rest. Gifted its own compound and walls, the earth swallowed its zenith where the wicked pulsing of red, violent energy fed from its source. The source. The vision dug into the rock. It crashed through glass and steel and paused at a circular, golden door. Larger than ten men abreast and just as high, it shuddered with an ominous creak, ancient joints straining to hold back what lay beyond.

Remember what you did.

"Rik!"

Rurik peered up from his back. Leylia sat on her knees with her palms alight with a golden glow she sunk into his chest. Sahira cradled his head in her lap with a concerned frown. The others gathered over him. Even Jerk looked on with interest.

Rurik coughed. Collectively, the crew exhaled, though Sahira's concern turned to anger.

"Stop that!" The Ishite slapped him.

"Oi!" Rust said.

"I'm done with this! It's all bad! Portals and runes and walking dead men!"

"Walkin' wha'?" Rust blinked.

"Yes," Sweets said, sheepishly rubbing the back of his head. "Souls reclaimed from Myrdion."

"Like any'a us knows wha' in tha'void tha' means!"

"Enough!" Sahira yelled. "We're over our heads. We're graspin' at nothin'! None of us have slept or eaten. We're done. Much more of this and there won't be any of us left!"

"Sahira," Rurik mumbled. "My face." Her nails dug into Rurik's skin where she held him. She snapped her hands back. "You're right. Help me up."

Feral grabbed Rurik at the waist. She set him upright and brushed his shoulders with a nod. He responded by patting her arm. A few of the crew snickered. No one liked being manhandled by the wastelander.

"I'll explain everything I know." The others slouched with fatigue, beaten to lesser versions of themselves. "Let's get our asses home first."

"I am pretty hungry." Hal clutched his stomach.

"Do we possess a plan?" Jerk placed his elbow in an open palm and cupped his cheek. "I suspect our luck does not last."

"We head south." Rurik pointed in a random direction. "We should be just north of camp. I know. Don't." He cut Jerk off, the man's mouth half open.

"Qora's joy, more walking." Sweets leaned against Feral with a dramatic sigh.

·　　·　　·

Rurik's plan stalled at high walls of blackened steel. Sheer and sleek, it separated the inner tier from the outskirts. A gate loomed at the end of the road in the form of a solid sheet of metal embedded into the wall proper, wide enough to fit four wagons side-by-side. A marvel, he mused, and one he did not understand. The random bits of knowledge he glimpsed from what he assumed was the ring did not bother to reveal the secret of their egress. Rurik cast his gaze skyward and issued a quiet prayer. All that greeted him was a pair of winged statues atop the wall.

"Ah yes, the plan. To be stuck." Jerk grumbled aloud. The group dispersed in a huff. Most of them took a seat on the curb. Sahira leaned into her spear and peered intently at the slab of solid steel.

"Soooo." She tilted her head and eyed Rurik who hooked his thumbs into his belt. "Any grand ideas?"

"Maybe. We have time. And we have a shaper."

"Eh? Thank ye fer tha confidence, Rik." Rust sat with Leylia and beamed with pride at the mention. "But ach. I know stone an'iron, tha'there is a job fer a true shaper, it'd take me days to shape steel on a full stomach, let alone exhausted."

"Not to mention the runes, no?" Jerk snarked.

"It'll be a break, just like the rest of them. Leylia." Rurik barked.

"Melody!" Sweets piqued up.

"Fine, Melody."

"Yes!"

"Melody, did you sense any corruption earlier? When you summoned the light?" Leylia rested her hands in her lap and squirmed until his gaze.

"No, Foreman, I–" She frowned. "None. I am certain."

"I think it was the ring. Before. That allowed Melody to cast like that. That might work for Rust."

"Why, that's dangerous, Rik." Sahira deepened her voice to mimic Rurik's husky tone. "Don't worry Princess, my sudden trust in Thalian artefacts and sorcery will somehow convince you to believe I'm right. Oh! Of course, great lord, why question such ancient wisdom!" She spat and folded her arms, letting her spear rest inside the crook of her elbow.

"Why runt alpha argue herself?" Feral leaned in and sniffed at Sahira. "Is bleeding?"

Jerk snorted. Sweets covered his mouth and Hal flushed a bright red, while Sahira glared daggers at Feral. Rurik suppressed a smile.

"The alternative is another portal."

"I know!" Sahira huffed. "I just. A break? Now? What if Rust ain't quick enough and they reform?"

"Rust?

The shaper pushed up from the curb. He studied the metal for a moment, his head tilting in consternation.

"Better'n through another portal, eh? If ya think it'll work, boss, I can do it."

"That means you're up, Sweets." Rurik nodded to the thin, wiry man.

Danger plagued the life of a breaker. Exploding runes, rotten food, ambushes from rival teams; most of them ended up dead or dismembered, but few faced death so bluntly as a runner. Sweets collected himself and made for their last sledge. Feral parted with it reluctantly, taking in its place two curved daggers liberated from the cache.

Sweets advanced while the others backed up. Their precision matched their experience–they performed their ritual, each observer whispering prayers to their gods. Rurik listened to the others. Jerk, despite his sneer, wished for the best of luck, while Leylia, Rust, and Hal prayed together to the Sky Father. Sahira mumbled too quietly for the others and Feral's hands balled into white-knuckled fists.

Rurik dared to hope. This one time no one would die. He ran a finger over the ring in his anxiety.

Sweets tapped his fingers against the haft of the sledge. He exhaled and bounced from one foot to the other, shaking out his arms, his shoulders squared. Limbered up, Sweets lifted the sledge over his head and swung, the hammer meeting its target in a calamitous roar of vibrating metal. He ran. A sudden twist and several wide, leaping bounds brought the wetlander away from his venture, boots pounding against smooth obsidian in a graceless retreat.

Sweets ran from nothing. Nothing?

Rurik's brow furrowed. Rust muttered a thankful prayer, and Sahira launched a fist into the air with an exasperated whoop. No runes? Impossible. Doors, portals, thresholds, whatever one called them, were the worst offenders. Runes reformed in seconds. Then how?

Sweets stopped in front of the arc of bemused and excited breakers. He grinned, that lopsided expression of satisfaction and confusion spreading over his sharp chin and weathered cheeks.

"I am alive?" Sweets panted.

"Maybe tha' Vari fella finally listened, eh?" Rust barked out a laugh and enveloped the shorter man in a bear hug. Rurik scanned the wall. Victory seldom came without a cost. Something drew his gaze upward along the sleek surface. A distant rumble, the faintest echo of stone dragging against metal. Above them two obsidian forms peered over the ledge.

"Get back! Everyone!"

The constructs leapt. The breakers dispersed in a chaotic flurry, spreading to the sides of the road as the stone creatures landed with a quake that split the ground at their feet. They moved in perfect precision, their massive spears brought to bear. Wings of stone expanded from thick, sculpted shoulders, as a misting purple aura bled from empty eye sockets. Cracks of a similar color webbed out from that source, spindled in lines over their bodies.

Too late he realized he stood alone. Did he stiffen out of resolve or fear? His hands shook. Fear. What appeared as eyes latched onto the movement. Both constructs swiveled to face him, their stone spears leveled in Rurik's direction. They launched into a run, faster than their size demanded. Too fast. He fumbled for the blade tied clumsily at his waist, eyes wide as his body failed to respond. Fight. Run. Nothing. A spear ripped through the air, its pointed edge seeking his skull.

Impact. A blunt trauma crashed into Rurik's side. Side? He tumbled to the ground and struggled beneath a heavy weight. Panicked, he tossed the corpse aside. Corpse? Gray, dead eyes stared up at him. Lord, they pleaded, save me.

"Hal? Hedrik?!"

A primal howl matched the rumbling gait of a construct. Something clashed and Rurik lifted himself as Feral locked her dual daggers with the head of a spear. She cast the weapon aside, the raw, brute strength of the wastelander a match for the guardians.

"Quick move, Chiefman. No hit or die." Feral arched her back and vaulted away from a thrust from the second construct. Rurik scrambled to his feet as their attention refocused. His face burned red. No one else. He groaned and drew the blade from his side. Ready or not.

They came as one. He avoided a strike to his chest with a quick step, angling his body flat as the air rushed past his face. Rurik struck the spear and sliced through the stone, cleaving the weapon in two. What a sword. His marvel was short-lived as another blunt force broke his arm with a snap. Pain seared into his mind and a sense of weightlessness sent the world spinning. He landed with a gasping exhale, his lungs emptied by the collision.

Another clash. Rurik looked up in time to watch Jerk bury his axe into a construct's back between the wings. It sunk deep into the obsidian, and he guffawed, his celebration cut short as the weapon stuck. The construct grabbed Jerk's leg. Rurik grimaced and pushed himself to his knees with a groan. He knew what happened next. It lifted Jerk into the air, his fate sealed until Sahira appeared and jabbed her spear into the statue's wrist. She twisted the weapon to sweep the curved blade under the stone and severed its wrist. Jerk hit the ground with a yelp.

"She said no hit, Chiefman!" Sahira shot Rurik a smug grin.

"Down!" He exclaimed, back on his feet.

Sahira whipped her head around. She dipped her torso backward and threw her body into a summersault as a spear cratered into the street, sending glass shrapnel into the air. Rurik willed himself into the foray, teeth clenched. The construct flung its handless limb at his head, and he ducked the assault, stepping close as he sliced through the stone at the shoulder. Its arm clattered to the ground.

Another howling roar lost itself to the cavernous night. Feral clasped an arm around the weaponless construct's neck as she held onto its back and stabbed the shoulder. Her dagger sunk in again and again, fracturing the solid obsidian. Movement drew his eye. He dipped from a spear only to be clipped by a stone wing. Nothing broke this time, but his right side burned with pain. Joyous day. He staggered and caught a glimpse of Sweets leading Leylia and Rust away from the brawl. Good man.

Jerk rushed the statue again and gripped his axe as Sahira distracted the creature. It wove away from her strikes, faster now without its arm.

Jerk freed his weapon as the construct spun and jabbed its shoulder into Sahira, who took the hit mid-step. She crumpled.

"Hey!" Rurik waved his sword in the air. "You want me? Come get me!" The motion caught the guardian's attention. It rounded on him. Oh. Bad idea. Rurik bolted.

The statue charged with thunderous echoes that steadily increased in speed and gained on him. Think first next time. Think now. The gate didn't hold runes, but the rest of the city? Rurik halted his momentum and spun. He changed direction and flat sprinted to the city block. He twisted his heel into the ground and faced his pursuer, close enough to touch him. Rurik heaved an exhausted exhale and dove, throwing his weight into a gambit at the creature's disarmed torso. Its head followed the motion, and it jammed its spear into the ground, slowing it, but not before its balance gave way. Rurik scrambled up and ran, his heart pounding, adrenaline dulling the fiery ache that radiated over his body.

The construct collided with a storefront. Red energy arced from the surface. Runes flashed, red and jagged and the construct exploded in a burst of fire. The fireball nipped at his heels. Heat washed over Rurik and blew him off his feet into the arms of Jerk who caught him in a clumsy embrace. A few obsidian stones fell into the street, parts of the monster rolling away in no cohesive form.

One.

With heavy breaths Rurik searched for the other construct. It had hold of Feral, a hand around her torso. She brought the daggers to bare, unfazed by her predicament; blood stained her chest and face, yet somehow the statue looked worse than her, its body chipped and webbed, fading. As if annoyed, it tossed the wastelander aside. She hit the ground with a roll, recovered, then shuddered, standing with effort. The creature hefted its weapon into the air and reared back. Rurik struggled free from Jerk's embrace and limped toward it. Too slow.

Sahira's spear flew through the air. It slammed into the construct's head, the blade sticking out one of the purple sockets. It swayed and its movement stalled. Feral followed, growling and near foaming at the mouth, she brought her daggers on the fracture at the beast's shoulder.

Rurik and Jerk charged. Jerk sped ahead and swung his axe into an obsidian leg, removing it. The construct lilted, then crashed. It cracked the earth beneath, and Rurik followed. He plunged the sword into the statue's remaining eye, the blade sinking deep into the stone. It fell, cold, the purple veins fading to nothing.

Rurik released the sword.

He limped over to Hal where Rust held the young man, his head bowed while Leylia watched, her hands folded in prayer.

"Melody!" Rurik dropped to his knees. "What are you doing? Heal him!" His eyes flickered over the wound. Too deep.

"Rik." Rust's voice was soft. "Rik 'e's gone."

"No, not for me!"

Someone gasped at his side. Sahira held a hand over her mouth as Rurik reached for the boy. He stopped, his hands shaking.

"Sunlord. Why? Why for me?"

Sahira lowered to a knee and placed a hand on Rurik's shoulder, her nails clutching the leather of his coat.

"Rurik. He's gone."

"No! No damn it! Melody, help him! You can heal him!" Rurik fell onto his backside. Two sets of footfalls came to a rest behind him. He heard Sweets whisper a prayer. "No one else was supposed to die." Sahira caressed his cheek. She hugged him and rocked him along with her own body. "No one else."

"We're breakers, Rik." Sahira squeezed him tighter, and he wrapped his fingers around her arm. "It's what we do."

Excerpt from the high Loremaster's Journal

O F ALL THE THINGS I am thankful for it is, assuredly, the absolute precision of the Sunlord to keep regular. I've looked for inconsistencies, for mathematical errors and they do not exist. I'd doubt my own calculations for not for the sheer simplicity of the cycles that dominate what constitutes a single year of the Thalian Calendar.

Twelve Months, all consisting of exactly thirty days. Each day accounts for twenty-four hours, and every six hours marks a phase of the "Sunlord's fight against chaos." Ridiculous religious superstition. Fulldark (Midnight, as more enlightened cultures call it), at the beginning of a day, as it is the moment after that he "emerges to shed his grace upon the realm" (is that a euphemism?). Dawn, or Half Light (really?) follows at the sixth hour, Full Light (Noon, elsewhere) at the twelfth, and of course Dusk, or Half Dark (absurd) at the eighteenth.

Seasons are particularly interesting, as the "Sunlord" rises to its zenith in the depths of winter and lowers to the realm in summer. And what does this bring us to? Three-hundred and sixty days; or a perfect circle in degrees.

Chapter 7
Nuance

S OME RECEPTION."

    Kali sat at an ornate square table with a detailed map of Ilvicar etched in runes on the surface's center. The Republic, Lindorum, and Haven were rendered to the east, Aul'Thannon to north and Isha'Rhi at the southern range; someone penned in the vagabond tribes of the lowlands to the west, doing their best to name those that frequented the border towns. South of Iskvar and off the western coast a glowing red circle marked Dula'Thalier.

    "To put it lightly. As you do, Arkalis." Solara's chilled tone stung Kali's ears. She stood at the head of the table with the rest of the council. Dinkira and Gariant flanked Kali, the latter's coat covered in dried blood. He managed without injury but kept his own council. Zevra, the resident Sunpriest, took her place by the diviner. She wore her hair free, long, black curls running to the small of her back. Her plain white robes contrasted the telltale mocha skin of Xyr. Slender fingers fiddled with the golden sunburst amulet at her neck. Middle age suited her face with a graceful texture, deep dimples and sunken cheeks under exhausted eyes.

    "Let's save the jabs, shall we marshal?" A fresh face joined them. Clad in his parade armor–an exquisite display of small plates layered over one another for ease of movement, joints reinforced by chain with thick gauntlets and hefty pauldrons, all black and trimmed with red—a knight, with four sword pins next to the gold clasp of his cape. He placed his helmet in his lap, revealing the thick mustache and same style goatee as Lesandre. Blond and light skinned. Lesandre sat opposite the knight. "Whatever happened, this was a monumental failure. I lost a dozen men. All knights, mind you. To gunfire! Who armed them with live weapons?"

"That," Solara flicked her attention to the captain. "Is a good question." She absently brushed at the blood on her surcoat. "Care to explain, captain?"

"Pulled those guns up from the old armory." Gariant's gaze haunted the floor, his shoulders hunched, Kali had seen him counting the servants' bodies. "No way they were loaded.

"The captain would never risk the life of his liege. Arkalis wasn't more than a few paces from Lesandre." Dinkira nursed his bandaged forehead. "And she put herself in danger, should you recall. It's because of her he remains among us, or did you attend a different ambush?" Still sassy. Kali nudged the elder man with her knee and a brief humor flashed in his eyes.

"Let's see this for what it is." Lesandre leaned in and every head turned to the lord. He blinked at the sudden attention, hesitating. "Ah—the mercenaries? Whatever they were. I believe the marshal has people interrogating the survivors now. My death was a secondary motivation. Their primary target was the duke. His mental state is well known. No better time to strike at such a renowned warrior."

Kali exhaled. She looked away from Lesandre and let her vision wander. The council room brought little comfort: gray walls, no windows, stone floors. A natural, white light filled the chamber via rune-lined lanterns. The servants called them sunlamps. Not quite accurate, but they bespoke a mystery above the standard issue equivalent.

"Who benefits from the death of an Iskarion and an Adirian? The other dukes swore allegiance to my father after the battle of Ilduan—"

"The betrayal, you mean." Kali's eyes flicked to Lesandre.

"I ah–the point is they swore allegiance, naming him Grand Duke. But this marriage solidifies his control of Dula'Thalier, and I very much imagine the others will try to prolong that as long as possible."

"A political hit?" The knight grunted his distaste. "Murdering the nobility? Such a thing is not done. And for what, a pile of ancient rubble?"

"Excuse me, Sir Elys, but that ancient rubble houses the Cathedral of the Sun and the Runecaster's College. Aklesia has representatives interested in those sites. Even if they are allowed minimal access." Zevra said, her tone neutral.

"She is quite right." Lesandre interceded and silenced the knight.

"The High Loremaster made his research public. There is undoubtedly a great weapon at the heart of the city. One he believes may have been essential to the Desolation. It stands to reason that not just the dukes have an interest in preventing my father from consolidating his power, but the rest of the continent as well. And who else? The Eindir Helmstates? Tsaodun spies were spotted in the embassy at Haven, and there are reports of Tuldrathi privateers at port in Caul. Foreign powers are wary of what we may discover at Dula'Thalier if you've not noticed. Signs of war are everywhere."

"We're to accuse foreign powers of espionage?" Dinkira scoffed.

"These mercs were Cavari. All of 'em. With training. It takes time to get that good with an arquebus." Gariant lifted his eyes from the floor.

"Not all of them." Kali spoke with a fiery intensity. "The things that went after my father? They were voidtouched." The room silenced. Zevra mimed a sunburst.

"Preposterous. Such things only exist in Lindras and Xyr." Elys grumbled and stroked his mustache. He spoke more to convince himself than the others.

"Go take a look at the bodies. When was the last time you heard of wastespawn east of Veldinan? Everything fits with the Litanies. Zevra?"

"I've not had time to investigate properly. But. From the Litany of the Void: 'They shall appear as wights, pale of skin; snow white, yellow eyes and blood of fire.'"

"Dramatic, but that's pretty fucking spot on."

"Enough of this!" Solara hissed. "These are distractions. Someone smuggled weapons and hired mercenaries on my watch. Diviner Dinkira, as steward you control the house, and you. Captain. You are responsible for recruits of yours and their arms. Had Lord Lesandre not. . ." She flicked her vision to the young lord. ". . .forbade it, I'd have taken both your heads hours ago. As I see it, you are responsible for the murders of multiple knights and attempted assassination of the nobility."

Kali's face flushed red and her nails dug into the table. Voices whispered rage at the edge of her hearing. That smug grin. Every fiber of her being willed to strangle the life from those arrogant, perfect eyes. Distractions? Voidtouched existed only in stories, and she saw three alive, well, and real. Now she pushed for the deaths of what few Iskarion retainers remained. Kali blinked. Her rage subsided as she pushed the buzzing away from her mind, replaced by a singular thought.

"You approved the training."

"What?" Solara returned the confused tone with a blank stare.

"There were no guards on the walls, no gunners. Why allow a loyalist garrison today? The guards for my father's chambers were gone, like they knew to clear out."

"Careful with your accusations, Arkalis."

"Those soldiers aimed at the knights, not him." She gestured to Lesandre. "They wanted to inflict damage, distract us. My father is still reigning duke. Only his death promotes his children and you. You." Kali fingered the black, leather-bound hilt at her waist. She replaced her old sheath, one that fit the runic, fiery blade of the voidtouched. A blood red ruby crowned the pommel.

"How dare you, whelp! I'll see the last of your blood spill in this room at your wish!" Solara drew half her saber from its curved sheath.

"Marshal!" Lesandre stood. He knocked his chair over, a hand adjusting those thin frames over his eyes. "What a trying day. There is much mourning to be done. Pyres to be built. My house may differ in name, and our people may split traditions, but tonight we are all Cavari. I invoke Riah's Peace to be observed until dawn a week hence. Enough time for us to pass on the souls of the fallen. Zevra, is it? Please, speak your blessing."

"May Riah's hand guide us to the Sunlord's wisdom. Peace is invoked, and it shall be observed, lest one abandons their faith and covets the Void." Zevra spoke the blessing too fast to decipher. The others relaxed at the withheld aggression. Elys removed his hand from the hilt of his saber and Gariant did the same of his blade.

"Diviner, I trust you have some trusted heralds? Have them declare this holy blessing and an evening of mourning followed by celebration. I'll replenish any silver from the Iskvar treasury for a feast. The keep and the town. That should show some solidarity. And that should be enough for the day?"

"As you wish, Lord. I'll work up an expenditure report for your scribe." Dinkira rose and placed a hand on Kali's shoulder. Gariant and Zevra went with him. Kali lingered, locked in a staring contest with the marshal. Neither blinked.

"Lady Arkalis?" Lesandre popped his head inside her vision.

"What?"

"Your blessing? For the feast?"

"Oh. Yes. Sure."

"Great! It's official. Marshal?"

Solara nodded her agreement. Elys left with the rest of them, his plate creaking. He mumbled something about a privy and bowed, leaving the chamber. Dinkira and company followed, with Zevra hot on his heels. Kali paused at the door. She set her attention on the marshal.

"Touch my father, Solara, and the Sunlord himself will not stop me from collecting your head."

•   •   •

Kali slumped over the western parapet. She rested her head in the crook of her arms, her hair scattered to the wind. It reached only her shoulders now, more efficient, but that did little to ease her depression. It took her a full year to cultivate that look. Maybe it fit her battle-weary physique. The ripped dress clung to her body, the neckline torn through her chest to her stomach with only a few heroic buttons left to the corset.

She listened to the crackling funeral pyres. Over the din of the flames Zevra led her chorus of sunsingers in prayer-song, their harmonies pleasant, if dark. Her nose twitched at the scent of burnt flesh.

At dusk, the sun waxed with darkness from top to bottom and hundreds of glowlamps appeared from the harbor and town. The commoners heard the message: Riah's Peace invoked, a week of feasting and rest–most celebrated, their cavorting carried by sea borne breezes and delivered to the envious ears of a lone woman. Tradition prevented nobles from drinking on the night of mourning. Riah and her voided rules. Alcohol didn't start brawls, fragile egos and dull wits threw punches, though perhaps the wine helped.

Despite the truce more than double the standard guard patrolled the walls. The entire Adirian garrison took the evening shift, armed with fresh arquebuses.

Bonfires roared from the courtyard gardens, blustering smoke billowing upward. She imagined the souls of the dead pilfered from their bodies by the winged messengers of the faith, carried home to the Isle of Cinder, the holy home and domain of the sun. Imagined. She saw only ash.

Solara's words echoed in her mind. The last of her blood. She refused to believe it, but with no word of Rurik despair crept into her thoughts. Always she felt his presence. At any distance, the familiar aura of her twin lulled her to comfort. As children they crossed wooden swords on this very wall; she won, of course. Her brother was slow, the clumsy oaf. Gariant's boisterous chuckle would sour the boy's mood and he'd take cheap shorts at her. She recalled the welts. And now his presence escaped her. No aura, only a hollow pit she filled with wine.

Nearby shadows took shape as Lesandre's visage approached. Kali closed one eye and did little to hide her twitching lip. She slid down, her rump hitting the ground with a soft thud and slouched against the stone. She mused her hair, eyes low, watching the circle of priests at prayer in the courtyard.

"I hope I'm not disturbing you." Lesandre said.

"You are."

"You met one of my sisters once. Lynette. She spoke highly of your– hah. Your honesty." The lord removed the frames from his face and wiped them with a thin cloth from his pocket. He held them up, squinting at the glass. "Though I doubt you remember."

"Short, right? Curled her hair like an Ishite. Portly, gabs for hours on end?"

"I'm surprised she caught your attention."

"I remember things that annoy me."

Lesandre's lips spread into a grin. He fit the frames onto his face, adjusting them until they sat parallel to his eyes. He swatted blond bangs out of his vision, slicking his hair back to the best of his ability. Several days carriage ride followed by full panic made it difficult to keep one's style.

"My father once described her as a simpering tool. Perhaps an accurate assessment?"

"My father once described yours as a maniacal void-fucking whoreson. How's that for accuracy?"

"More hyperbolic, I'd say." Lesandre smiled. Kali glanced up at him and searched for the sardonic expression she expected in Adirians but found only humor. He scooted over. "May I?"

"As you will." Lesandre sank. He rested his arms on his knees and mirrored her posture. His frames caught the light of the fire and almost absorbed it. Her mind drifted to the runework atop the beacon tower.

"I believe you," he started. "About the voidtouched."

"You don't need to placate me. They can make me your wife, but I'd bed a sword before you."

"Oh, I've no desire to placate."

"Eunuch?" Kali eyed the man's crotch. That could explain the baggy pants. "Seems counterproductive to a noble line."

"Hah. No. I prefer men."

Kali flat stared Lesandre in the face. He returned the look with a downturned brow. A full minute passed in silence. Then, without warning, Kali burst out laughing. She kicked her feet against the stone and slapped her thighs. Lesandre tapped his fingers together and issued a confused chuckle, stopping once he realized he missed the joke.

"I'm sorry." Kali spoke in fits of laughter. "No, really." She wiped a sleeve over her eyes to clear out the tears. "Oh, Sunlord be praised. And here I was worried you'd be ugly. Thus ends the Iskarion line, its children blown to ash and sex starved to suicide."

"I'm not thrilled with this union either. Less so now that my father wishes me dead."

"What now?"

"I noticed the missing watch also. Sir Elys is a powerful man but lacks wit of any sort; few men in his position are so apt to be caught unaware." He shrugged and tilted his head back to watch the sun disappear into darkness. "And Solara is, let's say, singular in her loyalty. Had I perished, or your father? The Adirian forces would have every excuse to claim absolute rule over Iskvar. Fortunately for us, you're every bit as fierce a warrior as the Iskarions claim to be."

"So all that pandering? Spies and pirates, why not confront her?"

"Forgive me, Arkalis, you are brave and honest, but you lack nuance." She glared at Lesandre, but the slight rang true. Hard to fault a man for honesty. "Push her too far and she reacts before we are ready. Better to buy time to maneuver. As I see it, I've purchased us a week with the Faith's most useful social ploy."

"We? I don't even know you," Kali grumbled and lifted herself upright. Below a line of servants took turns tossing the personal effects of those departed into one of the pyres. The other burned without an audience; the final grave of the mercenaries.

"Like it or not we're in this together. A common threat makes us easy allies. I don't know you either, yet I've little choice but to trust you."

"Let's say I believe you and this isn't some contrived plot. What's the plan? Stall forever?"

"Yes." Lesandre crossed his legs and sat upright. Kali turned over a shoulder, meeting his self-satisfied smirk with a skeptic's deadpan.

"Care to elaborate, lord?"

"It's simple. I intend to set you free."

Excerpt from hardent's Bestiary

KNOWN FOR THEIR relaxed temperament the Ruhks of Veldinan make for the most loyal and true companions. Assuming one possesses the near limitless resources to feed the otherwise gigantic eagle-like creatures, of course. They stand three times the height of a man; their wingspans twice that, with voracious talons capable of ripping armor to shreds. White and gold feathers span the length of their bodies. Powerful beaks mark them as predators, used often to break flesh.

Their strength pales to their rather daunting intelligence as I have personally witnessed the noble creatures use tools to solve daily incursions. Which does question their origins. Many believe them to be wastespawn, but how could such a majestic, gentle creature be such?

Chapter 8
Both Ends

Kali pulled her cloak tighter about her shoulders in defense against the sea borne winds of the beacon tower. Lesandre's meeting called for the entire trust. Dinkira stood off her shoulder, using her as a shield against the cold. Crafty bastard. Gariant took his place beside the seated duke, more so out of habit than intention, with Gwin, the attendant, opposite. Lesandre wedged himself awkwardly next to Kali. He struggled to keep space between them.

"This isn't suspicious at all." Kali scooted closer to Lesandre. "Meeting in broad daylight. In full view of every guard ever."

"Solara isn't a fool, she'll expect us to try something. Better she feels secure in our whereabouts." Lesandre shuffled closer to the barrier's edge.

"What's this about?" Gariant's breath carried thick tidings of alcohol. Lowborn played by more generous rules. In exchange for expected obedience, of course. "Say the word, Kali, and I'll dump the boy over the cliff."

Lesandre's eyes bulged.

"That shouldn't be necessary, captain. Yet. Let him speak."

"Ah, yes." Lesandre took a deep breath and smoothed over his countenance. "Arkalis and I agree there is a plot afoot. If the duke dies, she inherits Iskvar and is bound in marriage. If I am murdered my father gains the justification he needs to execute whoever is most convenient."

"Fucked on both ends," Gariant grunted.

"Charming colloquialism." Lesandre turned from the captain, trying to speak and breathe through his mouth. "If Arkalis were to flee the castle, we can't be married. She also will pose a genuine threat–an errant ducal heir whose home is beset by enemies? The barons won't tolerate ancestral lands seized by murder. It buys us time."

"And? She'll be hunted, the Diviner's Guild is not easily evaded," Dinkira added.

"On land. By sea she can reach Haven and claim sanctuary. If memory serves, the Magisters don't allow guild activity."

Dinkira rubbed his chin, thoughtful. "That may just work."

"Fantastic. We're all onboard." Kali clasped her hands and eyed Gariant before he could refute her claim. "Les and I agree that we'll need some of the household onboard."

"Les?"

"Roll with it."

"Okay." Lesandre adjusted his frames.

"Won't get too far with knights on horseback, so we'll need a distraction. If Solara sees one of us with Balen, she'll have his head. That leaves you."

Lesandre laughed, nervous.

•   •   •

Lesandre wrinkled his nose at the rough scent of barnyard living: hay, sweat, and unwashed animals. He straightened his jacket and strolled with squared shoulders into the stable. Several stable hands milled about, less than he expected of such a large castle, carrying buckets of water and bags of feed interspersed with waste removal. A day's respite rarely applied to essential staff.

The occasional grunt and whinny of kept horses hounded him as he wobbled his way up a narrow, wooden staircase, first at a walk, then an anxious jog as the boards creaked beneath his steps. His heart fluttered halfway up. With no rail to grab he pulled his tome closer to his side. The High Loremaster's journal eased the tension in his shoulders with a sense of responsibility. Or something.

A dozen or so hay bales decorated the stable's second floor with a notable duo built high enough to suspend a hammock between them. Balen lay with a leg crossed over his knee and his arms outstretched, a book held a little too close to his nose to be convincing. Four outlets connected to the central landing, each housing worn, weary linens and pillows large enough for a creature three times the size of a man. Ruhk pens?

"Balen?"

"Oy?" The boy poked his head up. He chewed on a straw stalk. "Oh ah, do sumfin' fer'ya lord?"

"You know me?"

"Nadda bit." He tossed his book aside. "But'cher too clean, no calluses. Thin. Poncy shoes."

"Arkalis mentioned your irreverence."

"Ahuh." Balen chewed. "Big'n words. Lord it is. Need'a horse? Fellers below'll rear'un up fer yah."

"No. Thank you. I've come with business." Lesandre eyed the discarded book. *Gilderan's Casting Analysis of Thalas.* Really? "If you're not busy."

"Business ay? Well' if'n Kali sen'cha I'm guessin' yer all up tah shenanigans."

"Shena–? Yes. That. Her life is in danger, you see. It's imperative that you–"

"Keep'n my mouth shut, ahuh. Listen'ear Lord Ponce, 'ow many country boys yah see livin' in a castle? Kali sees me one day, says: 'Hey! It's cold as shit out here, take care of my horse and you're set for life.' Now'n, as yah can see, tha' promise was kept. Who'd'ya think I'm in'a mind to rat on? My meal ticket, or yah red-wearing boot lickers?"

Lesandre stood with his mouth agape. He tapped his fingers against the journal, the dull thrum interpreting his dumbfounded state. Balen sat upright and dangled his legs over the side of the hammock.

"After the feast, before high dark, we need you to disable the horses."

"Wha' now?"

"Disable? Incapacitate? Make unrideable?"

"Ahuh. Yah want me disablin' the whole stable, an' Kali asked fer it?" Balen shifted his stalk to the other side of the mouth. He chewed at Lesandre.

"Yes. She said if you gave me any lip to–to. Well." Lesandre approached Balen and slapped him across the face. The stable master chewed, his face otherwise impassive.

"Yep." Balen rubbed his cheek. "A'ight, lord, but I'mma need supplies. As much as you can give me."

"We must remain subtle. What do you require?"

"Beer." Balen grinned. "Fuck load'a beer."

• • •

The duke coughed. The full-bodied sound distracted the trust. Gwin glared at the group, sour to their distraction of his duty. The fit ended with a grunt. Denrik cleared his throat and wiped his mouth with a sleeve then settled into his viewing chair. His royal coat tousled in the wind, fur blown about by ever present sea breezes.

"What's next?" Kali asked. The group realigned their attention.

"We've got no fighters. At least none trained at it. Some'a the servants blame the Adirians for losin' friends, but they'll make for a piss poor offensive. How're we going to get by the guards? The inner wall's open, but the lower gate's sealed tighter than the marshal's legs. Not to mention hirin' a ship." Gariant huffed.

"I may have a solution." Dinkira rubbed his palms together. "As I recall, despite the Faith's insistence on its closure, Arkalis, you declared a special decree that the dock side brothels remain open and untaxed?"

"Hah. Yeah."

"No doubt the proprietors of these institutions would allow us their services for a night, free of charge? I've often lamented such a steady source of revenue. Perhaps, even, via a madam we may purchase the services of a merchant to ferry you."

"Why Din," Kali snarked at the old man, grinning. "Didn't know you had it in you. Can you get Solara to approve it?"

"Of course not, but he can." Dinkira gestured to Lesandre. "And if, perhaps, a few rumors of hearty entertainment were to spread to the garrison? I've known few better remedies for low morale."

"Whores'll do to distract most of 'em, but the marshal'll have a reserve she's keepin' sober. Doesn't take long to rouse a prepped barracks."

Kali perked up. "I've got an idea."

•   •   •

The deep bedrock of Iskvar's foundations grew green with mold, its basements spanning from wall to wall, tunnels that ran throughout the compound. Despite its utility, few of the residents utilized the convenient paths if only because of the unfortunate sewer plan. The original architects pilfered the Lindorum concept of aqueducts to bring a constant supply of water throughout the keep. While Kali appreciated the use of indoor toilets, the original builders overlooked a key factor: the smell of feces.

Kali pinched her nose with a clothespin. She repurposed a sunlamp as a lantern to guide her path among the darkness with Cerric in tow. He carried two kegs of powder under each arm, unable to protect himself from the fetid scent. Poor fellow. Together they navigated the raised waterways, mounted aqueducts tailing their path with the open-faced drainage ditches beneath them. Runic ports built into the cliff face brought in the sea water where another set of infused markings siphoned the salt and deposited it in nearby cauldrons.

They halted beside one such portway. The scent abated, instead replaced by fresher, if mildewy, air. The tunnels opened up here to an open space with spare beds arrayed in too close of quarters to be comfortable. An ancient, worn ladder led from a sealed hatch where a previous duke thought it clever to expand the garrison. The practice stopped after an outbreak of what a Sunpriest referred to as 'Shit Fever'. Vestiges of the attempt lingered, however, such as the old armory. A set of chains secured the lock to those doors.

"Set them there for now." Kali removed her pin. Cerric set the kegs as instructed, weary.

"Lady, I'm always willing to serve but–"

"Kali." She interrupted.

"What?"

"Me. Arkalis. Kali. We're past titles, Cerry." She winked. Cerric blushed. "Now, what can you do about those chains?"

"Chains?" Cerric peered over Kali and fixed his gaze on the metal links. "I suppose cut them with a file? I'm no locksmith."

"We need to get in and make sure no one knows we were there, yeah? That last bit is important."

"I've not the skill, lady."

"Sure you do. You're a shaper's apprentice. I'm not asking for glasswork, just a little bedlam."

"I suppose I can try." Cerric's voice wavered. She offered an encouraging thumbs up. The young shaper appraised the lock and, with her urging, closed his eyes, his lips moving without sound. He muttered something about forging and iron. Elements, maybe? She shrugged and watched the tunnels, shifting her weight from one heel to another. A minute passed. Two. The telltale green glow of the art emitted from his hands. Weak, but suitable. A link frayed until it snapped.

"I did it, la–uh. Kali. I didn't think I cou–"

"Shh!" Kali placed a hand on the shaper's chest. From the hall voices echoed against the stone.

"Saw 'em go over 'ere." A deep, husky voice spoke.

"Marshal'll have our heads if we lose her." Still deep and husky, but noticeably feminine this time.

"You see that? Looks like a sunlamp."

Shit. Kali searched the sunken barracks. Moldy, moth ridden linens and beds too small to hide under. If Solara caught her now the whole plan was dust. Think. Kali met Cerric's terrified countenance with a blink. Oh. She unlaced the top of her bodice and pulled her shirt beneath her breasts.

"Take your pants off." She whispered and pressed her torso into his. He hesitated, stuttering. "Do it!"

Cerric hastily untied his belt and dropped his pants. Loud, ruckus footfalls marched down the dark corridor. Kali pressed her lips into Cerric's.

"Hold it right there!" Two red coated guardsmen rounded the corner. They burst into the room waving sunlamps and promptly turned away. The woman at the front dropped her lantern and stammered. "That is. I. We. S-sorry, Lady Arkalis, we maybe. We thought–well."

Kali broke her contact with Cerric. The shaper's bent in for more. She almost regretted using him. Almost.

"You thought?" Kali grinned and exposed her breasts and the shaper's crotch. The man kept his gaze averted while the woman looked, then reconsidered. "It's the perfect place to hide, you know. In case you two were looking." She winked.

"Oh! No, no. Lady. We were tasked with keeping watch. To. Make sure. Well, you know."

"How dutiful. If you haven't noticed, it's one of the few spots that doesn't smell, hm? Makes it more enjoyable."

"Yes. Lady. Thank you for the advice. If that is all we–we beg your leave."

"Please do."

"Thank you, lady!" The woman bowed low–very low, picked up her torch then dipped back. They retreated in haste. Kali waited until their lamplight disappeared and the sound of boots with it. She released Cerric to lace up her bodice. Cerric stared.

"You've seen them before. Cover that up and use that passion, we've got work to do."

•   •   •

"What if they catch you? Solara will have guards tracing your movements." Lesandre said.

"I'll figure something out. Don't fret over me, I'm resourceful."

"Is that the term now?" Dinkira sassed her.

"You're old." A valiant retort, to be sure. Gariant barked a laugh. She always counted on his support.

"I don't want to know the details," Lesandre added.

"Not with your preferences." Kali shifted closer to the lord. He stepped away, only to find himself on the duke's side, squished by two Iskarions. Lesandre fidgeted in the trap.

"Yes, but here's one problem that needs resolving. The feast will be distraction enough, but the marshal gives detail its definition. She will notice any absences. By any of us. Especially the heir of Iskvar. What are we to do with her?"

The lot of them exchanged looks. Dinkira opened his mouth then stopped to fold his hands beneath his robes. His face contorted in consternation. The rest followed suit. Below, servants hurried about in the courtyard, raising canopies to service the staff and its guests. Canopies? She looked upward and spotted a bundle of dark clouds off the coast. The castle banners, a mixture of Adirian and Iskarion heraldry, blew inward. What timing. Sunsingers considered storms to be an ill omen.

"As to be expected." A nasally voice spoke from the tower's doorway. Gwin stood with his hands over his hips. His thick, white brow made that judgmental face of his all the more powerful. Narrow, sharp eyes and a beak-like nose stared down at the group. "You are ignoring your most valuable resource." He spoke with a highborn accent. Years of service molded him in a lord's image. "Servants are beneath the notice of lords and retainers and your details. Do not worry yourself. Solara will be handled."

Kali shared a glance with Lesandre. She shrugged.

"May the Sunlord bless us. If he doesn't, we're fucked." Gariant said.

"On both ends." Lesandre echoed.

Excerpt from the Cavari Lowborn Charter

A NY HOLDINGS of significant population are to be overseen by officials appointed by the resident Duke or Baron, known officially as the Commoner's Council. This group, no less than five, but not to exceed thirteen, is led by a Patriarch or Matriarch chosen by their apparent liege who possesses the ability to rebuke decisions of the council. They are given oversight of taxation, trade, and are expected to administer justice on behalf of local laws and are considered an arm of the local nobility. To this end they may create and maintain a garrison.

While the Council is allowed to operate under their own power, they are first, and foremost, accountable to any of the nobility and must consider laws and decrees issued by those above their station before all else.

Chapter 9
The Last Guardian of Iskvar

The feast hall sang with light and music. Sunlamps lined the exterior, bathing the crowd of demi-nobles, retainers, and working servants in natural light. An endless banquet of food and wine made its way from the kitchens on silver trays; succulent pork and veal filled the air with a distinct maple aroma of Cavari tradition. A roaring fire burned in the hearth behind the royal table on its stage where Zevra and two of her singers kept the blaze alive with their voices lifted to song. Each note matched the flicker of the flame.

Kali sat beside her father. She surveyed the hall where Dinkira filled the benches of half a dozen long tables on short notice. She recognized those of import. Baron Shadowsong sat closest with her family–the only other landed nobility present. The middle-aged woman kept her back straight and oversaw her teenage children, all four of the red headed nobility caught in thralls of readily available wine. Their dark green clothing blended well with the Iskarion blues. The baron caught Kali's gaze and offered a gentle smile reflected in a single eye, her hair strategically groomed to hide a patch. Dinkira swore her aunt wore the visage of her mother. Not that she would know; the only image of Ilya Iskarion on the grounds resided as a rather dreadful painting in her father's chambers.

The center table held the remaining Adirian knights and Sir Elys dressed in their best surcoats sans armor, but not without weapons. The servants filled their cups with water. Smart. Kali eyed her goblet. Untouched. Nothing more suspicious than the local lush keeping sober. She raised the glass and tipped it back.

Apart from the shouting, chair scraping, and clinking of silverware, minstrels filled the atmosphere with a merry rhythm over the pious fire-song. A fiddle player kept pace and led the woodwinds and a light percussive beat in practiced harmony. Kali embraced the joy despite the rehash of the abundant feast clichés. She caught sight of Dinkira on the end of the royal table waving his hand to the music and her father bobbed a bit, focused as he was on his meal. Gwin stood dutifully nearby, leaning over and whispering into the duke's ear.

Lesandre sat on Denrik's right. Rurik's seat. He made a show of stuffing his face. Not a single morsel that touched his plate was safe from such ravenous stress. He shared a space with Solara who wore her finest attire: her marshal's uniform, blood red with black decals of Adirian heraldry and a thick, leather coat trimmed in gold. Kali's smile turned to ash. Show off. Her first plan involved shoving a dagger in Solara's throat.

"Not hungry?" Denrik jabbed Kali in the side. The lightest contact made her wince. She looked at her plate: venison. Any other night and she would devour it in seconds. "Don't stress your figure, girl, all blooded Iskarion women are thicker. Lets you cleave more heads. Hah."

Which father was this? Perhaps their matching attire helped his memory. Dinkira found her another dress on short notice–this one gaudy, blues and grays with sequins sewn into the lining at the hem, the neckline made more for spectators than the wearer. Two black ruhks took flight beneath the chest. A noble sign for a house of head cleavers.

"I think I'll stick to wine tonight." She flashed a toothy smile. Denrik chuckled and downed his wine.

"You'll want to, sure. How else to keep an evening in high spirits? Best piss someone off, hm? Get a brawl going. Shadowsong'll knock someone out, I'm sure. Steeled woman, that one, unlike your mother. She preferred to rip you apart with words instead of a blade."

"Father." Kali laid a hand on the man's leg and squeezed. "How much do you remember? Right now?"

"Hmph." The duke snorted. He dug into his meal, silver flatware pausing halfway through the cut. "There are gaps. Holes. I know your brother is gone, but I don't know why. I know that this clarity will fade. And I know I failed you, Arkalis. Somehow. And that I continue to do so. Certainly, it has to do with all the blasted red in my hall." Denrik instinctively reached for his greatblade and grasped at nothing. Solara confiscated most weapons upon entrance to the hall. Kali's decoy blade as well. "And I know you're leaving." His hand rested upon hers and he clutched it gently.

"I must. To keep you safe. It's the only way I can protect you," Kali said. Denrik smiled, his eyes focused, intent. She matched the stare until his widened in a moment of confusion.

"You changed your hair. What's the occasion?"

Kali inhaled and rolled her shoulders, settling herself. "It was too long. For training."

"Oh." The duke settled into his chair. He rediscovered his plate and popped half a chunk of meat into his mouth. Enough stalling. She caught Gwin's eye and pointed at her cup, snapping twice. The attendant bowed. Kali watched a servant ascend the stairs to the incline; a portly woman, near five decades worn. Throughout the night she managed to spill half a pitcher of wine on her apron, as well as drop a tray or two in transit from the kitchen. Quite the show. The woman made a fuss and yelped, falling toward the table and dropping her container. Red, luscious liquid spilled in Solara's lap.

The room grew quiet as the minstrels, sensing the mood, cut their music. Only the chant of the faith persisted with the crackling fire behind it. The aged servant apologized in a flurried panic. She made a show of fawning over the marshal. Calmly, Solara stood and slapped the woman across the face. The servant collapsed, blood running from her nose and staining her blouse. She simpered as Solara, without a word, crushed her boot into the woman's stomach. A sickening gasp escaped the servant and Solara brought her heel down at her face.

"Marshal!" Lesandre stood. He waved the minstrels on and they resumed their tune, if shakily, and the hall took to a low, cautious buzz. Lesandre whispered into the marshal's ear. She blinked, that placid face on the verge of igniting. Her eyes locked onto Kali.

"Very well, lord." Solara brushed her surcoat off. Her irises grew dark and for the briefest moment Kali saw them flicker yellow. What? An image of the voidtouched flashed in her mind. "Attendant, see to your peer." Solara spoke to Gwin who knelt beside the woman. Blood ran down the side of her head and her breath came in slow, raspy draws. "I must change, this soiled attire is not suitable for such an event. You." She spoke to Kali. "Remember who you risk should you not be here upon my return."

To the collective relief of the hall the marshal took her leave. The mood lifted and conversations continued in earnest. Kali signaled Lesandre with a glance. The Adirian lord brushed his collar and picked up his cup, tapping it against his plate twice. From the table on the far right Gariant–deep in his cups–slammed his fists against the wooden surface. Most of the skilled laborers attended the same seating, including the shaper and his hapless son. Once the captain stood Cerric excused himself, disappearing into the kitchens.

"S'that is how an Adirian marshal acts, eh?" Gariant slurred some of his speech. His head lulled as he faced the table of knights. Stellar performance. "Eh?! Caaaan't handle'er wine, can she? I think not! And on the last feast of Riah's peace. We-heh-ell! That'd make'er damned to the Void I say!"

"Hold your tongue, sir!" Elys slammed his cup down. A noble sign of disrespect. Lesandre knew his man. "Save your insults for the gutter! This is a lord's hall, and you shall act as such!"

"Oh. Oh. I see, got'a thing for that *bitch* eh?" Gariant snarked. He drank too much for real.

"How dare you sir!" Elys stood. Most of the diners watched, weary. "Withdraw your tone."

"Withdr–hah! You can't order me. What're ya? Some dressed up flounce? Cavalier." Gariant spat. "You ever held a pike line, Captain Cock? Ever faced down a legion? I bet you wouldn't last a minute in a real brawl." Guardsmen stepped in. They raised the halberds and navigated to the tables, only to cease as Elys waved them off.

"What are you proposing, captain?"

"Pssht. You. Know. I challenge you, Knight Fucker, to first blood."

Lesandre planted his palm against his forehead, bemused. Wine helped everyone fit their parts. Meanwhile, Dinkira slipped out the back of the room, following Solara's egress. Kali stood. She raised her empty glass into the air.

"Let's liven this feast up! Gariant, Captain of Iskvar against Sir Elys, Knight Retainer of the Grand Duke Adirian. Come now, Sir, you won't impoverish us such a sight?"

Baron Shadowsong raised her mug into the air. She stood, revealing a half-set sun embroidered on her coat.

"Seconded. I'll put a runed halfpenny on the captain."

"There we have it. What say you, Sir Elys?"

The knight examined his opponent. Half of Gariant's meal made its home on his tunic and for effect the captain took another swig from his cup.

"My honor is impugned. I accept, scoundrel."

"To the yard! Let's give everyone a show, hah!" Kali yelled. The knights at the center table cheered and several of the staff joined them. The diners took to a mass exodus, most grabbing their cups and absconding from the feast hall, Gariant and Elys among them. Baron Shadowsong made eye contact with Kali. She nodded then joined the others. Unexpected, but welcome.

"Gwin." The attendant lingered after servants carried the wounded woman out of the hall. His face paled. Kali stood and tenderly hugged his arm. "Gwin. She'll live. I need you to take father somewhere safe. His quarters, or the tower. Quick now." Gwin bowed and cooed to the duke, helping him up to his feet. Kali embraced the giant of a man.

"I'll be back for you, father."

"I'm sure, girl." Denrik chortled and returned the hug. He tousled her hair. "Where are you going, hm?"

"I've errands. Gwin will take care of you. Be kind to him." She broke her hug and stood to her toes, kissing his cheek.

"Such a sweet girl you are."

To the onlooker Kali bid her father a goodnight. They did not see her lips twitch before she descended from the platform without so much as a glance back.

Outside, a crowd formed within the central glade. Dozens of canopies with hastily erected tables lay beneath a thick, black sky with angry clouds that blocked the light of Riah's Moon. Dozens of sunlamps lit the festivities where the off-duty servants, guardsmen, and less essential household members made their frivolities. Stiff winds fluttered banners and linens alike. Half the spectators consisted of drunken guardsmen with an assortment of prostitutes among them. Few kept their weapons. The others, those standing in favor of House Iskarion, wore commoner's garb and serving attire, household loyalists. All Cavari, yet, distinctly foreign from their Adirian counterparts. Someone scrounged up a bastard sword for Gariant. He stood at the center of attention, flurrying the weapon without an inch of skill. Elys stood across from him, his posture perfect.

Kali slipped into the crowd beside Baron Shadowsong who looked on to the contest, arms folded. Kali shivered and cursed the flounce of a dress. Sure, a breeze up the legs felt nice, but nothing warmed quite like pants. They watched the men bray, each side eliciting cheers. A light drizzle pitted against the natural and erected canopies, though no one seemed to notice. A red-headed girl clad in green Shadowsong heraldry separated the duelists and eloquently dictated the rules.

"What're you planning, Kali?" The baron spoke without breaking her focus.

"People are about to die. You'll be safe in the basilica. Zevra will lock it down."

"And you? I'll not have my sister's last child fight alone."

"You've your own children to worry over, Airil. Besides, if I die one of them inherits this cozy little home."

The only sign of Airil's irritation was in the way her fingers clutched the fabric of her long-sleeved tunic. "Were Ilya alive she'd find the words to embarrass you. I've not the wit. Be safe. Ilvicar needs you."

Lesandre approached them. He bowed to the baron then to Kali, his face bright red. Airil ignored the greeting then excused herself. In the circle Gariant barked more insults at the stone-faced knight. The Shadowsong girl raised her arm to hush the crowd.

The ground rumbled. Kali wobbled and grabbed Lesandre, steadying herself. They didn't put that much powder in the foundations. Did they?

An entire section of the southwestern wall erupted in a massive fireball that carried up into the sky. It sent a torrent of debris into the courtyard. The voracious maw of heat swallowed anything in its grasp, igniting nearby canopies and engulfing those unlucky few nearby. Screams followed, then chaos as the gathered crowds turned to outpace the falling shrapnel. Kali placed her body in front of Lesandre and pulled him to the ground. She curled into a ball and waited.

"What the shit was that?!" Kali jumped up. Gariant and Sir Elys abandoned their duel, the former suddenly alert and able to run without a stumble.

"The marshal ordered the castle's powder supplies moved into the upper armory! A saboteur must've found out." Sir Elys stared at the resulting catastrophe in horror. Cries of pain took to the night, wailing into the sky at those struck by debris or set aflame. "Sky father, all those people."

Kali exchanged a look with Gariant. He winced. Kali shrugged. Fewer guards to deal with.

"Sir Elys!" Lesandre issued precise orders in his best lord voice. "Secure the area and lock down the castle, now! Captain Gariant, take the outer gate, make sure no one passes without my or Solara's order!"

"Yes, lord!" The two men spoke in tandem. One eyed the other before they split and rushed to their duties.

"How many people did we kill?" Lesandre paled.

"A lot. Don't lose focus, Les, we need you to be safe for this to be worth it. Go find Solara and do whatever she tells you. Tell her I manipulated you. If you want to stay alive she has to believe you. Understand?"

"I suppose this is farewell?"

"Too bad. Just starting to like you, Les."

"Considering the circumstances, I suppose it could be wo–hey!"

Kali bolted. She waved over her shoulder and navigated her way through the crowd to the stables. She slipped off her heels, her bare feet slapping against the wet ground as she crashed into the doors, throwing them open without resistance into the frantic mass of stable hands, most either hiding or brandishing pitch forks against the assumed assault.

Balen poked his head out from the second level balcony. He rushed down the stairway and shooed the hands away, depositing a sword belt and a pair of pants in her arms. She slipped into the warming linens and tied the belt to her waist. The ruby hilted blade stuck out from its sheath.

"Boots, Balen? Really?"

Balen snickered. He whistled and a saddled white mare rotted out from the back of the stable. Kali grinned and snatched her boots from the horse. She stood on one leg and slipped the footwear over a shin.

"And the rest of the horses?"

"Oi, 'ave faith Kali. Been feedin' the lot beer since half-dark, this'uns the only 'orse'can still see straight. Quickest palfrey we got too."

"You got the entire stable drunk?"

"They like the taste." He shrugged.

"Be safe. They'll want to question you."

"Me'n the boys'll be fine. Git, Lord, yer the'un should be worried 'bout'er head."

Kali mounted the mare. She took the reins and adjusted into the saddle, straightening her back and kicking the skirt of her dress aside. She ripped the hem from the bottom to give her legs room to breathe.

"What's her name?"

"Snow-Driftin'-Flower-Petal."

"What?"

"Git!" Balen slapped the horse on its rump.

Kali burst into the courtyard and overran two guardsmen en route to the stables. Heavy rainfall poured in earnest, drowning out the calls for aid and sending the feast goers seeking shelter. No ill omens here. Kali mimed a sunburst. She rode Snow at a full gallop beneath the inner portcullis, most of the guards distracted by the chaos of destruction.

Kali guided her mount to the cobble road of the outer defenses. A full story taller than the inner wall, the gate stuck into the hillside in a half-circle, covering all approaches and leaving no choice of entrance but its singular portal. She allowed herself a moment of triumph. The swirling wind sent chills down her spine, but freedom warmed her bones. A full solstice passed since she last left the keep. A prisoner in her home, her own walls.

Snow slowed as she approached the gate. Where Kali expected to find a token garrison distracted by the best workers in town, she instead found a line of guardsmen and a closed portcullis. No more than ten paces away, Solara stood at the head of her men, her saber held at Dinkira's neck. The rain doused his robes and for the first time in her life Kali saw shame in the old diviner's eyes. No sign of Gariant, either. Kali laid a hand on her sword.

"Reconsider, Arkalis." Solara dug her blade into Dinkira's flesh.

Dinkira spoke through clenched teeth as a bead of red dripped from the wound. "Leave me, Kali!"

"Silence!" Solara forced him to his knees. He cried out, his old body cracking under the strain.

"Don't!" Kali raised her hands and slipped a leg over the saddle, sliding off the mare and landing with a wet slop, her heartbeat in her ears. Overhead, lightning flashed, followed by a clap of rolling thunder. "Let him go, you have me."

"Do I?" Solara twisted her boot into the cobble. Her controlled countenance twisted to a wicked grin, a violent expression that highlighted yellow eyes. "I warned you, Arkalis. And I've shown too great a leniency."

"Solara. Please, let him go. He had nothing to do with any of this." Kali begged. She stared into Dinkira's eyes, those old browns matching her own. Tears rolled down his cheeks–not for himself, she knew. His lips moved. *I'm sorry.*

"I disagree."

"Please, do–"

Solara's blade slid across Dinkira's throat. His eyes grew large as he clawed at the wound, his breath coming in gasps. He heaved and clasped his fingers around his neck, squeezing, desperately trying to stop his death. The old man swayed. His eyes rolled back into his head as he collapsed.

"You fucking monster!" Kali ripped her sword from its scabbard. The runes along the spine of the black blade took a fiery glow in the darkness. Droplets of rain turned to steam as they hit the steel.

"Me? You brandish a weapon of the Void and call me a monster?" The line of halberdiers shifted. "Surrender, Arkalis."

Kali's knuckles whitened. More boots rushed down the road as Sir Elys and his knights cut off her retreat, their faces grim. Fucked on both ends. Solara knew. They played into her trap.

The voices came. Distant, yet clear, they crackled in her ears, dark whispers in concert with one another. They spoke in rhythm, echoes of screams, somehow soft yet jagged. They turned her blood to ice.

We offer power.

We offer life.

We offer vengeance.

She saw the promise in her mind. Strength like her father's. She could lift a man with one hand, tear him to pieces on a whim. Speed. Grace. Anything she wanted, all she needed was to listen.

Open your mind.

Join us.

Free your soul.

"WHO DARES THREATEN MY DAUGHTER?!"

A clarion call banished the voices. It echoed with a flash of blistering, white light and roaring thunder. At the top of the hill stood a beast of a man, Denrik, unarmored, his coat soaked. He hefted an ice blue greatblade upon his shoulder, dwarfing the slight form of Gwin beside him. Elys and his knights cowered.

Solara cursed. "Get her! Now!"

The guardsmen charged. Five, armed and armored. Kali pivoted on a heel and bolted from the road onto muddied grass and soil. The polearms tried to match her movements as she rushed to their flank, forcing them to abandon formation to maneuver. An axe head flung at her neck. She lowered her body and slid, the mud and rain propelling her beyond the strike. Her sword followed, the edge slicing clean through a knee, bone and all. Clothing ignited at contact and screams joined the cacophonous chorus of nature and blood.

Kali spun, catching the spear point of a halberd. She pushed in and swept her weapon beneath the pole, lifting it and curling inside its reach. Sparks flew as she disengaged the sword and hooked it around her side. It cleaved without resistance. The blade sunk into flesh and ripped through half the guard's torso. He fell. Out of the corner of her eye Kali caught glimpses of carnage. Seven knights faced the duke. One of them lay in halves at his feet.

Something pierced her left shoulder. Kali reared and spun again, flailing her weapon at the halberd and knocking it aside. She backed up, sword raised, with the remaining three guards on her heels. Two took her sides while another came to her front. She tried to lift her arm and winced at the sudden pinch. Blood stained the blue dress, masking it with red.

"Kali!" Thunder echoed off the walls followed by a thin plume of smoke. A bullet pierced the head of a guard. He dropped. Gariant poked his head out of the gatehouse in the pulley room, arquebus propped up against his shoulder. "Stop playing girl! Get to the gate!"

Kali leapt to her side and slammed her shoulder into a distracted foe. The woman exhaled as the wind rushed from her lungs. A quick stab to her stomach finished the job. She kicked the lilting corpse away as her clothing took to flame and turned to the last one standing. The man stared at her, his eyes wide. He glanced at the fire, then the sword.

"Run." Kali hissed.

He cast his halberd aside and broke, ending with a saber through his neck. Solara seethed. She ripped her weapon from the flesh and sent a splatter of blood at Kali's dress.

"Useless!" Solara growled. They faced each other, Kali's chest heaving from effort and pain. She favored her left side while the marshal stood with her torso at an angle, one foot out and a hand behind her back. From the gate the whining of metal joints signaled Gariant lifting the portcullis. Solara blocked her path.

"Let's see how good you are, Iskarion."

Kali rushed Solara. The saber flourished in response and its wielder sidestepped the assault with a clattering deflection. Kali stumbled and Solara invited the next foray. Another attack, an overhead chop met with the base of the saber and caught in the guard. Solara leaned into the lock, a smile crossing her lips. Too strong. How? Kali stumbled as Solara slipped her weight and spun along her side. She slammed the end of her pommel into the back of Kali's head.

The world blurred. An overwhelming sense of dizziness knocked Kali to her knees. Solara rounded on her prey, flurrying her weapon in a wide arc. Kali lifted her sword too slow and the steel bit into her arm. Blood ran free from her wrist. Solara laughed in triumph and stalked in a circle.

"That's all? Pity. I expected more. Perhaps this was unfair?" Solara stood above her. "But, then, life is not fair. Know that I will enjoy this. Greatly." Solara brought her saber down. Kali gripped her blade's hilt and swiped at the weapon to knock it off course. A knee followed. It caught Kali in the side of her face and she hit the ground, coughing. Something crunched in her mouth.

Atop the hill her father fought with the ferocity his legend spoke of. Though his coat was cut to tatters, only four knights remained, the rest dead or dying. Denrik swung his greatblade and a knight valiantly placed his weapon in its path only to watch as the Thalian craftsmanship split his saber and his body after. Kali watched in awe. In time she could have been such a sight. Now, though, it took all her energy to stay conscious. A streak of lightning crossed the sky and Solara's shadow darkened her vision. In that last moment the duke found his daughter's eyes.

Solara straddled Kali's chest and pinned her arms, blade pressed to her chin.

"Stupid, foolish girl. You thought to best me? Me?! Marshal to the greatest house of Ilvicar. You are nothing. Nothing!"

Kali grunted. She faced Solara and spat blood in her face.

"You talk too much."

"Goodbye, de–"

"ARKALIS!"

A shadow soared through the air. Solara turned as Denrik's icy greatsword pierced her chest and threw her back, pinning her body to the ground. The marshal gasped, a wet, sickening death rattle mixed with a heinous cry. Kali inhaled and groaned as she searched for her father. They shared a glance. Denrik smiled, his eyes alight with knowledge, aware and focused. He bled from multiple wounds with blood soaking his coat. He did not defend himself when the sword entered his back.

"No!" Kali cried. She pulled herself along the ground. "No!" She came to a knee and watched the remaining knights descend on her father, yelling as their steel punctured his body. Kali limped, the black blade dragging in her hand. "No!" A sudden force pulled her back as Gariant ran to her side.

"Let me go! I need to help him!"

"Kali!" Gariant held her and whistled, calling Snow from the road.

"You have to run, girl. Do you hear me?" He cupped her face, his eyes broken. "You have to run." Tears streamed down her face, her gaze flickering to Dinkira's still corpse then to her father. The remaining knights finished their work. Sir Elys pointed to the gate and called for haste. From the keep more guardsmen appeared, at least a dozen, rushing to join the melee. With Gariant's aid Kali mounted Snow's saddle.

"Come with me. Gariant, please. I can't lose you too." Kali searched his eyes for something. Anything to convince him.

"You can. You must, Arkalis. Now go! Before I die for nothing."

Kali stared. He saluted her with a fist to his heart. Kali kicked the flanks of her mare and the palfrey took to a gallop, all too glad to be moving. She glanced back, rain and blood staining her vision, watching as Gariant pulled the duke's sword from its bodily sheath. He raised the weapon in contest, meeting insurmountable odds with a battle cry. His silhouette faded into the night and with it so too did the last guardian of Iskvar fall.

Excerpt From the high Loremaster's Journal

W HILE THE NOBLES rule, the true power of Ilvicar is silver. An acceptable currency at any port of civilization. For large transactions Cavari call upon "writs." Financial agreements promising, or simply transferring, a portion of wealth from one party to another, hoarding their silver (or other valuables) in a central location. Any fool can create a writ (I once read a contract that simply read: seventy-five to Big Lore Man) as long as they have ink and paper, but is useless without a personal, unique seal issued by banks, preventing the rich from needing their servants to carry their coin.

For those not fortunate enough to be born into privilege, the value of a coin is delineated by its weight with most common transactions occurring in small sums commonly referred to as "halfpennies," or a "halfer," most likely because they weigh (within varying degrees) half an ounce. A runed half penny is altogether a different sort. Their worth is dictated by the complexity of the rune, but the smallest denomination is equal to a hundred of their mundane brethren, whereas I've seen the largest ascend to that of a thousand for a single coin. For sanity purposes it is accepted that a loaf of bread is worth a single half penny.

Chapter 10
Sahu

R urik shoveled the last bit of gruel into his mouth. Gray paste with dried oats mixed in for texture. He grimaced at the taste; wet, with too much salt to mask the lack of flavor. He set his bowl aside with a wooden clink and washed the concoction away with cool, fresh water. A glass cauldron with two spouts at the bottom rested atop a runic stone base nearby, the white inscriptions alight with a soft glow. He stuck his mug under the left tap and pulled on the release lever, filling it. Best damn find in the whole city.

A stubby, fat hand grabbed his abandoned bowl. The owner–a squat woman with fiery red hair and a stained apron–unceremoniously dropped it in a stone basin with the other flatware in the stall-styled "kitchen" of the Lanatir compound.

No self-respecting Cavari made do without a cooked meal.

Rurik scratched at his half-grown beard, his elbows resting against the countertop. He rolled his shoulder to a series of crackling muscles; sore from the break but healed. Melody worked wonders.

Variably sized tents made up the majority of the camp, most empty as only six breakers returned from the last job. He flicked a finger over the sapphire ring. Fueled by its power Rust managed to cut a hole into the outer tier. They left Hal's body behind. A breaker's funeral: left to rot in obscurity too far from home for anyone to notice.

The others droned in their routines. Feral managed to construct a larger pile of bedding to sleep on. Jerk and Sweets silently rolled dice at each other, using what few personal effects remained of their peers as collateral. Rust fussed over the weapons secured at the site, his face now more scar tissue than coal while Melody prayed in a corner, her head bowed against the palisade encircling the compound. No more than sharpened logs, the makeshift fortification existed more for privacy than defense.

Rurik watched the runes overhead shift and fade. They wove into one another–deep blues torn from his memory of the sky, shedding their ambience to those below. In the distance a rune exploded in a shower of sparks and faded not far from their origin. A crew broke into another cache. How many died?

"This seat taken?" Sahira said. Rurik waved his wrist at the suggested stool and Sahira sank low, her arms on the counter, elbows down. She wore a sleeveless blouse, revealing the unbroken line of gold tattoos from her cheeks to her shoulders and to the back of her hands. They flowed, delicately etched shapes in a cohesive pattern throughout.

The camp chef slopped a ladle full of gruel into another bowl and set it on the counter.

"No word in the market yet. About us. Entire camp is talkin' about it though. Sayin' it's voidwork. Lucky us," Sahira said, breaking the lull. She sniffed the bowl's contents then handed the meal to Rurik. He snagged it.

"Sunlord be praised." Rurik shoveled a spoon of slop into his mouth. Salty. "What about the detachment?"

"Nada. Maybe they let it slide."

"Thought you were smarter than that."

"Girl can dream."

"They won't move without justification. The barons would riot if they knew Adirian leveraged the diviners in Catalin for information."

"Try again?" Sahira waved the chef down for a mug. She leaned over the counter and filled it up, a hand clutching Rurik's shoulder for stability. He shifted his weight into the touch.

"Diviner's Guild is based out of Catalin, Adirian seat of power. They act under a neutral contract with the nobility. Financial writs in exchange for services. Oswin lets them operate above the law and doesn't collect taxes on land deeds. In return the guild breaks its seals with the other houses. One of the best kept secrets of the age." Sahira settled onto her stool. She paid her mug more attention than his meandering.

"You think that's how they found us?"

"Same trick they pulled at Ilduan. The other duke's pulled u–"

"You tryin' to bore me into leavin'?"

Rurik snorted and shoveled another spoonful of gruel into his mouth. He skipped chewing and swallowed before the taste hit his tongue.

"I'd like you to stay."

Sahira watched Rurik who stared absently at the central tent. A white and black banner hung from each side with a Lanatir rune emblazoned on the surface. Sahira leaned her weight against his side. They sat together in silence, for a time.

"You smell awful."

Rurik laughed. A full, hearty sound that escaped his lips loud enough to draw the attention of the crew. Rust looked on in concern before Sahira overcame her shock and joined in. The two of them reveled in the throes of their joy, Sahira's light soprano humming harmoniously with Rurik's melancholy. They caught their collective breath in a few snorts and giggles.

Rurik wrapped an arm around the woman's shoulder and pulled her closer, her head snuggled under his chin. He drifted. With his eyes closed Rurik envisioned the beach of Iskvar, the rolling tide, a waning sun and fresh air. Sahira smelled of citrus–not quite the homely scent of the ocean, but warm. How did she manage perfume this deep below the surface?

"Foreman!"

High pitched, haughty. Rurik opened his eyes with a scowl. Sahira glared openly at the nobility across from them. Dressed in a black surcoat, the middle-aged Cavari sported an assortment of finery; no less than two bracelets per arm, a ring to each finger, and a golden clasp for a half-cape that drifted to his left side. He wore breaker's gloves and thick-soled boots without a blemish to either.

Baron Lanatir placed a hand on his hip and waved Rurik forward.

"Lord." Rurik straightened. He towered over the baron who sneered and chewed on his too-thin bottom lip. "What warrants this rare visit from the manor?"

"Spare me your barbs, Rurik. Come. We have a visitor, and you have an opportunity to reimburse me for thirty death salaries."

"Those weapons will pay for a hundred contracts. I owe you nothing."

"Ah." The baron raised a spindly finger into the air. "I purchased your writ. You owe me your life. Unless you'd like me to sell it back to Celesti? She'd be glad to put a sledge in those manly hands of yours." Rurik sniffed. Lanatir glowered. "We done?"

"Lead on, great lord."

The baron spun on his heel and waltzed to an over-sized tent with Rurik in tow. They passed two coated guardsmen with arm mounted arquebuses and heraldic headbands into the canvas shelter. A covered bed sat in the corner of the interior with a full body mirror and a set of ceremonial plate armor beside it. A wardrobe lay in various states of scattered amidst a series of couches and rugs. How like a Cavari noble to bunker down in comfort.

Lanatir rounded a large table with a charcoal map spread over the surface. Goblets and a pitcher bolted the parchment to the table with the occasional red stain marring the detailed render of the outer city, it's wall a perfect circle with only a single breach. A red mark near the entry point indicated the camp and another pinpointed the forum. Or the ruin of it. Lanatir filled a cup with wine and handed it to a woman seated at the table.

The woman met Rurik with a smile. Thin eyes with a wide, flat face, she stuck out from her Cavari company. She wore her dark hair free in the front with bangs framing her countenance and the back half pulled into a ponytail. A hide vest covered her upper torso and a leather collar imprinted with a small scroll case hung from her neck.

"Foreman Rurik, this is Le-ah-a-oah. Or something." The baron poured himself some wine and rolled his eyes. "I've no gift for the lowlander's tongue. She is a loremaster, if you can believe it. She has a, well. She insisted we include you." Lanatir bowed, haphazardly, and flourished his cape. He sat. "I cede the floor."

Rurik clasped his hands in front of his belt. He approached the table, his vision wandering to the inward curved knife belted to the woman's hip above a thin skirt, slits on the sides allowing easier movement. Kukris killed easy as any sword.

"Oa? That's the Oadua tribe, isn't it?" Rurik started. The loremaster's eyes lit up.

"It's heartening to see a duke's education extends beyond his own lands." She spoke with a heavy alto and a Cavari accent.

"I know enough to not try to pronounce your name."

"Le-ua."

"Lyue."

"Good, good, we're all acquainted, yes?" Lanatir twirled his finger in the air and took a deep draught from his goblet. "Tell him the bad bit. What you told me."

"Bad bit?"

"The baron's talent for understatement is a thing of wonder." Lyue produced the slate Rurik sequestered from the study and laid it on the table. That explained the presence of a loremaster. He felt a pang of guilt at turning it over. "The bad bit is that this artefact is a bastion of blasphemy. Its every facet is a pontifex's nightmare."

Rurik shifted from one foot to the other. The slate mentioned ducal houses by name.

"The bad bit is that we can't sell it for dick." Lanatir drained the rest of his wine. "Just having that makes us heretical. I've no stomach for a pontifex."

"Well said, baron. There is the other matter, of course."

"Of course." Lanatir echoed.

"The explosion you and your breakers fled. It created a Voidtear."

"What?" Rurik snapped his attention to the loremaster and fiddled with the ring on his right hand. "How is that even possible?"

"The explosion was runic in nature, I expect. That much energy released at once? Akleasn Litanies exaggerate a great deal, but volatile power like that is why they inhibit sorcery and technology. And you're at the center of its confluence."

"Fuck." Rurik grumbled.

"Indeed." The baron refilled his cup. "We have a dead Adirian knight, a Voidtear, and your crew magically back at camp."

"For your fortune," Lyue gestured to the northern entrance of the breaker encampment on the map. "Guards reported your arrival from the other side of the city, and no one who matters knows you tarried so far east."

"Except for Celesti." Rurik interrupted. "And her diviners. May as well be everyone."

"Divination isn't so precise. Feelings, impressions; nothing so deterministic as faces or names. They suspect, but your position grants you clemency. Should one noblemen be so easy to dispose then the rest fear for their station. You're relatively safe. Until proper evidence is found. Which brings us to the point of this engagement."

"Oh joy. I was waiting for the exploitative part of the proceedings." Rurik pulled a chair to the table's side and sat, his arms dangling over the back.

"You've limited time, Foreman. But I believe you've a unique advantage. How, exactly, did you and your people make it back?"

Lanatir glanced expectantly at Rurik. He and Lyue watched the foreman who returned the stares with a blank expression. How much information to give? The baron responded to profit and vanity. Easy to manipulate. And the loremaster? Secretive bunch of bastards, as much as Rurik disliked diviners, their motives were clear. The loremaster's College operated under their own funding and rules.

"Luck?" Rurik tested the joke with no success. "Fine. We discovered an artefact. A portal. It let us cross the city in an instant and took us to the inner wall. Rust managed to get us through the gate."

"Rust?" Lyue asked.

"Our shaper. One of the baron's more inspired purchases." Lanatir leaned in his chair and crossed his legs. He smiled at the compliment.

"Brilliant!" Lyue clasped her hands together and hopped up. "The webway is real! I've come across mentions, hints. No hard evidence. And you say the inner sections are open now? Baron, this is exactly what we need."

"Yes." Lanatir waved away the excitement. "Get to the part about how much this costs me."

"If we work quickly, foreman, we can reach the tower in the center of the city. The High Loremaster believes it holds an ancient weapon. And from what I was able to gleam from this." She knocked on the slate's glass exterior. "That belief is backed up by personal experience. If we can beat the others, if we can reach it before Celesti does? We would all benefit."

"I get it." Rurik narrowed his gaze. "Lanatir gets his wealth, and power. I get my freedom. And you? Why not go to any other camp? Why not one of the dukes, to the Adirians?"

"Frankly, foreman? They're not so desperate. Their excavations are for wealth, for trinkets and baubles. Their focus is on avoiding civil war and keeping Lindorum at bay. You, on the other hand, have motives I can exploit. Your goals are convenient for my purpose."

"Your purpose? Somehow, I doubt it's for the greater good."

"Do you want Duke Adirian with a potentially apocalyptic artefact? Such men led us to the Desolation. He's managed to consolidate Ilvicar with the blood of your people, imagine what he would do to Lindorum. Aul'Thannon, Xyr? The Lowlands." Lyue's eyes took to a raw intensity, her voice lowering. "I do not wish to see my people chained. Selfish reasons need not be of evil intent."

Rurik exhaled through his nose. Two years of toil brought him little more than death and regret. Of waiting to die. Now, this woman offered him a chance for freedom. Or revenge.

"Rurik," he said.

"What?"

"My name is Rurik. Rik, if it's easier. I work for him." He motioned to the baron. "I don't have much choice in this venture and it's better than all this wallowing."

"Good man. Who says Iskarions are thick skulled." Lanatir polished off his third cup of wine which he set too hard against the table. "I expect I'll reap my share of the profits for my discretion."

"Of course, baron. The college will reimburse you for your aid as well. Assuming we are successful."

"We'll need numbers if we head out. Supplies, sledges. Anyone will suspect a crew without the right equipment. Which means we'll need at least two shifts. That's twenty-four new writs. How are your coffers?"

"Minimal." The baron shrugged. "Enough to guarantee six contracts. Twelve if we hire foreigners."

"That won't do. We'd be outnumbered if any of the other crews followed us." Rurik rubbed his temple. "We'll have to sell those weapons first."

"Weapons?" Lyue tilted her head to the side.

"Mhm. Thalian Steel."

"That should be quite the profit, no?"

"Not anymore." Rurik folded his arms under his chest. "If we had time to find the right buyers, sure. Under the table deals with nobles, escalating bidding wars. We need to offload these fast, which means black market."

"Which means," Lanatir frowned as he tipped the pitcher to no result. He flipped the container over in an effort to coax out the last drops. "We get ripped off. A pity. I'd like to keep one for myself."

•   •   •

Breaker's Row, the solitary line of civilization among the ruins, busied with the jostle of hundreds of glowlamps. At the far end, near the breach in the outer wall, lay the civilian holds and noble compounds, a sea of tents and haphazard fortifications arrayed in a half-circle towards the city proper. The Thalian gatehouse was rubble, pummeled and scorched from an endless assault of gunpowder that acted as the singular threshold into the ancient city. The only source of natural light poured in from the hole there, an incline to the surface. In the initial expeditions the explorers cared little for preservation. Only foundations remained near the entrance, their black, metal surfaces bridged as single-story structures cobbled together for temporary habitation.

A throng of traffic traveled along the obsidian road split between the merchant and "volunteer" compound, but most ventured to the row itself: open stalls with boisterous merchants that hawked a myriad of luxuries.

Rurik took up his perch outside one of the alleys of makeshift constructions, specifically the Sunsinger's Basilica, the lone, two-story building along the row. A gold and orange banner hung from the roof, displaying a full sun wreathed in flame. Below it two paladins guarded either side of a stone archway appropriated for a grandiose entryway. They sported a set of thick armor: layered plates from shoulder pauldrons to bladed gauntlets, with a tapered sheet over the breast and black chain that spilled out into plated greaves. From their waists hung golden half-capes fastened around the front with blue tassels and a sunburst shaped clasp. They wore angular full helms with a horizontal slit over their eyes and wings flared out from the head. Few from the road came close to the sentinels, weary of the visage and large swords sheathed at their sides.

Rurik rested against the corner of the building with his fingers hooked into his belt. The reverence allowed the basilica gave him the space to watch. His attention rested on the Breach Gate–the official title for the giant hole in the outer wall–and the full detachment of guards that monitored its traffic. Halberdiers and gunners, all adorned with Adirian pins, stopped every cart and wagon for the proper paperwork. No documents and they confiscated your as-of-then contraband. Pay to enter, pay to leave.

From the corner of his eye Rurik caught the subtle sway of Sweets' gait as he sauntered out of the crowd. Without the threat of fire and flame Sweets left his hairless, almost gleaming, chest bare, covered only by a loose vest.

"No interest from the shapers. Too many weapons for one haul, yes? They suspect something. With rumors of the. The." He eyed the paladins and dipped to Rurik's other side, whispering. "Voidtear. We need pray to Vari's blessing to find a buyer."

"Which one is Vari again? He a colossus or sentinel?"

"Bah, *Cavari*. The Colossi *are* Sentinels. Vari bestows luck, good and bad, so we ask his blessing. Too many sun rhymes for you to recall? No room for foreign truths?"

"Lot of truths to remember these days."

"Clumsy language. I think I misspeak."

"No, Sweets, I don't think you do."

"Fine, fine. What do we do now? No buyers, no crew, yes?"

"Either we wait for Vari to emerge from Myr-whateverion or check on the others. Princess and Feral are supposed to be canvassing the ale house."

"Better than courting heresy." Sweets knocked on the wall of the basilica. Together they joined the flow of traffic. They shuffled behind a band of breakers who walked by a line of solicitous men and women in various stages of undress. Silver halfpennies changed hands and patrons disappeared into a building or an alley with an escort. One of the men on the end, a large Cavari wearing scant small clothes and sporting a thin mustache, waved coyly at Sweets and blew him a kiss. Sweets returned the favor.

Their trek drew them to the front of the ale house. No windows, no roof, only a single-story box that kept the inhabitants in one place. The owner of the establishment erected the bare minimum for a business in the Ilvicar tradition. At least they managed a door.

A waft of alcohol and sweat assailed Rurik's senses as the dull roar of a busy market silenced, replaced now by the din of drunken murmurs and cavorting. Despite the lack of structure Rurik recognized the trick—a few runes at each corner of the building and an invisible filter absorbed the noise from either side.

At the far end of the enclosure Feral sat with Sahira at a well-lit table who lorded over several stacks of silver. Rurik joined them while Sweets disappeared into the crowd.

"No buyers I take it." Rurik sat.

"Oh, no no, they're all linin' up to buy. Everyone's thrilled to court heresy with all those Akleasn priests in an uproar. Somethin' about a tear in the fabric of reality." Sahira eyed the consistency of each stack, studying the oddly shaped circles. "I'd say there's a good fifty halfers here, at least. Good start."

"Fifty? That buys us, what? One tenth of a writ? For a one-legged old man."

"So judgmental. Maybe Gimpy's got a stunning personality."

"Princess."

"Rik."

Feral sniffed.

"Come on, Rurik, it's a bit'a fun. Don't know if you've noticed, but this place is on edge. Breakers weren't weary enough, now that we—er, someone—opened a Voidtear?" She lowered her voice. "Explains those walkin' dead men, doesn't it? I asked around, ain't no one goin' to risk a buy that big. Paladins and diviners are sniffin', there's even talk of a pontifex comin' to Ilvicar. Who'll risk that? This might be the best we get."

"I bring nourishment!" Sweets buzzed contentedly. He set four mugs at the table and sat. He looked at Rurik and Sahira. "Ah yes, thank you Sweets. Our thirst silences our tongues. This I understand. Sahu!" The wetlander toasted and brought a mug to his lips. Rurik grabbed one and tipped it to Sweets. Feral followed suit and consumed the liquid in one shot.

"A fraction of the Iskvar coffers and all this ceases to be a problem." Rurik drank.

"Sucks to be poor, doesn't it?" Sahira winked. She finished stacking her coins. "Sixty. Hah, closer to old Gimps yet."

"Here's to incremental progress." Rurik raised his mug.

"I'll drink to that." Sahira clinked her cup to his.

The ale house reveled with conversation. Breakers came and went to no set schedule with the occasional merchant or guard interspersed within. Rurik and the others refilled their cups often enough to break into fits of laughter with Sahira's mysteriously acquired stash losing volume with every round. Swept up to their revelry, none noticed Jerk saunter through the revolving door.

". . .Gariant–Captain Gariant, Knight Commander of Iskvar, mind you, the man is a sheet of iron in a coat–is running into every ally screaming for Kali." Rurik, his cheeks flushed red, mimed the stony-faced soldier with one eye bulging wider than the other. "Terrified of my father, thinking he lost her. He pulls a knife on a dock worker and there she is, nine years old, hiring a brothel worker with his purse!"

The table livened with laughter. Feral, having changed her mug for a pitcher, studied the contents and peered over the edge at the others, her brow raised at the jocular tone. Sweets snickered.

"And we got you, huh? Think I'd prefer the other Iskarion, I bet she's better looking." Sahira nursed her mug.

"We're twins. I suppose she is well developed?"

"Oh? You identical?"

Sweets spit a mist of liquid over the table. He cackled and rolled back in his chair. Feral placed a palm over her pitcher and growled at the unwelcome expulsion. Sahira's lips curled in a foxlike grin while Rurik matched the curiosity with a shrug and another sip.

A wooden scrape accompanied the arrival of a new chair. Jerk swiveled it about on one leg then pulled it to the side, smoothing the tails of his jacket to the back of his legs as he sat in a fluid descent. He folded a leg over his knee and laid his arms on the table.

"Hard at work, this I see."

The group collectively booed the Singuli. In response he flicked his black bangs from his eyes and brushed his hair over a shoulder.

"Ease up, jah-nipper," Sahira said.

"Ju-ni-pè-r. It is simple, no? Pè-r."

"Shari says Jerk is a better name."

"Valid effort, Princess, but try as you might you'll never get it right. Singuli have lithe tongues, something to do with their snake god."

"We have no *snake god. Merde.* You sun worshipping twits are so uncultured." Jerk inhaled. The table followed suit by sucking air in through their noses a moment after. They laughed. Jerk glared. "Ah hah, laugh at me, but I am the only one with news, hm?"

The frivolities quieted.

"Well? What news?" Rurik asked.

"I have a buyer."

"This is truth? Swear to this by Saiqua."

"By Saiqua, let's hear it," Rurik said.

"Pah, nonsense. I will declare my own death if I lie. This is good enough, no? Singuli suffer from Cavari trade bias–taxes, always taxes! But this? We sell at a one to twenty discount, she pays in Cavari branded silver. We are screwed but unless there is a better deal?"

"Opinions?"

The table silenced. Sweets glanced at Rurik, he to Sahira, then all three to Feral. The wastelander lifted her pitcher up and chugged. Some of the liquid spilled out the sides of her mouth to her tunic, and when finished she slammed it against the table, cracking the clay cup.

"If slaver lies, I rip off arms and beat to death with hands."

"That's good enough for me." Rurik raised his mug into the air. "Sahu!" Sahira and Sweets joined the toast. They drank.

Excerpt from the high Loremaster's Journal

SINGUL IS QUITE the oddity. Vast wealth flows from the western nation in the form of luxury goods and slaves. They worship no god or gods, priding themselves as stark atheists of logic, reason, and natural law, though their culture has some infatuation with the proliferation of snakes that inhabit the region. So much so that they revere an illness I've dubbed "scale sickness," a disease that turns flesh to hardened, leathery scales. While it makes you sterile and rids you of all tactile sensation, it is not inherently lethal.

Many Singali merchants and warriors will infect themselves with this illness intentionally. Often, by covering themselves in snakes in an elaborate, and terrifying, ritual. I've traced this as the source of the charming Cavari colloquial insult: "Snake Fucker."

Chapter 11
The Viper's Kiss

R URIK STARED down a line of steely eyed women. Singali
Vipers. Each wore a suit of sleeveless chain tucked into a pair
of baggy hemp pants. Sirwal, according to Jerk. A mask of
chain obscured their lower faces, woven into a hooded cloak. Absent
their standard spears the slightest bite from the dual jambiya at their
hips still meant certain death.

The roar of the market diminished to a distant collection of
whispers this far from the row. Half the buildings here lay in ruins, walls
and roofs collapsed from early attempts to bypass the explosive
defenses. They met inside a burnt-out storehouse with Sweets on watch
from a second floor-turned-balcony.

"They are intimidating, no?" The smooth, sultry tone came from
the women behind the vipers. Less deadly, more annoying. And shorter
than her guards, whose foreheads only came to Rurik's chin. The Singul
merchant wore a colorful robe with white speckled over square patches
and draping sleeves. Her face, angular and thin, flushed with sleek,
leathery scales that ribbed around her slit green irises. "A mere
formality, I say. Junipèr assures me you are trusted."

Jerk flourished a bow, his back dipping while extending an arm. He
kicked the nobleman's foot. Rurik crossed his arms under his chest.

"Yes, honored sister. Cavari lack manners, but this one oozes a single minded integrity. Besides, we are broke. What guarantees faith more than desperation?"

"Mm." The merchant folded her scaled hands inside the loose fabric of her robe. "We will see. We must be quick, no? I see no weapons, this is a bother."

"Rust." Rurik glanced at the stony shaper. He wore a brown leather coat in place of his typical apron and produced an icy blue dagger with a jeweled hilt. Rust handed it to the foreman to a dissatisfied grunt from Feral. With a flourish, Rurik flipped the Thalian dagger in his palm and held it up. The edge of the curved blade reflected too much of the dim light from the runic ceiling, almost glowing in the ever-present twilight.

"Tah-dah."

"Tauh dauh? What does this prove? Many ways to make iron hold light, and despite assurances we have little trust, Cavari."

"I suppose a demonstration from my expert shaper wouldn't satisfy you?"

The merchant glowered, unimpressed. She tapped a foot against the ground and one of the vipers shifted.

"Of course not. Little trust it is. Can I grab one of those knives from your ladies?"

"Vipers are not *ladies*." The merchant spat venom in her tone. Could she spit venom for real? "And *jambiya* are not *knife*."

"Technically–" Rurik paused with a sharp inhale as Jerk jabbed him in the ribs with an elbow. They glanced aside at each other, Jerk's narrow brow raised. "Apologies, honored sister." Rurik squared his shoulders and bowed. Singali referred to one another as siblings when negotiating in some kind of vague game of filial piety. "It will help us build trust. Pl–"

Jerk cleared his throat. Right. Culture. Singali saw Cavari mannerisms as begging, begging meant weakness.

". . .it will please me to show you its legitimacy."

The merchant did not react at first. The nervous scuffle of heels on rock scraped to the rhythm of Rust's anxiety. Jerk smoothed over the ruffled tails of his jacket. Rurik waited, weapon held aloft. He felt foolish, exposed.

"*Katriene.*" One of the vipers–the same woman that fidgeted before–unsheathed the jambiya at her side. A silken, purple scarf hung down from the woman's wrist. It twisted its way up an exposed arm and disappeared into the cloak that obscured her right side. Rurik smiled. She glared.

"Just hold it. I won't hurt you." The slightest twinge of confusion rippled over the viper's face. With no more than a flick of his wrist he cleaved the metal and the edge of the jambiya clattered against the ground. The viper snapped back, her eyes wide, ready to pounce.

"*Non, Katriene.*" With one last glance at Rurik and a dissatisfied huff the viper, Katriene, returned to her master's side and caressed her broken blade. "This is trust, yes." The Singuli flicked a humored grin to the foreman, her eyes alight with hunger. "Give it here. They say it is light, like shed skin." Snake reference. Singul had a weird thing with snakes.

Rurik tossed the dagger over. Katriene caught the weapon on her mistress's behalf. The other three stiffened. He imagined them flighting between rude hand signs under their cloaks. The imagery made them less terrifying. Katriene weighed the weapon. She spun it in her fingers and handed it to her owner. Owner? The vipers did not strike him as slaves so much as guards.

"Ah, ah. What an auspicious day, no? Singali and Cavari have trust. You give me this without asking to see coin!" Rurik curled his hand into a fist at his side. His nails dug into his palm. Idiot. "This I say is good, if naïve. Still." She shrugged then plucked a pouch out from a sleeve. It jingled with a clink of silver. "This is half."

She tossed it to Rurik who snatched it out of the air. His countenance smoothed over and he tied the bag to his belt. "You take payment, and now you provide me the others, hm? Junipèr told me of much variety."

"Company!" Sweets' whispered from above. "Many lights, Shari advises caution!"

The merchant and Jerk uttered the same curse under their collective breath. Feral flexed her shoulders and grunted, her hands tightening on her sledge. Rurik, meanwhile, moved to an open hole in the side of the building. He pressed his back against what remained of the wall and peered around the corner, careful to keep hidden. Several glowlamps cast a myriad of shades, frantic in reflection and easy to spot. They encroached from both ends of the street, absent the usual shuffle of work weary breakers.

He turned and tapped his collar, drawing attention to where guardsmen wore their pins. The crew scattered with recognition, while Jerk translated the situation. Two of the vipers somehow disappeared into the darkness as the others stuck close to their mistress, escorting her and Jerk along

Sweets snapped from above. The wetlander held up both hands. Ten guards. They could take ten. Especially with those Vipers. Sweets snapped again and frowned, repeating the signal twice. Twenty. Rurik bit back a curse. Rurik motioned for Sweets to stay. It took a feat of acrobatics to reach the ledge, so long as he kept quiet, he was safe.

The clatter of plate echoed nearby. Footfalls followed. Too many. They halted outside to the cadence of a familiar voice; distinctly feminine, with an air of authority and contempt.

How did they know? The details were too specific for diviners. Either way, they needed to leave. Rurik waved at Jerk and they exchanged a glance, Rurik swirling his finger in a wide arc and pointing at the metal door. Jerk shrugged and tilted his head to the side. Charming. He pointed at Jerk then the merchant then the door and patted the coin purse at his hip. Jerk bit his lower lip and offered a thumbs up, collecting the other Singali to pass along the instruction. Rurik slipped away from the wall and stalked over to the corner where Rust and Feral waited, his movements pronounced and deliberate. Rurik led them to a thin rupture that allowed them egress. He stuck his head out, glanced left. Then right. Clear.

Gingerly, Rurik lifted a leg up and squeezed through the split. He set his boot down and exhaled. The roads were open, flanked by the ruins; they could bounce from one storehouse to the next, or navigate the alleys and risk discovery in the narrows. Rurik took several strides into the middle of the street for a better look.

"Hoy, let's keep an eye on this road, yeh? Easy to spot som'un."

Rurik froze, the hairs on the back of his neck bristling. The voice came from the side of their storehouse. He raced back to the crevice with panicked steps as a glowlamp poked around the building. Rurik paled and he hurled himself at the space where he fell into Feral's muscular embrace. She caressed his hair and set him beside her where Rust watched with a stark, wide-eyed countenance. What a plan.

Rurik held up two fingers and pointed toward the guards. Feral raised her sledge. From the other side of the wall they listened to ponderous bootsteps and rustling plates against leather. Again, Rurik pushed up against the wall and pointed at Feral. He pulled his fist close to his chest then mimed a blow to his head. She huffed and assumed the position opposite him. Good enough. Rurik unsheathed his long knife and scraped it against the stone.

"Was'at?"

"Nothing. Debris, most like. Falls all the time."

"Oh yeh? Or it's thems we lookin' for. C'mon, lazy."

Rurik frowned. Good soldiers following orders. How many of his subjects did he kill with an order? Regret, he supposed, came as a luxury of survival. They approached, their footsteps deliberate now, careful. One tapped his halberd against the wall while the other held his lamp up.

"I'm not putting my head in that hole. That's stupid."

"Da'w, northerners really are a bunch'a pansies, yeh?"

"You do it then. Very model of courage, you are."

"I'm mannin' the light, see. 'Sides, was jus'a rock."

"Fine, but I get the *easy* job after. And no complaining." The lighthearted cackle of the second man signed his agreement. With some hesitant scuffle the guardsmen stuck half his torso into the hole and came face-to-face with Feral who grabbed his neck and pulled him into the opening. Rurik sprung up. He leapt into the street and crashed into the lamp wielding guard, his considerable girth enough to daze. Rurik rose to a knee and crawled up the other man's body, his knife piercing the flesh of an exposed neck. Fear stared up at him. Wide, wild eyes. They darted to the side, desperate, seeking. The guard grabbed his throat. Blood covered his fingers as he grasped the knife. His mouth opened then closed, his vision meeting the cool gaze of his murderer.

Rurik watched. Not his first kill, nor the last, but justified. Always justified. Either this man died, or Rust died. Or Feral. Someone died. Someone had to die. Did Hal? The image of the young soldier's face stuck at the forefront of his mind. How long could one moment haunt a man?

Forever.

Rurik sat on the dead guard's chest, the offender long since limp. Rust jostled the foreman and he regained his composure, plucked his knife free and wiped the blade on the red coat of the dead. Adirian pin. Of course. Rurik spotted Feral already across the road, her silent footfalls out of character for one so large. He followed suit and jogged to catch up, Rust on his heels. As a group they ducked into another blown out storehouse with holes aplenty. Their luck held.

Until the gunfire. A series of pops echoed nearby to no set rhythm. Void be damned. Rurik's face flushed red.

"We need'ta move, Rik. They're distracted. We can make'a break for it." Rust urged.

"That may be the merchant. We need the rest of that coin, who else is going to buy after this?"

"Won't matter if we're dead. They want ya alive. Us? Nae so much."

Rurik huffed in frustration. He knew the truth. Breaker, foreman, he bore noble blood, and that earned him clemency. So be it. Rurik untied the coin pouch from his belt and gave it to Rust.

"Take it and go. I'll distract them. Finish the deal, Lanatir can figure the rest out."

"Rik–"

"Don't. They want me alive. Now shut up and go, we don't have time."

A final, resigned nod signed the shaper's agreement. He mimed a sunburst and blinked back the redness of his eye. Feral grunted. She joined the older man and held up a thumb from a closed fist. Snarky savage.

From the road a chorus of discordant voices reached him. What was the plan? Think first, right? Not this time. Rurik mumbled incoherently under his breath and darted up the road.

· · ·

Two vipers lay in the road, One missing half a jaw, the other skewered on the edge of a halberd whose wielder lay beside her, his hand attached to the haft. Beyond them Jerk and the merchant stood with her protectors, their blades out, bodies hunched low. Half a dozen guards lay strewn about as fresh corpses, while others retreated in howling pain, holding their guts and retching the current contents of their stomachs. The Viper's Kiss took one's dignity before it killed them.

A line of guardsmen arranged themselves nearby, four on a knee and another four standing with their long-barreled guns pointed at the survivors. At the head of the formation stood a woman in white armor.

Ornate, rich. The armor covered her body with layered plates, tapered at the joints and fitted to the athletic form beneath. A gold inlay swirled from the breastplate to the fingers of the gauntlets, themselves narrowed to clawed extensions. It stemmed down her legs where angled greaves connected to a pair of sabatons. When she moved, the metal matched the motion like flesh. Blonde hair flowed to her shoulders in voluminous waves over unblemished, pale skin. Her mouth curled into a predatory grin.

Rurik watched from the corner of the storehouse. He recognized the armor as runecasted. Agile, thin, yet strong enough to stop a direct shot from an arquebus at close range. Only the most skilled shapers even attempted it, and the cost could outfit a small army. No chance of glory here. By the looks of it the wearer preferred to sacrifice her soldiers than risk dirtying the armor's finish with blood. Adirians. This one he knew by name.

"Quite a show. I would pay dearly to acquire one of your girls. Though I suspect they're not for sale? Hm? No? Fine, fine. Look, the whole noble resistance thing is admirable, but *such* a bore. So, I'll speed this up. First one to tell me where dear Rurik is gets to live. Easy! Go ahead. Whenever you're ready."

Rurik cringed. They needed time. Jerk whispered something to the merchant who returned the suggestion with a muffled scoff. Take the deal and risk it. He needed them to live, to finish the deal. And how did his presence help? One man with a knife against trained soldiers with guns. The sapphire of his ring caught a glimpse of twilight. The ring. He recalled the falling ceiling, the explosion. He used the ring to conjure a shield. How?

"Oh! I see some lively discussion. Progress is good, friends, but we're on a schedule you know. I'll do us all a little favor. I count to ten and if I don't get anything? Everyone dies."

Jerk and the merchant whispered at each other.

"Onetwothreefourfive." The woman laughed with mirth, a hand holding her stomach as she raised the other out in front of her thin lips. "Hah! I wish you could see your faces! I'm joking. Come on. That's so unfair, we need *some* kind of dramatic tension." She smiled. "Six."

Four seconds. Rurik scoured his thoughts. He made no conscious effort before. He saw the golden woman. The Sunmother?

"Seeeeven."

That sparked something. A memory. Darkness encircled him. Not him. Her. She wore *her* ring and stood at the peak that would be Iskvar. Shadowed figures approached.

"Eight!"

The voidspawn launched their tendrils at her. Sickly, wild limbs. The memory knew that touch meant death. She raised her arms and warped the energy around herself. She took it from the wind, from the light of the sun.

"Ten! Time's up! Any takers?"

Energy. He needed energy. The runes! Rurik rushed out and raised his hands. Ease guided him, experience of something he knew nothing of. He glanced up at the cavernous ceiling and felt the power coursing through each line of woven power. It beat to a steady pace, a heavy thud that moved in time with his heart. He reached out in his mind and grasped at the river of energy, It flowed free, following his whim as an old friend.

"Wait! We know–"

"Fire!"

The guns clicked and popped with a puff of white smoke. The scent of burnt powder wafted into the air. Where Rurik expected to see four fresh corpses, the Singali stood, dazed, but alive. An expansive blue aura cackled in and out of sight, humming with a dull thrum. It spanned from one side of the road to the other. Jerk's jaw dropped and disgruntled murmuring rose from the guardsmen.

"Jerk, run!" Rurik's voice boomed. Every eye turned to him. Oh. He shuddered and let his arms fall, knowing somehow the shield would remain. He stumbled, weak, blinking away the sudden spots in his vision. Jerk and the others took their cue. They bolted to the frustrated yell of the armored woman.

"What are you doing?! You, all of you! Go! Don't let them escape." The detachment split off and ran after the survivors. The others trained their weapons on Rurik. The woman unsheathed a jeweled saber and stalked to the front of the column. She stopped, blade up.

"Hey there, Rurik. You look like shit."

He grunted and steadied himself against a wall.

"Celesti. Nice to see you again, still presenting yourself as a lifeless husk I see."

"You wound me so, my lord duke." Celesti closed the distance.

"Forgot how things work again? I'm not a duke."

Celesti stopped inches from Rurik. He measured his breath, forcing himself to take slow, deep draws to hide his exhaustion while she took stock of him.

"No one told you, did they? Oh, I suppose your *lowered* position doesn't afford you a great deal of communication from home."

"What? Told me what?"

"You're a smart boy, Rurik. What elevates your position?"

"What?" The realization sapped his strength. Rurik sank to his knees. Tired. The tides of power left him, the drumming beat that filled his ears fading to silence. A chill gripped his muscles. His father, dead? "How?"

"You'll love this." Celesti circled her prey. "Your sister? You know, big girl, more bear than woman? She tried to take back Iskvar. Blew some stuff up, *including* Denrik! Hah! The Knight of Cinder burnt to ash. Ironic."

"Arkalis?" The mocking tone fell flat.

"Dear sister. I forgot you two are–" She paused and clicked her tongue with a *tsk*. "Were. Sorry. Were twins." She mocked a frown. "How sad."

His chest sank and he slammed his fists into the road. All this for nothing. What was the point? Escape. Die. His family was dead. That meant the household went with them. Dinkira, Gariant. Grief came as a wave and burned to anger. His face grew hot. Rurik screamed. He snatched the blade from his waist and snapped up, his eyes alight with fury. Celesti snorted and a halberd haft slammed into his temple. He whipped around and fell.

"So dramatic. Take him."

Rurik's vision blurred as another blunt end knocked him into darkness.

Litany of the Duskmother, Tenets of the Faith

RIAH'S PEACE celebrates the armistice brokered by the Duskmother between Thalia and Lindorum that led to their unification against the Void Gods. Riah calls for a week of ceased hostilities and sobriety by the invoked parties and a holiday for the common peoples. Blessed by a Priest of the Sun any encroaching offense shall be laid at the feet of the perpetrator and be branded faithless, a heretic, and put to trial by a pontifex.

Alas, to make mistakes is to relish the will and want of the Sunlord. Any conflict that does not draw blood shall be treated with mercy, as the Duskmother granted such generosity to the Lindrisi Warlord in his violation of the original truce.

Chapter 12
Better Lucky. . .

L UC SLID the cylindrical wrap around his mouth. He inhaled, the bitter smoke running over his tongue with a cool mint aftertaste. Oh. Cavari knew their vices. They called it char. He bobbed his head in appreciation and swayed with the whimsical fiddle from the floor below, its playful tune meshing with a steady accompaniment. Raucous and chaotic, one conversation bellowed over the other in conjunction with free-flowing alcohol, the occasional clink of boisterous toasting mixing with scraping wood from too-full tables and not enough chairs.

A kick to his shin woke him from his reverie. Luc grinned and leaned forward in his rickety chair. He studied the cards in front of him. Someone explained the rules briefly, but he often tuned out during most of the important bits. He caught the name at least. Sun's Fortune? From what he gathered the cards held some significance to the easterners' faith. Something about a Sunstar. Gibberish, really.

He held five cards, four of them a different phase of the sun: full dark through midday. Why not call it full light or midnight? From the spread he recognized a render of the deity Riah. He frowned at that. The goddess' likeness summoned a profound sadness within him.

"Hoi! Mercenian! Your ante, traveler. Or you passin?" The tan woman across the table leaned in on a tattooed arm. Her leathery skin adorned itself with more decorative imagery than most paintings. All blue, a complex series of connecting shapes and lines wove vague oceanic references into every bit of exposed flesh, which was considerable. Much in contrast to his heavy, patchwork coat and thick woolen shirt. "No shame'n foldin', traveler, more than obliged to take your coin."

"I'm not from Mercenia." Luc's trembling voice contrasted the woman's coarse alto. Nui possessed such low tonality.

"Eh?" She raised a thick brow over a deep, ocean blue iris and ran a hand through tightly knit braids adorned with beads and other jewelry.

"I'm from Aenia, it's farther west. How much can I bet?" He glanced at his remaining stash. Three stacks of silver, ten coins high. Not awful, but the pile in the center contained enough to stifle his greed.

"Bosun, fill 'em in."

Another fellow at the table whistled in annoyance. One eye bulged larger than the other, from what he could see beneath his long, matted, and otherwise facially obfuscating hair style. More importantly he kept a hand on the cutlass at his hip. Always.

"Minimum bet be five half-pennies. Any time ye raise the ante it always doubles, five ta'ten, ten ta'twenty. Or, if ye want to starve, ye can bet all-in. Er'one has to match or ye win the pot."

What kind of gods awful accent was that? Asuk maybe. He nodded in response, half-smiling to avoid any more conversation with the black-skinned fellow. What then? He posed the question to himself. Minimum? No. All-in? Ah. He felt a tug in the back of his mind.

"Okay! Well then, I will. . ." He pushed all three of his stacks into the center. "Go all-in! How exciting!"

The other five players groaned. One threw his cards and spouted off what he counted as ten unique curses in the Ilae trade language. A slender, graceful tongue, filled with the vilest curses in the world.

"You positive, traveler?" The woman folded a leg over her knee. "Usually you ask for new cards first."

"Oh! How many can I get?"

Bosun snickered. He and the woman exchanged a glance and the other players made little effort to hide their humor.

"All five, but usually you play for three at most."

Luc pursed his lips and eyed his cards again. None of them held any particular pattern or synergy. He placed all five face down and pushed them away. The table itself seemed to snicker at him.

"Five new cards please! And all-in!" He smiled, the expression taking up too much space on his thin jaw. The minty taste of his char repeated itself as he blew out a draft. Happily, the woman picked up a stack of cards and dealt him a fresh hand then pushed her far more considerable stash into the pile.

"I'll call. Won't pass easy money." Bosun followed suit. The other two bowed out. "I'll save you some time, too." The woman played her cards face up. She revealed four full suns, midday, with her fifth card, the mortal rendering of the Sunlord, shining crown and gold white robes and all. Luc never understood why he possessed pale skin. Religion, so silly. The Bosun grumbled and tossed his cards away and the woman moved to collect her lucrative reward.

"Shouldn't we look at my cards?" Luc chimed in, sheepish.

"You know the odds of beatin' four full suns?"

"From context, it's highly improbable?"

The woman rolled her eyes. She sat back and circled a long, thin finger in the air, gesturing to Luc. Satisfied, he reached out and flipped the cards over one-by-one. Dawn. Mid-day. Dusk. Fulldark. And Riah, the Sunlord's champion in her rendered glory. He took that to mean High Solstice, or the new year.

"Is that good?"

The table silenced. Bosun leaned in and stared at the cards, his bulging eye somehow wider. A few onlookers turned at the sudden lack of joviality and watched for curiosity's sake. The woman folded her arms over her chest and pushed her leather vest tight against her skin. She wore only a strip of tied cloth beneath it, testing the bounds of civil decency.

"You win," she said, calm. Too calm.

"Great! That's great. I could use the money." Luc jostled the square bag strapped over his back and opened the top, pouring the stream of coins in. He drew another gout of smoke into his lungs. What a night. He collected the last of the silver and hopped up, eager to be free from increasingly skeptical glances. "Well then! Thank you for teaching me your game, friends!"

"How'd you do it?"

"Excuse me?"

"How? I've seen the best cheats, traveler, but none as good as you."

"Oh. I didn't cheat. Turn of luck."

Didn't he?

The woman slammed a fist into the tabletop. The wood shuttered and the other three men rose, weapons unsheathed. Not good. Luc stepped back. He glimpsed the stairs from the balcony and a grizzled looking man with a weapon blocked every path.

"Don't lie to me, Mercenian."

"I'm not from–"

"Don't care!" The woman stood and advanced. Luc backed away and patted down his waist, his legs, baggy pants and all the way to his soft soled leather boots. Lastly, he removed the floppy brimmed hat that covered a mess of unkempt, curly black hair.

"Nothing! See? No cards. Hah. Just. Me! And no weapons. It's Riah's Peace! Isn't it? The festival! No blood shed under Akleasn Law!" Luc scanned his surroundings. Seaside towns in Ilvicar used brick and stone in their construction–admirable, really, despite the company the Cavari held a singular mind for advancement. They also tended to build up. Over his shoulder he saw it. An open window, its shutters drawn out for some fresh air. Again, something tugged at his mind. The window? Really?

"That's fair. No blood. We can do no blood, can't we gents?" The woman overturned the table. Her hair jostled with a rattle of trinkets.

"You're all together. Hah. That's nice, friends celebrating a night out."

"Aye, and there are few Cavari willin' to step in for a Mercenian."

Luc matched the slow progression of his aggressors in retreat. He stood out among the locals, dressed so in his bright, patchwork coloring to their muted, dark tones and stylish doublets. Cutting edge, they were, with the women in their silken dresses and corsets worn outside their blouses. His coat hung off his too-thin frame and his boots looked two sizes too large. Even his face, hawkish in form, gave him away to lighter skinned company. Good thing long legs meant larger strides.

Luc dug inside his bag and his fingers curled around a small pouch.

"I can return the coin! No harm done. You get everything back."

"Cheats need be taught a lesson. You're runnin' out of room, traveler."

"Quite a point! Well then. I–hah!" In a snap of Luc withdrew the pouch from his bag and threw it at the woman. It bounced off her chest and hit the floor, the tie unfurling to reveal a pile of black powder. She glanced at the concoction and snickered, her hip jutting out as she placed an open palm aside, supporting the scathing attitude. The group of irate card players chuckled. So did the crowd of spectators. Some placed wagers on the intended punishments.

"That is not how that works, you know this, eh?"

"Point! To you, again." Luc plucked the lit char paper from his mouth and flicked it at the exposed pouch. It sailed through the air to the horrified gasps of the nearby onlookers. The skill and accuracy it took to sink the spark of flame into the partial opening took years of training, countless hours of trial and failure.

Luc possessed none of these things.

Nonetheless, the char flipped over itself in one-to-many perfect circles and landed, lit side upon the powder.

The woman and her cohorts did not move as the powder lit. A small gout of flame sputtered and released a puff of smoke that underwhelmed but by the time they looked back to Luc he was at the window. He jumped, headfirst and over himself midair and landed on a sloped, leather overhang above the tavern's entrance. His body slid, hit the edge, then tumbled into a small gathering of Cavari by the front door.

Luc brushed off his shoulders and rolled off the groaning individual below him. Not the best landing. Hat? He brushed the brim. Still there. The wetlander appraised his surroundings. Half-dark took the night, or dusk. Really, the naming conventions made little sense. With it came his favorite bit of Cavari artisanship. Instead of gas lanterns or torches a series of rune powered sunlamps lined the streets on wired metal poles. Most of the road clattered boisterously with celebration of Riah's Peace, with string lights hung from one sloped, tile roof to another. Crowds clogged the cobblestone road, wide enough to fit two full wagons abreast, buildings smashed together on either side with not but a single arm span between them.

The group responsible for his safety stirred. Two men and one woman, they wore red leather coats and carried long-barreled firearms. What a strange choice during a festival.

"Hey!" The tan woman struck her head out the window and yelled. "He stole my coin!" She pointed at Luc. The guards hurried themselves to their feet and scowled in tandem. One leveled an arquebus at Luc. Oh. His luck turned sour.

"A misunderstanding! For sure, you see she thinks I–"

"Shut it! On your knees, you're to be taken under arrest for assault on the Adirian Guard."

"Ah." Luc held up a finger. "If you let me spea–"

"On your knees!"

"Or!" To the surprise of his captors the lithe man slid by them and came out in a flat run. They shouted as he dipped into the throng of festival goers and shoulder checked a woman mid-bite into a roll covered in glaze–it smelled of sweet, baked sugar–who screamed in protest and sent him stumbling into a street performer who blew a spout of flame from his mouth. He paused and nodded appreciatively. What a skill. Luc clapped.

Shouts called after him. Luc veered to the side of the road and hopped into a gutter carved into the cobbling. Water splashed at his stride, the stream flowing over a series of runes that generated a current.

Luc only noticed the scent of waste once it soaked into his trousers. What lovely technology.

Something popped. Gunfire. Gasps and screams parted ways for the guards. Two of the three dropped to a knee and braced their weapons against a shoulder. He splashed left. No right. Something tugged at his mind. Down? Dreadful. Luc grimaced and dropped into the gutter. Two bullets whistled over his head and collided with a waterwheel at the end of the stream. Luc lifted his head out of the water and spat, shuttering at his predicament. Ahead, he spied the wheel, perpetually in motion from the gutter water and siphoned energy back to the runes.

The line of buildings ended and the road split into a -T where a bridge took the traffic over a thin inlet from the sea. From where he lay Luc glimpsed the town below the alcove of the cliff that housed Iskvar. Or, as he called it, a dead end. He hopped up and bound away and vaulted onto the wheel. And it spun downward. Wrong side. He held onto the ledge and closed his mouth as it completed a revolution, assaulting his face with sewage. What a day.

Luc clung tight against the lure of gravity until the motion brought him to the top. The guards peered over the bridge, searching for a body, or anything. Again, Luc took flight, kicking off the wheel and into the side of a building. He latched to a windowsill and scampered up, pulling until he lay flat along one of those sloped rooftops.

Luc rolled onto his back, panting. He stared up at the evening sky. Black clouds obscured any divine presence and threatened rain. A drop of which took the opportunity to hit him in the face. Better than piss water. A light sprinkling refreshed the man to his feet. He folded up the collar of his drenched coat and patted himself down. No holes, no blood. What luck.

Countless sunlamps illuminated the crooked streets below. As the rain intensified it flicked off an almost imperceptible shimmer emanating from each pole, guiding the stray droplets into the gutters. The dull grays of construction fit the occasional splash of red from tile and brick. Ships made berths along a dock that ran the length of the town; from the alcove to the front gate, it could house dozens of vessels, all guided by the powerful beacon that blazed atop Iskvar. Luc cast his gaze skyward, content to peer up at the marvel of a lighthouse.

Until the wall exploded.

A massive fireball blasted outward from the lower castle wall. Debris launched from the cliff, trailing smoke and flame. The wall shuddered. It's base cracked, spasmed, then collapsed, the tower at the edge cascading over in a waterfall of stone. The projectiles landed first, crashing into roof and road alike, breaking into pieces and crushing whatever lay beneath it. Wails rose from the people. They scattered in any direction, some seeking the shelter of the alcove while others chose to shelter within their homes. Next came the stone.

The deluge of carved rock overtook a terrified mass of people, their screams silenced in an instant. Houses were torn to shreds. A precise pressure against Luc's shoulder forced him back as a rock the size of his head crashed into the rooftop. He teetered, flailed his arms out, and came to a steady balance. Whew.

"There he is!" The call came from the street. His pursuers caught up to his ruse, drawn so to the events above.

"Are you serious?! Go help those people!" Luc pointed wildly at the mass of dust and smoke.

"Surrender, saboteur!"

"How are you so dense!" He growled out some kind of mix of grunt and hiss. Best to lose these fools.

• • •

The rain sped to a downpour. It slid from the invisible aura above the street and created a cascade of clear water. A crack of thunder rolled over the coast, lighting the sky in brief flashes.

Where to go? Luc glanced west where the docks lay. Nothing. North? More town, albeit away from the mess of destruction. Nothing. East! That drew him. Luc brushed some of the rain off of his shoulders and started off, free from his trio of trailing morons. Most of the traffic retreated to the safety of indoors while others yet looked onto the devastation and watched flames dance upon the cliffside.

Ahead loomed one of the two major gates of Iskhold. Wide enough to fit a dozen men abreast they led into a square of roads clogged now with a mass of fleeing merchants and terrified commoners at odds with confused travelers. Two men screamed at one another, wildly gesturing at a wagon with a broken wheel that blocked half the road. A child wailed into the night amidst the panic and Sun Priests managed groups in attempts to stem the tide of fear. To the exit then. No response. Luc paused. He turned in each cardinal direction to no avail.

She appeared first as a haze. A woman slumped into a saddle upon a white palfrey. Her blue, sequined dress shimmered in the light, soaked in blood. Luc's gaze latched onto her. He felt it then stronger than ever. The sense burned in his mind. She weakly guided the mount through the current of bodies, few taking note of her unique person. And those that did wore red coats.

Luc rubbed his hands together. He inhaled, stomped a foot, and glimpsed about. A guardsman with half a golden cape flung over his right shoulder pointed the rider out. At his direction, the few soldiers remaining shoved their way past the crowd. His mind tugged at the woman. Again. Luc exhaled. He wrung his hands together and spun about to leave the mess and head into town.

"There he is!"

The gun wielding trio blocked his path and waded into the crowd. Luc scraped a heel across the cobble. He tossed his hands up and dipped backward, disappearing within the traffic. The woman's palfrey forced its way past the gate. Splotches of red wove amidst the sea of black, gray, and brown, convening from all directions and tearing a path to Luc and the rider. A tug sent him spinning to the right to avoid a burly Cavari man in a rage. Another pulled him aside, then back again as a guard took his place.

"The Mercenian! In the hat!" A voice called from the ether. Luc ducked to the new guard's side as he moved to investigate and slid to his back. And so he danced. One pull after another, he doubled back then bound forward, slipping through the confusion until he came face-to-face with a drenched horse. The mare snorted. Luc laid a hand on the strap of the bridle and came to the mount's side. His nose twitched at the acrid scent of blood mixed with mud. The woman bled from her wrist and head.

"Hello. This is going to sound quite odd, but I need you. D'you mind?" Luc spoke in a hushed whisper. The woman turned her head, one eye swollen shut, and spoke in a coarse, broken voice.

"Docks." She coughed. "Please. I need." Tears streamed down her battered, bloodied cheeks. "Help. Please."

"I'll take that as a yes!" Luc flashed her a toothy grin and ascended the saddle without a fuss. He settled in and wrapped his arms around her hips. She groaned and slumped farther.

"You! Stop! By the name of Duke Adirian, I demand you halt!" The caped guard yelled.

Luc jostled the reins and kicked at the mare's flanks. She responded in kind, unleashing a wild whiney and leaping into a full gallop. Unable to match the ferocity of a mount at full speed the crowd parted enough to avoid being trampled underfoot. Several pops preceded more screams. Pellets whistled by Luc's head.

They left the square to the constant clack of horseshoes on stone. Lightning arced across the sky above. To the docks? The sense pulled him to the west. To the docks it was. With a yank on the reins Luc directed his surprisingly acquiescing mount, the wind buffeting his face while his new charge faded in and out of consciousness.

Sailors scattered about the harbor in various states of confusion. Pockets of lightly armed mariners protected caches of cargo near their moorings, some retreating to their vessels while other, calmer minds chatted up nearby festival goers for information. Luc followed the road that would normally be a circle of mobile merchant stalls. Fishy scents of ocean life hung in the air, mixed with billowing saltiness as the cant of his mount turned hollow and wooden at the pier proper.

"You have a ship, yes? Please tell me you have a ship." Luc jostled the woman. She murmured something too quiet to comprehend and bled a little on his coat. He grimaced. A glance revealed a lack of pursuers, but with so few ways out of Iskhold did they need to give chase? The storm raged over the sea and few vessels showed any signs of departure. Except for two. One, a regal military vessel, scouts alert, watching for passersby. Farther down the harbor a mass of sailors unfurled the square sails of a worn carrack, laden with dozens of sunlamps. Hurried, disparate. His mind tugged him to the latter. Really?

Luc hailed them as they drew closer. He raised a hand and waved. Some of the crew paused their work and eyed the disturbance. Luc pulled back on the reins and brought the mare to a steady halt. Carefully, he slid off the saddle.

"I need to speak with your captain! Please, it's urgent."

Those sailors that did pay him heed raised a brow. One leaned over to the other and spoke in some foreign language. Nui. The men abandoned any sort of torso covering, displaying the ocean blue tattoos indicative of their people. Some wore baggy pants tied off above the ankle while the women sported little more than wrapped fabrics and skirts that exposed a leg and part of the other. What a coincidence to meet more of the islanders. Luc smiled at them and summoned his best accent.

"If pardon. Many tidings. Must broker trip. Am offer monies. Many monies. Will money you now. Speak to boss person?" He blinked, butchering his way through the heavy tonal consonants. The wrong inflection made all the difference between an insult and a request. One of the Nui laughed. The others crackled a bit then they returned to their work. Luc flushed red.

"Traveler!"

The wetlander froze. There, on the side of the vessel's rail, sat the Nui woman from the card game. She opened her arms and fired off a few quick commands in her native tongue. The sailors around Luc withdrew hatchets and cutlasses. He swore he saw a man turn a cannon from the deck on the horse.

"How good of you to return! I think Kiliku smiles on me this day. You owe me some coin, I believe."

Noτe ϝroɱ Arkɑlɪs

DIN! Where in the void-fucked-wastes is that wine merchant? Whatever. If you see him order the following, in order of perfection:

Aul Red - I'm down to one bottle. Order a case. Can we still get this? I will never forgive you if we can't.

Singali Rosé - What it's called? Chateau de Biliviue, or something? That. Two cases.

Mercenian Debina - Sparkling white. From the Wetlands. You know. Can we get barrels? As many cases as you can.

And however much of that Veldanian cider they have. Buy all of it. Literally. By thee Lady you are commanded!

Chapter 13
Everything You Wished For

Consciousness seemed a silly thing. Flashes of life came to her in brief waves of nausea and pain. Shapes plagued her vision, unfamiliar, vague shapes. Her mind reeled at their comprehension. Thoughts came as sluggish things. Blood loss? Parts of her body burned while others ached. Somewhere, distantly, she heard screams.

Her screams.

Kali's mind drifted, stunted by the dull light of the small enclosure. Too woozy to bother with description she focused on the sensations. Ginger fingers pressed on her skin. Their light touch brought momentary relief, a blissful lack that highlighted the stinging pains that wracked her body. Was this death? Did the Adirians catch up to her? Memories slipped through her grasp. A horse. A dock. A man. She glimpsed enough to realize she lay flat on her back, her throat hoarse.

Water. No, wine. Yes. That. She wanted it, desired it. Needed it. She thrashed and asked the shape for a cup. Not much, just enough to wet her lips. A muffled laugh responded. Kali lifted her head. Terrible idea. Pain exploded in her skull, a pounding ache that sent her into an involuntary shake. The shape laid a gentle caress upon her cheek. Bright, blue light blinded her. She felt her face scrunch in distaste, her flailing arms weakly buffeting at the invasive shape.

The pain dulled and Kali stilled. Her body relaxed and a sense of relief washed over her mind. Yes, time to die.

·   ·   ·

The shapes were gone. Only darkness remained. The world spun. Wine. The thought occurred to her before any other. A drop, even. She could manage that. Kali lifted herself, then didn't as her wrists stuck at her side. What? She pulled, they resisted. Shackles burned against her flesh. Bindings? They did capture her. She rested now in a dungeon, a dark, lonely cell.

No wine here.

Again she screamed. She pleaded. Begged? Maybe. No one came. Time passed, but with nothing to measure it she mused at what must surely be hours. Days? Weeks? Her throat ached and she ceased her cries, instead turning to sobs. The aches persisted and on occasion her body shivered to add insult. Her teeth clacked against her will despite the distinct sensation of heat, her body too hot for comfort. Then, in the same breath, she felt cold enough to freeze.

The Void then. Somehow, they found a tear in the world and tossed her in. Better to just slit her throat. She sobbed and turned her head to the solitary pillow beneath her head. Pillow? Did the Void have pillows? Evil pillows. Dark, infested linens woven by voidspawn. What did Dinkira always say?

"Even our enemies sleep."

Kali's eyes snapped open. That voice. Dinkira sat at her feet, his face pale and gray with his throat open, blood dried and stained to his flesh.

"I saw you die," she stammered, her voice no more than a harsh whisper.

"Quite right. I am dead."

"What?"

"You should know, Arkalis. You killed me." The visage of Dinkira rocked up, his old knees cracking from the strain. A cold sweat drenched her forehead. Her body.

"I didn't. I didn't mean–"

"Mean to? Of course you didn't. You don't mean to do anything do you? We live to serve." He mocked a bow, his head listing a bit too far forward. "At your leisure. At your whim. So you can drink and fuck? How many died to free you? All for you to ruin it. For nothing!" He gurgled. Taller than she remembered the shadow that was Dinkira loomed over her as he wrapped his hands about her neck.

"Why do you get to live?"

Kali choked. She twisted her shoulders and thrashed at her bonds. She fought for breath.

"Why do you live?!"

The shadow vanished. Kali gasped for air while her body convulsed. Not real. None of it was real. She tried to scream but nothing came free.

•   •   •

Years, certainly. Years passed. She woke, she slept, only to wake again exhausted, panting, gasping. The shadows waited for her. They taunted her with her failings. The only way to pass the time became listening to the sounds of her own sobbing.

•   •   •

Kali's eyes fluttered open to the flicker of candlelight. The cabin rocked to some gentle lull, a nondescript rhythm that made her innards churn. Her senses returned to the sound of water crashing against creaking wood. Then came the pain. A fiery jolt stung her arm at any hint of movement. She groaned and clutched her stomach. Cramps. A pleasant addition to a thorough beating and desperate ride. Ride. Horse. Images flooded to her mind's eye of taunting shadows. Gariant standing in defiance, Din's slit throat. Her father's body impaled upon a blade.

"Ah, you wake." Arkalis shielded her eyes from the rays of sunlight, her hands free. A figure stepped into the room. Dark skinned with cropped black hair, she wore a slip of a dress with a single strap that held a blue-green material loosely over her bust. The woman sat next to the bed where she laid a wooden bowl on a nearby stand. Kali sniffed at the concoction. Garlic and onion mixed with the unmistakable odor of boiled fish. She caught her breath and held her nose.

"Mm, no appetite? *Tut.*" The woman wagged a finger. "You must eat. Regain strength, you sleep for days."

"Days?" Kali balked at the sound of her own voice. Weak, and hoarse. "How many?"

"Five. You eat. But no wine. Do not ask."

Strained, Kali rolled onto her side and put her weight on her good arm with a grunt. The blanket that covered her body slid to reveal a bandaged torso and a myriad of bruises. That explained the utter agony of movement.

"Where are my clothes?"

"We toss them." The woman shrugged. Her accent clumsily tied words together, but she enunciated her consonants with a biting finish. Easy to understand, if odd. "No worries. We keep the boots. Everything else blooded. And ugly."

Fair. Kali glimpsed her surroundings with disinterest. Her boots lay on a nearby stool next to a few folded articles and her blackened sword. The barren cabin held little else of note. Was that all she had? A blade and a pair of boots. Kali exhaled and dropped her head onto the voidpillow. Even her hair felt foreign. Dry, matted, and short.

"Sad girl." The woman hoisted a bag onto the bed and fished out a fresh roll of bandages and a tin of clear jelly. She removed the old wrappings. Kali lay still. Calloused and cold, the woman's tough fingers were nonetheless gentle. She rubbed the gauze into her wounds to a familiar relief. "You regain strength. This brings joy. Pretty, clean face. Except for scar here." She tapped the side of Kali's forehead. That's where her headache stemmed from.

"Whatever you say. And just who are–hey!" Kali bolted upright and wiggled away from the woman's touch. She placed a hand over her crotch and glared daggers at her nurse. "Not without wine first, woman."

"No wine! You survive demon, eh? But now you bleed. Sheets hard to clean. You take care, or me? Choose." Her stare cowed Kali's own irritation. She laid without protest. Verbally, anyway. At least that explained the cramps.

"You have a name? Usually I'm familiar with the person attempting to violate me."

"Leinani."

"Pleasure, Leinani. I'm Arkalis."

"Am here to clean. No pleasure."

"No I did—sure."

Leinani finished with her bit of uncomfortable meddling.

"Captain Niati wishes to speak when you walk."

"All business, huh?"

"Cavari words clumsy. Not speak for joy."

Kali eyed her guest. Leinani shoved her items into her bag and appraised her charge with one last scan. She pointed to the stew.

"Eat. Not great, but spice is fresh. Ghar-leek, this Cavari grow. Makes fish taste less fish." She dipped her finger into the stew, stirred it, then deposited the digit in her mouth with a wet smack. "Is good. Not great." Leinani shrugged. "Eat, sad girl. Drink broth."

Sufficiently convinced, Kali labored her way to a seated poise. A momentary flash of light revealed a clear blue sky and a fluttering sail as Leinani departed. The door clicked shut, sending a gust of salty air to her tongue. Her stomach rumbled.

"Sky Father, if this shit makes me queasy." Kali grumbled and proceeded to force the contents down. Better all at once. What a motto. The howl of hunger calmed itself in due course as she shoveled the slimy gruel in the relative silence of her hovel.

It washed over her, the quiet, in a sudden wave of anxiety. She crossed her arms over her breast and sank her head into her hands. Here, away from home, she sat alone on a thin mattress, her body broken. She sucked in the air and forced herself to breathe. Inhale. Her chest heaved and burned. Exhale. She emptied her lungs. Rinse, repeat. Kali sat until the candle lost half its height.

Better to not keep her savior waiting.

Sad and slow, Kali slipped out from under her blanket. She wobbled to her feet and stretched to a series of pops along her arms and back. She used the wall of the cabin to reach the folded clothes. Kali slid into the wide, brown trousers, grateful that Leinani concealed her groin in bandages. They only reached as far as her shin. If the rest of the crew were Nui that made sense. They were not tall people, more so known for their general thickness of body. That she related to. Once she tied the waistline, she slipped into a frilled shirt. It buttoned in the front. What a concept. Kali made sure to leave the top two undone then finished with the uncomfortable, but at least familiar, riding boots.

A foray of activity greeted her on the deck. Dozens milled about. Some replaced the lines of the sails while others coated the wooden sides in some kind of oil. She swore one man rubbed some of the ropes with tar. Not one Cavari. Tan skin, blue tattoos. Nui. They ignored her, caught up in their routines. Kali swayed with the ill balance of the vessel to keep her footing, making use of the various lines to hold herself steady at an errant wave. None carried weapons though she spotted a few mounted cannons and some bombards for good measure. Well-armed merchants? Not military, the crew lacked discipline. They tended toward bare chests and loose bottoms, men and women sporting bare skin wherever they could manage.

Her venture took her from the raised front of the vessel where her cabin lay to beyond the masts–massive trunks with square sails where a few brave souls climbed about in some form of maintenance or another.

"And here she is, our mysterious princess!" A woman's voice cut through the seaborne breeze. She stood with one foot resting on the railing of the second-story platform at the rear of the vessel, short in stature but no less authoritative. Kali lifted her gaze to the voice. Sharp, narrow features, sunken cheeks with a devilish grin. Her long, braided hair blew with the winds, chiming to the tune of the jewelry and trinkets scattered to elegant styling.

"Ilvicar doesn't have a royal family." Kali's voice cracked, her tone strained.

"Eh, speak up dear one, or has Kiliku taken your voice?"

"Ilvicar doesn't–" She paused at the sharp grin of her tormentor. "Who are you?" Kali coughed in an attempt to clear out the persistent lump in her throat.

"Me? *Ei, ei,* dear one, you must be a princess to be so rude." The woman snorted. She rose up onto the rail without a hint of a misstep as she paced back and forth. One hand rested on the hilt of a basket-hilted rapier while she winged her other arm out at her side. "It is custom in Nukati to introduce oneself to avoid such frivolous anonymity, eh? I suppose, yes, these waters are Cavari, but this boat? This boat belongs to Kiliku, my very tall friend, and it is captained by a faithful servant of the Wind Mistress, Niati Kanhe." She bowed, flourishing a hand outward, her orange-red skirt blowing in a sudden gust. "And this be the Hepsu and her delightful crew."

Nui traders then. Kali took in her surroundings with a degree of skepticism. Nukati made it a point to field their own Water Treaders; agile vessels lower to the waves. Carracks carried more cargo. And cannon. Few of Din's lessons detailed Nui customs, mostly their naval tactics and trade prospects.

"Captain Kanhe? I am Arkalis I–" No. Better to keep her status quiet. ". . .Iballa. Second heir to Patriarch Alukan of Iskvar." Rich, but not important.

"Hah! No princess, but still with the titles. You see? They breed themselves for a specific stock, the Cavari. You too lift one of those giant swords, I think." Niati spoke over her shoulder. "I find this odd, though, dear heart. Do Cavari ladies run from their guards often?"

"Not a lady." Kali interrupted, her voice gaining strength.

"Eh?"

"Lady is reserved for high-born women. Nobles." Niati's eyes darkened. A few of the Nui sailors chuckled. "The daughter of a patron has no title."

"Balls aplenty girl!" Niati hunched onto her heels, her balance impressive. "That makes you a useless captive, eh? If you speak truth that is."

Kali's face flushed red. Commoners never dared speak to her in such a way. No doubt her tone would switch with her knights in tow. On horseback. On her lands, where her livelihood and family relied on her kind whim. Now? Kali struggled to stand upright, but she managed a fierce stare that left the captain unamused. She glowered, the noble, gold tinted blood in her veins boiling over in a flash of rage. She exhaled through her nose and twisted her heel into the deck.

"Calm, dear heart." Niati hopped up from her perch. "May as well enjoy the ride. Besides!" The captain turned her speech to the ship-proper, speaking now to the crew more than Kali. "Where are you to go? You cannot row, you have nowhere to swim. Do not worry your head, we send word of ransom to your father. You'll be home in weeks, maybe."

"You're pirates." Kali said, annoyed.

"*Ei*, privateers, dear heart. We don't want to be throwin' accusations around now do we? Unless you'd like to spend your time aboard below." Niati flashed a wolfish grin.

From one prison to another. Kali's head spun. Whether from her weakness or this revelation she didn't know, yet somehow again she managed into the hands of another with designs on her future. Kali bolted for the side of the ship and hung her torso over the rail, expelling the remains of the fishy stew into the rolling blue of the ocean.

She coughed the vestiges of intolerance out of her body and hung for a moment, catching her breath in short, shallow pants. The chattering voices blended. Some laughed, others returned to their chores.

The spectacle faded to the ambient creaking ropes and drumming wood. A gentle wind caressed face, cooling the hot bluster of her cheeks. An unending horizon of water and sky loomed in the distance. The sun lingered, full and bright in the throes of summer. Kali closed her eyes.

Lord of the Sky. She prayed. *Master of life and light, hear me. I am not your most faithful servant, not your most pious. I sleep through most of the cantings, really. It's shameful. But Zevra is so monotone and her acolytes are tone deaf. Anyway. I am in great peril and I know I don't deserve it, but I am begging you. For something. For anything. Please. A sign.*

So earnest a prayer.
So great a plea.
On deaf ears you call, Arkalis.

The voices whispered at the edge of her mind. Sharp, cackling, they took form in static, distinct in tone. The first spoke with a sweet, sultry tenor timbre that rolled its tongue. A female voice took the cadence next; lithe and airy, it lulled her into a state of comfort. The last bled confidence, command. Dark and low, it rumbled with all the authority of a god.

We offer life.
We offer vengeance.
We offer power. Your soul is mired, unfulfilled. Let us free you.

"What are you?" Kali whispered. She focused her mind on the voices. A sharp whine lay beyond them. It pierced her hearing and drowned the ambience of the ship.

We are what we offer.
We are the truth beyond the veil.
We are everything you wished for.

Kali's eyes shot open. The Void? Her fingers brushed the red ruby of the obsidian blade at her side. She need only accept their offer, to say yes. Again, she saw herself in a dream. Sheathed in power, strong enough to return home, to claim it. Freedom. True freedom lay within her grasp.

"*Tut,* sad girl."

The voices vanished. Reality rushed to take their place. Kali shook her head and exhaled, flexing her sword hand above the ruby. Leinani approached, hands on her hips. Beneath the Sunlord's gaze the caretaker looked younger than her imagination painted her in the cabin. Almond-shaped eyes, round, chubby cheeks. Kali admired the dress and the lack of what her culture thought of as decency. Two slits at the hips separated the bottom into two distinct pieces, allowing her legs freedom of movement. A proper feminine garment aboard a vessel. She held a mop and bucket.

"May be stew is too rich. This I give apologies. You finish?"

"For now. May have some left for dinner." Kali sat and dropped her chin to stare at the deck.

"*Ei, Nani!*" A few of the Nui chattered at the woman in their native tongue. They chuckled, speaking with an almost laid-back cadence while slurring their vowels. Leinani responded by sweeping her hands at them with a chiding tone. The words meant nothing, but Kali knew a taunt when she heard one.

"What are they saying?"

"Them? *Enwue*, pay them no heed, sad girl. Nui are birthed on ships. Land walkers take time to ajoost."

"Adjust."

"Aad-just."

"Close enough. Doubt you're here for a Cavari lesson. What do you want?"

"*Ei*, so sharp. You are like stone coral, pretty, but no touch. Kiliku encourages curiosity. Expand mind? Nui need no reason to speak and trade ideas. But in this trade?" Leinani set the bucket and mop beside Kali. A soapy water sloshed inside. "You work. Or *Niati* tosses you into waves. Easy idea, eh?"

•   •   •

Long tangles hit the floor with a wet lurch. Kali dragged the mop head across the wooden beams with a malaise of intent; slow, sloppy, and arrhythmic. Inside the bowls of the carrack–or the *Hepsu,* or home–a twilight sort of darkness prevailed. With no openings, only a few, scant sunlamps lit the interior. The dull blue aura did little to distinguish one object from another, leaving her to stumble about to the occasional stubbed toe. Painful blisters now adorned the soles of her feet.

With her newfound duties Kali familiarized herself with the ship. Most of the nautical terminology evaded her, but she distinguished one deck from another, which side was port and starboard. The only thing of note her sleuthing revealed was Snow kept below deck. Remarkable temperament, that horse. Otherwise, escape seemed beyond her reach.

She swept the mop to and fro, the soapy suds mixing mildew mold and brine. And piss. After days of ceaseless, menial labor on the main deck Captain Niati assigned her progressively worse details. At least above she got fresh air. And sun. Now she glared more often. She grumbled at the passing crew and cursed in low tones. Few spoke to her with the notable exception of Leinani. The woman checked on her wounds daily, changed her bandages, and allowed some semblance of contact with their broken conversations. She spent most of her day in silence, stuck to the confines of her own dismay.

The whispers followed her. Since her first rebuke they persisted in their pursuit, distant yet clear, they offered the same deal. Power. Freedom. They swelled when she acknowledged them, the fierce static eschewing reality in its sudden onset. Her motion ceased. Now? Her ears rang. The shrill, high-pitched wail exploded in her mind. She cradled her head into her hands.

We are the truth.
We are power.

"Sunlord please, release me from this torture," she whispered. "Cast out this darkness, raise me to the sky so I might be free."

"He's not listening. Not to us."

Kali jumped, startled. The voices silenced. Silenced? She scampered up and whipped her vision about the hold, the mop held out like a blade. No dark figures, no threats, only an assortment of crates and a lonely cell; a sad bunch of metal shoddily installed for a bad seed or two with a lamp hung overhead. Its glow swayed to the gentle lull of the boat's keel and cast a weary shadow of the bars, illuminating a strange man in thin strips of light. He lay on his back with his hands cradling his head, elbows winged out and long, golden brown hair scattered over his face in thick tendrils to his neck.

"Who are you?" Kali tapped the bars with her mop.

"Whoever you want me to be." The man flicked open a hazel eye and smirked. Despite the expression his lips pointed down. Maybe from the hollow cheeks or stubbled chin. Kali detected a distinct sardonicism that oozed from the prisoner's manner. "But, if you seek a name? Nihilus."

"NI-hee-loos? You're from Lindorum?"

"Correct, *Pulchra*." He switched from a fluid, western Cavari accent to the sharp annunciation of his people. Perhaps to prove a point. "And you deem to use high speech. Do your captors know of your nobility?"

Kali's hands twisted around the haft of the mop.

"They don't. How interesting. A Cavari noble with a mop, hiding her identity. You must be in trouble." Nihilus exhaled. He swept up in a fluid motion and brushed the thick red shawl wrapped about his neck to drape down his back. He wore a sleeveless tunic that narrowed at his hips into trousers flared at the waist. Loose fabric bunched where it tucked into a set of thick boots, buckled up from his shin to the heel. All red, toned to match his dark skin. He leaned against the bars, muscular bare arms hanging out from the cell. Kali pointed her weapon at his head.

"Have no fear," he continued. "I've no cause to reveal you. I am, as always, where I need to be."

"Never met anyone that needed to be locked in the hold of a ship. Guess we can't all be privileged enough to be forced into menial labor." Kali set her mop down and bore her weight into the handle. It slipped. She scampered to keep her balance, twisting herself enough to not fall. She coughed. Nihilus raised his narrow brow but otherwise kept silent on the display.

"I'll trade you buckets." He tapped his makeshift chamber pot with a toe.

"That why they threw you in here? Smart mouth?"

"I required a ride, and here I need not earn my keep."

"Being intentionally cryptic doesn't make people like you much. Ever tried straight answers?"

"Once. It led to my incarceration."

"I get it now. You're an asshole." She responded with a taunt of her own. "I guess that means we can be friends."

"How prodigious. An alliance could prove fruitful. Especially with one of your nature."

"One of my what? Sweet Sunlord, is this your first time talking to another person?"

"Your nature." Nihilus said, matter-of-factly. He spoke with a deep bass that didn't fit his shorter stature. "Do you not know you are cursed?"

"Cursed?" Kali's brow narrowed. "How do you–what did you mean? That the Sunlord isn't listening?"

"To us. Those out of favor. Those that dare to break the rules." Nihilus' eyes sparked red for the briefest of moments. Kali brandished her mop once again. "Calm yourself, lady. I said I have no intent to reveal you and I do not. Your condition is fragile."

"Hey!" Kali slammed the mop handle against the bars. Nihilus' gaze flickered to the impact, but he remained stoic. "My *condition* is fine. I didn't break any void's damned rules!"

"You did." He straightened his shoulders and let his hands fall to his sides. "And you know it. Tell me, do the voices speak to you? I would hope you are not yet their puppet."

Voices. She heard them spark to life at the edge of her hearing, distant, but powerful. A torrent of emotions flooded her mind. Did she bring this on herself? What rules? The escape, the deaths. Dinkira and Gariant. If something else forced her hand then the blame lay elsewhere. And yet. She acted. She chose. They died, her father died, because she chose. Anger swelled in her mind. Her hands trembled and she lost to rage.

"I am not *cursed*!" Kali reared back and swung. The wood splintered and toppled to the floor with a clattering echo.

You are, Arkalis.
Cursed. A prisoner. Trapped.
Take your freedom. It waits only for you to act.

"Get out of my head!" She screamed. The mop hit the floor and she clasped the bars, her knuckles white. "Get out!" Kali's body trembled under the strain as a groaning wail twisted the metal around her clenched fists. The white noise that invaded her mind washed out the world. It all needed to burn. This prison, the ship. This man. Her captor. They promised her that much, the voices. The Void. They promised her power.

Something wet splashed her face. The static ceased and Kali withdrew, her nose twitching at the stale scent of urine. Nihilus stood over her holding a bucket. Her breathing came in quick, shallow pants but her legs quivered, suddenly sore, and she dropped, catching herself. Her back arched and she vomited.

"Ah." Nihilus dropped the bucket. He poked at where Kali released the bars and the metal flaked, so brittle now that a solid chunk of it collapsed as soot. "So not yet under their control. This is good."

"W-what?" Kali hacked. She spit then wiped her mouth, groaning. A raucous thumping interrupted them and marched into the hold. Niati and a group of her sailors rushed toward the two of them, weapons drawn, the captain sporting her rapier.

"What is this? What did you do to her, spawn?" Niati said with a glance between the two.

"Me?" Nihilus shrugged. "I am behind bars." He kicked the cell for punctuation. Two of the bars dusted at his touch, crumpling to ash as if they never existed. A low murmur emerged from the sailors. Niati pointed her rapier at Kali who righted herself and sat. She rested her elbows on her knees, her head hung low, matted, sweaty hair obscuring her face.

"He did nothing." Kali spoke.

"You did this?" Niati asked with a venomous hiss. "Explain this. Now!"

"I can't." Kali sniffed. The sweet stench of piss wafted over her nostrils and stained her frilled shirt. She flexed her hands, feeling the heat that radiated out from her palms. The voices did not need her permission, they just needed time.

Excerpt from the high Loremaster's Journal

P RECIOUS FEW SITES of faith remain in the world, no doubt a casualty of the Desolation. Lindras, the home of the Sunstar Religion, is nothing but a sterile desert. So it is that I find myself utterly distraught at the lack of access to the Basilica of Light. All other contemporary Sunhouses are based on this temple, one of the sole surviving structures of an utterly forgotten past and the Hierophant herself wrote me a letter of denial of passage.

All I need is a single, surviving Thalian archive, and I know those charlatans have one! Only one of the Faith's ranks may enter, and even then, they must be a Priest at the very least. Figures that an institution that condemns the use of "high" technology would possess the last remaining bastion of it.

Chapter 14
The door

LESANDRE ATTENDED the slate-colored map table. He traced new lines on the meticulously sourced borders while referencing the open tome: the High Loremaster's journal, itself an artefact worth more than most castles. A flat, black slate with a glass surface lay in a carved depression of what should be pages. It displayed a column of runes on the top that Lesandre used to explore a render of the countryside in alarming detail, from the width of rivers to the height of the most extraneous hill. The journal worked without exposure to sunlight. Unlike most runecasting, such as the table that drew its power from the sunlamps, the slate never waned, forever aglow.

Thalian artefacts served as wonderful distractions. Lesandre retraced the border of eastern Ilvicar and Haven, the beacon of neutrality separating a sordid history of warring nations. The lines erased and reappeared at his whim, settling once he tapped the table's surface. Work well done, at least as a distraction.

Outside the war room delegations from every faction in or near Iskvar waited to speak with him. With the duke and marshal dead heritage should fall to Arkalis, who–according to plan–was missing. That left one lord with noble enough blood to handle high affairs of state.

Also according to plan. His plan.

Possession of Iskvar brought new challenges. Those that fit Lesandre's skill set, if not his disposition. Cavari government did well autonomously. Peasants ruled themselves, with the notable exception of taxes and arms, and loyal, estate hungry knights did everything in their power to please their superiors to the extent of keeping peace.

Lesandre adjusted his spectacles to better frame his face. He tapped the side with his index finger, activating the embedded runes in the cosmetic lens. A stream of information flooded the edges of his vision. Details and compositions invisible to all but himself. Another gift, and far more useful than any sword. He focused on the doors and adjusted the frames to change perspective. They pierced the heavy wood and gray stone of the castle walls.

Gwin stood dutifully on the other side. The poor servant took to following him since the death of Denrik. Around him a delegation of colorful individuals waited at the door. Elys did what he could to stall them.

"Let them in!" Lesandre's voice cracked. He coughed. So regal. He rubbed his chest over his light, leather jacket. "Let them in!" He tried again with sufficient volume and closed the book. The door swung open to reveal the host of impatient, important people.

First came Baron Shadowsong. Airil. With her long, red curls and green trimmed breastplate. She wore a long-sleeved coat that dipped below her waist and tight, leather pants, complete with a green cape clasped around her neck. A fresh scar ran from her forehead to the left eye to her cheek. It took five guardsmen to secure her when she learned of Denrik's death and only two of them survived.

Next came Alukan, town patriarch. Old, wrinkled, but hardly frail– the man filled out his brown robes a little too well, bulbous around the waist. A wizened, gray beard hung from his chin to his chest, giving him an air of wisdom. Lesandre's spectacles revealed the dagger he kept buried in those robes and various pouches stuffed with char and halfpennies. The plain circlet of his office decorated his bald head to distract from the splotchy skin. Zevra next, always in her sunsinger garb, followed by Gwin and Elys, the latter shelled in his parade armor, though helmetless, where half his face prickled black and blue from a vicious bruise. A host of other officials filed in; Wessen, the shaper, representatives of the commoner guilds, and even a guard captain from the Adirian forces, gold half cape slung over a shoulder. Before long, the room felt stuffed, with only enough chairs to seat the highest-ranking attendees.

"You're all full of questions, I know." Lesandre started, mustering as genuine a smile as possible despite the artificial joviality. "With Arkalis' disappearance."

"Duchess Iskarion." Airil's voice cut through his.

"With her grace's disappearance." He offered her a nod. She glared back. "Stewardship falls to me. Make no mistake, these are *Iskarion* lands, though with their capitulation to the treaty of Ilduan that makes this a legal proceeding. Any disputes?"

"Yes, yes," Alukan grumbled. The old man's jowls rumbled as he spoke. "We all know how this works. You assure us nothing changes then everything changes. Come off it boy, you could've just sent a missive. Why are we here?"

"That *boy*. . ." Elys slammed a gauntlet into the table, ". . .is a *lord*, Patriarch. And he is yours. I suggest you show some respect."

"Or what?" The fearless old fool stared up at the better armed knight. "Denrik appointed me patron before you were old enough to stab good men in the back, and now his killers summon me to offer excuses? I'm too old for games, *knight*." Alukan barked the word in insult. Lesandre saw the flicker of rage infest Elys' countenance.

"Alukan, peace." Zevra grasped the patriarch's shoulder. The eerie calm of the sunsinger silenced his complaints. "We are all remiss at Denrik's loss, but this does not help. Let us hear out Lord Lesandre. What else is there to do?"

"Thank you, Zevra," Lesandre continued. "Let's skip the pleasantries then. This house is a mess. A duke is dead. One heir is missing, accused of insurrection, the other is held for voidcraft in Dula'Thalier." A shocked whisper erupted from the crowd. Only Airil and Elys ignored the hype. "The Church of the Sunstar proclaimed it this last week. With that and accusations of infestation in Iskvar the Hierophant is sending a pontifex here. So, while I do not require, nor expect, your respect," he glanced at Alukan, "I need your cooperation. For your own sake. That is why you are here, patriarch."

"A pontifex? You're sure?" Zevra flashed a sunburst.

"A messenger arrived last night with the news."

"What do the people care for a pontifex?" Alukan asked.

"They care." Airil leaned back in her chair, arms folded over her breastplate. "Pontifices are liberal with fire."

"Very." Zevra echoed.

"Fine. Fine!" Alukan threw his hands into the air, defeated. "You want cooperation, *lord*? I need guarantees that taxes remain untouched and special funds for the town. It had part of a castle fall on it."

"As I said, patriarch, these are Iskarion lands. I will have no part in those decisions." The mob quieted. Good. "I've appointed Gwin as acting steward. I will serve as the signature." More murmurs. Most of the minor officials signed their approval in some fashion. Gwin scratched at his mane of a beard. It spread up his ears and bled into a wavy, well-kept mop of hair, fluffed and combed for his new office. "No one here has more experience with the Iskarion House than he. And Baron Shadowsong, I would like for you to take a temporary position as Guard Captain for Iskvar."

Elys balked visibly, assured as he was of the position. Where before the delegation seemed suspicious, they now moved to downright approval. Trust so easily garnished.

Airil's response was slow, measured. "I accept. Under the condition that–"

"That you may hire and train a house guard? Yes. Had Solara allowed more freedom we may have avoided this conflict. Adirian soldiers will maintain a presence, but under the command of Sir Elys and based below in Iskhold. And who will report to the Common's Council. I believe that eases their continued presence, patriarch?"

"For now." Alukan wrung his hands together.

"It's settled then." Lesandre smiled coolly. Those that mattered grew distracted by their new duties. A reasonable Adirian shocked them all enough. "We have suitable witnesses for official proclamations. Which includes some major revisions to the interior wall. As the patriarch said, portions of it were relocated. I've asked Wessen here to clean up what he could. Your report, shaper?"

Wessen addressed the crowd at the behest. An overweight fellow, his chubby cheeks held a permanent red tint and beady eyes made home beneath a sunken brow that he hid with a deep blue headband. Lesandre mused that the only clean-shaven man in the host would benefit the most from a beard. Double chins were out of style.

"Yes, lord. Few lads from the Shaper's Union in town an'me been cleanin' out the rubble. Explosion blew out the barracks and wall section, most'a the foundation too. But we found somethin' odd by the old armory." Lesandre knew the words before the man opened his mouth. Better another speak your piece for you, integrity oozed credibility when issued by another.

"Odd? What do you mean?" Lesandre spent years perfecting an air of genuine interest.

"It revealed, well. Not too sure, lord. Deeper foundations?" Of course it did. Lesandre ordered the extra powder stored in the barracks for its 'protection'. Nothing short of a few tons worth of force would break low enough. "Not sure how to describe it. It's like nothin' I've ever seen. Obsidian walls smooth as ice, an' a door with no handle. Tried shapin' it myself."

Perfect. The others had heard such descriptions. Tales of Dula'Thalier traveled with merchant caravans: a black city, dangerous to the touch. Obsidian walls that defied imagination. If one ruin could be buried so deep, why not another?

"Obsidian? You're sure, Master Shaper?" Zevra spoke, as she often did, without looking at anyone. "Dinkira often mused that Iskvar's construction was far too rudimentary for its age."

"Sure as a ruhk shits in the sky." Wessen spoke with confidence. What a charming colloquialism.

Lesandre raised his voice for all to hear. "Best to keep this to ourselves. If a pontifex is due in Iskvar, better we not invite additional inquiry."

"What'a, what are we to do then, lord?"

"Seal the breach, of course. I'd like to take a look if you feel it's safe." Harmless curiosity. A lord set in his duty. Lesandre observed those with enough influence to be suspicious, his augmented vision translating the various twitches of body language. Nothing of concern.

"Safe enough for the lads. Can't see why it wouldn't be for you too, lord."

"And me." Zevra fingered the sunburst pendant around her neck. The jewelry identified as some sort of artefact, one his frames failed to perceive in depth.

"Anyone else?"

"Aye. You'll need an escort, just in case." Airil volunteered. "My lord."

A moment of doubt pierced Lesandre's veil of complacency. If most of the Iskarion household was too trusting, then Baron Shadowsong made up for all of it.

"Point, lady. That ends these proceedings. Any further issues can be discussed with the new steward."

• • •

Hidden for centuries beneath a clever ploy of foul odors, the collapsed foundation revealed a partial wall, its obsidian exterior smooth, darkened despite its exposure to light. If not for the pronounced seams the door in its center would be all but invisible. A door that Lesandre examined now. He scanned the material while Airil helped Zevra down, the computational babble of his lenses useless as they identified limestone, or nothing.

Only Thalian artificers possessed the expertise to create that kind of interference. Anyone divining beneath the surface of Iskvar would see nothing. Easy to confuse with a deep concentration of rock, certainly not an underground structure. Now, how to open the door? Lesandre knocked at its center. A solid, hard thrum matched the rhythm of the tap.

"I doubt anyone is in," Airil mocked.

"I wouldn't be so quick to assume," Lesandre responded, his fingertips gliding over the gelid seams.

"This wall. It is the same as the Basilica." Zevra approached the wall. She abandoned the more voluminous robes of her station for a more efficient, tightly fit kaftan with a single draping flap that flowed down her back. It was clean, with golden embroidery shared by the white sandals that wrapped up her heels to her shins.

"*The* Basilica? You mean within Aklesia?" Lesandre's interest piqued.

"The very same." Zevra's hesitantly reached out. "To think something so familiar rested below us all this time."

"Familiar? Can you open it?" Airil shot Lesandre a cautious glance.

"Perhaps? If it works the same. Every sunsinger must open the doors to the Basilica of Light and recite the Litanies. It is a test of faith. As most things are."

"And?" Lesandre tapped the binding of the journal, his shoulders tensed and back rigid.

"And. The Basilica of Light is a relic of the original Sunstar Faith. So too is the Cathedral within Dula'Thalier, but there are no markings here, nor mentions of a third holy site in the Litanies. I fear what rests behind these walls."

"Fear is the death of progress. Think of what we may discover! Ancient texts, lost litanies? This structure predates the Desolation, Zevra, and it's here. Now."

"Careful, lord, you're in danger of sounding overeager." Airil looked on with muted disinterest. Lady Shadowsong often grew bored with things she could not stab.

"Of course I'm eager! We're here. Now. What if what we find renders this madness with the black city moot? What if-"

"It's a weapon," Airil interrupted.

"Better we have it then. Or would you prefer my father?"

"He's right." Zevra lowered her arm.

"He's motivated, Zev. Who cares about a dukedom when they can have a Thalian weapon? All this pomp, he's up to something. Wouldn't surprise me if he orchestrated the whole damn mess."

The baron was smarter than he gave her credit for. While the others contented to follow their assigned distractions, Airil watched him and his designs. True, he may have moved too quickly, something to remedy.

The sunpriest voiced Lesandre's defense for him. "That's what you're here for, Airil. For now, let us see what the Sky Father has in store for us."

Zevra wrapped her delicate fingers around her amulet. She closed her eyes and her voice rose to a high, solitary note, her crisp soprano ringing within the enclosure. A soft yellow glow sprung from the amulet as it absorbed the light of the sun. It began as a thin aura then swelled with her song, a sweet melody in perfect pitch that plunged the heights of her register. The room darkened as the aura grew, any and all light drawn into the jewelry.

Lesandre tapped his lenses and a shade covered his vision.

Luminescence blazed in a mock star that enveloped Zevra. She sang her wordless aria and pressed her hand to the obsidian frame. Flares of swirling energy orbited the metal; chaotic in their paths, they spun to some unknown accord until the sunsinger's voice quieted, fading to an empty silence. The sphere sank.

Lesandre clutched the journal in both hands, bouncing with excitement. Every last vestige of energy disappeared into the door. Then nothing. A hollow melancholy filled the space in its anticlimactic glory. Zevra's eyes opened to a blank stare and Lesandre frowned, his gaze latched onto the point of contact. All of them shared a disappointed look.

"Neat trick." Airil broke the silence. "Thought you priests just made fires. Guess that explains why the basilicas are always so well lit."

"Mirrors." Lesandre removed his spectacles and cleaned them with the sash at his hip. "They use mirrors to highlight the dais. The stained glass separates the light and it–you get it."

"You sound like a loremaster."

"I studied under the High Lore–"

"It should've worked." Zevra's voice quivered.

"You don't know that Zev. Place is what? Thousand-years old? And buried. Our only instruction is this little twat of a lord."

"I could do without the insults, baron."

"And I could do with my niece back. Trade?"

"Enough." The sunsinger snapped. "It is as He wills; may He light the path ahead." She bowed her head and laid a hand on the wall.

From where her skin met the obsidian an ephemeral, blue gossamer rippled over the surface. Lesandre inhaled sharply. A streak of light formed in the center of the door and took shape as a perfect hexagon, thick lines that emitted pale illumination. Runes formed within the shape, no larger than a hand each, rendered in complex script.

"That's Thalian!" Lesandre exclaimed. Zevra startled at the occurrence and withdrew her hand. "You did it!"

"I did?" Zevra, eyes wide, stared at the symbols. "Yes. I did."

Lesandre activated his frames again and a torrent of information flooded his perspective. Data came as he identified a static pulse within the wall: currents of energy that snaked through a matrix-like structure.

"Congratulations. You turned it on." Airil said, unimpressed. "And yet, it's still closed."

"It's locked. *Magically* locked. If Thalian design is anything it's remarkably consistent. What's next, Zevra? How do you open the basilica doors?"

"There's a sequence. You touch the runes in order, but these are." She squinted. "Different. Some I recognize but most are new."

"Can't be that hard. We've got nine runes? How many do you need to enter?"

"Nine."

"Oh. Well, that's only–do they repeat?"

"Yes."

Lesandre rubbed the bridge of his nose. "Three-hundred and sixty or so combinations. Assuming the string remains the same."

"A few hundred? Get to it then, Lord Loremaster. We've got time." Airil snorted.

"Three-hundred and sixty *thousand*."

"Oh, shit."

"Quite."

From above came the echo of a horn. More guests. Lesandre exhaled through his nose. Here he stood, so close to his goal, inches away from the fruition of years of study, only to fall afoul of a door. "I'm sure I needn't impress the importance of keeping this between the three of us.

"Please don't." Airil started. "Anything to spare us your voice."

They retreated up the slope of scattered earth to the ruinous remains of the sea facing tower. Lesandre tasted salt, the new ocean view stunning. Beneath the soot and blackened, scored stone pools of dried blood persisted. In excess. The guardsmen deserved no such fate, their only crime being born of the lower classes. Unfortunate, but acceptable losses.

Airil brushed past him. He caught himself with a stomp, a flash of anger taking his countenance. The woman meant trouble. He may need to keep Elys closer than he planned.

"Lady Shadowsong, if you would guard the breach until we can get a proper watch?"

"Your will is mine, Lord Adirian." Airil brought a fist to her chest. Lesandre almost tripped at the lack of attitude.

"Right. Good. Thanks. Zevra, if you'd accompany me? I have an idea who our guest is."

He and the sunsinger made their way from the ruin to the inner gate where riders rode up the hill, the echo of powerful hoofbeats bracing against the cobble that preceded their arrival. Lesandre took up as lordly a pose as possible, smoothing out his jacket and tucking the journal up under an arm. Zevra made no such effort. Nearby he spied

Balen draped on a few bales of hay, peeking over a book at the gate. Another oddity, that one.

Five riders crossed the threshold into the yard. Four of them, armored paladins, circled their charge at the center who halted before the duo. Lesandre shifted his weight from one leg to the other at the arrival.

"Lesandre, House Adirian. And Zevra Onyilogwu. Wise of you to not summon more." The pontifex spoke with a metallic tone, his face obscured behind a featureless white mask. A purple cowl covered his head and shoulders, the edges spun with gold tassels. Lesandre swallowed. Hard. An oppressive charisma exuded from the figure. One that made him small. "You know what I am. Do you know who?"

Zevra bowed her head. "Pontifex Aluntir, Order of the Fading Dawn."

"Very good, sunsinger." Aluntir slid off his saddle and landed into a walk. He clasped his hands, his pace one of directed leisure. Tight blue robes inlaid with gold clung to a tall, thin frame; he stood at height with the Iskarions, gangly, almost unnatural. He adjusted the cuffs of a long-sleeved coat that only covered his chest, the collar folded up to reach his chin. Narrow slits wreathed in an orange glow accounted for eyes on the mask. "You needn't do that."

"What?" Lesandre tilted his head. He thought about bowing.

"It's not worth the explanation. Reshod and feed them." The second line he addressed to Balen who stopped midstride, already en route to greet the party. "Come. The paladins will take care of themselves. We have much to discuss. The Sunsinger will accompany us as a witness."

Aluntir strolled off toward the keep proper. Lesandre watched him go, a single thought on the tip of his tongue.

"Fuck."

Excerpt from the high Loremaster's Journal

AND OUR LESSON comes to the unfortunate Battle of Ilduan. An otherwise unremarkable hill, the land and the nearby village will live forever in history with the greatest blunder of the Iskarion House. The young Lord Rurik fell victim to greater Adirian cunning, committing his cavalry and knights to an early offensive without support. In his blindness? Folly? The confusion remains unclear in its origin, but the resulting destruction of the Iskarion forces is undisputed.

Rurik unwittingly engaged the Salivar infantry, Iskarion friends, previous the blunder, and in doing so fell victim to a vicious counter from Adirian gunners, having left the high ground in their charge. With the news, Kalthier forces abandoned their ancestral alliance to the Iskarions, leaving them alone against a newly combined army of the remaining dukes. One that granted mercy to only the nobility.

Chapter 15
Merde Idiote

R URIK SCREAMED. A hoarse, guttural howl came from the back of his throat that ended with his bare chest heaving in a shallow pant. Blood flowed from his fingers to his wrist and splattered onto the chains that held him. The first fingernail came easy. He watched the extraction without a wail, but the second cracked. That led to a more involved procedure, one undertaken with an intentional lack of care.

"Don't be dramatic," Celesti said between bites of a pitted date. She abandoned her armor for a white frock coat and high waisted trousers, off to one side, away from the blood. "It's just a nail, they grow *back*. Or." She tilted her chin up in thought. "Do they? I never stick around for that bit. Hah."

"They do, my lady." The sniveling response came from the slouched son of a bitch that held the pliers. "After six months, with a proper diet." He spoke without emotion and set the tool on a metal tray next to a bloodied knife. "I believe he understands your threat now."

"I think he did before. They're just stubborn, these Iskarions. This one, for example, refuses to die on his own. Much to my family's dismay. Shall we give it another go, Rik?" Celesti tossed her fruit aside. She traded places with her torturer, leaning her face into his. The clear, sky blue of her irises met his own. Bored, disinterested. She traced a finger up his stomach to his chest, her touch aggravating the superficial cuts on his abdomen.

"I see swinging that hammer does good things for the physique. Do you remember when we were betrothed? I must admit, girl could do worse." She tugged his beard; a scraggly, wild thing. "Northerners lack the dark, brooding complexion; I prefer it. And so tall. Hm. You mind if I?" She winked.

Rurik swirled his tongue in his mouth and choked up what he could from his throat. That would do it. He spat an impressive amount of phlegm with considerable aim at Celesti's eye. Dead on. A small, victorious smirk spread out over his lips, and he managed something akin to a chuckle that turned to a dry, rasping cough. Rage replaced the general nonchalance of his tormentor. Celesti picked up the knife from the tray and cut off Rurik's nipple.

He screamed. Again. The chains rattled as he fought against them, muscles tightening as he thrust his chest forward. He railed against the bindings, his hands balling into fists. They gave an inch. Enough for him to bruise his back against this accursed chair. His breath came out in spurts, wordless complaints issued in anger.

"Satisfied?" Celesti discarded the spare bit of flesh. She flicked her hand in the air, her face scrunching up in disgust as she dropped the knife. "Why fight, Rurik? There's no one left that cares for you. Even your own people betrayed you! How do you think we knew about your little deal? The Ishite? She bargained for her freedom with your head. You have no one. No friends. But us! Rurik, us. We could be such good friends and put all this unpleasantness aside. You've already lost, why lose more?

"Fuck off," he managed. Sahira? He didn't believe it. Not her.

Celesti pouted. She shimmied his pants below his waist and glimpsed his groin, her gaze fixated. "Such good friends. Mm. No?" She ran a hand through her hair and stretched with a cat-like grace. "Fine. Have it your way! But I tried, darling. All yours." The torturer returned, armed now with a fresh, runed blade. Rurik glared at the imp of a man.

"One more time, Rurik. We know about the webway. Where it is, what it is. The only thing we don't know is how to activate it. Tell me how. Pretty please?"

The torturer held the knife over Rurik's waist. He recognized the design; the runes stymied any blood loss, making them ideal surgical implements. These were altered. Made to burn instead of soothe.

"Not sure if you understood me. Let me try again." Rurik's voice was soft, but firm. "Fuck. Off."

"You don't want to be the last Iskarion, do you, Rik?" Celesti bit off the -k, clicking her tongue. "Careful now. This gets worse. Much." Her eyes grew sadistic. "Much worse."

"Nothing." Rurik inhaled, looking away as the torturer lowered the knife. He felt it press against his skin. "Nothing is worse." He breathed in short, rapid gasps. Looking anywhere but the knife. "Nothing is worse than your fucking voice."

"So be it. A pity. Such a pity."

Even the enclosure could not dull his cries.

•   •   •

Rurik laid with his face against the cold stone of his cell where the chill soothed his scalp. The pain of consciousness came in slow details: shoddy iron bars, a bucket, and a single glowlamp that hung from a too-low ceiling. He recalled the knife, the cutting. Then nothing. Only black. The pain in his groin told him all he needed to know. He flopped over onto his back. That ached too. Dried blood stained his chest and face with his wounds bound by fresh bandages. They needed him alive. Death, he thought, would be easier. A strained groan escaped his lips as rose and laid against the bars.

Unlike Lanatir's sad wall and temporary housing, the Adirians built for longevity. And with that needless display of power they added a jail. A long, narrow hall with cages on either side. The gray stones of Cavari architecture made a lovely comparison to the obsidian outside. It reminded him of home. Despite present circumstances.

Home. The word felt foolish now with his family and household dead. Dinkira, Gariant. Did they get Balen too? Without them what was a pile of stones and a bed? And now, Sahira betrayed him? The idea threatened to overwhelm him as tears stained his cheeks. He mourned, silent, his head lulled forward, eyes downcast.

"Still alive?" Lanatir said from the cell over. "Thought you were done for this time with all that screaming."

"They can't kill me. You know that."

"Yes yes, keep the *lower* nobles in line and all. We are such petty malcontents."

"Give it a rest." Rurik struck the bars with a rattle and Lanatir yelped. Hah.

"Did you tell them anything?" Another voice asked from across the hall. Lyue sat with her legs crossed. Calm, and composed, she watched Rurik, though she flicked that scroll about her neck with an anxious twitch. Nearby, he caught a glimpse of a new prisoner sequestered nearby, her head held between her legs. A spy? He figured Celesti let Lyue and Lanatir nearby to listen in on their conversations.

"No, but they know most of it. About the webway. Apparently, they can't turn it on."

"Of course they *know*. I told them that much." Lanatir recovered enough of his pride to participate.

"You what?" Lyue grabbed the bars.

"Come off it, girl. I've not the constitution of the Lord Iskarion here. They would've gotten it out of me one way or another, and they *refused* to bribe me. Such a lack of civility."

"Damn you, Lanatir." Her voice betrayed a venomous anger.

"He's right." Rurik temples pulsed. A headache too? Wonderful. "Lanatir is a coward, but he's not an idiot."

"Thank you."

"There's no sense in him enduring. This." Rurik touched the bandage on his chest. He never thought much about his breast. His fingernails would grow in time, but not that. Among other things.

"My thoughts exactly," Lanatir agreed.

"You're still a royal asshole." Lyue rolled her eyes. She released the bars and smoothed out her hair; out of its tail it stretched to the small of her back. Her anger cooled to mild discontent. "We need to find a way out of here. It's only a matter of time before they cut off something irreplaceable."

Rurik snorted. He would have laughed if not for the creeping dryness in his throat. "Escape? Why?"

"You *want* to stay here?"

"We're fucked, Lyue. Even if we do get out, where do we go? We're heretics. Can't take refuge in the basilica, can't fight our way out."

"So we give up? We rot here?"

"We have nothing." He shrugged. "No crew. No silver. When I make decisions people die. When I fight, everyone else suffers. The best thing I can do is rot here. Do what you will, just leave me out of it."

Lyue stared in stark disbelief. Good. Rurik sniffed and rubbed his nose, his head dropping to his shoulder. He caught a dumbfounded visage of Lanatir out of the corner of his eye. They allowed the baron a cushion and to keep his noble regalia; wrinkled, but passable, his normally quaffed hair now a mess that hung over his eyes. Lanatir slumped onto his cushion, stunned by Rurik's lack of fight, though more likely by his own incarceration.

"What about your freedom? You're still alive, Rurik. Why resist Celesti if you've given up?" Lyue tried again.

"Because fuck the Adirians. Why do you think I'm in this pit in the first place? She's the one that betrayed us at Ilduan. Suckered me right into that voidfucked trap." He tapped his bare foot against the stone. "I sent hundreds of my people to their deaths, Lyue. Thousands. Me. No one else. Thought I was brilliant. I murdered half of our allies before I realized what happened. I watched them *butcher* my people." His cheeks flushed red. "She sacrificed her own to turn the rest of the dukes against us. And what could I say? She won. And Cavari law grants me clemency."

"I knew what coming here meant. I could pay for my crimes, give my sister a chance to be better than me. I thought. When we met, if I could stop Celesti, I could do it for her. That would be enough to make amends. But what's the fucking point?!" Rurik heaved his waste bucket at the wall. It shattered, wood splintering in a mess of shrapnel and muck. "There is no freedom for me, loremaster. Trapped here? In Iskvar? Everywhere I go I live with *myself*. The Fool of Ilduan. Murderer. Idiot. I should've died then. It's time now."

The silence that followed was deafening. Rurik laid back and folded his hands behind his head. The glowlamp above served as a poor substitute for daylight. He imagined it as the sun anyway, full light, with his toes in the sand, the water lapping against the shore in a gentle rhythm. All of it gone. Forever. He closed his eyes, his anger enough to dull the pain of his torture as he fell deep into the throes of sleep.

●   ●   ●

Dreams came in wild fits of distress. He saw Arkalis' face surrounded by flame and his father impaled on a sword as Dinkira's head rolled over the cobbles of Iskvar's courtyard. Shadows stalked every image. In one instant he presided over a grand hall; the remains of his crew suspended from the ceiling by tendrils of black energy. In another he rode free on the back of a great war mount wielding his father's sword. The blade cleaved his enemies with ease. Not his enemies. His friends. His people. Corpses stared in horror from the blood-soaked field. Among them Celesti's face smiled up at him. She appeared at his back and kissed his neck.

He faced her only to find himself alone on the beaches of Iskvar. Blessed with white sand and gentle waves it brought a calm to the parade of horrors. Above the Sunlord took his throne, but not without contestation. A black lens surrounded the star as tendrils latched themselves to and drained its light.

"They never left."

Her voice stoked his memories. Yellow eyed demons. Friends turned foe. Cities lost to the Void. The golden woman stood beside him in her intricate armor; form fitting and sleek, it curved with her body, ridged down the shoulders and arms, with winged gauntlets and loose black fabric suspended at her waist like robes. A furred mantle sat over thick pauldrons and a tight gorget. And more. It glowed. Vibrant, white lights lined the joints, casting a soft aura in thin strips of power.

"I don't need this right now." Rurik rubbed his forehead.

"What you need is a swift kick in the ass."

"What?" She never spoke to him directly. Only in feelings and impressions.

"You don't get it yet? How thick are you?"

"Never been good at interpreting vague, mystical visions. Must've left that out of my tutelage." The snark came easy.

"These aren't visions. You *know* what they are. Think. Listen to yourself."

"I don't know wh–"

Shorter, but stronger, the woman forced him to his knees and slammed her palm into his forehead.

"Remember what you did!"

Images flooded his mind. A room covered in red runes. A figure on a throne of shifting obsidian. A city, vibrant and alive, hundreds of thousands of people running in fear. Clouds swelled above, deep, gray monstrosities that parted to emit a beam that struck the very heart of civilization. Black fire followed. It bellowed out from the city center, burning all in its path to nothing. Unmade by its touch. A circle of armored men and women coated in runecast garments argued with one another nearby in violence exchanges. Rune Knights. Salivar, Lynesse, Kalthiar, Adirian. Iskarion. Heated exchanges. The others pointed at Iskarion. At him.

At him.

Not images. Memories. Her life flashed in his mind's eye. A lifetime of battle and conflict, ancient stories of clashes against the Void and its spawn. He remembered the sinking of Dula'Thalier. Why? He saw the figure on the throne, the black lens around the sun.

Rurik inhaled and fell to the sand. Somehow, he possessed the memories of Iskarion herself. With them he could navigate the city; he could do whatever he wanted. He could seek his revenge.

"You sank the city. To protect it. From what?"

"Not to protect the city." Iskarion grew distant. She turned away, her helmet inclined to the waning light of the sky. "We went too far. We needed to be stopped, but it meant our enemy went free. They never left."

"Who? Who never left?"

"You must find me. Now is not the time to give up. *Find me.*"

"Why me? Why should I care? Give me a reason!"

Iskarion faced him. She knelt and laid a hand on his shoulder as she removed her helmet. That face. The visage of Arkalis held his vision. He knew this was not his sister, but she mimicked every detail. Every sardonic twinge.

"No one can *give* you a purpose. We make our own way, Rurik. What do you want? Forgiveness? Revenge? Find a reason to live or do us all a favor and end it."

•   •   •

Rurik opened his eyes. The pale light of the glowlamp greeted him. He sat up to the complaint of every muscle in his body and a new, sharp ache in his neck. He tousled his hair–the matted dry mass slinking over his face to his chin. The others slept. Lantair snored peacefully. What a wonder. Cumbersome and slow, he managed to stand, his joints cracking in sequence. He walked to the front of his cell and leaned against the bars, lost to thought.

Why did she have Kali's face? What way did he go? Too many questions. He wished for freedom, and all this time he knew that meant death. From a break, from a knife in the back. It never occurred to him that his end would come from his own hand. The last question loomed in the forefront of his thoughts. Which end made him the bigger coward?

A shadow of movement caught his eye. The new arrival watched him near the front of her cell with deep blue eyes, one half-shut from abuse, her head shaved and mired with cuts and dried blood. Singul, by the looks of her; she wore sirwal and a sleeveless leather jerkin.

That stare stirred a memory. She was a viper, the one the merchant called Katriene. She seemed expectant. Interested, even. Katriene waved a bruised hand and pointed at his feet, at the shards of his bucket. Not the smartest move. What did she want? He glanced up. She redoubled the aggression of her pointing then mimicked chopping.

"What?"

Katriene rolled her eyes at him.

"*Donne-moi le tesson, merde idiote!*"

"*Dis juste ça la prochaine fois.*" Rurik quipped back. His accent left a great deal of desire, but his meaning came through with the visible shock on Katriene's face. Rurik tossed one of the larger pieces of wooden shrapnel across the hall. and the viper snatched it, studying its edges. Not the worst idea. Rurik followed suit, sorting through the remaining bits and shuffling the rest of the debris toward the back of his cell. He rolled the shard in his palm. Sharp enough.

Do us all a favor.

Could he end it? Rurik mused at Iskarion's words. Kali's words. Arkalis. He tightened his grip around the wood. Arkalis. Denrik. Gariant. Their names burned inside him. Maybe he would, but first someone had to pay.

Lɪⲧⲁɴy ⲟꜰ War, Teⲛeⲧs ⲟꜰ ꜰⲁɪⲧꜤ

A S THEY SERVED Riah in her campaign against the Void, so now shall Paladins act as the elite guardians of the Faith and its loyal followers. Raised from the ranks of valiant Crusaders, these men and women shall be monk and warrior both, beholden to all oaths of a priest and schooled in the art of warfare, both martial and mental.

Tasked with the protection of all the Faithful, Paladins' first and foremost duty is to seek and hunt all corruption of the Void under the purview of the local pontifex. Second, should a civil arbiter or clergy member be unavailable, they are to rule on matters of justice and faith in their stead—authorized, if necessary, to bring a resolution through any means available.

Chapter 16
Cathedral of the Sun

URIK SAT against the wall of his cage, elbows on his knees, head hung low. The wounds that scored his chest and head lay exposed. A scar ran from one shoulder to his stomach. Another over his abdomen, all bare, bandages coiled around his palm.

The jingle of keys fumbled with the lock of his cell, followed by a soft click and the creek of metal joints. A trio of guards followed, their leather boots clattering against the stone.

"Up you get, lord."

"Maybe later." Rurik sniffed.

"Excuse me?" One of their number brandished a long blade, its ring echoing in his ears.

"You peasants deaf? I'm disposed."

"If he tries to run," the armed man said and handed the key chain to his second. "Close the cell on him. Wouldn't mind a bit of stress relief."

There. Rurik flexed his neck to the cracking pop of the knots in his shoulders. Two guards advanced, their blades up, ready. He shoved a hand down the front of his trousers.

"The lady doesn't like waiting, lord. Don't make me convince you."

With a sudden jolt Rurik seized the edge of a sword with a bandaged hand. The guard recoiled and Rurik vaulted up, twisting the blade away.

From his pants he withdrew a wooden shard and thrust it into an exposed neck. The second guard howled and slashed at Rurik who shielded himself behind the fresh corpse. He ran one body into the other, taking his opponent down into a staggering tackle. Pinned, the guard squirmed to free himself, only to end as Rurik redirected his pilfered blade into his side.

The third guard stared in horror. He backed away as Rurik stood and slammed the cell closed. Terrified, he turned to run only to have thin, calloused fingers wrap around his face and pull him into the bars of another cell. Katriene sniffed and used her shard to slit his throat. She rescued the keys as they dropped and set about freeing herself.

"Whoa! What was that?" Lyue rose in shock.

"Don't get too excited. Katriene," Rurik addressed the viper, "tu viens avec nous?"

"*Je n'ai nulle part où aller, putain de connard débile.*" Katriene rolled her eyes. The lock thunked at her touch and she slipped out of her cell.

"You speak Singali? More importantly, who is this? What is happening?" Lanatir was on his feet.

Rurik waved Katriene over who responded in kind by opening his cage. "This is Katriene. She's an assassin." He took the keys from the viper and liberated Lyue. The women armed themselves from the dead guards.

"You aren't going to leave me?" Lanatir asked, "Are you?"

"Thought about it." Rurik paused in front of the baron's cell. "But you're another body to shoot at." The door's joints swung open with a metal screech.

"*Perdre du temps.*"

"*Détendez-vous, nous allons,*" Lyue responded with an impeccable accent.

"Am I the *only* one that can't understand this girl?"

"Yes," Lyue and Rurik said in unison.

"Adorable. What's the plan, then? There are dozens of guards in the compound alone and we are near the breach. There's no food or water in the city. Nowhere to hide the diviners won't sniff out."

"Sunsinger's Basilica," Rurik said.

"Come again?" Lanatir poked one of the dead guards with a toe and a scowl.

"Trust me. We run, and we keep running until we reach the basilica."

"In your words: we are *heretics*. Need I remind you what paladins do to heretics?"

"No. You needn't. Come on."

The four of them rushed down the hall and Rurik tossed the keys to a stray prisoner. They followed the stone to its end and spilled out into the Adirian compound: a courtyard complete with a stone wall and gunners. Across the way Celesti stood with her back to the prison, engaged with a detachment of her soldiers. Fucking Adirians. None of them glanced in their direction. Quietly, they crept along the base of the wall.

Two soldiers staffed the open gate, hands affixed to halberds, lazily watching ongoing traffic. Many, curious to the fort's purpose, made for its entrance which kept the sentries looking out.

Rurik pointed to the guards and ran a finger across his throat. Katriene shook her head and jabbed the air with a dagger. He shrugged. She shrugged. Together, they split off from each other and crouched low. Katriene arrived first. The steel entered the guard's flesh and severed his spine at the neck. Rurik cut half into his target's head with a sword. Both collapsed. From the road someone screamed. Not the stealthiest of ideas. The throng of traffic veered away from the violence and the compound woke from the malaise of routine.

"Run!" Rurik waved others on. He lagged behind and Celesti, alert, swiveled to meet his gaze. He spat and she blew him a kiss.

Rurik's grip tightened around his sword. He could reach her before the gunners took him out. All it took was one stroke.

"Rurik! We need to go!"

Lyue's voice brought him to reality. He growled and ripped his sight away, skipping off to a dead run. His legs burned from weakness, from days without food as he raced down the center of the row. Bullets whizzed past his ear with the pop of sequential gunfire fast on his heels. One hit an unfortunate breaker, another fractured off into the road into the rows of merchant stalls.

Rurik dove into a roll as a volley of fire hit several bystanders who fell or twisted from the impact.

Panic erupted in the market and screams rose in a chorus. Rurik rolled over and jumped up to his feet, glancing back to watch a column of Adirian guardsmen take to the road, pursuing the lot of them. He sucked in a deep breath then took to his pace again, abandoning the pilfered blade in favor of speed. Everything burned. From his feet to his lungs, his breath came in labored heaves, his mouth and throat dry. He moved to the side of the road with a majority of the inhabitants and ducked beneath stalls to avoid the indirect gunfire.

Wood panels pinged against lead bullets. Another volley, at him, scattered erratically about the market. Rurik vaulted over a Cavari merchant prone against the black road and landed with a stumble. He steadied himself against one of the temporary enclosures and caught his breath. From there he watched Lanatir face off against two black coated guardsmen. Kalthier attendants on patrol. Shit. The baron raised his arms and panted, sweat pouring down his forehead. The Adirians advanced from behind.

Rurik ran silent along the smooth road. No boots proved beneficial for something. Though he lost some weight during his incarceration, the full brunt of Rurik's girth met one of the Kalthier men with all the force of a horse in full gallop. He tackled and slammed him into the ground, committing to a violent tackle. Winded, the guard barely managed to complain before Rurik locked his head in his hands and twisted. His neck snapped.

"Lanatir, down!"

"What?"

"Down!"

The baron dropped and Rurik followed suit, pulling the body of the dead Kalthier guard over his own. Bullets riddled the corpse with a few stray shots tearing apart the second soldier. By then the road cleared itself of any activity. Rurik kicked the body off of him and hopped up again. He lifted Lanatir by his surcoat and brought him to his feet. Some of those in the Adirian column took a knee, guns on their shoulders, barrels smoking from the recent shots.

"You saved me!" Lanatir seemed shocked.

"Run now! Gratitude later!"

Off again. Rurik and Lanatir bolted a straight line from the encampment until the slanted rooftop of the basilica burst into view. Lyue and Katriene waited for them off the row, the viper holding one knife against her wrist with the blade down and the other out in front of her torso pointed at a pair of paladins. Both imposing figures glowered at the women, swords out, bodies lowered into stances with one leg forward, the other twisted and set. Defensive in nature.

"Sanctuary!" Lanatir yelled.

"Denied." The paladin's voice was dark and stoic.

"This man is a duke you imbeciles! He deserves a trial before a pontifex as is Akleasn law! Sanctuary!"

"Denied."

"Fuck!" Lanatir stomped his foot into the road. The Adirians neared, taking their time. They knew escape was impossible.

Lyue removed the scroll case from her neck. "Rurik, you're sure this is where we need to be?" She opened the top.

"The arch is a gateway. I can make it work."

Lyue slid a furled parchment from the container and snapped off a seal. The paladins advanced. Katriene hissed, her body low, stance wide, ready to pounce. The loremaster mumbled some words from the scroll in a language Rurik recognized. Or rather, Iskarion did. She recited a process, a simple distribution of currents. One of the first tricks a Rune Knight learned for self-defense.

The hair on the back of his neck stood on edge as a crackling energy sprung up around Lyue's arm. Her eyes sparked and flashed white as the paladins charged, raising their swords into the air.

"Katriene, move!" Rurik shouted. The viper rolled aside as Lyue twisted her wrist then flung her arm out. Lightning arced from her fingers in a blinding current that sunk into a paladin's armor. Electricity jolted over his body as it ran from one plate to the next, spasming until he fried. Burnt to a crisp. The stench sent Lanatir retching.

Rage overtook the second paladin in a vitriolic outburst. Lyue drew her arm back, the glow of her eyes settling to their natural hazel. One time use.

Katriene darted in, her sleek form ducking a wide slice in a graceful and deliberate spin. She sank one of her knives inside a gauntlet from the wrist and wrenched the paladin's hand away from his sword, then swept under his arm and shoved her spare dagger through the singular slit of his helmet.

Rurik stared. Katriene spit at the dead man as he fell to his knees.

"*Armure vous ralentit, putain de chatte.*" She withdrew her dagger then kicked him to the ground, her drama ending in a bow.

Right then. Rurik plucked a glowlamp from the road and smashed it against the obsidian archway the sunsingers co-opted for their front door. Inert, it served as little more than decoration. He removed the runestone; a small sphere carved with an absorption equation and pressed it against the surface of the arch, its control sigils appearing along the edge. Weak, but sufficient.

"That easy all this time?" Lyue marveled.

"The arch is solarstone." Rurik palmed a sigil. Its glow deepened to signify the lock. "The entire city is."

"What are you prattling about? What is happening?!" Lanatir slumped against the basilica and caught his breath. None of them were in prime condition.

"I'll explain–" More gunfire. A shot pinged off the stone as he depressed the last command. An inky blackness flooded the archway, replacing the basilica's stout wood. "Go!"

"In that? No!" Lanatir cried as Rurik grabbed his collar and tossed him into the blackness. Lyue saluted and ran after him.

"*Si je meurs, je vais te tuer.*" Katriene went in next.

Behind Rurik, a detachment of gunners took a knee, their arquebuses shouldered. Celesti stood among them, her previous confidence replaced now with a vicious scowl. He blew her a kiss and stepped into the portal.

• • •

Rurik emerged from another arch and slapped a run at its zenith. The portal dissipated and the rest of the runes fleshed white. Locked. Rurik's shoulders slouched and he hunched over. His legs burned, his arms ached. Breath came in short, pained wheezes.

"Where are we?" The awe in Lanatir's voice turned Rurik's head.

White marble walls stretched into vaulted ceilings of crystalline glass above, lined with balconies and bridges that extended over a massive hall made from a white-hewn stone. From a set of golden doors, stained glass encompassed the ground floor, figures of delicate construction painted into the windows with artistic precision. Knights and winged warriors, men and women riding giant eagles and mages aglow with power, all bathed in yellows, oranges, and reds, the sun at their backs as they rode into battle. They faced shadow. Creeping darkness that spewed forth wicked constructs, scaled beasts and cloaked, sickly creatures, yellow of eye.

Water spilled from the bridges into a clear pool in the hall's center, flanked on all sides by wild moss that spiraled over the aged marble. Brisk, fresh air. Gentle running water. It brought peace to Rurik's mind. A calm sort of clarity that lightened his exhaustion.

"The Cathedral of the Sun." Rurik stood. Something glinted in the distance: a giant, winged statue crowned with a sun. A smaller statue knelt before it. "I think."

Katriene found her way to the waterfall and stepped under it, scraping blood from her blouse. Rurik joined her and washed himself of sweat and grime.

"You think? I *think* you need to fill us incompetent fools in, Rurik. Not even the Sunlord knows where we are! And! We're being chased by trigger-happy Adirians! What is keeping them from following us here?!"

"I locked the gateway." Rurik washed under his armpit.

"You can do that?" Lanatir blinked.

"Yes. Anyone can. You set the rune at the top. It locks out the coordinates from any other gateway."

"Well! I didn't realize dukes trained their first-born heirs as full-fledged loremasters. That *may* have been useful to know two years ago!"

"Webway Theory is basic study for initiates." Rurik balked at his own words. Initiates? Webway Theory? The concept was foreign. Yet, Iskarion's memories flooded his own. He *knew* that the water came from the ocean. It flowed through a miniature gateway, through a filter that purged the salt, then into the pool where another portal sent it elsewhere.

"I know. You don't have to say it." He exchanged a weary glance with an upset Lanatir. "I don't understand, exactly, what's happening. But I have these memories. I can remember things when I see them. That's how I've survived this long. I found a ring that I think belonged to Isk–"

"Rurik!" Katriene snapped up at Lyue's call. It came from deeper in. The three of them rushed after the desperate lure in her voice. They skirted around the pool until the statue came into focus, its features that of familiar renders of the Sunlord: crown, and flowing robes, only this idol took form as a woman. Lyue stood rigid. Rurik halted and laid a hand on her shoulder, squeezing.

"What's wrong?"

Lyue pointed at the figure before that statue. It wore the armor from his visions. Iskarion herself knelt upon a raised dais, locked in a still frame of prayer, frozen in time. She held the runecarved shaft of a glaive, its blade as long as a sword with the edge embedded into her own chest. The tip pierced the armor, visible out her back. It emanated a soft white glow and a low hum thrummed from its visage.

"It's a Sunlance." Lyue slinked out of Rurik's grasp. "Maybe seven of them were ever recorded. They predate the Desolation. They predate everything. The oldest litanies say they were gifts from the Sunlord, weapons of his agents and protectors."

"That's." Rurik's voice caught in his throat. "That's her."

"Who?"

"Iskarion tir'Thalian. Rune Knight of the Black City. She's been here all this time. Waiting."

"How is that even possible?" Lantair asked.

"The lance." Lyue ascended the dais, her eyes hungry. "Her body is suspended. The theory is that these weapons siphon power to the wielder. This whole building is an energy sink. Or was, anyway. It's not far-fetched to believe whatever she drew from has kept her body intact. But Iskarion? All accounts have her death at the Tower of Haven."

Rurik's eyes narrowed. "She told me to find her."

"Told you? She spoke to you?"

"It's hard to explain." Rurik followed the loremaster up the dais. He settled on his heels, face-to-face with the helmet. "But yes. Since we broke into the forum. She's been sending me visions. Guiding me, I think." He reached out to touch the helm.

"Don't touch he–" Lyue's warning fell to silence. Rurik placed his palm on the armor. The hum died.

Light exploded from the glaive. It enveloped the dais and he and Lyue along with it.

Personal Log, 11.24.0260 C.E.

MY. LEGS. BURN. I understand being familiar with the Justiciar, but training with them? These guys have been fighting since birth. Hyperbole, but point made. It was worth it at least. I've altered the armor design to be a copy of the delegate ceremonial. Thinner, but runecasted, so thick enough to take a magus' flame to the face and live and still allow enough movement for their martial forms. Quick, light, but sturdy. Should give the Lindrisi a show.

Have Kal make you some of that ointment of his. You know. For "chafing."

Chapter 17
A Thousand Years Lost

Iskarion's fist left its imprint on the lacquered surface of her desk. She dropped a letter and glared at the ill-practiced penmanship. Paper, really? She scanned the missive for a second time.

> Mithirin is gone. There's no trace that the city ever existed. It's the same devastation that hit Lindras but we know that Lindorum no longer possesses Sunlances. I'm afraid your suspicions are correct. None of the Void Emissaries have shown any ability to replicate the weave effect, it must be the Avatar. We need proof. Vari says it's somewhere in Lindras, but we need more time. I need more time, mother.
> - Riah

"Fuck." Iskarion crumpled the letter into a ball. She snapped her fingers so that one crossed her ring and a flame scorched the paper to ash. "Fuck." She leaned into her chair. "Fuck!"

A series of three high pitched beeps interrupted her melodrama. She slid open a drawer and pulled out her slate, a rune flashing over the surface. She tapped it and a stream of information flooded the screen in the complex logograms of Thalian.

"Sorry, the delegate you've attempted to reach is experiencing an existential crisis. Please try again never."

"Where in the mother's tits are you, Isy?" The deep bass came from the slate.

Iskarion rolled her eyes. "Kalthier, darling, lost without me?"

"Don't sass me woman. You need to get to the forum now. Adirian is whipping the delegates into a frenzy. He wants to use the Avatar on Haven."

"What? We don't even know if the Magi have contact with an Emissary."

"I know. Get here. Now."

The slate silenced. Adirian, that snake-tongued spawn sucker. He knew her investigation stalled, and Haven stood in the way of a key tactical advantage over Lindorum. Iskarion groaned. She slid her ring off her finger and deposited it and the slate in the drawer. Best to avoid temptations in a political arena.

She circled her desk to where her armor hung, suspended over a gravity rune, the back retracted for easy access. Light, but annoying, she preferred the bodysuit she wore in its place. No one whispered about her scandalous personal tastes in the confines of her private office. She mumbled a few equations and ran her fingers over her head, her black hair tying itself into a tight braid over her scalp.

She stepped into the suit and shimmied her chest to fit as the backplate slid out to seal the exterior. The gauntlets and greaves followed, contracting until they fit her size. Inside, a white interface flooded her vision with a series of overlays and information dumps and a single message:

FEED THE RUHK SO HE DOESN'T BITE YOU AGAIN.

Shit. She tapped at a series of runes on the back of her wrist, wiping the message clear then dialed into her private webway gate. She brought up a coordinate display and entered the address for the forum. An inky, black sheet flooded the interior of the arch.

A sigh escaped her confidence. Iskarion gazed at the shelves of archaic texts that lined her little sanctuary. No one much preferred the old bindings anymore. One day she would find the time to read some of the more exhausting tomes. Today, though, she needed to yell at morons.

She emerged behind the speaker's stage. Bright, filtered light streamed from the glass ceiling, bringing with it the heat of summer. She left the gate and adjusted the internal temperature of her armor to a pleasant chill. Delegations from every faction of the city and beyond filled the pews: multi-colored robes from the Runecaster's College, the whites and golds of the faith, black clad council members and patrons.

Adirian's voice drew an involuntary twitch of her eye. Iskarion snuck aside as the gateway closed and took her place next to Kalthier who wore similar armor only colored black, green highlights pulsing over the joints. Lynesse and Salivar stood opposite them, clad in the same ceremonial garb. Their position along the platform bespoke their united front. The council of Knight Delegates, experts in runecraft.

"What the shit, Isy?" Kalthier whispered. "You know I can't hold off these skumsuckers alone."

"Riah sent me a message from Mithirin," she spoke quietly, beneath the robust pandering. "It's gone, Kal. Entire city. Poof. That was us."

"Are you sure? She said she found evidence of destabilization?"

"It's Riah, it takes her a month to plan dinner."

"Fuck."

"Right."

"How long do we succumb to the inaction of lesser peoples?!" Adrian's voice carried across the forum's stage, boisterous and charismatic. Runic acoustics, Iskarion marveled, Lynesse's idea. "The Cabal of Magi remains neutral despite the obvious threat of Lindorum! We have numerous reports that the consul is a pawn of the Emissaries, and yet we are limited in military action! We squander our greatest weapon! The Avatar allows us a source of unlimited energy and power!"

Some among the crowd voided their agreement. Others contributed to a disquieted mumble, measured conversations that weighed the benefit of such an action to their own agendas. Iskarion hands balled into fists.

"Colleagues. Peers. Is it not time we ceased this meek behavior? We possess unmatched technology. None can stand against us in total war. Let us be rid of these voidspawn for good! Let us cast down our enemies and bask in the glory of Cinderfall as we were always meant to!"

Sporadic cheers and applause came from the garden halls; civilians gathered to listen. The forum broadcast its proceedings to the entire city. Iskarion imagined they too latched onto war. The masses loved to feel superior, especially when they could participate from a safe distance. They rarely approved when asked to pick up a sword.

"Bravo!" Iskarion said. She ascended the platform and clapped. Adirian's shoulders stiffened. "Yes! Bravo, well said delegate." Her sardonic tone cut the anxious war mongering. "Let us declare war on a city that houses refugees and facilitates peaceful trade with most of the world. This has nothing to do with border disputes with your personal territories, who would even say that?"

Kalthier snorted.

"I see you deemed it appropriate to show up, Knight Iskarion." Measured, controlled, Adirian's red helmet swiveled to greet her, his armor lined with golden streams. He wore a thick robe over his plate, open in the front, bulbous, but a solid reminder of political position. The delegates stood above the various Thalian councils, but Adirian made it a habit to be among them as well.

"I figured I'd skip to the end of your tired foreplay." That drew a few laughs from the hall. Good. She needed the people on her side, council members be damned.

"I have not yielded the floor. The other delegates will have ti–"

"Motion to interject." She could feel his glare through her faceplate. Kalthier raised his hand immediately and issued an aye. Salivar shook his head at Lynesse who nodded her approval.

"Motion passes. Three to two. Councilman Adirian." She offered him a courtly bow, one hand with a fist to her heart with the other flared out to her side.

"Unmatched technology. Meek." Iskarion addressed the crowd. "Yes, our advancements are impressive. Useful. But these leaps come from peace, and study. Rune Lore is the study of creation, of all we are. We are already at war with Lindorum. But what of the plague of Xyr? Aul'Thannon's borders are closed for the first time in centuries and even the far reaches are beset by countless wastespawn. Our duty is to solve these problems, not start more!"

Too few within the crowd approved.

"Problems caused by the Void." Adirian cut in. No one made any motion to stop him. "Problems only we can solve. Our assault on Mithirin was a resounding success and already the Sunstar is reported as in a state of recovery."

"According to who?" Iskarion jabbed.

"The Avatar confirmed it."

"The Av–" Iskarion caught herself. She inhaled. Calm. He wanted to push her over the edge, but blatant lies? "There is no data to support that. Mithirin was hasty and ill conceived."

"And unanimous. If you forget yourself, all five Delegates sanctioned the use of the Sunlance."

"A mistake we need not repeat! Millions of civilians were caught in that blast. Not soldiers. I have reports that the devastation contains the same destabilization of matter found in Lindras." A shocked mumble took the onlookers. Some gasped, others sneered aloud. "We have no verifiable proof that any of the Magi are voidtouched!"

The council's unrest grew. Their dark musing filled the forum with doubt. Accusations flew. Men and women argued in a sudden torrent of worry and distrust. Good. Uncertainty was all she needed. A delay in a vote could last weeks.

Adirian gestured for silence.

"Fellow councilors. Delegates. Calm yourselves. These claims are ridiculous. The devastation of Lindras was the work of the Void. Evidence in Mithirin only solidifies the righteousness of our actions. What greater calamity would we have if not for our intervention? Not only do we possess a Sunlance, one of the most holy relics of the

Mother, but the means of which to unlock its unlimited potential. Join me! Let us end this hideous threat, let us destroy those that would dare threaten our way of life!"

Applause broke out within the forum. Whereas she sowed doubt and reason, Adirian brought them clarity of action. A sense of righteousness. They wanted war.

Iskarion stalked off the platform as Adirian continued his pandering. She heard him call for a vote. No need to view the outcome. She stopped beside Kalthier for a moment, catching Lynesse and Salivar raise their hands in favor.

"Meet me at the beacon."

"Beacon?" Kalthier raised a hand after the others. Iskarion did not blame him, solidarity helped the delegates push other agendas. She made no effort to follow them this time. "What are you going to do?"

"What I should've done last time we sanctioned the death of millions."

Iskarion dialed into the gateway. If Riah needed more time, then that's what she would get.

• • •

Iskarion emerged from the gateway within the beacon's compound: an open yard of solarstone generators, rectangular constructs that stored and distributed energy to the entire city via forking paths of embedded power lines. Kalthier awaited her at the base of the tower. A fortified wall offered some privacy, though no one else wandered the automated facility.

Two stone sentries stood guard at the not-so-grandiose entrance to the beacon proper. She scrunched her nose up at the sight of them. Ridiculous cosmetics, Adirian's addition of course. They took the visage of the famed Cinderfell guardians, rumored to bear jagged, metal wings and star shaped halos. Other units stood inert within the courtyard.

"We're meeting. What is this about, Isy?" Kalthier folded his arms as his helmet segmented and folded into the gorget of his suit.

"I locked out the central webway. We've got about maybe ten minutes until the others get here."

"You what now?"

"I need you for this, Kal. I won't be party to another massacre. Not again. How are we any better than the Emissaries if we murder civilians?"

"What are you going to do?" Wizened and old, a grey sheen hung over Kalthier's pupils–long since passed his natural death. The man refused to retire. "You're strong, Isy, but even the two of us can't take the others."

"Not us. Me." Her eyes drifted to the crystalline sphere at the beacon's summit.

"Isy, no. We have no idea what that will do to you."

"Then you should record the effects," Iskarion snarked and climbed the stairs.

"Wait! Wait. I know I can't stop you. Mother knows I've tried before. What do you need me to do?"

"Stall them."

Iskarion waved over her shoulder. The doors to the tower slid open as she approached, and she stepped into the cavernous interior. A spider-like web of power conduits snaked along the floor beneath as she trod a catwalk of metal-wire mesh. Trails of blue bled down the walls from the top of the beacon. With no visible ceiling they lit the blackened interior with an eerie, pale shine. The bridge ended in a circular platform with a thin column that rose from the floor at her arrival, images projected from the top in the form of Thalian script.

Iskarion punched in a series of commands and the lift shuddered. A metallic whir spooled up from beneath her feet as the detached flooring sped upward to the beacon housing. Icons flashed within her helmet. Warnings, alerts.

*Central webway is locked out. Is this a malfunction? The
Council requires a response.*

She snorted. Malfunction. What a creative choice of words for
sabotage. Iskarion glanced at her wrist and ran her fingers over the
runic display, bringing up a chronometer. Five minutes, maybe, until
Lynesse activated the sentries. She tapped her foot. How much slower
could this thing move?

The lift docked with a ca-thunk of sealing metal. Ceremonious, the
domed expanse sung with natural light, a transparent ceiling filtering
rays into prisms that cast a spectrum of colors along the interior.
Crystalline spheres further siphoned that energy, lining the walls and
chiming with clarion tones. They glistened with the noon sun.

Iskarion's easy pace increased in stride until she hit a full jog. The
sentries here abandoned their angelic visage. They stood in vague,
humanoid shaped forms, each a literal ton of solarstone with Thalian
steel embedded into their arms as wicked blades. No eyes or armor;
built purely as wardens.

Iskarion stopped short of a golden door. Circular, it held no
openings or consoles, instead layered in thousands of tiny, white runes.
Contact with any one of them meant the end of the aggressor.
Fortunately for her, she invented them. With a quick flick of her wrist,
she projected the backdoor equation she imbedded into the casting and
each of the runes winked out simultaneously.

The door took up half the wall and in the center a depression
encircled with five stone plates held the Sunlance. More a glaive, really.
Though she supposed Sun Glaive didn't have the same ring to it.

*All channels, this is an emergency. We have
intruders in the beacon tower.*

Iskarion eyed her chronometer. Right on time. Whoever decided
not to put gateways in the beacon was a genius. She mentally patted
herself on the back.

Isy! I've got a lot of upset company.

Right. She snatched the base of the Sunlance and grimaced. A wave of power coursed through her suit and into her body; raw energy, chaotic and shifting. She felt a brief connection to the source beyond the door. Their greatest victory. It reached out to her and Iskarion ripped the weapon from its housing. Sparks flew from the blade as it slid free, the sudden rush of energy dissipating from her grasp.

Intruders identified as delegates Kalthier and Iskarion. All privileges have been revoked, perimeter and central sentries activated.

Iskarion's interface darkened as only her personal data remained. Lynesse worked fast. The multitude of constructs hoisted their shoulders, red pockets of energy emerging in the place of eyes on featureless faces. Twelve of them. Iskarion shifted her weight, her feet sliding apart as she choked her grip up on the weapon's shaft. The sentries' lumbering bodies turned with thunderous groans.

A thought stirred in the back of her mind. Not her own conscious mind, something else. Knowledge. From the lance? No. This was a gift from another. Her eyes darted to the door. Did it know?

She needed only to guide her intentions, to formulate her will. A blinding white light erupted from the lance. Not a weapon, but a battery. Her helmet's augmented vision dimmed to filter out the flash. She felt lighter. Her suit enhanced her speed, her strength, but this power sunk deep into her bones. Iskarion bobbed her head and bounced from one foot to the other. Two of the constructs approached, assessing the proper threat response. She could take two. Maybe.

Iskarion raised the lance and hurled it through the air. It screamed with power and pierced one of the sentry's chests, the blade embedding deep. The construct slowed. It placed its enormous, stone hands on the shaft and pulled. Iskarion raised her hand and twisted her wrist, envisioning a rune of force. The lance complied. The glow that surrounded it focused, collapsed, then exploded. Debris scattered over the hall, swaths of stone shattering prisms and glass. A blue half-sphere of energy surged from her gauntlet and turned the incoming shrapnel to dust on contact.

Hah. More sentries sprung to life. One closed, faster than its size should allow, and scythed a bladed arm at her chest. Time slowed. Iskarion somehow saw the action before it happened. She reared back from the blow and rebounded, holding her hand out as she summoned the lance back to her grasp.

Iskarion sidestepped another blow, the blade slicing into the metal floor. She flourished the lance and cut the exposed arm from its base. More rumbles. Another three sentries approached. Iskarion huffed, ducked another swing from then launched into a full sprint, holding the lance against her arm.

They met in a flurry of blows. Six limbs flailed at her–or where she would be. Iskarion leapt, her newfound strength propelling her into the air, landing on the shoulders of an errant sentry. She stabbed the glaive blade into its head and a blast of energy followed, collapsing the monstrosity into rubble. She fell to her knees and a stone foot slammed into her back, sending her sailing into a wall. Her armor cracked on impact.

The light within the hall dimmed. The sentries drew from the prisms, absorbing energy and surrounded themselves in a crackling current. She set the haft of the lance against her shoulder and freed an arm, summoning her shield as concentrated arcs seared into the energy and rebounded into the beacon. Glass shattered from the force. With the light of the sun so close to the prisms the sentries drew from an unlimited well of power. Though, so now did she. The lance kept her safe.

What a day.

Shuttering roars burst out from the beacon tower as strands of weaponized light dissipated into her shield. The lift lay on the other side of the hall and two sentries broke off to intercept her retreat. Something had to change.

"Fine! Just. Fine!"

Iskarion collapsed her shield. The streams of energy collided, exploding in a torrent of flame as she leapt from the broken windows. She fell, the wind buffeting her form in a whistling descent. Below, she made out the other Rune Knights in tandem with a mass of sentries and Justiciars, all aglow with runecasted armor, their heads turned up to witness her hasty drop. Kalthier lay on the steps, half his armor melted to his flesh, black scorching visible along the base of the tower.

Iskarion launched the lance ahead of her. It hit the yard with a shockwave that knocked the gathered forces to the ground. She thrust her arms out and formed a gravity rune in her mind, her descent halting just before her collision. The rune faded at her will and she reclaimed the lance, floating to meet the ground.

Kalthier, most of his body charred, took his rightful place among the dead. Damn it all. Iskarion narrowed her brow at the knights as they picked themselves up. She depressed the seal of her helmet, causing it to section off and fold into her chest. Strange. Even without her helmet she was able to read the runic connections that flowed from the suits. More, even. She saw the gossamer strands of power absorbed by the solarstone and the webway's emergence in and out of physical space.

Her eyes are white. What does that mean?

She's bonded to the lance. How?

"Not sure how, but it feels pretty good." Iskarion's voice emitted a powerful echo, a deep, multi-toned expulsion. A few of the rising justiciars involuntarily withdrew. The knights exchanged a glance, aware now that their communications lacked privacy.

"It's not too late to stop this." Salivar started, his metallic tone pleading,

"Why don't we consult Kal. He's the wisest of–oh. Wait. We can't." The subtle twitch of her lip drew a full panic from Lynesse who hugged her white-gold suit.

"This is treason, Iskarion. The council has voted to strip you of your titles. Stall as long as you like, once this little outburst of yours ends you will have changed nothing." Adirian. The snake.

"You're awfully confident." Iskarion hesitated. He was right. Even if Riah found proof of their folly, why would they stop? The council voted for war. For destruction. They could find new ways of channeling. As long as the beacon stood, as long as it held its prisoner, it remained a threat. She needed to do more than stall.

"You'll want to evacuate the city." She spoke with a calm, threatening purpose.

Salivar and Lynesse eyed one another.

Iskarion slammed the haft of the lance into the ground. It quaked, shaking as cracks split the stone and rent power stations asunder. Some sparked, others burst into flame.

"Evacuate the city. Or stop me."

Power coursed through her body. It infested her, changed her. Every moment she wielded the weapon it became less a tool and more a part of her. The knights considered her terms. She felt their fear, their apprehension. Raw, oppressive power rolled from her in waves.

Adirian acted first. He lifted his arms into the air then brought them and his body low, pressing his palms against the ground. A gout of flame followed, a spiraling wave that exploded upward in a series of chaotic flurries until it reached her. Pieces of embedded stone flew into the air, ripping up the yard and casting hail and debris in the path of the fiery destruction. Crackling energy sparked from Lynesse's shoulders. She joined the foray by snapping her wrist and coiling the arc toward Iskarion, flashes of wicked lightning jolting out from her hand. Jagged spikes emerged from the earth below her feet as Salivar stomped, steam hissing from the cracks. A wave of rock rose from the ground and collapsed over her body.

The combined might of the knights left a static stillness in the air. Melted, black and scorched stone lay over the spot Iskarion occupied. They collectively relaxed as they surveyed the devastation.

Until light pierced the rubble. The winds shifted. Drawn into the mass of earth it swirled, lifting debris, revealing a bright, bristling aura. They flinched away from the sheer intensity of the flash. Iskarion stepped out, untarnished, her body bathed in a brilliant white sheen.

"Nice try."

She raised her fist to the heavens. A column of light appeared from the sky and burst with a piercing chime, washing over the Justiciar and sentries. The constructs broke to pieces as soldiers were reduced to cinders. She advanced at her leisure. More columns assaulted the courtyard. The knights formed a circle and summoned shields to defend themselves as Iskarion idled past.

She blew them a kiss.

Those that could ran while the detonations ripped the power structures to pieces, eviscerating any semblance of architecture.

She stopped at the base of the stairs. Her countenance contorted in anguish at Kalthier's burnt corpse. Her fault, she knew. No matter. This ended today. Iskarion waved her hand over the gateway and summoned a portal.

She emerged at the Cathedral of the Sun.

Shanty heard Aboard the hepsu

O'er salt I sail, with winds behind
My heart I leave with mine
Own sweet love, my calling divine.

You'll wait for me, for not too long
I'll see you again my love,
With treasure for you, sublime

My spoils brought for mine
Own sweet love, my land, my hope,
Horizons long behind.

O'er salt I sail, with winds behind
My heart I leave with mine
Own sweet love, my life, my darling divine.

Chapter 18
Cursed

A chorus of cacophonous grumbling buzzed in Kali's ears. She knelt, shoulders slouched, too tired to raise her head. She studied the construction of the deck. No cracks or hidden imperfections–a shaper's work. Expensive for pirates. The ache in her joints betrayed her confidence, stemming from a weary sort of exhaustion only the menial understood. No wonder then that the voices did little to catch her interest.

Captain Niati perched on the edge of an ornate desk within the spacious cabin, one knee bent with her arms crossed. The fur-lined, feathered mattress sequestered in the far corner drew Kali's gaze, past the captain, her eyes soft with longing and envy. Comfort. Sleep. Her splintered fingers and sore feet itched at the promise of luxury.

"Best be'ta slit 'er throat, cap, toss'er o'r board. Bad fortune, havin' a curse a'board."

Kali suppressed a groan. Not at the sentiment, but bosun's accent grated her sensibilities. Or rather, *the* Bosun. Titles took precedence over names. The man made a habit of reminding her of shoddy work, apparently all bosuns did was annoy the other sailors. Did she sound like that to the servants in Iskvar?

"Fah." Leinani settled a hand on her hip. "Most Nui hang Asuk with no thought, Kiliku has learned you no mercy, bosun?"

He grunted. A few of the others mumbled something in the Nui tongue. Kali recognized disapproval. She remembered the faces of the sailors when those bars vanished, fear, despair. Hatred.

"Mercy? Ya foolin, Nani, tha' is the only mercy we can give."

Appreciative grumbles this time. Getting closer to a solution then.

"Murder is not mercy, *alu ai so kae*!" Leiani spoke with venom in her tone.

"*Ufa kefe!*" Bosun fired back. Leiani launched into a rapid mastery of her first language, her hands waving aggressively, pausing only at the occasional snip from Bosun who struggled in his retaliations.

"*Kio!*" Niati barked. The argument ceased. Neither dared continue at the captain's displeasure. "You're both pretty. This helps nothing. I am the captain, yes?" Niati slid off her desk, lithe. She lowered herself to Kali's level, balancing on the toes of her boots. "Nothing to say, princess? Anything in your defense?"

Kali lifted her eyes from the floor. They met with Niati. Deep, blue pools of the ocean itself stared back at her. Bereft judgment, more curious than accusatory. Kali sniffed. Everything smelled of salt, though she caught a whiff of lavender perfume. Enticing.

"I'm not a princess."

Niati cackled, her uproarious laughter drawing confused stares.

"Out. All of you. Leinani, bring the red one. The Lindrisi. And leave the Cavari."

A haze of reluctance filled the air. No one moved, not until Niati thumped her foot into the deck. The crowd filtered out the single doorway.

Kali, dejected, divided her mind between reality and ignoring the sweet, alluring voices that plagued her waking psyche. She eyed the rapier at her captor's hip. One jab. Preferably through the heart. Make it quick, easy. She deserved no less.

"That's better, eh? Now we can speak." Naiti's tight braids jostled, the ringing chimes without rhythmic intent. Kali straightened her back and shivered. Did it get colder? She studied the captain. Or her hair anyway. The jewels. All different colors and all etched with runes.

"Who are you really, Arkalis? You don't hold yourself like a lowborn. Even this." She gestured to Kali's poise. "Rigid. Proud. You're not used to kneeling."

What would the truth bring? No doubt a renewed sense of value. Was that preferable? The voices said yes.

"Iskarion." Did she say that? "Arkalis Iskarion."

"*Ei*? This is a lie."

"Please." Kali grunted. She flopped onto her side. Her knees ached. "I'd rather be anyone else." Kali flourished a sort-of bow from the ground. Inelegant as ever. "Alas, you are in the presence of nobility, in all its splendor."

Niati's consternation grew visible at the twitch of her nose, her disbelief mired by the confidence in Kali's deprecation. They shared silence. One caught in the throes of contemplation, the other consumed in her sudden craving for cheese.

"If what you say is true," the captain started, "then why did your own soldiers chase you? Who beat you to inches of life? These things do not happen to Cavari nobles."

"Duke Adirian has owned us for years. I wasn't running from my people. I don't have people." She snorted. "They're all dead. All of them." Kali grinned, her lips parting in a slow laugh. "Got my ass kicked. Botched the escape. Then fell into the hands of pirates."

Her laughter took a maddening turn. "Sorry, sorry. Privateers. Quite the daring escapade. And now. I can see them. Everywhere I look. Everyone that died because of me. And the voices." Her voice quivered. They shushed her, the whispers. Best to not let anyone know. "I don't care what you do to me. Kill me. Sell me. Better to be done with all of it."

The door creaked open. The flutter of Leinani's light gait accompanied a near-silent padding. Nihilus entered with his hands tied. He wore a knowing grin, barely visible beneath a full, prickly beard.

Leinani latched the door and leaned against it, shivering. It was colder in the cabin. The woman twirled her wrist then pushed her palm forward, her fingers igniting briefly with a flash. A sorcerer? And a good one. Heat wafted off her body.

"Captain." Nihilus inclined his head. "Decided to listen, have we?" The Lindrisi's accent no longer held its Cavari tint, replaced now with a similar cant to their captors.

Leinani quipped something in Nui. Niati responded in kind.

"Correct, you can't trust me, but you want what I know." Nihilus interrupted the two and winked at Kali. The two women exchanged a glance. The captain spoke first, reverting to Cavari for what was obviously Kali's benefit.

"How much would a Lindrisi Consul pay for a duchess?"

"Ah, a large fortune in gold. Iskarions are a known thorn in the side of the Consulate. Quite a prize, *Soatau*."

Leinani gasped. Niati laid a hand on her rapier. "How do you know this title?"

"Calm, calm. We are speaking of our noble acquaintance. One subject at a time."

Kali shifted to her backside and rested her elbows on her knees. She tried to follow the conversation with ill effect.

"You asked the wrong question. How much, not important. But who will pay for *tainted* goods? Lindorum is solidly of the Sunstar Faith. Warcasters would sink your boat before you made berth. Likewise, Cavari will riddle you with cannons for the spite of capturing one of their own. Who then?"

"And this is why we locked you away. Too many words." Niati spat. She rounded her desk and slumped into her chair, lifting her feet up and pouring herself a cup of what smelled like spiced wine. Kali licked her lips. "I assume you have a who in mind."

"Quite perceptive of you, *Soatau*."

"Captain." Niati bit off the retort.

"Captain, do forgive me. You are correct. I have a who in mind. You are familiar with the Magi?"

"No sailor does not know of Haven. What of this?"

"Haven, yes, but the Magi rule there. They are free of faith, of political interest. Your gain does not lie in your captor's birth, but of her affliction. One in her state is a rarity. Tainted, yet not lost. Currency is cheap for the Magi."

Leinani joined in. "You think us fools? Why would the Magi not just take her?"

Niati gulped down half a glass of wine. Her head listed to the side as she lazily watched Nihilus. "The Magi tax whatever they want. And we've not the casters to stop them. Is this your best?"

"They would do no such thing. To privateers, but to you? The Nui bring much trade. If you fly a different flag, this is not a problem."

Kali felt the urge to slap the man. That smug arrogance sparked a wave of violence in her mind. Worse yet, did he know her original plan? Haven was the goal. Did it matter how she got there? Yes. Who pulled her strings now? Nihilus? Niati? From one prison to the next.

"That all sounds exhilarating." Kali coughed, her throat dry. "But I'd prefer you dump me overboard. Just." She clicked her tongue and slid a finger across her throat. "Easy. If I'm so terrifying. Give me a blade, I'll do it myself."

Rage came to her in a wave and warmth surged through her veins. The voices grew louder. They told her what to do. Her vision flooded with red and the world pulsed. Faces dissipated, replaced by color, heat. From Niati and Lenani blues and yellows beat to a hastening rhythm while Nihilus took a steady, dull pace, shrouded in shades of black.

Exhaustion grew distant. Kali flexed her shoulders. Heat rolled off her in static pulses as oppressive power filled the room. The captain clenched her teeth as she sank unwillingly into her chair, Nihilus flew back, pinned to the cabin wall, his breath ragged.

That's right. A seductive, feminine voice spoke in her ear. *You need only embrace it.* Your *wrath. They want to use you, Arkalis. You command the Void. Crush them. All of them.*

You command the Void. The words hung in her mind. A face appeared with them. Yellow eyes. Did Solara hear the same voices? Visions of her father's death cooled her mind. The air lost its weight and Kali slouched, the deep ache returning to her joints. Niati cursed and leapt to her feet. She recovered her rapier and ran at Kali, blade extended.

"Niati!" Leinani stepped in front of Kali and lashed an arm at the captain, palm out. The sharpened edge stopped at Leilani's eye. "No. She stopped, so must we."

"Fah!" Niati swung her blade in frustration.

"You musn't." Kali's voice trembled, terrified at her own display. "Don't stop. If you don't kill me now, they'll take me. I don't know if I can stop it again."

"Stop what?!" Niati spun, her brows knitted in frustration. "What is this?!"

"The Void." Nihilus spoke, calm. He brushed off his shoulders and muttered something in another language. "She is touched by it. And yet, she resists it. You cannot kill her, *Soatau*."

"Captain." Niati growled.

"No." Nihilus snapped back. "You are a Knight of Nukati, a Seeker of Kiliku! So must you act. This woman cannot die, not now."

"Why? I am as you say, spawn, and I will not tolerate such corruption on my seas. She asks to die! I will grant her wish." Those piercing blue eyes stared into the weathered countenance of Arkalis. This was it. No more guilt, no more prisons. This was freedom. True, final freedom. She nodded her approval to Niati, her eyes pleading. The captain brandished her blade.

"She cannot die!" Nihilus yelled, his accent failing.

What? Kali looked beyond the blade to Nihilus. The Nui women mirrored her confusion.

"I have chased voidtouched for decades. Hundreds. All of them turn, by their will or others. Yet she resists. She *resists*. This does not happen, has not happened. Tell me you have not seen the signs, Seeker. You journeyed to Iskhold by the will of your goddess. For what? For the same reason I allowed you to capture me."

"Allowed?" Niati asked.

"You felt it, you, and your priestess both. The corruption beneath the land, beneath the castle. It is no coincidence it arrives with the discovery of the black city. And she." Nihilus pointed at Kali. "She is a key."

Kali tilted her head. "Key to what?"

Loud thumps rapped against the door. Leinani jumped up, startled. She composed herself quick enough and opened the door to the urgent tone of the Bosun.

"Cap'n! Cav'ri Galleon off'tha bow. They'r flyin' runic flags."

Kali would pay good money to have that man's tongue removed. A series of muttering curses flew from Niati's mouth. She begrudgingly sheathed her blade, her gaze lingering on Kali.

"Cavari? They sail slow and clumsy. Leinani, give us some wind." The priestess bowed her head and left the cabin.

"Doesn't matter how fast you are." Kali leaned her weight into the wood. She closed her eyes. She knew they would come, didn't she? "They'll track you. Same way they found you. There's a diviner on that ship, and I doubt you have one to foil them."

"No wonder the Void touches you, princess. Always dark. You may long for death, but the rest of us enjoy living."

"To Haven then?" Nihilus interjected. He crossed his arms over his chest having slipped his bonds. Tricky bastard.

"And why would I do this?"

"Our dear duchess is correct. You cannot escape this diviner, and a Cavari galleon carries enough cannon to sink you in one volley. You can neither run, nor fight. A neutral port then?"

Niati cursed in every language Kali knew and ten more she didn't. The captain threw her hands in the air, spewing a diatribe of vehemence unmatched by the drunkest soldier on her way out onto the deck proper, but not without a rude gesture at the Lindrisi. Kali remained with Nihilus. They exchanged looks. His appraising, her's thirsty. Ah. Wine. Kali meandered to the desk. Sweet, sweet alcohol.

"No thank you?"

"For what? Continuing my sentence?"

"For your life."

"Cheers to you, Nihilus." She rolled her eyes as she scrambled to pour herself a cup. "You've bought yourself a nightmare."

Excerpt from the high Loremaster's Journal

THERE IS NONE so frustrating a ruler as the Cabal of Magi. Seemingly unconcerned with their holdings, they nonetheless hold dominion over the largest hub in all of Yaros. Haven, with its unique position, borders three major, wealthy countries, facilitating trade by both land and by sea, its ports able to hold hundreds of vessels.

The Cabal cares only for its experiments. A council of seven, each magus is thought to be immortal, perhaps predating the Desolation itself. Stewards of vast knowledge and unknown depths of power, they jealously–and greedily–guard their secrets, using it only to keep a firm hold of their power. None of their members are prone to public appearances and they keep no living servants within their tower, preferring indirect missives delivered via some subtle form of casting or another.

What then, is their purpose? I'd do terrible things for a single day of access to that tower.

Chapter 19
Preserve

ARKALIS SAT off the bow of the Hepsu, one leg dangling over the edge and a wine bottle in hand as the silhouette of Haven appeared on the horizon. Hundreds of ships approached its harbors, vessels of all shapes and sizes and cultures. An angular Tuldrathi galley passed on their side, dozens of oars adding speed to the triangular sails. She recognized the boxy design of a Tsodunese vessel, its rigidity apparent from top to bottom. Ilae trade ships weaved their way among the ocean traffic, their sharp construction easy to spot amongst the majority Singali and Cavari designs: clumsy, but powerful, shaped for war.

Haven grew outward from a solitary tower. The tallest structure known to the world. It scraped the sky, black as night and jagged at the top; thinning in its ascent from a massive, wide base, its four tapered extensions serving as walls and housing alike. The city grew between those roots. Flat roofs with structures snuggled close to one another at varying heights, some five, six stories high near the center with a sprawl that swept out into three distinct valleys, and all of that surrounded by tall mountains.

Kali swept her gaze over the deck of the Hepsu. Its crew worked with precision as they raised the flag of Nukati, a blue field with two crescents circling a lone island. Niati took the helm, altogether an uncommon sight having abandoned her loose, revealing attire for vibrant, furred robes. Leinani sat with her legs crossed; a position she held for the last week at sea. Her trance explained the unending favorable winds that kept them ahead of their pursuers, a galleon that Kali could only just make out in the distance on their stern.

"Impressed?" Nihilus appeared from nowhere. Kali managed to suppress any sign of alarm at his sudden arrival. A skill she only mastered recently.

"By you? Not at all."

He snorted. She returned to her dramatic viewing of the city. Closer now, the scale overwhelmed her definition of 'city.' Dinkira once told her over a million people lived there. She laughed it off, of course, that was impossible. Until now. "But the city is nice. Bet it smells wonderful."

"Each quarter has its distinct scent." He hunched. "The bay, like fish and salt. Like any. The south is all spices. This is by Lindrisi design. For trade. The west? Smells like shit, a Cavari influence, I think."

Kali laughed. The less wealthy Cavari cities held that distinction. They suffered a similar waste disposal problem as the bowels of Iskvar. Her civic pride could not refute the observation.

"You should be happy. All that work to get here and here we are." She said.

"Mm. Truth? From here I've no clue what will happen."

"Serious? All that brazen confidence and there's no actual plan?"

"The appearance of confidence is a better persuasion than an argument itself. You are a noble, a politician by trade. Your tutor failed you."

"The opposite. I was a terrible student."

"Time to learn yet." Nihilus clasped her on the shoulder. "I hope you've reconsidered that death wish of yours."

She brought the bottle to her lips, finishing the contents, then hurled the empty container into the sea.

"We'll see."

• • •

Kali's clumsy steps thumped against the walkway as she disembarked onto the quay. The Hepsu made its berth among several other vessels of its type, all flying Nukati flags. Logistic precision, how quaint. While Kali stuck out among the majority of tan sailors, none of them paid her much mind. Instead, they focused on their captain. Niati drew respect from the lot of them at her mere presence. Even Kali found herself dumbstruck at the newfound grandiose grab.

A cloak furled around the captain's shoulders, lined in fur, fluttering in tailored perfection. Intricate sandals wove themselves from her heel to the knee. They bled into a half-skirt, also fur, hooked around her hips, revealing her thigh. Kali looked on, jealous. Niati pulled off regal and could breathe at the same time. The Nui had the right of it.

"*Ei*, duchess."

"Yes, your apparent majesty?"

Niati waved her off. Since the night in the cabin the captain spared few words for Kali. Something about being a terrible curse. If not for the assumed payday her bloated corpse would haunt the ocean depths.

"Let us deliver you to the Magi. This itches." Niati adjusted the fur.

"Better than a corset."

"Why would you wear such a thing?"

"Ceremony."

Niati spit.

They disappeared into the crowded pier and its atmospheric bustle of shuffled boots and uproarious conversation. Kali wrinkled her nose at the powerful scent of fish and salt. They joined Nihilus who waited where the wooden docks met Haven's cobbled streets. They trailed Bosun and a procession of armed sailors, enough to draw attention and dissuade any sort of delay.

"Your priestess not joining us, captain?" Nihilus asked.

"She rests. Do we have need for a caster?"

"Assuming a lack of interruptions, no."

"Interruptions? This is Haven. Who would attack an official delegation?" Kali glanced about, paranoid. The voices warned her of danger.

"Politics are complicated, *Pulchra*. More to learn, yet."

"Perhaps not so complicated." Niati nodded to the road where the throng parted at the behest of boisterous commanders. Shuffling metal and synchronous footfalls approached. Soldiers. Kali groaned and withdrew the black blade from her side.

A useful tool. It will protect you.

Kali cringed at the voice, though she felt stronger at the weapon's touch. The voices, too, whispered louder.

A formation of Cavari halberdiers came to a thundering halt at the edge of the pier in red coats, their brigandine and helmets glinting in the light of day. A knight led the twenty or so, armored for battle. Eight men bearing arquebuses set up in front of him, their sights trained on the Nui. Passerbys retreated at their arrival.

Murmurs of discontent rose from the sailors. Nui were excellent sailors, experts at maritime warfare. But on an open field? Ilvicar ruled.

"*Ei!*" Niati addressed the column. "I know these fools do not point their weapons at a Nukati delegation." Her voice carried well across the empty space between the two forces.

"All I see are pirates," The knight responded. He carried a cavalier's saber at his hip, though he made no effort to draw it. "And cabal law states that any guilty of piracy may be apprehended by the local customs of the affected party. If I am not mistaken, that is a Cavari prisoner you are holding."

Niati glowered at the soldiers, but it was Kali that took the lead.

"Hey you, horse fucker." Gariant would be proud. "Do I look like a prisoner? How many jailors give their charges weapons? These Nui are my escorts, and I'm the rightful fucking duchess of Iskvar. One scratch and your duke will personally flay the skin from your bones. Now clear the voidsdamned road."

"Well said," Niati mumbled.

"My girl, Duke Iskarion and his daughter perished in a tragic accident not but weeks past. You've no need to follow this sorrowful ruse the Nui placed upon you! Come to us, if they try to stop you, we'll cut them down where they stand."

No room to argue here. With Lesandre at Iskvar did it matter if she survived? The people believed her dead, best if she died for real.

"They're going to attack no matter what I do." She whispered. "I'm not worth it, take your people back to the Hepsu."

"I did not sail this far to lose coin," Niati grumbled. She unsheathed her rapier. The sound echoed as the rest of the sailors brandished a series of cutlasses and axes.

"I see. Very well. These orders sanction my actions." He removed a scroll from his belt, sealed with a gold band lined with runes. "Fire!"

Kali wrapped her arms about the captain, her sheer size blocking her from the sting of lead. Another death on her conscience proved too great a strain. She waited for the pain. Yet. She opened her eyes to the stunned faces of Nui sailors, those in the front caught mid flinch.

A shield of shimmering energy hung in the air. It spanned out like a transparent wall before Nihilus, his brow furrowed.

"You?" Was the only word she could manage.

"Fight or run, *Pulchra*, this is difficult to hold."

"They have a blasted warcaster!" The knight shouted, frustrated. "Reload! Halberdiers, charge!"

Decision made. Kali separated from Niati, who recovered from her shock, unclasped the lapis chain broach that held her cloak together and took a stance beside her would-be savior.

"Duchesses are trained to fight, eh?"

"Nope."

Kali cut her jest at the onset of professional soldiers. They ran at the shimmering static absent the confusion of her allies while the gunners fanned out to the flanks to hit the Nui around the shield. For the first time in her life Kali hated the Cavari war machine.

Nihilus dropped the barrier as he dipped away from the mass of halberdiers, skirting to the outside of the imminent clash. Niati shouted something in her native tongue. The Nui charged.

Adrenaline pumped in her veins. Her hands shook. The voices taunted her with an easy victory. *Let us in*, they urged.

Steel met flesh in a sickening clash. The Cavari halted at the moment of collision with the Nui and steadied their halberds, allowing most of those at the front to skewer themselves. A cutlass deflected off the side of a soldier's sallet, the arm wielding it severed by an offending axe head. Kali maneuvered around a halberd and dragged her sword across a soldier's neck, the wound cauterizing as it appeared, sealing the severe as he choked on his own blood.

A series of pops preceded the loss of more Nui. Four sailors dropped, their flesh ripped apart by hot lead. Kali waded into a mess of a melee, the considerable numbers on her end cut down in seconds. Niati plunged her rapier into a soldier's armored breast and caught sight of Arkalis. The two exchanged a curt nod then dove into the fray.

You can end this.

Not the time. Kali rounded on another soldier with his weapon locked with Bosun, the man's bulging eye red with fury. She kicked out the Cavari's knee. He dropped and Bosun pushed the halberd from his grasp as Kali thrust her sword into his back.

"Down!" Bosun pointed. The remaining gunners positioned themselves with prime sight on Kali. She spun and stared, ready to die.

Nihilus appeared among them. He descended on the soldiers with no weapons, faster than she could track. He extended an arm with an open palm and twisted his hand before contact, resulting in a sharp, red burst of power that tore apart the soldier's armor and exploded out his back in a mist of blood.

One fluid maneuver flowed into another as Nihilus wove a palm over his arm to create three distinct spikes of energy and sent them sailing through a soldier's salette. He died instantly. The two remaining turned their weapons on the Lindrisi as he ducked beneath them, palms hitting their sides and tearing a chunk of their torsos to pieces.

Despite the initial loss of life, the Cavari's numbers dwindled. The knight watched from afar, his face obscured by his full helm, but his body betrayed his hesitation. Kali separated from the Nui as their numbers overwhelmed the soldiers. The remaining gunners fled after the brutal slaughter of their companions, leaving her free to advance.

"You want to see a ruse? I'll show you what a coward looks like with no arms!" She spewed vitriol as her stride turned into a flat run. Rage welled up in her mind. Adirians, everywhere.

The knight ran. Her blood pounded as she sprinted after the bastard, arms pumping, her breath focused, adrenaline beating in her ears. In mid stride her boots stuck. All of her muscles locked, her arms taunt. What? She twisted. Nothing. Neither the knight nor she moved. Nothing did. No sounds from the wharf, no screams of battle or cries of pain.

From nothing came the pressure. Formless weight crushed against her body. Pain erupted throughout her and she froze, unable to scream, locked in time.

They are coming. You will lose your chance, Arkalis. Let us in.

It appeared all at once. An inky blackness shaped like a doorway. It pulsed, shifted, then emitted the vague shape of a man. White robes draped from a gangly form, lined in intricate, gold designs, all runes, from top to bottom. The very air shimmered and bent at the figure's passing. A white cowl wrapped itself about the creature's shoulders, a mask designed with the likeness of a skull obscuring its face. The eyes glowed with a white energy that dissipated into mist.

A sigh rasped from what must be a throat. The creature, with a surprisingly pleasant tenor, paused in front of the knight and spoke.

"Tell Duke Adirian that if he tries something like this," it reached onto the knight's belt and removed the bound scroll. The voice echoed itself as the words came, giving it an otherworldly mysticism. "Again." It flicked the knight's visor. "Then we will cut trade with Ilvicar for a year." The creature continued forward then, twisting its neck with an intimidating pop. Human? The realization hit Kali.

It was a magus.

"I apologize for your sordid welcome, duchess." He addressed Kali now. An elegant stride brought him near. His robes tapered at the bottom to reveal white leather boots that made no sound as they met the wharf. "We did not believe you in immediate danger."

She mumbled something, the words emerging without form with her mouth sealed shut.

"Oh, sorry. Please do not attack me, I am not above disintegrating you out of spite." He tapped her forehead with a gloved finger.

"Fuck!" Kali stumbled to the ground, her legs burning, but relief came instantly with movement. "What in the void? How the–what the fuck?!" She picked herself up, careful to keep her blade lowered. His threat came off as a matter of fact.

"Peace keeping technique. Painful, but harmless. If you're recovered, we should be off. Into the webway, please." The magus bowed his head and motioned to the inky portal.

Kali righted. Her companions remained in stasis, Niati with her rapier through the chin of a Cavari soldier and Nihilus hot on her trail. "I'd rather not."

"Do forgive me, duchess, but that was not a request. We know why you've come. The captain will be compensated if that is your worry. Best not to tarry, now, the spell is harmless but if left active too long it does leave some psychological scarring."

To be taken by the Cabal of Magi themselves. If one of them was able to wield power like this, what could they do together? She glanced at the others. Did they mean something to her? Nihilus stopped her execution. Niati inadvertently rescued her from the Adirians. Allies of necessity.

No, she had no friends.

"Into the scary black hole then?"

"Quite."

She held her breath and entered the darkness.

•   •   •

Kali gasped and grabbed her chest at the sudden, icy chill. Hot, cold, she longed for the days of persistent body temperatures. The portal closed with a hiss, the magus on her heels. He tapped her shoulder and the heart-wrenching shock dissipated. Handy, that. He sauntered ahead and raised his hand, fingers extended, as a circle of light surrounded Kali.

"In the circle, please." Despite his godlike voice and powers, the magus was quite polite. No sense denying his patience. Kali stepped onto the platform. She caught the source of the light: hundreds of runes carved into what looked like metal. The rest of the room crept in darkness, a murky haze to her eyes.

Another voice came from outside the glow. A second magus emerged from the shadow. Identical to the first, she possessed an arrogance and impatience that strayed from her friendly escort.

"Is this her? She's covered in grime and blood." Her voice modulated in the same fashion as the other magus.

"What did you expect? We plucked her off the street." Another contender. This one male with a deep, rumbling bass.

"She'll bathe once we decide her fate, of course." Polite Magus–she named him–piped up. "But we are being rude. The victim of such deliberations should at least be able to face her jurors. Come forward."

Victim? Jurors? Her shoulders tensed. Kali whipped around as another four magi appeared from the darkness, all of them the same in form and manner.

"Happy now, Wyr?" Arrogant Magus, the woman, addressed the polite one. Wyr? Title or name?

"Is this really such a bother, Emerys?" Rumbling Magus spoke. Definitely names. "I'm sure your experiments are *riveting*, but we agreed to this."

The magus referred to as Emerys glowered, her spindly fingers locking in front of her stomach.

"We can make this simple. We can dispose of her, like any voidtouched, or issue her as a priority to Ymastu's study. A majority vote should suffice."

Ah. Summary execution or a specimen for study. One prison to another.

"You'd think this was the first time a bunch of assholes sat around deliberating my fate. Honestly, it's getting old. Thanks. But no thanks."

Kali sprinted at the magi, her blade shining with red runes. Her strike flew fast and true and sparked against nothing. A blue shimmer appeared where the blade hit the edge of the platform. Emerys did not so much as flinch.

"Interesting," the magus mused.

"Indeed. Did you see that surge? The sword is touched as well. We've not seen voided arms since the Sunstar's wrath." Wyr spoke with a reverence in his tone. "That she can even wield it without signs of outer corruption is a feat worth preserving. Could she house an elder soul?"

Kali blinked. Could they hear her? Did they even care? She shook with anger. Again, she struck her invisible cage. It flashed. Same result. She brought the blade to bear a dozen times and screamed as it did nothing.

"The barrier is weakening. Impressive. I would very much like to study her. I vote to preserve." That must be the aforementioned Ymastu. She sounded old, almost predatory.

"She is too dangerous. Dispose." Emerys tilted her head as Kali stopped her flailing, her eyes narrow as they met the glowing aura that served as the magus' vision.

"Preserve," Wyr said.

Rumbling Magus voted to keep her alive with the next two tying the vote. The seventh, and final, magus held her tongue. The others waited, though Emerys betrayed the stoicism of form by allowing her foot to tap in her impatience. It made no sound. They all turned to face the last of their number.

"Well?" Emerys spoke.

"My." Kali froze. "Isn't she just darling." Lithe and airy, the last magus' voice danced inside her skull. It calmed the air but incited Kali to real, blithering terror. She dropped the obsidian blade and forgot to breathe. That tone. She knew it. She lived with it. Everywhere she went, every action she took, it taunted her. It tempted her. "Look. She's terrified. My friends, how can we condemn this poor girl to death?" Kali stared, her eyes wide. She dared not move as a chill sunk into her veins.

Hello, Arkalis. It's about time we met.

"I vote to preserve."

Litany of the Void, Tenets of the Faith

BLESSED IS THE HOLY pontifex. His Lord's chosen agents, they are to be raised from the most fervent Priests, trained by Champion Paladins and the Divine Hierophant to seek out all creatures of the Void and cast them out of the realm. Arbiters of law, warriors of sunlight, with their unquestionable faith and loyalty they may face the temptations of vile, High Technology and destroy those that would covet the wrath of the Lord.

Blessed is the holy pontifex. A leader, a soldier, gifted their own order to carry out their harsh duties; lonely is their task, for a pontifex may never couple nor foster children, for all the Faithful are their wards, the Church their mate.

Blessed is the holy pontifex.

Chapter 20
Faith

ANOTHER SCORCHED BODY joined the ever-growing pile. Four now, discarded in an unceremonious heap within the basement of Iskvar. Where the pleasant taint of excrement and piss once filled the sewer-like enclosures there now gathered the even more appealing olfactory sensation of burnt flesh. Together the aromas mingled to bring tears to Lesandre's eyes. In the days previous he managed to avoid the canals of waste–though designed as a brilliant way to hide secrets, his appreciation lost its luster in proximity to literal shit.

Two paladins grabbed the newly charred corpse and tossed it onto the pile. Something cracked. Ugh. Lesandre choked back the bile that welled up in the base of his throat. He abandoned any show up strength, but he could keep some of his dignity. Some.

Aluntir moved on from the first cell, now empty, in what served as a dungeon for Iskvar: little more than a short hall with the most basic necessities. Prisoners lingered from the castle ambush and they stared in horror at the pontifex's approach. A steel cage creaked as one of the paladins pulled the door open. Imposing fellows, every step brought some sort of solid, steel clink, from plated boots to shoulders encased in metal. A poor soul was chosen at random and pulled from the cell, begging, pleading for mercy.

The paladin set a man, a Cavari, his eyes sunken, cheeks hollow before Aluntir.

"You've witnessed the fate of the others. Your reward for honesty is that your soul may return to Cinderfell. Otherwise, I will erase you." Aluntir's hollow, steel voice sent a chill riding down Lesandre's spine.

"I'll tell you anything!" The prisoner spoke with a northern accent. "Ask! Don't condemn me." A religious man. Lucky.

"Who recruited you?"

"The marshal! We served at Ilduan, under her banner. She smuggled us in as servants. Paid us silver to attack the lad." He pointed out Lesandre. "And any Iskarion we could get our hands on. Even the duke."

"This is not new information. Tell me of your company, the voidspawn Arkalis Iskarion swore she witnessed." Aluntir's stoicism turned to anger when he spoke of the Void. "They carried obsidian swords." Lesandre had taken great care to hurl those remaining blades over the walls and into the ocean.

"I never saw them up close, Faithful! Please. Please, don't make me say what I know. The others. I saw what happened to them."

"Speak. As a servant of the Sunlord, you must speak."

"I. They. They wore all black. Their faces, wreathed in sha-shad-shaaaad–" His words stilled in his mouth. A sudden convulsion took the man's body and black bile spewed from his lips. His eyes grew dark and his voice transformed into a howling shriek of otherworldly echoes.

"SHADOWS OF THE VOID. SHADOWS OF THE ST–"

Lesandre winced. Poor man. Aluntir grabbed the man's face, his clawed gauntlets piercing the prisoner's eyes and digging into his skull. He screamed with a supernatural exhale. Lesandre covered his ears.

It did not last long.

White, blazing fire coursed from the Pontifex's palm. It engulfed the man in short order, spreading and burning him from the inside out. He squealed and howled until he waned to blissful silence.

"I'm detecting a pattern," Lesandre said. Opening his mouth forced him afoul of the scent. He willed himself not to vomit. "A conditioning?

If the marshal was voidtouched mayhap she ensured their silence. We know precious little of what voidspawn are capable of."

Aluntir did not respond. That blasted mask rendered any reading useless. His spectacles made little difference. Everything about the Pontifex identified as some kind of technology he did not understand.

"Useless," Aluntir muttered.

Lesandre leaned in. Nihilism indicated some form of emotional involvement. Desperation?

"They are all tainted. There is no absolution for them."

"Perhaps, but with study they could rev–wait!"

Aluntir whipped his arm from his side in a vicious gesture. He yelled–a guttural, primal frustration that preceded a torrent of white fire that torched the cell in front of him and to either side. People screamed in a chorus of agony. The steel melted, the stone floors and walls scorched, with nothing left of the prisoners except for hideous, contorted char. All done with a single casting.

Lesandre lost his cool. He ripped the scarf from his mouth and doubled over, vomiting what little lay in his stomach.

A paladin snorted. A manly man, to be sure. Though his companion, a woman, joined the ridicule with a chuckle. Less man, albeit accustomed to the extreme barbarism of their charge. Lesandre coughed as the last contents of his stomach relocated to the dungeon floor. He wiped his mouth with a sleeve.

"Was that truly necessary?" Lesandre said, licking his lips. He needed wine. "At least one left alive for study could have revealed answers! A way to break the conditioning, maybe?"

"You labor under the assumption that we possess unlimited time." He turned to the last cell, the one farthest from the door. "One remains."

Lesandre followed the Pontifex's gaze. He settled on the odd person at the edge of the hall in an old, shaggy coat covered in patches. Each held a distinct pattern with varied coloring, leaving most of the original material replaced at one point or another, including the wide buttons that fastened from the bottom to the end of the high-necked collar.

Bronze skin. A wetlander? That wetlander. He watched them with wide, terror-filled eyes.

"He's a nobody. Guards caught him attempting to kidnap Arkalis as she escaped. Silly fool, he probably recognized her as a potential ransom. Some Nui sailors laid him out and took the heiress themselves."

"Kidnapped?!" The outrage took Lesandre by surprise. "I have been locked in here, subjected to this–this awful smell! For. I don't know. Forever! I don't even know who you all are! Or who she was! Is. Or what. Oh Vari. You're not going to burn me, are you?"

Lesandre defaulted to Aluntir.

"Should I?"

"No! She asked me to take her to the docks. There I was, minding myself when–"

"You were chased by the guard." Lesandre added. He tapped the side of his spectacles, shifting his vision. Aluntir blazed with a myriad of colors. Garbled texts appeared in a vain effort to describe the effects. He ignored them, his focus moving to the wetlander. Odd. A spark of something appeared over the man's head. It vanished before any kind of identification. A hiccup.

"Wrongfully! I was assaulted. By pirates!"

"Enough." Aluntir's metallic interjection silenced the room. "You've no signs of corruption. What do you know of the voidtouched at Iskvar?"

"Nothing?"

Aluntir stared. Silence from the pontifex commonly resulted in fire.

"Paladins, dispose of this one once you finish. What he has seen cannot be shared."

Harsh. Lesandre shifted his weight from one foot to the other, then jumped off after Aluntir at his sudden departure, leaving the poor fellow to a tirade of complaints.

•   •   •

Air passed through his lips in a mixture of anxiety and stress. Lesandre lounged on a delightfully fluffy couch, one arm over the back, the other nursing a half-full glass of wine. He admired the opulence and taste of the former lady of the room. Arkalis stored a significant selection of Aul Red secured in one of the greatest creations of the Cavari runesmiths: a cold box. Filled with wine. Bit of a lush, that woman.

He sloshed the liquid about in the crystal glass as Aluntir plagued his thoughts. Terrifying, smart, powerful. His presence risked Lesandre's mission in Iskvar. His life, even. One suspicious word. One discovery. So far, the shapers proved loyal and held their tongues. Loyal to Airil in any case. Baron Shadowsong proved useful. Hateful, to be sure, but her relation to the Iskarions kept the remaining household in line.

"Your brooding is well practiced, my lord."

Lesandre spotted Elys' well honed, muscular backside in the full-size mirror. The knight crossed the room from the posted bed and admired himself in the same reflection. Scattered shadows danced the stone walls, cast by a red-runed fireplace, the flame no more than a crackle. Lesandre looked a little longer than consideration allowed. He adjusted his glasses to enhance his vision.

"Do you ever take those off?"

"I feel naked without them." Lesandre spoke between sips, his eyes fluttering as the cool liquid soothed his throat and mind.

"Isn't that the point?" Every man showed their true personality in the privacy of intimacy. Elys became a flirt, less concerned with honor than he was with another ride. Ever the cavalier.

"Ah, ah." Lesandre wagged a finger. "That's no way to speak to your liege."

"Come to bed, this darkness does not suit you."

"Darkness? If you'd seen their faces." Lesandre flinched. He finished the contents of his glass with a gulp. "Grab another bottle, I'd rather not remember tonight."

Elys huffed, frustrated as he dug into the cold box. A simple enough construct: a metal cube with a sliding top that turned water to ice. Lesandre could read most of the runes that lined the exterior: freeze, chill, solid, capture. No chemical or mathematical compositions meant it needed targets. Most likely inscribed on the back. Elys returned and popped the cork on another bottle, distracting Lesandre from his scientific appreciation.

"Were they all touched? Truly?"

Lesandre rolled his eyes and shook his glass. Elys smirked, filling the container to the edge. Quite a game. Get him drunk enough and festivities were sure to follow.

"As if drawn from the Litanies themselves. They spat up this. Bile." He sipped. "Their eyes blackened and the howls. Ugh. The howls." Another drink. "Whoever took the Litanies at their word? Instructions for the masses, at best. You know. Don't rape, murder. But this? I believed Arkalis spun the tale to highlight the threat to her father. And Aluntir." He shuddered, drinking again. "Aklesia harbors greater power than I imagined. No wonder the High Loremaster seeks the true Iskvar. We're insignificant to them."

"You don't believe the Litanies? The son of a duke, an atheist? Now that, I cannot imagine."

"Oh come now. Worship the sun? It's a natural phenomenon, not a conscious entity. No one's ever spoken to the fucking thing."

"Lesandre Adirian, is that a commoner's swear? This place is affecting you."

"Don't be so narrow. This rural outing may be as grand a discovery as Dula'Thalier itself. And we may be here for quite some time." He drank only to find his cup empty. Lesandre frowned. "This place could rival Catalin. Even Haven."

"Catalin? Please, the most advanced structure this hovel boasts is a lighthouse."

"You may excel at war fighting, Sir Elys, but try to think less." Lesandre flopped his head back. His cheeks flushed red at a rush of alcohol to his mind, preceding the realization that he, very possibly, drank too much. From his new position he caught another glimpse of Elys' form. What a pleasant distraction. "Rune Lore is many things, but the greatest challenge is sustainability. You follow?"

"Not at all." Elys grumbled. Did Lesandre's position not demand such patience no doubt the general would find more pliable company.

"Power! Contraptions such as this one," he swooned, pointing out the cold box. "They require power. Yes? Simple runes are easy, they recharge from the light of the sun. Others take energy from movement, like waste canals. Sunsingers create fire then draw from the heat, it's all conversion. Yet. We've only scratched the surface of what they knew. Only just! The structure below us still functions, therefore. Listen!"

Elys glanced up having preoccupied himself with pruning his fingernails with a file. Women's rooms contained such wonderful treasures, a side effect of society requiring their perfection in appearance.

"Better. Therefore! It must generate power. Beneath the ground! What do we know of that can do that? Hm?" Lesandre cleared his throat. "Hm?"

"Oh. Nothing, I suppose?"

"Nothing! The Iskarions lived here for centuries and all the while they possessed such potential! Why, there won't b–"

Three raucous bangs came from the door. Lesandre started, his body stiffened. Elys resumed his beauty routine.

"Lord Adirian." A rough, confident voice pierced the privacy of the room. "Pontifex Aluntir requests your presence."

Lesandre groaned. Audibly.

"I'm not well, we'll meet tomorrow!"

"My lord, the pontifex warns that should you avoid his summons tonight he will come to you instead."

"Fuck."

"This vulgarity does not become you." Elys mused, unconcerned. "Perhaps you should take some wine with you, so you won't remember."

Lesandre glowered. Sometimes he wondered if women were any easier.

•   •   •

With considerable trial-and-error Lesandre managed his way to the basilica. What a waste of space. He mused at the display of the Sunlord opposing the feature of Riah, her long, blonde braid given as much detail as a brandished blade of shadow, the watchful guardian ever alert.

Lesandre associated the depiction with lessons of duality. Good, evil, order and chaos. Two sides of a coin.

He slipped inside the partially opened portal. Sunlamps lined the ceiling, bathing the empty, ornate space filled most of the worship hall with natural light. Aluntir stood upon a raised dais between two fire pits in the back where a sunsinger tended to the eternal flames, her voice at song, soft in the evening chill.

Aluntir's masked countenance faced east to the prayer window. Always meant to face the sun, a basilica's construction was a picky ordeal, though perhaps easier at Iskvar. The only view here was of stone walls.

Lesandre halted at the steps, hardly presentable. His coat hung open and his hair splayed unkempt bangs over swelled, tired eyes. He clung tight to the loremaster's journal, the one comfort that kept his confidence anywhere near the pontifex. Dangerous to bring but more so to leave it alone.

"You took your time." From his position Aluntir's voice gained a harsh echo. By design, the basilica's acoustics amplified the speaker. "How is the general?"

"Frustrated." Lesandre spent most of his life dodging bigotry. Only nobles cared much about who slept with who. "As am I, it's closer to dawn than fulldark, pontifex. What could not wait until the morning?"

"Technically–"

"It is morning." Lesandre cut Aluntir off. He expected the jest. What he did not expect was the chuckle from the pontifex. An odd, unnatural sort of thing. Did a human wear that mask?

"I am aware my presence here alarms you and the others. My touch is not light, and few witness the wrath of the Sunstar in such proximity." Some sort of apology? No. An attempt to empathize. An interrogation tactic. Friendships garnered more accurate information than torture. "I am not here to make threats, Lesandre." More of that pseudo mind reading. He focused intently on Aluntir's words and let his thoughts fall aside. "What you need to understand is that we seek the same thing."

"Do we?"

"Let us be direct." Aluntir raised his hand and spread his fingers out as he twisted his wrist. A white flash encircled them. The world quieted. "Now we speak in confidence. I know you've discovered the true Iskvar, the outpost hidden beneath this castle. I also know what those are." Aluntir tapped the side of his mask, at the eyes. "And that you carry a data slate in that false book of yours."

"How?" Lesandre's surprise betrayed him. He lost any sense of calm, his eyes wide. This level of technology labeled most as blasphemers, heretics. More than one 'voided' label found themselves attached to overstepping Loremasters.

"You told me." What?

"What?"

"In such a way. I don't read minds, invasion of the soul like that is beyond my scope. Scenarios present themselves concurrently and instead of experiencing one, as you do, I am able to sift through many. In other potential realities of our interactions you've let too much information slip, though I must admit I am impressed how you handle yourself."

"There's-"

"No way. Yes. I know. No, I am not the only one with this ability. We could spend weeks discussing the theory, but as you remarked upon your entrance, this will not wait until morning."

Aluntir lowered himself to the top stair, folding his leg over a knee. Gingerly, he removed his mask with a hissing click. Human indeed. Half of his face held horrific burns, nothing but scar tissue and a hole through his jaw. One of his eyes bulged, with no lid or flesh, it almost hung from his skull, unblinking and terrible. What remained was thin black skin, half a pointed nose and thin lips curved in a perpetual scowl. Wrinkles placed him as elderly, at least.

"I know what lies beneath. Rune Knight Iskarion's refuge and workshop. It undoubtedly contains marvels this world has not seen for centuries."

Lesandre's chin dropped. He reached for words and failed. His alcohol-soaked brain could only interpret one revelation at a time.

What did that mask do? Help the pain? Were all Pontifices so horribly maimed?

"In my youth I mounted a voyage to the Isle of Cinder. It did not go well. Lesandre, you heard me, yes?"

"Yes. Yes I." Lesandre dug his nails into the journal. He remembered to breathe then focused on what words were. Shocked stumbling was cute in a lover, not in a conversation with one of the most powerful men on the continent. "Iskarion, you say? The original? That would explain the ancestral holding. Do you suppose she hid it to protect her family from the Desolation?" There it was. Sense.

"Undoubtedly." Aluntir's unaltered voice wove like silk, smooth and calm. "The Rune Knights were geniuses of their time. I would suspect her capable of such a feat–yet, we know in hindsight that they suffered great maladies in their fight against the Void. We must assume that their legacy, too, may contain corruption."

"You're not implying–"

"I am. Why send a pontifex to Iskvar, hm? And with paladins. Those accompanying me are some of the fiercest warriors on Thalas. There is great danger here, and the signs of corruption are vast. Tell me. How close are you to breaching the door?"

Aluntir knew everything. From Zevra, or even one of the shapers. Why deny a man of the faith? Adirian was a dirty word to the locals. He reared his head back and stared up at the steepled ceilings, exhaling through his nose.

"I'd say we're about as likely to get inside as I am to bed Arkalis Iskarion."

"That's not encouraging."

Another sigh. Lesandre opened his journal and removed the slate. He waved his hand over the surface and it sprung to life, colored runes shimmering into existence above the smooth material. He swiped his fingers over a few commands to display an image of the door.

"I'll do us a favor and not ask how you got this." The pontifex poured over the information. He mumbled and ground his teeth. An unsettling event as Lesandre watched it occur. He begged himself not to vomit inside a basilica. Aluntir glanced at him. The grinding ceased. Oh.

"Even with all the black powder in the garrison we'd only dent it."

"Mhm."

"And you're sure of the possible permutations? Three-hundred and sixty thousand?"

"It'd fit the whole Rune Knight theory."

"I suppose, then, we will need a great deal of faith."

Lesandre rolled his eyes. He retracted the slate and wiped it clean. The images dissipated.

"That's what you're here for, isn't it, Pontifex? I've not the stomach for miracles. I imagine your station nets you one or two."

"One or two." Aluntir smiled, setting the mask back into place with a latching click.

Excerpt from the high Loremaster's Journal

Z ACHAR'RUHN. Mentioned once in the Litanies, the Cursed Mountain is said to be the origin of Lindorum's original folly, where they opened the Void and let loose the gods of destruction. Said to be the tallest natural structure of Yaros I've longed to glimpse its heights, but explorers have since reported the Desolation of Lindras to be filled with nefarious voidspawn, their density only increasing the closer one approaches.

A point of personal curiosity lies in Riah's oasis. The last stop in the Duskmother's journey before she ascended the mountain to seal the First Void. Local legends say that she encountered guardians that sealed the only path up, able to withstand the corruption and fight the spawn. If they could survive such power at the time of its height, might they still be there? And if they are, what requires guardians in a broken part of the world?

Chapter 21
. . .Than Good

DISPOSE? Luc swallowed. Blasted Sentinels. Where was Vari now? Champion of luck, patron of Aenia. Useless vagrant. Luc cursed every prayer he ever uttered in the deity's name. Trapped behind bars in a foreign land to die as a prisoner in a sewer. Oh what he would give for soap. He dug his face into the collar of his patchwork jacket and inhaled, the leather making a fine enough filter from the refuse. He dared not glimpse the ever-growing pile of death, nor the molten iron. The fellow with the mask drew inspiration from every cautionary tale Luc's parents used to scare him as a child. Don't piss off unholy sorcerers that can summon white fire from their hands. He issued a quiet apology to his mother.

Steel chains rattled outside his cage. Luc met the faceless visor of a grossly over armored zealot, one hand clasped around the hilt of a jagged blade as tall as the wielder. Luc squeaked. He backed up against the cold, gray stone of his cell, his teeth chattering. Whether from the chill or fear he did not care. An ominous creek groaned from the cell's hinges as the door swung inward. A thought appeared in Luc's mind. Rush him. Rush him?! Death sauntered towards him, his great wicked blade poised to strike. Luc's pack sagged against the wall opposite the cell. His pack. Rush him.

Okay.

Luc rushed the paladin. The man reared back, stunned, as the too-frail-too-thin vagabond unleashed a terrified scream and ran. Luc closed his eyes and put his head down. Wild strides brought him to his prey and he tripped over his own boot. Habit curled Luc's head as he pushed his weight into his clumsiness, his back hitting the ground and propelling him into a roll. Luc opened his eyes. He patted the top of his head. Hat present. Not dead. The paladin remained within the cell, shocked, his blade plunged into the stone. Oh. Well. Luc scrambled up and closed the door and twisted the key.

He apologized to Vari, whispering a short, gracious prayer.

"He escaped!"

Oh yes. There were two.

"I didn't do anything! Please don't kill me!"

Luc stumbled backward, watching the second part of his executioner approach, this one similarly armed. Pack. Right. Luc flipped open the top and pilfered the inside with the jittering clink and rustle of pouches and vials.

"Ahah!" Luc withdrew a vial of black liquid. "Don't come any closer!" The paladin stopped, confused. "You know what this is?!"

The woman tilted her head. She lifted her visor, revealing intense brown eyes beneath and a splattering of freckles over dark, sunken cheeks.

"No," She said, flatly.

"This is Zachar'dai'ruhn!" Luc's chin quivered. He hoped she mistook that as fear of the name. Whatever it meant. "I drop this and the fumes will kill us all! One whiff! We all drop dead." She lowered her blade and extended an armored palm, easing to the side. What? That worked?

"Waters of the cursed mountain? How do you have this?"

"Yes? Yes! The Void graced me with alchemical knowledge beyond your pithy understanding! Now back. Away! Let me free or I'll break it! The walls themselves will ooze with corruption!" Luc's eyes grew wild, his voice laced with hysteria. The paladin took to a knee and placed her blade on the ground. Luc inched toward the exit. He held the vial out, his hand shaking, a thumb held over the wooden cork that kept the liquid at bay.

."You stay here! Or else I will unleash every substance in this infernal bag, diseases and plague you'd not dare imagine!" Their eyes met, pure rage and hatred visible in her stare. An obvious ploy, yet the slightest possibility of truth begged inaction. Luc opened the heavy, barred door that led away from the dungeons and slammed it shut, ducking the corner. He pressed his back up against a wall and exhaled.

He uncorked the vial and downed the contents.

The sweet, sugary liquid eased a burn in his throat he never recalled. Something for the nerves, a tincture of his own concoction. Big hit in Cavari towns. He listened to a scuffle of activity from the cells followed by harsh, muted voices. Doubtful they would wait. Luc pushed himself upright and slung his pack over his shoulder and observed his new surroundings.

A cellar? A sewer? A hybrid of the two with internal aqueducts connected to pipes. Dim glowlamps lit the path, illuminating the darkness with their eerie, blue twinge. Which way? The water flowed toward an undoubtable escape, yet. Luc's sense told him to eschew logic. Upstream, it warned. Warned?

With a sigh and a prayer Luc scampered off.

• • •

He popped his head up from a circular opening behind a bale of hay. Luc inhaled deeply, ready for the sweet relief of untainted air. He choked, coughed, then spat. Again, the sweet aroma of shit plugged his nostrils. That solved the mystery. He died and woke to the great latrine in the sky. Other less offensive scents reached him, those common to a rural lifestyle. Horses and hay. Luc grumbled as he scrambled over the last rung of a rickety ladder, laying prostrate in a moment of assumed safety.

Luc crawled into an empty stall. Across from him the head of a black Cavari stallion stared from over a closed gate, chewing with no concern for the new arrival. That explained the smell. From a sewer to a stable, home to varying degrees of disease and stink. How wonderful. Luc thanked Vari for his luck.

He rose first to his knees, shaking as his adrenaline wore off. A fugitive from the law and now a voidtouched alchemist. In hindsight his gambit put him in greater peril. Then again, what would they do? Kill him more?

Luc crept to the edge of his hovel and poked his head out, his vision sweeping over the stables. A dozen or so horses occupied twice as many stalls. Their grunts intermingled with the occasional bark of a stable hand and scratching brooms. Some laughed in the distance, speaking lowborn Cavari with a harsh, yokel accent. Sunlamps lit the interior here. At least his station improved. He exchanged a look with the stallion, its bored, flat countenance challenging his apprehension.

"Quiet you."

"Hoi, it dun speak y'know. Las' I checked. Ya may be special tho', sneakin' outta th' foundations'n all."

Luc jumped. He whipped around and flailed his arms out in what he imagined a defensive posture to be. Mostly he covered his face.

"Don't kill me!"

"Wha'n th' void? Settle yerself, I look like'a friggin' boot licker?"

Luc peeked. His ambusher sat cross legged atop on a pile of hay, half a gaunt face sticking out over a comically large book, dark hair scattered across his scalp as if unwashed for weeks on end. His trousers frayed at the ankles, holes patched with haphazard stitching. In that they shared a likeness.

"No? My Cavari may be lax. Boot licker?"

"Yer 'Vari's better'n mine, prolly. Jus' meanin' the red ones. Silly Adr'n pricks."

"Adr'n?"

"Ho, fuck buddy, where'n tha' void ya' come from? Ya ain't local, judgin' by tha' skin'a yers an' tha' hat. Aenia?"

"I." Luc blinked. He smoothed out his coat, shifting his weight back onto his heels. "Yes? How did you–"

Balen waved him off. He shut his book, titled: *Hardent's Bestiary, Spawn and Fauna of the Western Wastes.* Lowering it revealed a mischievous grin.

"Iskvar's gotta voidin' spectacular library. Duke's holdin's an' all. More'ta tha' point, I heard tell'a wetlander was locked up in tha' cells. Assumin' tends'ta make fools outta th' originatin' party, but eh, in this case I'd be safe'in thinkin' tha's you, ya?"

"Yes." Luc agreed carefully, doing his best to interpret the onslaught of accent. From what he deciphered this man cared little for his daring escape. "And so?"

"An' so. Ya'd be responsible fer Kali gettin' away."

"Kal-who? You mean that half-dead woman at the port?"

"Sweet Sunlord, dead?" Balen's yokel charm faded to a cold despair. It lasted until he opened his mouth again. "Gah. See, Iskari'ns were good ta'me, so. I feel I owe ya one."

"Thank Vari's luck." Luc breathed a sigh of relief. "To start. Where am I?"

Balen snorted. He discarded his book and hopped down, knees cracking from the effort. The gangly stable hand took stock of his charge. He hummed, circling, appraising from head to toe.

"Castle up'n the cliff from'n the town. Knights'n nobles'n things. Name's Balen, by the by."

"Luss."

"Louass, huh? Weird 'un."

Luc shook free from the stunning oddity. "Good. Fine. Yes. Can you get me out of this nightmare?"

"Hmph. Not durin' the day. Pontifex got guards er'where. Airil may'n be able to help, tho. Sit tight, Louass."

"Any point in correcting your pronunciation?"

"Nah."

•   •   •

Luc woke with a start. Balen loomed over him, grinning beside an unfamiliar, scowling redhead with one narrowed eye. Ah. Death. So be it. Luc peered up from the most boring literature of his life, musing on something Hardent referred to as an Ice Wyrm. His last thought before sweet release.

"Sunlord, Balen, this is Louis?" Airil's nose twitched. She folded her arms beneath her chest, dressed like royalty.

"Eh? Lou-ass, Airil."

"Luc," Luc said.

"Don't care. Get up. We have no time." The woman hooked Luc by the arm, her ironclad grip digging into his skin with an excited yelp. He nursed his arm and collected his pack. Not death then. The haze of sleep lifted amidst a foray of chaos. Airil rushed him out of the stables and into a forested courtyard, greenery flooding his nose with sweet air. Crisp, with a salty taste of ocean bearing coast. For the first time in what seemed like forever Luc rid himself of any thought of sewage.

Balen pushed from behind while Airl took the lead, her hard soled boots clacking against the cobbled pathway. They trailed her, straying to the edge of posted sunlamps to bask in the cover of shadow. Airil skirted the walls and avoided the roving pockets of light. Patrols, no doubt. By the depth of Riah's Moon Luc figured it was early morning.

"I thought it'd be more difficult to move," Luc whispered at Balen.

"Whys'at?"

"Alarms? Escaped prisoner? You know."

"'Bout that. No'un said nothin'. Business as usual in Iskvar." He shrugged. Why did that not make Luc feel better?

Sea borne breezes buffeted Luc's form, blowing his coat out as the wind howled through a nearby breach in the wall. Ah. He remembered that particular bit of destruction from below. Though his senses drew his attention to the cavernous indent in the ground. He felt the tug. A ladder fastened itself nearby for descent. Go, it said.

Airil veered away from the hole. Luc followed her to the edge of the cliff where a woman in a white kaftan awaited them, her black hair woven in layers to her shoulders. A Xyran. She exchanged pleasantries with the redheaded one who motioned to Luc. They glanced in his direction. He waved.

"Come," Zevra beckoned. Or demanded. He did as instructed, shuffling over, weary of his sudden proximity to a two-hundred-foot drop.

"Balen, time for you to go. The less you know the better." Airil said, moving to block Luc from any egress. She withdrew an inch of steel from her sheath to punctuate her sincerity.

"Hey hey hey, now'n this fell–"

"Balen."

Balen shot an apologetic look in Luc's direction then cleared off, muttering under his breath. Luc swallowed. He shuffled and a dusting of debris fell over the edge.

"I'm harmless!"

"Guards reported you helped Arkalis escape. Where is she?" Airil spoke sharply. Zevra clasped her necklace with a whisper. It took on a soft, white emanation.

"I have no idea. Those Nui could've taken her anywhere."

"Nui?" Airil shared a glance with the priest.

"Traders or something. They knocked me out, stole my silver, and took the girl. I only helped her because. Well. Because." Luc scratched the back of his head. For once the sense quieted.

"Because?"

"Because who wouldn't help a person in distress! I did nothing wrong. And frankly? I'm exhausted. Exhausted! I smell like a sewer, I feel like a sewer, I am *becoming* a sewer. So please, I'm useless to you. Let me go, so I might bathe before I die."

Again, they exchanged a look. Airil sheathed her blade, her shoulders tilting back. His legs wobbled. He fell onto his rump and sat.

"My apologies, Louis, but this is a complicated matter. That person is my niece. If the dukes find her, I fear she will not be long for this world."

"Hence the severity," he huffed. How many more times could he avoid a violent end?

"Anything you cou-"

"Airil?" Another voice cut her off. Masculine, the source haphazardly fumbled his way toward them. A mess of a man, he looked fresh from a night of drinking, clutching a book to his side as if it held him upright.

"Fuck," Airil grunted. Zevra muttered into her necklace to kill the glow. Both turned to the new arrival, the latter bowing her head. "Lesandre."

Ah. The sense tugged at his mind. The ladder. No! If he ran they'd stick a sword in his back. Or worse, the sunpriest could set him on fire. Could she? No more chances. Vari be damned.

"You two out for a late-night trollop, hm? No need to hide it from me, I swing the same way." The drunkard snickered, amused. "You'll never believe what I-oh. Who is that? A new friend?" Lesandre edged closer, stepping out from the shadow of the wall. Luc's eyes bulged. He knew that face. In the dungeons he watched those prisoners as they burned alive. Shit. His mind tugged. Go.

Airil hissed at the man, speaking in low, harsh tones, though that seemed her persistent state. Zevra joined in. She vouched for the other while Lesandre grew more suspicious at each word. Go. It pulled.

Fine!

Luc crawled, his motions silent against the rubble. Distracted as they were, he reached the ladder before one cried after him. *Wait!* Not a chance. He descended the rungs with an acrobatic grace, hopping two at a time. Freedom awaited below. He jumped down at the end and sprinted face first into a dead end. A dead end with glowing symbols. Housed within a hexagonal outline nine, hand sized, glowing runes covered an obsidian metal wall. Above he heard his pursuers argue.

Luc examined the script. Complex, layered, like the panels of Vari's temple in Aenia. A door then? Yes! Luc licked his lips and depressed one. Its glow brightened then diminished to its original intensity. Exactly the same. His sense guided him. The symbols appeared near the top of the shape in the sequence in which he designated. He locked in nine. The indentations of the door hissed steam. A line appeared from the center and it parted, six individual panels separating and sinking into the walls.

Light sputtered to life inside a metal tunnel. Not lamps, but long, thin panels raised along the sides of the walls. They bled natural illumination. At the end, a separate panel loomed, framed by railings with a black stone stand in the center. Maybe not like the temple after all.

Gasps. Luc turned, greeted by stunned, slack faces. Airil, sword brandished, lowered the blade and stepped toward him. Lesandre cut her off. He rushed over, his eyes alight with wonder. With hunger.

"How?!" Lesandre's voice cracked. He tapped the side of his spectacles and tilted his head, his lips turning up into a crazed smile.

"You just push the panels."

"You just," Lesandre snorted. He laughed, grasping at words. "You just. Push. Who are–you know what, it doesn't matter. It's open! Do you know what this means?!"

"That you're going to let me go free?"

"Not a chance in the void." Lesandre silenced his laughter. What madness did this man possess?

"You're not going to wait until morning, are you?" Airil joined them, Zevra too. The priestess mouthed a silent prayer.

"No, Airil. And neither are you. Aluntir will know we opened it if he sees any one of us. We go now, and we're bringing our new, brilliant friend.

Luc frowned. His sense tugged him deeper. Inside. He supposed it could be worse. The hall did not smell of shit.

Excerpt from Gilderan's Casting Analysis of Thalas

NOT TO BE CONFUSED with a magus, the warcasters of Lindras are first, and foremost, sorcerers, with a touch of runecasting in their repertoire. What is the difference, you ask? In truth it is more preference than divide, specialty rather than inability. Sorcerers are masters of gesture casting, utilizing quick, simple movements to create simple effects such as electric discharge or forcing exothermic detonations. This makes them well suited for combat but inhibits any true complexity.

A magus, otherwise, employs the use of preparation in the form of foci. Foci allow them the use of more complex spells and castings with stored energy, batteries, which save their own constitution. Magi too are learned, dabbling in sciences outside the realm of casting. Indeed, in order to attain the title of Magus one must master a more mundane category of study. Alchemy, Metallurgy, Natural Law, or something of similar achievement.

I'd be remiss to not at least mention runecasters. Rare, even before the calamity of Void Gods, these individuals craft complex equations and elemental compositions into complicated symbols, able to "enchant" mundane objects or improvise vastly intricate spells.

Chapter 22
Fight Good

R URIK BOLTED upright. He held his stomach where the glaive pierced his flesh to find his body absent pain. This is where he died, wasn't it?

He pressed his palm against his forehead. Memories came in a haze of confusion. Dula'Thalier first, in two versions–one of its original splendor, spiraling towers, thriving markets; tourists gated in from around the world to share the culture of the ancient rune masters. Next came his version. The black city, a void ridden nightmare.

Next to him knelt the body of Iskarion. His body. His? Huh. No life lingered in that empty shell, its mass no more than ash and dust. Mere moments passed since he summoned the full power of the lance, his body used as a conduit above this very amplifier. He saw it now, the solarstone construction that drew from crystal foci he once thought were only windows. A perfect spot to unleash a cataclysmic shockwave. One that could bury a city.

Lyue sat up in a fit, her eyes wild. The same haze that took him repeated in her. They found each other in a deranged stare. What did she witness? Rurik remembered the sting of every blow and each mistake. He glanced down at his thick, calloused hands, hands he did not recognize. His hands were soft and worn with runic burns. No, that wasn't right.

Lyue wobbled to her feet. Recognition flooded into her countenance. She felt herself up as if trying to understand her body.

"You alright?" His voice took him by surprise. A masculine tenor. One set of memories flooded to the forefront. A twin sister, a dukedom, Ilvicar, a country founded in the aftermath of the Desolation. After the what? An apocalypse. His life ended before it started.

"I cannot honestly answer that," Lyue responded, confused.

"Are you?"

"Am I me? Yes. And no, but yes? It feels like me. All of it feels like me."

"In different places." Rurik grunted. His body reminded him of the now, the torture, the exhaustion. He nonchalantly twisted his wrist and curled his fingers before he dropped his hand and extended an open palm. Warmth crept into his bones. Better. The days of malnourishment and insomnia drifted away.

"Rurik."

He didn't respond at first.

"Rurik." Rurik? That was him.

"What?"

"Did you just use sorcery?"

"Of course, it's cold as shit in here."

"And you became a sorcerer when?"

He learned the gestures by sneaking into the college when he was nine. He would watch from the rafters between thefts from the kitchens. Kalthier, already aged, caught him when he blasted a hole in the ceiling. He entered the Rune College as the youngest candidate in history. Or was he learning Singali from Dinkira at that age?

"A runecaster. Not a sorcerer."

"*Putain de merde, vous êtes vivants tous les deux?*"

The voice came from the pool. Katriene jogged to the base of the dais, her knives coated with a fresh layer of blood not her own. More memories. The interrupted deal. Rust and Feral escaped and Celesti captured him in place of the others. Anger flushed his face red. Celesti.

"Where's Lanatir, Katriene?" Lyue descended the dais.

"Le sac à merde est entré par le portail. Il l'a laissé ouvert. Fallait tuer deux connards avant de le verrouiller!"

"I knew that bastard lacked a spine. Probably assumed we died."

"Je suis content que tu sois encore vivant. Je me croyais foutu."

"You're not." Rurik rubbed his forehead. He recalled more of his life over the last two years. His crew, his servitude.

"I don't see how we're not fucked."

"I do."

Rurik grasped the haft of the Sunlance. It thrummed at his touch and slid free from the remnants of Iskarion, whose armor clattered to the dais as her body turned to dust. Rurik lifted his wrist and envisioned a rune with the motion. The suit hovered, its segments swirling about at his behest. Each piece snapped to his body as if made for it and sealed with a mechanical whine, concealing all but his head. Iskarion loved gravity runes, and now so did he.

"Qu'est-ce qui se passe?"

Lyue's jaw slacked. "That's Iskarion's armor, Rurik. The Iskarion. The *traitor.*" She recoiled at her anger, almost surprised by her own vehemence.

"It's my armor," He said matter-of-factly. Another gesture brought the helmet up to his palm.

"Wait. You saw *her*? You have the knowledge of a Rune Knight?"

Her. Rurik remembered himself as a man in both lives, though he expected a more feminine physique in his reflection. Her reflection? Did that matter? His sense of self was muddied, caught between a dual set of consciousness.

The helmet snapped into the armor's gorget with a whirring snap. Runes sparked to life inside as the opaque faceplate turned translucent. Novel, familiar. Experiencing two different simultaneous emotions took some adjustment. A series of warnings flashed in his peripheral, not least of all the alarm from the gaping hole in the lower abdomen and insufficient power to repair the damage.

"You okay in there?" Lyue knocked on the side of his helmet.

"Mhm." Too many distractions sought his attention. "There's a lot to process. Like how the webway is still active."

"Something is sustaining the grid," Lyue interjected. "The beacon? It's almost perfectly preserved. You don't think it could be the Avatar? After all this time?"

"Is there another explanation?" Rurik engaged with Lyue like a peer, her fresh memories matching his own. "I tried to destroy the beacon. It must have been able to shield itself somehow."

"Quelqu'un peut expliquer?"

Lyue answered Katriene. "Sorry, I'm–we're still processing what happened. The only clear thing now is that we need to leave. With Lanatir they'll figure out where we are soon enough."

"The breach is the only way out of the city." Rurik spoke and descended the dais, strangely light on his feet. The armor added little weight. "I cut the webway lines out of the city before–well. You know. We could fight our way through with this." Rurik punctuated the point by clicking the lance's haft against the tiles. "But I'd rather not leave an Adirian with free rein over the ruins."

"You're right. That woman is a psychopath. If she gets access to the Beacon, she could free the Avatar. I'd rather not start another cataclysm, thank you."

"Mais qu'est-ce qu'on fait? Il n'y a que trois de nous." Katriene's tone bled frustration. She threw her arms into the air, exasperated.

"Not just us. We have my crew." Rurik returned to the arch with the others in tow, its power spent. Two Adirian guardsmen decorated the floor, puncture wounds replacing their eyes. Katriene kicked one and giggled. Rurik tapped the lance against the solarstone. It sparked, lighting up the array of runic inscriptions.

"Handy."

"Immensely. But it draws from my soul without any excess power source."

"Probably ease off it, then? For now." Lyue eyed the lance, weary. She took a step back. "So. Where to? Your people could be anywhere."

"Not anywhere. They need food. Celesti is looking for them, so no chance they're at the camp. We only had one break with anything resembling those conditions."

•   •   •

Rurik emerged in the council chamber. A snarl greeted him followed by the towering violence of Feral. She charged and whipped a sledge at his head, her thunderous footfalls shaking the stage. Rurik sidestepped the blow and shoved the lance's haft under Feral's leg and sent her to the ground with a skittering collapse.

"Whoa!" Rurik raised his hands. His typical fighting style relied on brute strength and luck, but that? Decades of training with the Thalian Justiciar came to him in a burst of technique. "Feral! It's me, Chiefman!" He depressed a plate on his neck and the helmet sunk into the armor.

Feral sniffed. She lowered her sledge as Lyue came through next.

"Sunlord fuck me. Rik!" Sahira ran down the stairs, spear in hand, wearing a set of white-gold tinted brigandine with matching coat and greaves. Lynesse colors. She stopped by the rabid wastelander, calming her with a light touch.

"You're alive. We thought, void. We." Sahira rubbed her eyes with the sleeve of her coat. "But you look. Shit. You look good. What happened?"

"A lot." Rurik brushed the furred mantle over his armored shoulders. He watched Sahira with a keen eye, her betrayal still circumspect. "You pledge service to Lynesse?"

"This?" Sahira smirked. "Nah. We bushwhacked some Lyn guards outside the camp. Let us bail without too much fuss, Celesti's lookin' for us and all."

"Us?"

"Rik!" Another voice. Rust and a gaggle of others: Jerk, Sweets, all in similar armor. A viper trailed on their heels. Katriene smiled, wide, abandoning any pretense of stoicism and rushed to her sister.

"Shari blesses us!" Sweets laughed, joyous.

"How'n the forsaken void are ya here?" Rust slapped his bald scalp above his burned face. "An' is that? Sunlord blind me, tha's runecrafted armor."

Singali chattering echoed within the chamber as the vipers embraced. One brought the other up to speed. Their mother–the merchant–waited in the garden.

"Celesti had us in her dungeon. Managed to trick our way out and found something to help along the way. Wasn't sure any of you'd be here."

"Princess's idea. Shari approves."

"Princess?" Why hide if she betrayed them? The lie lost its credit. Who then?

"Yeah." Sahira cracked a grin. "Wasn't easy. That Voidtear is close, turned all the dead we left into those yellow eyed things. Started callin' them ghouls, ya know. Like the Litanies. But, don't gotta worry about soldiers pokin' around. And there's food. Been here for a few cycles now. Shit Rik, thought we were gonna all die here."

Rurik wrapped Sahira in a tight embrace. She stiffened at first, shocked, then returned the hug and buried her head beneath his chin. All that confusion and rage melted away.

"Where is Lanatir?" Jerk eyed the gate, frowning at the display of affection. He looked silly in his guardsmen outfit, too thin to fill it out. "We heard he was taken, yes?"

"He was." Lyue spoke up. "No doubt the Adirians have him now, which means they'll have a better understanding of the webway. We don't have much time."

He broke the embrace with Sahira, neither doing so with any hurry.

"Chiefman is strong." Feral nodded, approving. She leaned close and sniffed Rurik's head. "Pure magic."

"Rik?" Rust interjected.

"There's a lot to explain. Too much. Lyue is right, we're on a crunch. Celesti has my ring and slate, which means she'll figure out how to use the gates soon enough."

"You expect us to understand any of this?" Jerk added. The group collectively booed him. He pinched the bridge of his nose and closed his eyes.

Sahira perked up. "The ring. That make her dangerous?"

"It's a channeling artifact." Lyue took this one. "A shortcut, kind of. Even an amateur caster can use it to siphon ambient energy."

"Ahuh."

"Melody still with us?" Rurik asked.

"Aye. She's in the garden with Sarette."

"Sarette?"

"The arms merchant," Jerk said, "she has forgone payment, taking protection in its stead."

"Let's go then. I'd like to not repeat myself."

·   ·   ·

They gathered around the inert arch while Rurik measured the ambient energy readings. They peaked near the pool. Runes glittered like stars through the transparent ceiling, shedding enough light for the focusing crystal to fuel the old enhancements to the garden's ecosystem. By theory, energy from the runes should be absorbed then transferred to the new effect, except the ceiling regenerated itself.

The crew fared better than he expected. His augmented vision bounced between them, outlining their respective physiologies. The analysis caught subtle shifts in body language: raised heartbeats, aberrant health issues, nothing much of concern except for Melody's advanced leprosy. Though the chill did them little good. Rurik tapped at his gauntlet over a series of projected runes and raised the garden's ambient temperature.

His companions shared an uneasy glance as warmth crept into the room. None of them trusted Thalian technology, their minimal exposure being general death and dismemberment.

"Is that?" Sahira asked, weary.

"Me."

"Worth it to ask?"

"Nope."

"Well then." Lyue clasped her hands. Her stance was rigid, posture perfect and pristine. A stark contrast to her previous swagger. "Let's get to it."

"Let's." Sarette flared her forked tongue. She sat on the edge of the pool, her daughters to either side.

"We need to stop Celesti," Lyue said.

"Aye. An' how?" Rust chimed in. Melody lay on his shoulder, her eyes latched to the glaive. "Got any more'a those suits?"

Rurik cracked a grin. Not that anyone could see. "Just the one."

"T'ey got us on numbers." Rust continued. "Never seen'a fight end well tha'way."

"We have an advantage." Rurik tapped the lance's haft.

"That is what I believe it to be?" Melody lit up.

Sweets peered over Rurik's shoulder. "What is? This fancy stick?"

"It is."

"A Sunlance," Melody said, awed. "This is the weapon within the city? If we have it, we must leave, only Aklesia must have this power."

"The lance is a weapon, but it's not what I'm worried about," Rurik said, "the real problem is in the center of the city. Something we sealed in."

"We?" Sahira set her hands on her hips. She was disheveled, curls tangled into one another with grime and dirt under her fingernails.

"The Rune Knights, it's–"

"Hard to explain. Ahuh, we know."

"Anyway. Celesti can't reach it. Not just for us, but for Ilvicar. Potentially all of Thalas."

"This is what Cavari call hyperbole, no? There is no power left capable of such concern." Singali skepticism. Sarette did her people proud.

"There is. And it's here. It's why all this still works." Rurik gestured to the fountain, the garden. "Why the runes reform, why they're so powerful. It all comes from the Avatar."

"*Av-a-tar? Quelle est cette absurdité?*"

"It's not nonsense. We found it in the wastes." More memories. An image of five knights came to him. They fought as one against an almost formless mass of energy. "It cut a swath of destruction and madness across the continent. It took the power and mind of every great magus of the continent to stop it. The college, the Magi, even Lindorum warcasters. We stole it, sealed it inside the Beacon of Dula'Thalier."

The others hung on the edge of his words, all except Lyue. The loremaster wore a scowl while he felt the guilt of his actions creep in. Dula'Thalier's destruction was to stop the war, to end pointless suffering. Instead it kick-started a cataclysm. Perfect hindsight came with knowledge a millennium into the future. The avatar engineered its own salvation with him as its patsy.

"And we used it to commit terrible atrocities. What you know as Omen, the Ghostlands of Dastanir, we called Mithiren. We destroyed their cities because they threatened us, because we believed them corrupted by the Void."

"The Litanies say Omen was named such for its dalliance with the Gods of the Void." Melody's brows knit together. "That their masters turned against them."

"Sorry to disappoint. It was a bunch of assholes with a toy. A powerful toy."

"But their lands were unmade. Power only of the Void."

"That's what you get when an apocalypse wipes out centers of learning. We called them Emissaries, not gods. They were powerful, yes, but they could never literally disintegrate things. They undermined the Sunstar and wooed cities to their side with technology and knowledge. They were a threat to our way of life, not our existence. That power never belonged to them. It was ours."

"The armies of the Sunlord descended in our defense! The Litanies say–"

"Cinderfell was always impenetrable. We never knew what it housed, but there are only three entities powerful enough to summon so much power. The Avatar, the Void, and the Sunstar. Why would the

Emissaries wipe out what they worked so hard to covet? I didn't survive the destruction of Dula'Thalier so I can't say for certain."

He lost them. Interest faded to confusion.

"Stay with me. Whatever these armies were, they're only recorded in religious texts. A religion based around the only great power to witness the events. Some alien, malign presence wasn't responsible for the Desolation, we were. People. We took too much from a power we didn't understand, we misused what we knew, and it took the opportunity to fight back."

He never intended to drop so much on them, nor did he realize it until their stark faces stared at him in disbelief.

"And that's why we need to stop that bitch." Sahira took in a deep breath. "If all that is true. Which, ya know. It's a lot. But fuck me, I've trusted you this far, Rik." Her eyes softened as she looked at him. Belief or affection? "If she gets access to that Ava-whatever then we're all dead. I'd rather go out fightin'."

"It's all fascinating. Mind bending, yes." Jerk pinched his nose. "Not even all of us are fighters. How do we overcome so many? They have weapons. Numbers"

"Easy," Rurik interjected, "we build ourselves an army."

Feral grunted, her mouth half stuffed with a turnip. She spat out the vegetable and grabbed her sledge and slammed her foot into the ground.

"Fight! Good."

Excerpt from the high
Loremaster's Journal

E SSENTIAL, but otherwise expendable, the Cavari Lowborn leads a life of almost perpetual servitude. They are beholden to the local House from birth and are considered aligned with a duke or baron, their rights able to be stripped at the slightest whim from one of noble birth. Their education is stunted, for obvious reasons. No good in your oppressed population learning how terrible their freedoms are.

No able-bodied commoner is safe from conscription, and it is almost expected of a lowborn to have served as a soldier at one point in their lives. A double-edged blade to be sure, for the rate of desertion and banditry is particularly high in Ilvicar but makes for fairly safe rural villages. Not much gain to be had when anyone you'd rob has a chance to stab you first.

Chapter 23
Allies

L YUE'S BRIGANDINE ARMOR chafed against her bust. Oadua
women prided themselves on their broad shoulders and hips. A
trait she regretted in the present. She'd rather the body of her
past: a man's physique. Easier to convince other men to listen that way.
Rurik took to his new memories easier than her, though she suspected
he had more practice, exhibiting signs of the merger since they first met.
While not as grand as a Rune Knight of the ancient world, Lyue
respected her new skillset. A Thalian Justiciar's training made it easy to
disable a lone guard out for a piss.

She entered the breaker compounds and navigated the various
camps until she found a specific palisade, one flying a flag with a black
rendering of a runic -K, the extensions curved with separate dots in the
curls on a backdrop of white lilies. Not as large as the Adirian hold, but
grand enough to fit two full breaking crews and a complement of
soldiers.

Her disguise allowed her to bypass the dual, black-coated
guardsmen on guard outside the gate and waded into a mass of uneasy
tension. Over a hundred men and women crammed themselves into
the fortification. Lyue's nose twitched at the scent of the unwashed:
sweat and body odor mixing with whatever the boiled slop was they
served en masse. Her red coat drew eyes from soldiers and breakers

alike, but no one stopped her as she came to a halt at the open-faced tent. Cavari nobles benefited from a lack of danger. The elite spared one another punishment for even the worst atrocities, and those beneath them depended on their fair rule. All except for Rurik of Iskvar.

At least the Kalthier lord possessed some semblance of humility. His tent contained a single cot, with him poised over a runic table rendered with the image of Dula'Thalier, shirtless. She lingered a little too long on his muscular frame before announcing her presence.

"Hm?" Karil flicked his gaze up from the table and pushed his hair away from his face. Jet black, it reached his shoulders and a full, trimmed beard framed a square jaw. Light brown eyes peered at her, thin brows raised at the intrusion. "Here to defect?"

Lyue set the arquebus down, letting it clatter against the ground. "No."

"I'd think not. Soldiers respect their weapons more, so what are you?"

Not who. Lyue never met a Kalthier. Observant, even cunning. Next to his maps Karil kept a Tsö Board, a circular, red and white marble surface that housed stones of varying shapes. A game of patience and strategy. Lies here would do little good.

"A loremaster."

"Mm. I know you. Not many lowlander loremasters. Oa, right? You're the heretic Rurik escaped with. He swallow his pride and deem to seek aid?"

"In a way. He's organizing an offensive, to take the encampment and free the breakers. To stop Celesti."

"How many guns do you have?" Karil asked, his deep bass inquisitive. "Lanatir is back in Celesti's clutches. No support there. I'd guess. One?" He eyed the discarded arquebus.

"We have surprise. And an artefact. With the gates we won't need conventional weapons."

Karil responded, unamused. "I heard about the gates. Useful. I don't care much for using Thalian weapons, but." His chest heaved. "Frankly, loremaster, my men are tired and I'm sick of this cage. Celesti is sadistic.

Her people gunned down two of mine in the market, who knows how many more. If you've got a plan, I have soldiers."

Lyue opened her mouth to speak then closed it again. She would suspect a trap if not for the sheer insistence in his voice and countenance.

"I know what you're thinking." Karil stood upright. His muscles gleamed in the sunlamp in the corner of his tent. "My father lost himself to a bottle since he abandoned the Iskarions at Ilduan. Lost his honor, he says, would've rather died fighting. We owe Rurik this one. I'd rather skip the pleasantries and begging."

Lyue explained the details.

•   •   •

Sahira ducked into a stray wagon riddled with gunfire. The marketplace was eerily silent, most of its patrons in hiding. Most, except for constant Adirian patrols. A column of soldiers, a dozen or so, marched past without so much of a glance in her direction.

Despite the crackdown sparse pockets of people haunted the wide street. Subject to close inspection they suffered their indignity with obvious intention: alcohol. Little else existed to entertain the masses since the emergence of the Voidtear and even Celesti was not arrogant enough to forbid bread and circus. She left the safety of her temporary hideaway, her head low, forlorn, like the common breaker, back in her blacks.

She darted into the alehouse, assaulted immediately by stale beer and depression. Sahira choked back a violent rebuke of the sad scene. While packed to the brim no one spoke above a whisper. Groups congregated according to the sigils on their headbands, some engaging in intense, hushed conversations while a steady stream of mugs made their way to and from the bar. Sahira touched her band, the Lanatir brand replaced by Kalthier's.

Sahira procured a pint of hoppy Cavari beer–a hearty, thick breakfast–using the remains of the silver she conned from her last visit.

Her eyes darted from one table to the next as she sought the hotheads and malcontents, an assured faction of the exploited.

"What can we do?" A burly Cavari woman hissed nearby. "They've stopped paying us. No work, no pay. Can't even cash in on a death salary."

The group grumbled their agreement. Suicide forfeited your earnings back to your writ owner. Either you died on the job or you got nothing. Sahira eavesdropped a moment longer. None shared the same sigil here.

"You want out there?" An exasperated Xyran flashed a sunburst. "I was on a breaking when the tear formed. We were lucky, not many dead, but those that did?" His eyes hardened. "They got back up. Killed a few before we realized what happened. Took three sledges just to kill one! Worse than the blight!"

"My foreman told me a crew is responsible for all of it. Broke without a diviner's approval." A boy no older than sixteen added. His voice cracked.

"Bullshit." Sahira made her entrance. She set her mug on the table with an intentional harshness, spilling some beer. Their collective gaze poured over her. Not unusual, Sahira drew more than a few stares when she entered a room. "I heard from Kalthier himself that the Adirian bitch found somethin'. That's why she stopped the breaks, doesn't need us anymore."

Some of them grumbled over rotten luck. The Cavari woman leaned in, crossing stares with Sahira. She wore a sigil with a golden - H, the ends turned into one another with the central line capped with crosses. For the first time in two years Sahira regretted zoning out when Rurik went on about the barons.

"Who in the void are you?"

"Princess." Sahira raised her mug at her introduction. She took a swig. Warm, flat beer. Only the best for the workers. "Kalthier."

"Hoglet." The woman retorted. Sahira raised a brow. "Used to be fat. Haccord. You heard that? How?"

"Was cleanin' out his chamber, saw him meetin' with someone that looked important. Didn't say nothin' until I left. Stopped around the back of the tent to listen." Believable, the nobles used the breakers as servants while not out on a site.

"What'd she find?" Hoglet's interest drew in the others.

"Heard about the mess in the market? Foremen and a loremaster escaped in a portal. She knows how to open them now, so all this breakin' is pointless."

"No shit?"

"None."

The table collectively drank.

"What'll happen to us?" The boy said from behind his mug.

"Depends on the writ ya signed." Sahira shrugged. This bit she did listen to. "Barons knew this wouldn't last forever. Only payout death salaries if ya die on the job, but it's a service contract. They own us. Prisoners though, execute 'em or send them back to a dungeon."

"How you know all of this?" Hoglet snarked, skeptical.

"I can read."

A few at the table chuckled. Education of Cavari lowborn was abysmal. At least in Isha'Rhi they schooled their children.

"I'll level with you." Sahira looked about, feigning paranoia. "Kalthier is plannin' to attack the encampment. Take power himself. He promised any breaker that fights to tear up their writ."

That caught their attention. Some mumbled to each other. Hoglet tapped her fingers against the table.

"You're recruiting," Hoglet said.

"Betch'er ass I am. There's more of us then them. Think about it. If the soldiers kill themselves off? There won't be enough of 'em to stop us from taking what we want. We can burn our writs and get out of this cesspit with enough silver to start over. If we lose." She drank. A solid chug guzzled down most of the liquid. She didn't realize how much she missed beer, even the crap variety. "We're fucked anyway."

Hoglet mulled the proposition over. She nursed her mug, the others watching her lead.

"Kalthier is going to fight?"

"Mhm."

"Tell us more."

.   .   .

Rurik surveyed his handiwork. Little endured of the landing outside the forum garden. Piles of black debris, scorched stone and glass ran the length of the original hall. Destruction spread beyond the forum's entry, shrapnel launched from the chaos into nearby structures that erupted on contact. He spent the younger years of his life haunting those buildings. Meetings and delegations, special councils, official complaints, and other political nonsense. His last life. Fitting that he oversaw their end.

From here he caught his first glimpse of the runic ceiling. Memories did it little justice. Complex formulas wove themselves into a myriad of colors. They seemed random. Long strings of symbols woven over one another again and again, patternless, unless taken by layers. He imagined a section, fingers tapping against the back of a wrist. Funny, Rurik was left dominant in one life, right in the other, and now ambidextrous. Piece by piece he separated the strings, merging them onto differing flat planes. In his wildest dreams he never imagined such intricacy. An entire section existed only for projection, placing runes dictated by another layer onto specific materials. Another cast interference throughout the cavern. It kept the city a secret, safe from divination.

Who created these? Not him, none of the other Rune Knights. The Void? Emissaries did not use runes.

The tear hovered nearby. Little more than a jagged, pulsing line, it appeared as if someone cut the universe with a knife. Purple energy bled from the wound, dissipating the farther it emanated from the source. His helmet's augments identified it only as an anomaly. No shape, form, or any source of sense.

His vision swept from the gash in reality to the darkened horizon. There, within the shadows of ambient light, he saw the beacon, the single tower that rose above the rest, its crystalline peak buried in the world above. Could it be the source? The runes encircled it, spread from it. He could go alone. Open a gate nearby and do what he should have done a thousand years ago.

Could he? Trapping the Avatar took more than what he had. No. Lessons learned in this life and the last. He needed help.

"Focus, Rik." The name sounded familiar and foreign in the same breath. Iskarion fit his sensibilities better, accurate for the two of them.

Scrambling clatters of clumsy feet drew his attention below. The staircases to the landing collapsed, leaving only a few perches, one of which he occupied by half a railing. Ghouls collected en masse. Tortured visages of dead breakers and soldiers, some with armor fused to their flesh, others dragging broken limbs along after their jagged steps, but all with yellow eyes and purple, bulging veins over rotten flesh. Searching, hunting. They did not breathe, but they howled. Cries of pain, of dismay. Did they know what they were? They gathered below Rurik now, drawn to his movement. And because he threw stones at them. Too dumb to climb–or too clumsy–he watched them watch him. Waiting.

He recognized one. A Cavari man, thin. Half his jaw hung to his neck.

"That you, Slackjaw?" The ghoul groaned, incapable of the normal howls. It chittered, its tongue wagging from its open mouth. Rurik wished that made him queasy. Two lifetimes of horrors numbed his sensibilities.

"Sorry. It's my fault you died. Twice over." And now he planned the deaths of more innocent bystanders. How many this time? Dozens? Hundreds? Always at the mercy of his own self-importance. He slid his hand to the shaft of the Sunlance, feeling its hum, wanting to draw from him.

Rurik levitated another chunk of stone to his hand. He threw it at one of the ghouls, pinging it in the forehead. It screamed at him, a terrible, ferocious wail that echoed into the darkness.

"Calm down. You'll get your chance." He looked into the distance, mapping out the immediate proximity with data stored in his display's runic memory. About five hundred paces or so he found another gate.

"Foreman."

He turned to the lithe, melodic voice. Melody waited, her hands folded in front of her stomach. Fresh bandages graced her face and hands, a gift from Lyue on her return from Karil. "The others are asking for you."

"Of course." His usual warm gaze and smile did little behind the stoic faceplate of his helmet. Together, they walked through the garden to the open gateway.

Barons and merchants circled the garden's pool, most examining their surroundings with an acceptable degree of awe. Some wore guard uniforms, others donned breaker blacks, all disguised to belay suspicion. Not that Celesti wouldn't notice their absence of lords and ladies.

He recognized most of them. Karil led at the front, the only ducal heir of the bunch, with the barons pledged to his house and a collection of Lynesse nobles behind. Nothing from Salivar. Sarette organized a gaggle of merchants, some sick from the gate travel, though Sahira, Sweets, and Rust had yet to return. He frowned at that. The breakers gave them the necessary numbers to win.

"Sweet Sky Father." Karil's exclamation turned the attention of the nobles to Rurik's direction. The Kalthier lord stood shorter than him, but he never lacked for physicality. He wore the armor of his guardsmen. "Is that you, Iskarion? Oa mentioned a surprise."

Iskarion. That felt right.

"In the heavily armored flesh."

"Good to see you found your balls."

Oh. That stung.

"Close enough. Everyone here aware of the plan?"

"The concept. Not the details." Karil took the role of rebellion representative.

"Simple enough. Move quick, take the Adirian compound, get out of this forsaken voidscape."

"We can start with the Salivar loyalists. The Lynesse nobles not here will sit tight, they'd rather play neutral and side with whoever wins. We've enough to do that simply, but if the Adirians have time to form up. Well. They outnumber us by themselves," Karil said.

"The breakers will make up the difference."

"Unless they catch on and make the same offer. Adirian barons are sycophants, not morons."

"We've got another option." Rurik lifted the Sunlance. Karil eyed him, weary.

"That part of your surprise?"

"I won't use it unless I have to. Too much energy will make the Voidtear larger. Last thing we need are more ghouls."

"Ghouls? Litany ghouls?"

"You got it."

"This place grows on you." Karil spat. What a charmer.

Excerpt from Gilderan's Casting Analysis of Thalas

S UNSINGERS ARE A BIT of an anomaly. Somewhere between a sorcerer and a magus, they implement foci and are somehow able to replace gestures with incantations via recitations of liturgical works and precise tonal manipulations. Mainly, song. No loremaster or magus has been able to replicate these effects to any success, but I believe the secret lies within the particular foci these priests employ.

Of interest, they have managed to focus their expertise on the precise control of fire and light, able to create impressive, subtle, or if necessary, immense destruction. Thematic, to be sure. This is not to mention their unique ability to heal the body. Neither magus nor sorcerer has such a skill in their lexicon.

Chapter 24
A Miracle or Two

THIS HAS TO BE the way." Lesandre kicked the chest-high column at the end of the hall. Aril watched him struggle with a satisfied smirk while Zevra mumbled a prayer. Meanwhile, Luc made himself useless. He leaned against the nonsensical railings fashioned around the platform, arms crossed. Every few minutes the blue lines pulsed. That meant nothing to him, but nothing good ever came from erratic glowing lights.

"Am I the only one looking here?"

"Yes," Airil spoke, eager. "You're the loremaster."

"Mayhap our new friend could assist me?"

"Me?" Luc blinked. "My name's Luc."

"Yes. You cracked the code. You have no other ideas?"

"Oh. No. Sorry. You're the loremaster." He parroted, unaware of the implicit insult.

"Just what I need. More snark." Lesandre scoffed and tapped the side of his lenses, cursed, then argued with himself. Luc watched with interest. Since his departure from Aenia he encountered a number of unstable individuals, most of them in Iskvar. He vowed to never leave the wetlands again.

Another pulse. Lesandre decided. He opened the tome at his side to reveal a thin, black slate. Airil's expression darkened.

"What is that?"

"It's a Thalian Dataslate. Translated, of course, by the High Loremaster. He entrusted it to me along with the task of unearthing this facility."

"This whole time you came here looking for this?" Airil gripped her sword, her shoulders tense.

"Yes. It's why I recommend the explosives beneath the barracks, and why I was quick to be rid of Arkalis. Her freedom was a fortunate byproduct of my aims. I care not for my father's political interests and I'd rather Aklesia not add more power to their already overreaching shadow. Now you know everything. So either wave that sword around or skip the drama. I've not the patience."

Zevra ceased her prayers as Airil considered her options. For the briefest moment Luc wished for the sword. He frowned when she lowered her hand.

"Fantastic. Now if you could help?" The glass screen of the slate lit up. A circular symbol with a vertical slash in the center appeared as the very same image projected itself from the column.

"I think that goes there," Luc said. How helpful.

Lesandre rolled his eyes, but otherwise kept silent. The lord dropped the fake book and laid the slate atop the column where it snapped into place. More symbols appeared. They hovered for a moment then translated themselves into Cavari. Select level? Lesandre pursed his lips together and motioned toward one of the options.

"No!" Luc lashed out and slapped the hand away. "Not that one." He panted, eyes wide. His senses screamed at him.

"And, pray tell, why not?"

"Just. Please. Trust me. We need to go there." He pointed to the last selection. "Cracked the code, right?"

Airil and Zevra exchanged worried glances.

"As good as any, I suppose." Lesandre pressed his finger against the slate. The floor beneath them hissed. The platform rumbled, and all four of them sought the rail. Not so nonsensical. A loud whine screeched from beneath and the platform descended into the floor.

Their descent rid them of any sense of depth. The lift passed four halls, all arrayed as the sterile entry. Luc studied the apparatus that allowed such lateral movement. A single hitch attached to the wall ran along another strip of blue light that pulsed when they reached a new level.

Their destination opened into a wide chasm of a room. Surrounded by metal on all sides it sang with a dull buzz, multiple strips of light arcing out from the floor to the walls. They stemmed from a rectangular box embedded into the floor, its surface covered in runes, blue and red and yellow, all interwoven with lines of sickly, purple cracks. They pulsed, accompanied by a hollow thrum at every interval.

The lift secured itself with another hiss. Lesandre removed his slate from the column and aggressively tapped his lenses, his eyes darting about the room. Zevra's prayers grew more intense as she and Airil followed the lord. Luc looked up to the far-too distant retreat.

He came off last, giving a wide berth to the sickly runes. If it looked bad, it was bad. A motto to live by. While the others stayed close Luc skirted the perimeter. He hopped over one of the blue strips and stumbled through the ambient lighting, his fingers gliding along the wall, taking a strange comfort in the cold steel.

Another hiss startled him. He screeched and jumped. This was it. The end. He waited, anxious, for nothing to happen. He popped an eye open to an opening in the wall. A black stone archway preceded a simple office shaped like a hexagon with a mahogany desk in the middle, flanked on all sides by bookcases embedded into the walls. Huh. Luc ducked inside, shrugged, and went to pilfer a random book. Nope, not that one. Left. His hand wavered, more left. There. He slipped a red cover out and spied the gold lettering on the front. Words? Most definitely. Language? No clue. Luc dropped it into his bag and slung it over his shoulder.

The exit nagged at him. A blackened arch alight with blue runes stood in front of the sliding metal hatch. His senses nagged at him as a combination appeared in his mind.

"Hah! Got it!" Lesandre's voice reached his ears.

Luc popped his head out of the room. The dread returned with greater intensity. One word came to him. Bad. Quickly, he jogged from the room to the source. Lesandre waited on the far side of the rectangle, his slate connected to another one of those columns. Closer now, the structure soared a dozen paces above him.

"Don't mess with thaaaat!" Luc warned.

"I agree," Airil echoed. Zevra stayed close to the baron, one hand over her amulet, chanting.

"Please. How old is this place? If there is something here, it's been dead so long there aren't even bones left. You're all so paranoid. This sort of discovery will catapult our civilization centuries into the future. Can you imagine? Technology that will rival Dula'Thalier in its prime. All you need is a sense of adventure. Ah. See? If I had to guess, these are commands to the facility and!"

Luc felt a searing pain rip through the back of his skull.

"No! Don't!"

Lesandre tapped the slate.

The rectangular construct shuddered. High pitched whirring preceded a loud grinding as the top of the box hissed. Red lettering appeared on the slate.

CAUTION, VOIDTEAR OPEN. FAILSAFES ACTIVE.

The color drained from Luc's face. He ran for the lift, forgoing his accomplices, only to watch as the platform ascended on its own. Electricity arched from the runes. It made the hairs on his neck stand up and sent an aching chill down his spine. Luc whipped around in time to see the two halves of the seal atop the structure pull apart.

Solid, black energy erupted from the opening, washing over the room and knocking Luc off his feet. Glass shattered in his pack. Time to run. Luc rolled up from the floor and scanned the chamber for an exit. A red rune appeared over the now visible outline of multiple doors embedded into the walls, one already open. Exits? His sense pulled him. The arch.

Airil and Zevra caught on. They ran with him from the other side of the structure, the baron's sword unsheathed and the sunpriest's amulet aglow with a blazing white light. He caught a glimpse of Lesandre, his countenance grim, hurriedly swiping commands on his slate.

"Go for the arch it'll—what is that?!"

Purple tendrils of cracked, scaled flesh burst from the opened seal. Six of them threw themselves into the room, shaking the ground on impact: thick appendages that fused to the metal. With their appearance the runes around the box flashed, exploding in a black flame that erased their inscriptions. The foundation quaked, followed by dull roars below the surface.

Then came silence.

The lights flickered. Zevra's amulet illuminated a small section, shedding pure, white warmth that brought a small sense of peace. Luc inched closer to her.

"I think I stopped it. It's a power sink! It draws from something below it. In this case a, ah—a Voidtear." Lesandre sounded unsure. "Something activated a failsafe. It stopped." He paused, his eyes widening as he read the screen. "It sto–oh."

Guttural clicking leaked through the opening. Since his venture began Luc never felt true, unavoidable danger, yet now something primal screamed from within his mind. Run. Go. Flee. His fear latched him in place, every muscle in his body locked.

It came from the blackness. A too-long, pale body floated upward, leathery skin pinched to its thick muscles. Exposed bone jutted out from his elbows and shoulders, sharpened to a point. It wore no clothes, but neither did it possess any discernible sex. The bottom half of its face opened with more teeth than flesh, no nose, and two thin slits for eyes that held only a deep blackness. Hairless, a bone protrusion sloped up from its skull and angled like a cowl down its neck.

It hovered in the air for a time. No one moved until Lesandre disconnected his slate from the column and slipped to the other side.

The slightest click spun the creature around, its head twisting toward the sound. Luc grimaced. It had no ears.

Peculiar.

The voice whispered in Luc's mind. Sweet, beautiful, and hideous, it contained hints of light feminine and masculine tones at the same time. By the confused searching from the others he figured his madness spread.

I expected another. I suppose it does not matter. You've freed me, yet by your expressions I think not intentionally. Where is the knight?

Knight?

I see. Much time has passed.

Luc cringed. No one spoke, not that he heard. Then again, this thing did speak directly into their minds. Did it read them too? No matter, time to go. Luc made a break for the door.

Sorry, no.

Luc slammed into a wall of energy. He planted flat against it with a painful crunch. The creature lowered, clawed feet clicking against the metal floor. It moved with a cumbersome weight, twice as tall as Luc. Elegant, deliberate. Terrifying.

I appreciate your unwitting assistance, but I am quite famished.

Oh. Oh no. Luc fell to his backside. He dug inside of his pack, his hand shaking as he felt for vials. Ruined. All of it. His senses told him to wait. Wait?! The creature paused above him.

How delightful. You possess sight, but do you not know how to use it?

It reached for Luc's head with four fingers, long and slender, covered in more bone. Red flame appeared from under it. From nowhere, the fire seared into the creature, eliciting a chuckle. Wet, deep, and monstrous, its breathy laugh did not fit the voice. More fire spread from the barrage, creating a ring around the beast that surged from the ground.

Zevra stood nearby with an arm out, the other clutched to her amulet, her voice low as she chanted, eyes locked onto the creature with desperate focus. The chanting grew in intensity, her fingers curling inward. Sweat poured from her brow as the fire roared. Luc crawled away, the heat flushing his face red.

Your source is above ground.

The creature stepped out of the blaze, unharmed.

And your soul is too weak to harm me.

Zevra gasped and released her amulet. The white light flickered out, leaving them in pale ambience. Quick footfalls preceded Airil as she charged the monster. Her blade swung up from her side, the edge clashing against the creature's bone plated thigh. The sword sparked. Airil withdrew her strike then assaulted it again. More sparks. The steel dulled as it hit, resulting in a terrified grunt from the baron. It grabbed the blade.

What is this? Imperfect steel?

It snapped the sword in two.

So far you've fallen. How convenient.

The beast wrapped its hand around Airil's neck. Zevra screamed. Luc bolted to his feet, his eyes wide, but his senses guided him. Run, they urged. Run. He did. Luc ran to Zevra's side and urged her on.

"Come on!" She resisted, her eyes following the baron as the creature lifted her into the air. She fought, grunting, kicking, she stabbed the shattered blade into its arm again and again. Its exposed teeth curled into a snarling grin, extending too close to its eyes. "We need to go!"

Zevra gave in. Luc dragged her along. A wet snap trailed their escape and Airil's protests ceased. They ran. Closer now. No sight of the fool of a lord, but Luc considered that a positive. Best he reaps the rewards of his actions. They neared the open door, his sense pulling him toward the arch. Why? Was it a weapon? Something sailed over his head. He jammed his leg into the floor and stopped as Airil's body splattered against the wall in front of them, blood spraying over the grey metal. Zevra screamed, fraught with tears, staring at the mangled, broken body of the baron.

Please. I am ravenous, do not prolong-oh? What is this?

A metallic whine screeched from above. The lift soared down its track, the blue energy that guided it sparking as the platform descended faster. Lesandre stood at the base of the lift, his fingers flying over the slate. The bastard used them as bait.

．　　．　　．

Lesandre held his breath. The creature–no, he knew what it was. An Emissary. That's what the Thalians called them. The stuff of legends and religious nightmares. That solved one point of curiosity. Thalian technology worked from solar energy, absorption and distribution. Iskvar, the true Iskvar, stole its power from the Void itself. Dangerous, but brilliant.

Peculiar.

It spoke into his mind. Not only, he figured, otherwise why not address them with its mouth? It had one.

I expected another. I suppose it does not matter. You've freed me, yet by your expressions I think not intentionally. Where is the knight?

She's dead, a thousand years in the past. Lesandre addressed it in his own mind.

I see. Much time has passed.

Ah. Direct communication. Yet it did not respond to his thoughts. Did he need to address it? He had precious little time for theory. Lesandre pushed his back up against the structure and crept along the side, his fingers tapping against his slate. He pulled up a few commands, projecting a map of Iskvar, new and ancient, on the screen. With the door opened signals could pass. He heard frantic footsteps.

Sorry, no.

Shit. Lesandre froze. It knew his thoughts without his aid. He tensed, set in his heels, and prepared to run. A solid thud came from the other side followed by a clicking. From the clawed feet? One of the others drew its attention. Hah. The clicks moved away from the structure and Lesandre continued to the lift. He pressed his finger against the map, on the single emanation of red light.

I appreciate your unwitting assistance, but I am quite famished.

He grimaced. It wanted to eat them? The clicking ceased. Someone would die. Lesandre tapped furiously, imputing symbols. They were close. He depressed the red light once again.

That is interesting. You possess sight, but do you not know how to use it?

Sight? Not him, obviously, but who? The wetlander? Something off about that man. Better him than Airil or Zevra, despite their distrust of Lesandre he respected them. Maybe even liked them. Light and heat blazed from the other side. Fire? Zevra. Admirable folly. Lesandre pushed free of his hiding spot and ran to the base of the lift. He examined the power readings with his lenses. He activated them on minimal interference now, unable to process the constant slew of data from the terrifyingly brilliant auras of the Emissary.

Les placed the slate in the secondary column. It merged with the facility's systems displaying an interface for the lift controls. Now for some luck.

Your source is above ground.

Come on. Sweat dripped down his forehead.

And your soul is too weak to harm me.

More taps. He opened a second display on the lift. The facility drew residual power from the Voidtear, giving him limited access to other systems. He redirected what he could to the lift. The fire died, replaced by the sound of heavy boots. Airil. He winced. She wouldn't stand a chance. Two rings echoed across the room.

What is this? Imperfect steel?

Something cracked.

Not very intelligent, are you?

Damn. Damn damn damn. Lesandre watched the slate. Zevra's screams filled his ears. Finally, an alert pulsed in the upper corner. He tapped it.

We are here.

Lesandre activated the lift. He held his breath. More footfalls. The others ran. Someone ceased struggling and by the sound of the grunts he knew it was Airil. Brave woman. Stupid woman. The baron's body clattered against a wall, dropping in front of Luc and Zevra. The beast flared its shoulders out, stretching.

Please. I am ravenous, do not prolong–oh? What is this?

A metallic whine screeched from above. The lift soared down its track, the blue energy that guided it sparking as it descended. Lesandre met Luc's stare, his eyes hard, angry. He moved aside as the platform landed.

"Your miracle, my lord."

The pontifex stepped off the lift.

•   •   •

Aluntir placed a hand on Lesandre's shoulder. The poor boy shook, his fear palpable. "Go, Lesandre. Gather the others and run."

The lordling bowed his head. He retrieved his slate from a column and skirted off to the far side of the room. Smart. Aluntir shifted his thoughts to the abomination. It watched him, its rows of heinous teeth curled into an amused smile. The paladins spread out. Two to each side, they withdrew their blades. Aluntir lifted a hand, turned it upward, then closed it into a fist. The swords took on a white aura, shining with all the glory of the sun. Aluntir winced. No light here. His spells stole their power from his own soul.

Now THIS is exhilarating. Who are you?

"Silence, demon," Aluntir growled in response. It spoke into his mind. All of their minds, but he only perceived one occurrence of the speech. Did it block his sight? No. It possessed the same ability. Every reality countered the other. Random chance then.

The beast chortled. Its physical voice the stuff of nightmares. One of his paladins faltered, but the others kept his morale from breaking.

So be it. Your civilization has forgotten even its manners.

"Ignore its taunts. Work together. You've yet to face a foe such as this."

You have no idea, little creature.

The paladins charged. They spread out, giving one another enough room to maneuver, straying from the range of their blades and forcing their opponent to track more than one set of strikes at a time. Aluntir walked after them. He wove a hand in a small circle and formed a series of quick gestures, channeling energy to his arm. Powerful spells took time. From the corner of his vision he caught Lesandre meet up with Zevra and the odd fellow from the cell. Aluntir smiled, knowingly.

Something crunched. The creature held the head of a paladin in its hand, the helmet crushed as blood seeped out of it. The other three struck. One found his blade caught by the spawn's hand mid-swing. An uncontested blow cracked the creature's thigh plate as another broke its shoulder open.

It roared and kicked at an offender, sending the paladin flying, his back breaking against the rectangular housing with a dry crack. It swiped next, taloned fingers ripping off the breastplate of another. She groaned and withdrew, ignoring the bloody marks. Another strike, the paladin behind it scored a second wound in the beast's armor. It faced the aggressor, arm raised, exposing its back to the pontifex.

Aluntir lashed out. Projections appeared around his extended limb, three circles made up of runes, one at his wrist, elbow, and upper arm. He dug his heels in and sped off toward the fight. A paladin fended off a wild attack, putting her blade between herself and a terribly large fist. It saved her life, only to break the weapon in halves, the glow dissipating. The creature raised his arms for a following assault only to falter as the plateless paladin returned to the fray. The damage widened.

Annoying gnats!

Aluntir swept his palm outward. A gravity rune appeared on the ground and propelled him into the air above the spawn. He repeated the process, creating a second rune around his body, his momentum shifted, directed at the creature. The runic ring from his wrist expanded outward, sinking into the cracked shoulder plate as he reached it.

Aluntir landed, one hand on the ground, his knees bent as an explosion rippled through the demon's body, blasting its arm off at the joint.

Flesh fell with a heavy thud. The creature roared, more frustrated than pained. No blood dripped from the wound. Odd, spawn always bled.

Enough of this!

A black pulse of energy erupted in a flash from its body. Aluntir placed his arm out, the second ring moving to his wrist and expanding into a shield. The force pushed him back as purple veins appeared over his defense. Aluntir groaned. He twisted his torso, spinning, twirling his arm and launching the disk back at the demon. It embedded itself into its torso, tearing through its boneplate.

Another paladin lay on the ground, her body limp, sickly, purple veins infesting her armor and flesh beneath. Another gripped her sword as a shield, its glow dissipating from taking the brunt of the black energy.

Three dead. Aluntir cried out. "Go! You can no longer help me."

The paladin faced him, panting, her clawed chest heaving, bleeding. "Go."

Yes, go gnat. I'll be with you soon.

Aluntir nodded to the others as they gathered in the open doorway. The wetlander slapped the black archway, grinning wildly as a black portal emerged from nothing. A webway gate? The paladin saluted Aluntir then took off a dead sprint to the arch. Good. No more distractions.

"I've read stories of your ilk," Aluntir said, giving himself some time to breathe. This beast enjoyed talking. Might as well let it. "They mentioned strength but never how ugly you were."

The beast chortled again. What an awful sound.

I am impressed, little human. Your civilization has not lost all its strengths.

"Spare me your judgement. You are but another test, a vile spawn to be stamped out in the glory of the Sky Father."

Sky Father now? Your obsession with gender is unevolved. Your precious star cares not for you. It doesn't even care for itself.

"Enough of you! Be silent and die."

The creature leapt. Its raw strength sent it high into the air at Aluntir. He projected another gravity rune that sent him aside as the spawn landed with a crash, creating an indent in the metal floor. Aluntir bounced back and ran up to the creature's side. He grabbed the open center of the disk and ripped it out of the body and slipped it around in time to catch a violent blow. Aluntir buckled under the weight. The spawn pushed, barely straining, as the pontifex put all his strength into resisting. He dropped to a knee.

He twisted his wrist. A rune appeared between them, aimed upward. The creature tilted its head as a blast of energy sent it careening to the ground. Straightening, Aluntir raised the disc and shoved it into a gaping wound, slicing the beast in half at the torso.

It died, laughing into its last breath.

Aluntir groaned. His bones ached, his ribs burned. Gravity runes wreaked havoc on the body. He allowed the disc to dissipate. He sat, breathed, and stared at the gross corpse. No blood. He thanked the Sunlord and mused on his fate, his eyes cast to the corpses of his greatest allies. His friends.

Ready for a second round?

What?

One of the tendrils rose from the floor. It encircled the top half of the creature. A piece separated from the base as its body absorbed the scaly flesh, the matter sinking in, molding, shifting, taking shape as it emerged from the lower torso, forming a pelvis and legs. The demon rose, its wounds gone, showing no sign of impediment. Grinning, always grinning. It laughed.

Aluntir grimaced. The spawn he hunted over the years were symptoms, leeches, drawing power from a tear or from some left-over heretical technology. The creature was no different. A puppet controlled by something greater. The voice came from the roots, the corrupt mass that snaked out from the darkness. He could fell this beast a thousand times and it would always rise. Unsteady, he brought himself to his feet.

Fine. He ran at the monster. It snarled, flared its arms out and hunched over, issuing a violent challenge. One final strike. Or not. Aluntir projected a rune beneath himself, angled toward the open structure. It fired him away from the spawn. He landed on the edge, the beast screaming, hot on his path. Aluntir placed his hand over his heart. The runic circle sunk into his body. He channeled, focusing, but made no gesture, imagined no runes. He felt heat well up in his chest. Not much time to dwell on his life. No time to feel sad, to consider his choices, his regrets.

Aluntir signed a sunburst, his palm placed in front of his face, fingers spread wide, and jumped. His eyes burned white as he descended into the darkness, as a raw, explosive power built within him. In his final moments he faced the maw. No tear, no portal to another realm, only a colossal mass of flesh and bone in a cavern leagues below the surface, centuries of corruption that dug into the very foundations of the world. Sweet Father. No demon he faced possessed such power. His actions here would do no good. Another, then. His death could be of use.

The pontifex ripped off his mask. He siphoned the energy into another trick, forming the image of complex calculations in his mind. It would lessen the damage, but this was more important. In a flash the mask disappeared. With luck, the right one would find it.

Aluntir's last miracle before his body turned to dust in a blast of light and power.

Personal Log, 3.11.0273 C.E.

T HIS ONE IS FUN. By creating a ring of shielding runes in a perfect circle on a metal surface you can use any heat absorption to power the shield. Conservatively, anyway. It won't be enough to stop, say, any kind of casting, but a single person? Their own body heat would generate power. I'll take this one to the college before I make it public. It's neat, but someone is bound to exploit it.

Chapter 25
That's Nice, dear

I VOTE TO PRESERVE."

Kali beat her head against her magic cage. She felt the pressure, but no pain. A blue aura appeared where she hit the wall. It flashed at her. Taunted her.

"I vote to shove my fist down your throat," she snarked to no one. Despite the presence of similarly runed circles none of the other cells boasted occupancy. Only her, in the open, sterile dungeon. Smooth black stone filled the interior: walls, floor, and ceiling. No windows, one door, and that stupid archway. Three score of the enchanted prisons ran the gamut of the floorspace, long enough to lay and tall enough to stand. Little else. They didn't even give her a pot. Not that she needed it. Wyr did something to her. A simple touch and she felt full and hydrated without the need to use the privy.

That made things worse. Of all her trials the lack of wine pained her the most.

Kali entertained herself by walking in circles for a while. When she grew bored of that she exercised. Once that lost its luster she kicked at the magic aura. It flashed at her. Fun. She beat her head against it, holding it steady against the static if just to feel some contact. Her clothes smelled. Her new clothes, if they qualified as such. Bandages over her breasts and pelvis, for decency's sake. Ymastu complained at first, arguing clothing interfered with her observations. Wyr provided what he could in spite of the protest. Politeness extended to modesty.

Ymastu. The name burned in her mind. Surly, old bitch. She poked, prodded, and violated Kali with an arsenal of pointy and prodding tools. Some devices stung more than others. They dove below the surface somehow, despite never touching her. Technology of ruin, similar tools responsible for the foundations of the Desolation.

The door slid open. Slid. Not swung or pulled, it slid, opening from the center, separating, and disappearing into the wall. Kali spat. Only one person used that door.

Ymastu strolled to her cage. Long and thin like the rest of the Magi, this one moved with a sense of frailty. Her voice rattled when she spoke, rasping, always hoarse and impatient behind that skull mask. She imagined the magus to be particularly ugly. Wrinkled, sagging skin, uneven eyes, a cleft lip. The degradation of character eased the nausea at the mage's approach.

"How are you feeling, Arkalis?"

"Fuck you."

"That's nice, dear."

Ymatsu responded the same way: "That's nice, dear", no matter what she said. Despite her single-minded hatred of the vaguely old woman Kali relished the encounters. With no way to pass the time Kali fell out of touch, sleeping irregularly, unable to even count meals. How long had she been here? She clung to the one occurrence that brought her out of the present into the future.

That's nice, dear.

"I'm going to deactivate the cage. Will you be a good girl?"

Kali dug her freshly clipped nails into her arms.

"Yes." She uttered the word with clenched teeth, her anger flourishing.

Sweet Arkalis.

The swell of anger drained from her cheeks. A magnetic thrum died as the mage released Kali from her cell, unaware of the sudden shift of emotion.

How much longer will you endure this? You need only take what you already possess.

That static returned. Deafening, horrible static. Kali knew of what she spoke. A thread in the back of her mind, it begged her to tug on it, to release it. An image of Niati's cabin flashed in her mind. The heat, the power.

"Arkalis, come."

The shriveled hag's voice silenced the static.

"I'm cold," Arkalis said, the lack of the field allowing the dry chill of the dungeon to assault her senses.

Ymatsu laughed. Or tried to, anyway, it came out as a series of snorts, something like the chuckle of a dying pig.

"That's nice, dear."

•   •   •

Kali bit down on a wooden file. Ymatsu shoved it into her mouth during their second session. It made her drool, but better than biting her tongue again. She lay flat on her back, arms and legs secured to a clinically cold table made from metal. A system akin to her cell bound her wrists and ankles, a coherent red aura, impossible to wiggle from, though not for her lack of effort. The same gray material made up the composite of the chamber. A domed sunlamp hung from the ceiling, its directed light bathing Kali in an uncomfortable blindness.

Ymatsu operated a chest-high column embedded into the floor. She attached a thin slate to its angled stand and began a series of "hms" followed by long pauses. Tools lined the counters built into the walls, instruments of all shapes and sizes: a jagged knife, a thin set of tongs, a curved wire with a hook on the end. All steel. Every time the same thing. She *hrmed*, she awed, then after a few minutes of channeling a circus crowd she approached the table and started the prodding. Today was no different.

The shadow of the mage blotted out a part of the light. Despite her rage, her fight, her hatred, Kali's countenance grew fearful. Once again a prisoner. Once more at another's mercy. The static returned.

No.

Kali pushed it away. She could lose her freedom but she would not lose herself. Out of her own will? Aboard the *Hepsu* she contemplated taking her life. That was her choice. Her decision. So, she resisted. Out of spite.

"You're fascinating, dear."

Kali glared at the dark outline of the magus. If she spoke Ymatsu would not put the file back in her mouth. Last time proved too painful.

"You're able to resist my instruments. It's wonderful! I've waited so long for a subject like you, you know? I could kiss you."

She swallowed the bile that rose in her throat. Please don't, Kali willed. It worked. Ymatsu pinched her cheek instead.

"Let's get started!"

Kali squirmed away from the cold, sterile metal against her skin. She closed her eyes and bit, her teeth near breaking the file in half.

• • •

Sleep came in fitful, restless spurts. More often than not Kali woke to the pressure of her fist against the cage, or a toe bent from an involuntary flail. She did not remember her dreams, yet she knew them to be nightmares. Often, she woke to the static, the high-pitched wail revealing the thread, begging her to grasp it. She resisted. Again. And again.

Same dungeon, same life. Time progressed without her. Did it? She lived only in the present with blissful, sweet trips into the past.

"Go to Haven, huh Nihilus?!" She yelled into the emptiness, a new habit she adopted to keep herself stable. "What a brilliant plan. You'll be safe in Haven, Kali! You're nobility. No one cares! Add that to your lessons, Din!" She kicked the cage. It retorted, flashing. "No one gives a shit about blood." Did she? Not anymore.

The irony of her success fed her anger. She made it to safety, only to find demons lying in wait. What was her purpose? Was there such a thing? Nihilus knew, Niati knew, the Magi, the leech in her mind. All of them held some divine knowledge beyond her scope.

Another punch. Another flash. Kali screamed. She rested her forehead against the cage, listening to the sound of her own breath.

The door slid open.

Ymatsu appeared from the hall.

•   •   •

Another session. Fresh bandages lay on the counter beside the obsidian blade Ymatsu occasionally directed her instruments at. Lately, the magus placed it on Kali's stomach while she enacted her experiments. It provided clearer results. It also made the voices more difficult to fight.

How long must you endure, Arkalis? Have you not suffered enough? Give in. Let it end.

Kali envisioned something she saw at a brothel once and projected it at the voice in her head. It disappeared. Victory.

"Lay down, dear."

Kali winced. The table loomed in the center of the chamber.

•   •   •

The cage glimmered. Kali rested her cheek against the red aura, arms and legs curled up in a human ball. Small cuts ran the length of her body. They itched. Ymatsu warned her not to scratch. She scratched. Nearby, the hiss of the opening door soured her mood.

•   •   •

She stared into the light now. It comforted her. Without the shadow it meant no pain. Her eyes glazed over, staring. Thoughtless. All she heard was static. It hummed and she did not cast it aside. For a moment, the briefest moment, she considered accepting the offer.

•   •   •

Kali lay in her cell, arms and legs splayed out, her chest lifting in lifeless, patterned breathing. She no longer walked in circles. All she did was listen. To the silence, to the crackle in her mind. The sound lulled her to sleep. It greeted her in the morning. It punctuated her conversations. She concentrated on it when Ymatsu experimented on her. It soothed her, reminded her that something else existed beyond the tower, beyond the dungeon.

Why not give in?

Why not? What awaits you in this life? More suffering, more pain. You can be so much more. You can have so much more.

Tempting. The voice railed against her mind. It intruded now, coming as it desired instead of by her trigger. Could she give in? Power waited there, she knew. She remembered the cabin. The sudden influx of possibility.

Take your life back, Arkalis. Be free of these chains.

Kali sniffed. She rubbed her eyes, stretching her fingers over her cheeks. She dug them into her skin. Why not? At least then she could get some wine. Kali rolled over, pushed, and ascended, standing straight. Her joints cracked down from her shoulder to her arms as she stretched. Time to move on.

Or.

A rune appeared atop the stupid archway. What? She scrambled over to the side of her cell and pressed her face and arms and torso against it, looking at the only new thing to happen in weeks. Days? The symbol glowed with a blue light. Soft, different. It hung and did nothing. Fascinated, she could watch it for hours. If just to do something.

An inky blackness sprang to life from the arch. It reminded her of the portal Wyr opened in the harbor. Another magus? No. No no. One hurt enough, two would surely end it. The thread. The static guided her.

"Close it! Close it!"

Luc stumbled out of the gate screaming.

"Close it!"

Next came Zevra, her cheeks wet with tears, a splatter of fresh blood staining her white kaftan. She covered her mouth with her hands, muffling her cries. Lesandre followed. They collided and Luc caught the priest while the lord frantically scanned a device similar to Ymatsu's.

"Close it!" The wetlander howled.

Kali watched, dumbfounded, her mouth halfway agape. She lost it. Her sanity abandoned her for sweeter pastures.

"I don't know how! Shut up!"

"Closeitcloseitcloseit!"

"I. Don't. Know. How!"

The portal shuttered. An armored woman bereft her breastplate ran through, knocking into the others and sending them careening to the ground. Three wicked claw marks bled from her chest. She surveyed the area then spun and sunk the edge of her great blade into the top of the arch, slicing into the rune. The portal died, wafting into nothing.

"Oh thank Vari. Thank the Sunlord. Thank everyone." Luc rolled onto his back and exhaled. He panted, then laughed, then stopped. He laughed again. And Kali thought she had problems.

"Don't thank anyone yet." Lesandre stared at his slate. "Wherever we are the readings are intense."

"And where," the voice of the paladin matched her muscled form. Full, deep, and commanding, she spoke with an accent that enunciated one vowel clearly, struggling to connect to a second while hitting consonants with her tongue higher and further back in her mouth. "Would that be?"

"Haven," Kali raised her voice.

All four startled. They turned to her.

"Blessed Sky Father." Zevra shuffled up to her feet. "Arkalis?"

"Hey." She waved, not convinced what she saw was real.

"How did we?" Lesandre examined the chamber now that the portal sealed itself. He wearily eyed the wetlander at his feet then brushed by Zevra who trailed him over to her runic cage. The paladin retrieved her sword from the stone, distracted. Luc stared at Kali.

"How did you know where I was and open a door from thin air? Funny, I had the same question." Voices. Words. No condescending dear, no prodding. Kali decided sanity was overrated.

"It's a webway gate. We managed to open it in Iskvar. The real Iskvar, that is."

"There's a fake Iskvar?"

"Not fake, per se, newer?"

"There is a godforsaken voidpit with a real, living, demon Iskvar!" Luc hopped up. "And you!" He pointed a finger at Kali. Rude. "You brought me into this! All this!"

"I'm sorry am I supposed to know you?"

"Know me?! I. You. I." Luc's face flushed. He dug a heel into the stone, flustered, exhaling. "I guess not!"

"Okay. What's this about a demon?"

"Beneath the foundations." Zevra spoke, depressed. She wiped the wetness from her face. "The explosion of your escape. It unearthed an ancient structure of Thalian design. Within we." She paused, her eyes narrowing as she looked at Lesandre. "We. Unleashed a monster of the Void."

"That explains the blood."

"You're taking this all very plainly." Lesandre ignored the accusatory glance.

"Les, I'm locked inside a magic cage wearing bandages talking to people who I'm not sure aren't figments of my imagination. Do I look like I haven't seen some shit?"

"Ah, well then."

"Well then. How about we play catch up later and you figure out a way to get me out of here."

"I don't recognize this technology." Lesandre adjusted his frames. "It could be extremely difficult to puz–oh." He lifted his slate and tapped the glass exterior. "Huh. This is more advanced than I thought, I can connect to it remotely." Kali punched the cage. Lesandre flinched.

"Don't care, do something."

An atmospheric thrum accompanied the cage's deactivation. Kali stuck her hand out. No flash. Nothing. Carefully, she stuck her foot outside the runic circle. Nothing stopped her. Hah! She jumped out from the runes, embracing the chill, the cold on the bottoms of her feet more than a dreadful march to her torture chamber. Kali laughed. An awful, repressed madness filled out her tone. The others shied away until she hugged Zevra, embracing the much smaller, thinner woman. She smelled of metals, like a mixture of iron and sweat.

"You're real." Kali's shoulders slouched with relief. "Don't ask. We all have a lot to drink about, but we need to get out of here before she comes."

"She?" Lesandre asked.

"Tower of the Magi remember? Happens to have Magi in it."

The door slid open.

•   •   •

No one reacted. Rather, none of them could react. When the white clad magus entered the dungeon, she raised a hand into the air, the simple motion enough to freeze any movement. All of them, except Luc.

Don't move, his senses warned. He listened. Luc stiffened, finding a new appreciation for his baggy coat and brimmed hat. He puzzled out the room. The paladin found her way to a corner near the door. She stilled with her hands on her blade, the weapon poised to strike. Ymatsu appraised the new arrivals with a prolonged "hrm." More unbearable power. Luc almost screamed. He kept his lips shut, sure that the slightest gesture would end in his demise. To survive a creature of the Void only to end as a mage's inconvenience. He lived a charmed life.

"Playing around in Thalian ruins were we?"

Ymatsu picked Lesandre's slate from his hands.

"How intrepid. Rescuing a damsel. That's nice, dear." The magus ran a long, thin finger over Arkalis' cheek. Luc swore he saw her move the slightest inch. Ymatsu paced, taking her time to inspect the motley collection of intruders. She tossed the slate into the air where it hovered in her periphery, scanning its contents while moving. Her palm grazed the top of Zevra's head.

"A sunpriest? You lot make life difficult, you know. I've special experiments reserved for one of you. How fortunate for you to arrive in my little home."

Careful. Luc knew he was next. She wanted to touch them. Cast something? He knew he should've studied magic instead of alchemy. What to do? Distract her. With what, a joke? His sense urged him, it begged him. Save Arkalis. Luc's eyebrow twitched. Save her? Every fiber of his being desired to help her despite the risk. Everything guided him here. Here, to help this woman.

"Oh, a Mercenian? We don't get many of those." She glimpsed beneath his hat. "Welcome to Haven."

Luc wrenched his fingers under her mask and ripped it from her face. She gasped. Beneath it lay a face like any other. An old woman, wrinkled, comely in her time, her eyes white with blindness with saggy skin. Luc reared his head back and careened his forehead into the bridge of her nose. The woman groaned and withdrew, blood flying.

The others stumbled. They collapsed, weakened, all of them moaning in some way or another.

"What are you?!" The crone wailed, flailing. She extended a hand at Luc as electricity crackled from her wrist and out her palm. Another voice joined in. Chanting. A flash of white enveloped the air in front of him, creating a spherical shield that absorbed the bolt. Zevra, grounded, continued to chant, her amulet flickering with what power she possessed. A greater surge arched from the magus. It buzzed, snapped, then sunk into the white aura, disrupting it. The shield exploded leaving Luc to duck.

A cry rose from the corner. The paladin swung her blade and met with an invisible force, glancing the blade aside. Ymatsu twisted to her attacker, her hands up, holding sway over the weapon. She forced the blade away and fought against the paladin's strength, turning it toward the exposed chest. The bright, red wounds. They battled wills, one brute against another.

Until Arkalis tackled the magus. She took Ymatsu down, tumbling with her. The magus reached out only to have her head meet the ground.

"How are you feeling, Ymatsu?!"

Arkalis shoved a knee into the magus' chest. She wrapped her hands around the sides of her face. They were large enough to circle her head. Ymatsu spat up blood with a wet cough.

"That's nice, dear." Arkalis said, shoving the back of her skull into the metal floor.

Again.

"That's so–"

Again.

"Fucking–"

Again.

"Nice!"

Luc stared. This was what his senses told him to protect?

The paladin placed a hand on Arkalis' shoulder. Blood lined her face, her chest, it pooled beneath the now limp body.

"I believe she is dead."

"What a day." Luc mumbled. He spared himself any gorier details and returned to the company of Lesandre. Joy.

Oath of the Knights of Kiliku

I RISE A SOATU, a Guardian of Kiliku, keeper of salt and pathfinder. I will seek corruption upon the waves and end its reign. My life I give to my Elders of Nukati, my soul to my crew. Never shall the winds see me home until they carry my name in whispers, in voice, and so I shall serve. A Soatu now and forever.

Chapter 26
The Grand Duke

NIATI HATED FUR. It tickled. She resisted the urge to adjust her skirt, to rip out the stray material that brushed her exposed stomach. Such behavior lacked the expected grace of a captain and Soatu. Never mind that her promotion came only a month ago, that her first assignment to gather trade prospects along the Cavari coast landed her as a target for the Cabal of Magi, that she now stood as the ranking representative of Nukati among some of Thalas' most powerful lords.

Leinani sniffed and itched her nose. Traitor. Niati's eyes hardened.

They met in the audience hall of Isca, the southern border castle to Lindorum. Polished marble floors housed rows of concrete columns plastered to look like stone, supports for open air balconies. An open domed ceiling allowed natural light to highlight the intricate carvings of runes and more mundane designs. Marble statues decorated the interior structure at random intervals; grand, lifelike depictions of heroic warriors and deific figures, shapely, muscular, and nude. The quiet din of chatter flushed in from one side of the hall and out the other, swaying into the closed compound that consisted of Isca's holding.

Niati took her position to the side of Nihilus. Despite his utter lack of grooming, he possessed the clout to broker a deal with the southern consulate. After his display of prowess Niati grew weary of his presence. That cold, calculating stare gave her chills.

"*Nihilus, curare ut faciam in honoribus?*"

A middle-aged, dark-skinned woman spoke from a lacquered throne, hunched to one side with an elbow propped up on an armrest, her palm flat against her cheek where a jagged scar ran up her brow. Arrayed in black and purple, a linen cape spilled over a set of lamellar plates that embraced her chest and shoulders. A black helmet adorned with a gold finish and a plume of horsehair rested on her knee.

Nihilus stepped out of formation, distinctive from the other dozen Lindrisi soldiers in a half circle behind the general. He addressed a lone figure clad in black not but ten paces away, his back straight, and blond hair tightly cropped, his countenance impassive, attentive.

"Consul Silsara welcomes Grand Duke Oswin Adirian, his presence is most–"

"Enough Sil, you don't care, and I don't have the time to dance around pleasantries." Oswin straightened the high collar of his long Cavari-style coat, black leather gloves groaning with a leather creak. "My gambit at the Nui pier failed. Now you've a pontifex beside you and I received a threat from Wyr to my doorstep at Catalin." He spoke with finality, every word demanding attention. Thin of face with a strong clean-shaven jaw, he looked younger than his five decades demanded.

"*Tuum leporem, numquam deficit imprimere.*" Silsara leaned into her chair, intense, green eyes locked with the stoic gaze of the duke. Niati spoke enough Lindrisi to recognize a slight. "I will speak your tongue, I think, to spare myself the butchery you do to Lindrisi. In truth, Oswin, I signed the summons only to bring you here from your cushions. And to arrive so quickly? How many horses did you kill to bring you at haste?"

"Two." His answer ignored the hostility of his host. "And?"

Niati twitched. A gust of wind fluttered from the open ceiling, swaying the fur so that it brushed her skin again. Her foot tapped on the marble. Quiet clicks from her sandals drew a momentary flicker from Adirian.

"And. Your retainer assaulted an agent of Aklesia, whose order is housed in Lindrisi lands. By extension, you attack Lindorum. Cabal law says you must pay by the customs of the wronged party. A concept you are familiar with?" Humor entered the consul's tone. From what Niati knew of the Cavari duke he deserved the ire.

Oswin showed no sign of irritation. "Did I not mention my lack of time? Get to the extortion, Sil."

"You Cavari are no fun. Nihilus has offered to drop charges. He defaults to the other harmed party, *So-a-tu* Niati Kanhe. Captain?"

Her turn. Niati unclenched her hands and drew them across her stomach, running a finger under her skirt with blessed relief.

"Two penalties." Her voice didn't crack. Good start. "In Nukati, undeserved death is met with a gift and a favor. For the gift you will pay in Cavari silver."

"Straight to the point. How pleasant. Per man slain I will grant half their weight in silver."

Leinani choked behind her. They agreed to a lesser sum, enough to bring on new sailors, restock and sail. That much silver bought them a new ship.

"Yes, this will do." Despite her attempts to remain calm, Niati spoke too quickly. The corner of Oswin's lips curled into the slightest of smirks.

"And the favor? You did not orchestrate this for money, I hope."

"For the favor," Niati echoed. She practiced most of the lines at Nihilus' behest. He suggested this course, making good on his promise of payment. "You will relinquish the heretic Arkalis Iskarion into the custody of Pontifex Nihilus."

"That is interesting." Adirian glanced between herself and Nihilus. "You know I don't have her. Which means you want me to petition the Cabal, as a subject, into my care for crimes committed. My judgement will then relinquish her to your keeping and avoid your unanswered justice from reaching the Magi. Do I follow?"

"I uh," Niati faltered, "yes."

"I can do this, under one condition."

"You are in no position to demand consideration," Silsara interceded.

"Ah, ah. Your ploy is creative, but it rests on the assumption that I care. You tell the Magi I did not cooperate. What will they do? Bar me from a year of trade? Please. I'm not some provincial warlord. I'm playing nice to avoid inconveniences and I suggest you do the same." There it was. The teeth. His voice never raised, yet he wrestled control from them in an instant.

"Name it," Niati conceded.

"Why?" He asked.

"Why what?"

"Why do you want Arkalis?"

"That is your condition?"

"A pontifex uses a clear-cut advantage over the Grand Duke of Ilvicar for a neophyte, noble brat. I have access to many things, Soatu, so yes, that is my condition. Tell me why."

"She is a heretic," Nihilus said.

Oswin wagged a finger. "Magi do not show up to apprehend common heretics. Try again."

"She is possessed," Niati blurted out. Nihilus cursed under his breath. Silsara perked up, spared that detail. "No use in hiding it, eh? He would find out. The girl, Arkalis, has power. She unmade things."

"*Hoc est verum?*" The general slid into her native verbiage as she and Nihilus exchanged a heated diatribe in hushed tones. Oswin seemed content by the outburst. He winked at Niati.

"Honesty is rare in this age, Soatu." While the two Lindrisi argued, Oswin addressed her, quietly. "A thing can be both foolish and wise. The trick is to weigh the outcome, deem what matters to you more. Your pride, or your victory. More often than not," he paused, eyeing the consul. "Most choose the former."

Nihilus finished their argument with a bow, his countenance ridden with irritation. He opened his mouth to speak only to be cut off by the duke.

"I'll help you."

Nihilus exhaled, his posture unsure.

"But not in the way you want. The Magi will not relinquish Arkalis if what you say is true. You'll need more than petitions and politics. Black powder, for instance."

"You want to attack the Magi?"

"They have no army. Only a garrison of their bladed contraptions. They've not the numbers to stop a combined force."

"One of them froze over a hundred men. I was at the harbor." Niati recalled the pain, remembered the magus that surfaced from nowhere.

"A problem, my spies tell me, Lindrisi warcasters have worked out."

Silsara's expression darkened. She gripped the edge of her armrest, breaking off the edge. "You have spies in Isca?!"

"Of course. You have two in my consulate. Why would I not put some in yours?"

Did Oswin's arrogance help or harm him? Both, Niati decided, and it was fun to watch.

"Bah." Silsara released the chair. She stood and paced, a hand resting atop a crown of laurels. "Why would I aid you in this? What does this do for Lindorum?"

"The Magi are powerful. Too powerful. It was their ilk responsible for the Desolation. I want them gone, for the same reason I want to find and crush the powers left in Dula'Thalier. Or would you prefer apocalypse? We can end their reign here, Silsara. Cavari and Lindrisi working together? What can stop that?"

"What of Caul? They will come, fight against us." The consul paced.

"No. Caul is only a proxy to Aul'Thannon, and the queen will not threaten their isolation."

"You've had time to plan this, I think, Adirian."

"Two horses worth."

"Hah!" Silsara exclaimed. She sunk back into her chair. "I am convinced. You will have my warcasters. So boring, this is, this peace. Nihilus, you will be joining us." Not a request.

"And of course," Adirian mused, "the intrepid Soatu as well, hm?"

A year ago, Niati apprenticed under a Keeper of the sacred tree. She completed her inscriptions, swore an oath to the Wind Finders and was gifted a vessel, a crew, a priestess. She looked now to the passive form of Leinani. The Wind Finder offered her an encouraging smile. A year ago, Niati thought herself capable of great deeds. But nothing so much as bringing about the fall of Haven.

"My crew and I are in. Do not think this erases your obligation of gift."

"Never crossed my mind." Oswin smiled.

Excerpt from the
high Loremaster's Journal

THE MINOR HOUSES of Ilvicar hold the title of "Baron," or "Baroness." Typically, they possess a holding or two, three at the most as their liege dukes tend to stilt those sorts of ambitions by "reshuffling" properties. Not that this is difficult. There are a plethora of knights vying for ascendancy into the nobility at any time and bestowing a previous hold on to one is a common practice of allegiance. Barons themselves are divided into a pseudo ranking system of their own, with Tributary Barons forming the base, recently landed knights with a singular settlement. They tend to be fostered and allied with high barons, nobles with enough land to not be stingy, but haven't the name to take on the title of duke.

Barons form the aristocracy of Ilvicar and will often war with one another for land, revenge, resources, or boredom, as there is little risk to a noble in direct warfare. The loser is always ransomed (though sometimes jailed if particularly nefarious) back to their estate for a war prize along with any retainers and other individuals of note. Lowborn, of course, are expected to serve their captor without dispute. Mere pawns.

Chapter 27
The Battle of Oula'Thalier

A N INKY, BLACK PORTAL sprung from the archway. A squad of Adirian gunners formed a firing line across from it, arquebuses up, aimed at the portal that took the place of the basilica's doorway. Two paladins joined them. Along with a half dozen sunsingers, uneasy with the forbidden technology in motion. A red rune at the top locked the gate. How then did it open?

The answer arrived in the form of Rurik. Plated in gold, Iskarion's armor bristled with energy. Someone gave the order to fire and smoke drifted upward from the line. Pellets collapsed against the plate, useless.

As the paladins charged, he sidestepped the gate. A yellow eyed ghoul sprinted from its murky depths and snarled, half its face burnt, the other thick with purple veins that spread over its melted brigandine. Another emerged from the gate. Then another. And a fourth. They poured from the webway en masse, shredding anything that stood in the way. One of the paladins went down as three piled on top of her, bashing, clawing, ripping into steel and mangling flesh.

The firing line broke. Some continued to fight while others retreated. The sunsingers steeled themselves and chanted, weaving runes of fire. Until Rurik stopped them. A column of white light appeared above their heads. It streamed into the sunsingers, creating a spherical expansion that engulfed them in moments. Their screams never left their throats.

The soldiers fled and the ghouls followed. One split from the group and pounced at Rurik who cut it in half. It squirmed, its black, purplish blood splattering his armor. Ugh. He wagged his gauntlet, clearing some gore away. After the last ghoul he tapped the lance against the gate's side, draining it of whatever energy it possessed. The others would see the column.

* * *

Cries of struggle emerged from the western camps as the Salivar barons paid the price of their loyalty. A hoard of breakers, a sea of black leathers, descended like a flood. They made quick work of the few soldiers that roamed the palisades, the very defenses that kept them safe and separate now proving their greatest threat. Breakers flooded into the compounds like locusts. No matter how many fell more joined as the wave expanded and their numbers swelled.

Sahira never considered the translation of hitting walls with hammers to hitting people with hammers. The realization came as Hoglet and her crew barreled into a line of Salivar gunners, their deep blue coats overtaken by screaming terror. A volley of gunfire dropped a fourth of them but did little to wound their morale. Facing one's imminent death on a daily basis changed a person.

Feral crunched her sledge into a soldier's sallet. It caved, blood spewing and staining the wastelander's chest. Sahira pushed the image from her mind and joined the fray to face a duo of confused guardsmen. They awoke in their tent to the clash of battle. Half-dressed and unarmored, a steel spear head erupted from a chest. His companion fell to his knees in surrender.

"Stay down," she said. He did.

Sahira darted in and out of the small melees within the compound. She ran into a group of halberdiers, her spear dragging across an armored coat. The Thalian steel seared through the leather and brigandine, severing a soldier's spine. His companions moved to meet her challenge as more ferocious breakers hit them at the distraction, beating them to pulps with sledges. She rallied the squad of breakers and circled, finding the remaining pockets of guards under siege by their own crews.

The fighting lasted minutes. With their numbers and surprise, they lost few. It all seemed too easy. Sahira mangled the leftover corpses of the assault, decapitating bodies. No one knew how ghouls worked or in what timeframe they took hold. Better safe than mauled by vicious void-infested corpses. Feral joined her once the compound ran out of soldiers.

"Mind takin' over girl?"

"I take. Princess go be important." Feral placed her palm on Sahira's head. She wondered if the wastelander saw them as pets sometimes.

"Thanks. Just make sure they can't walk if they, ya know. Reanimate."

The sound of crunching bone chased her away from the pockets of death. She wandered near the center of the compound where Hoglet lined up the surviving soldiers, their liege out front on his knees. A richly dressed, chubby man, he begged for the nonsense to end. His face flushed red from rage and embarrassment as the towering, muscular woman argued with another from her crew.

"We can't kill a voided noble!"

"Why not? Bastard killed who knows how many of us. So what, he was born rich, that means he's safe?" Hoglet leaned on her sledge.

"Without nobles," the baron interjected, puffing between words. "There would be chaos. We are agents of civilization. We keep order! I demand to be ransomed."

Sahira's spear found his throat. The baron choked. He clawed at the wound, blood running free over his grasping fingers.

"Huh. Doesn't feel like nothin's changing," Sahira said.

"Shit." Hoglet sniffed. "Guess that's solved."

A distant echo of sequential gunfire pierced the raucous clashes nearby. The occasional bang popped from the camps, though most cries turned to the wet slap of a metal on tissue.

"Hear that?" Sahira wiped the curved blade of her spear on the baron's pristine, green tunic. "Sounded like a volley. Kalthier is on it. Need to wrap up here and circle around or they'll be outnumbered."

"Don't we want them to get roughed up?" Hoglet poked the noble's corpse, as if she didn't believe he was dead. Lowborn saw plenty of their own die. Never nobility.

"Ahuh, don't want them to lose though. C'mon. Bash that asshole's head in and leave a few to watch them." She pointed out the prisoners. "Got us a battle to win."

•   •   •

Rurik stretched his palm outward. A swirling mist coalesced into a coherent shield that spanned the width of the road and intercepted a volley of lead.

"Fire!"

He released the energy and his formation returned the assault. Adirian soldiers dropped from the loose array of gunners positioned ahead of Kalthier's halberdiers. The chaos of the ghouls gave the soldiers time to overtake most of the row, but their advance stalled as the encampment's construction forced a gauntlet of pitched battle. The Adirian gunners retreated to the wings and took up new positions, some kneeling, others standing behind as they reloaded. Red-coated halberdiers flooded to the center of the formation. Cavari soldiers trained to fight against Lindrisi warcasters, leading to swift action against magical interference.

Rurik split his gunners up, mirroring the retreat. The shield would not stop a charge and the more power he used here the less he could bring against the Avatar.

Lyue and Kalthier advanced with their own column of polearm wielding soldiers. Kalthier wore a black suit of runecasted plates bearing a visored bascinet; layered metal that flared at the shoulders and rounded at the chest with a steel skirt from his waist down. Lyue outfitted herself for battle in a sleeveless suit of brigandine. She wielded the blue tinted long blade liberated from the forum and had shaved the sides of her head with thick braids slung against the back of her scalp.

"Fire!" The shout came from the opposing side.

Bullets zipped from the flanks, harassing Rurik's center as he conjured the shield to small pings of shattered metal. The halberdiers charged. Rurik released the spell as dozens of Adirian soldiers closed the gap and turned to face them.

"Brace!" Kalthier's imposing bass came with a uniform shift. The front line dug their heels into the blackened street, their polearms held low, centered, with soldiers behind filling the gap. Rurik joined the line.

"Fire!"

The Kalthier gunners unleashed a volley into the sides of the Adirian charge. Soldiers dropped out of formation, but not enough. Steel clashed against steel. Flesh ripped and tore, leather split as sharpened metal pierced leather and steel alike. Warriors impaled themselves on extended edges while others pushed weapons aside as bodies met in a ferocious melee.

Rurik waded into the mess. He thrust the lance outward, the glaive-blade searing into armor and bone. Two soldiers rounded on him. He knocked an offending spike away with a gauntlet and allowed the second to deflect harmlessly off his suit. A countering sweep took off a leg. He choked up on the haft and circled the blade to cut through the sallet of the second, taking off half a skull.

Lyue wove within the clash, blade flourished as she ducked an axe head and impaled a soldier on the sword, unconcerned with armor. She kept close to her opponents, working her way into the reach of their arms and wreathing chaos amongst their ranks. Every assault brought another kill. Her strikes flowed from one to the next, fluid, her sword never stopping in a whirlwind of terror. Rurik recognized the forms of a Thalian Justiciar.

The Kalthier halberdiers pushed. The gunners fired in an arrhythmic cadence now, resulting in the oddly timed pop of scattered shooting. More red coats fell than any other, their numbers endless. Rurik cut his way into the mass. He caught a glimpse of Kalthier and his men follow suit, the lord wailing on anyone close enough with a maul akin to a breaker's sledge. He cracked a soldier's helmet, breaking the skull.

The Adirian's numbers thinned. Aware of their weapon's futility against Rurik's armor most ran at his presence. Others caught on. Gunners and halberdiers heeded a sudden call for retreat. Rurik spied the source of the order, a knight in pristine white armor. He twisted his wrist and projected a gravity rune. The man screamed as he sailed through the air and found himself passing by Rurik, who took the opportunity to separate his head from his neck.

The retreat hastened. Rurik raised his arm, stopping any of his soldiers from chasing. The gunfire diminished with sporadic pops until it silenced in full. Kalthier and Lyue jogged to meet Rurik, covered in blood. None of it their own.

"That was too easy," Karil said, catching his breath

Lyue nodded. "I agree. We should regroup."

Lyue and Karil assessed their strategy while Rurik observed the scene. They managed to pass the ale house and the basilica. The market started here, and beyond that lay the Adirian fort and the breach. He took a closer look, augmenting his sight with the helmet's enchantments. The retreating Adirian soldiers ducked into the fort, manning the walls in an anticipated siege. He scanned the market, the upturned stalls, the abandoned wagons. Shadows bounced beyond the breach and movement caught his vision atop the buildings.

"Damn it," Rurik mumbled, "Form up!" He tapped the display on his forearm, increasing the intensity of his voice as it left his helmet. "Gunners, above you! Karil!" Rurik whipped his head around. "We need to move!"

Soldiers appeared from the rooftops, hidden from the initial clash, their fellows sacrificed to lure the allied troops into the road. Gunfire rained. Men and women collapsed under the volley until Rurik thrust an arm into the air as another shield erupted over the formation. Runes sputtered and died from the ceiling as he drew from their power.

The gunfire stopped. From the breach a fresh host of armored soldiers appeared, led by knights in shining plate. More Adirian loyalists. At their center a column of paladins marched in formation, massive blades brandished in contents. Akleasn reinforcements. Hundreds of red coated halberdiers and fresh gunners, mercenaries bolstering their numbers in cured leathers and gambesons wielding swords and pikes.

Kalthier reformed his soldiers into a line. Thinner now, they stood too-few ranks deep even with seldom Lynesse barons joining the assault.

"How long can you keep that up?" Lyue asked.

"A while, so long as I'm not distracted."

"We may need to withdraw, Rik, regroup and use the portals to hit them in small groups." Karil spoke between barked orders.

"And give them time to bring in more? No. We stick to the plan."

"Rurik! Up!" Lyue cried.

Soldiers hoisted barrels up over the rooftops with lit fuses. Rurik released the lance. It hovered of its own accord, and he summoned a gravity rune as the soldier released the barrel. It flew up and exploded midair at height with its owners. They and part of the building took the brunt of the blast, sending stone debris and body parts flying. Two barrels landed on the shield. They ignited into a gout of flame and splintered wood, the shield stuttering from the impact. Rurik created a second rune at yet another cask. It flew halfway back to its target, killing the gunners. Rurik groaned as his defenses waned. Gunfire followed.

"Scratch that, shield is almost done!"

"Won't matter for long. Here they come!"

A cacophonous clatter of metal rose as a wave from the charge, paladins out front, their wicked swords brought to bear. Rurik felt his power wane under a constant stream of ricocheting bullets. If he dropped it to fight they'd be ripped apart from above.

"Fire!" Karil bellowed.

Arquebuses from their flanks opened with volleys of concentrated fire at the advance. The paladins' armor held up against the attack. Some blew back from the force, but others ignored their wounds and pushed on.

"Fire!"

A second round of shots finished off too few holy warriors. Rurik strained as he drew more from the runes, their regeneration too slow to hold for long. Either keep the shield, or stop the calamitous charge. How many did they have left? Dozens? A hundred at best. He could not do both.

Rurik grabbed the Sunlance. Now or never.

Boisterous shouting came from beyond the row. A guttural roar broke from within as a sudden mass of breakers crashed into the Adirian forces. They spilled into an unguarded flank, sledges swinging and crunching bone and armor alike. A smaller group came from the eastern bend. Singali vipers intermixed with mercenaries met with the breaker attack, cutting the Adirian forces in half. Rurik spotted Katriene and her sister among them, their Thalian daggers glinting. A gift for a botched deal.

"Now Karil!"

"Charge!"

Paladins and halberdiers clashed. Kalthier forged ahead as Rurik refocused his efforts on the shield. He worked out a series of projections in his mind, weaving a complex matrix of effects into a single, runic form. His shield shuttered, then lifted at his behest, cresting the rooftops to the confusion of the gunners. All at once the flat disk of energy collapsed into a sphere. Arquebuses took aim. Rurik flattened his hand and spun his wrist as the sphere shattered into thousands of pieces. Shrapnel exploded in a circle, impaling guardsmen and ripping their guns to shreds.

Rurik joined his forces, the bleak, brutal efficiency of the paladins tearing them to shreds. He reached Lyue who held her sword at the center of the blade and caught a paladin's weapon mid strike. She slid in close, bucked an attack and flung the Thalian Steel at his helmet, tearing into the metal visor and spewing a thick splatter of blood in its path. Rurik arrived in time to intercept a blow, his lance sundering a sword into two halves. The paladin stared, his shock locking his muscles as Rurik bashed in the side of his helmet.

"I'd give my left testicle for a company of Justiciar about now." Lyue spit, sliding her back up against Rurik's rear.

"You don't have testicles, Lyue."

"Right." She chuckled, using a sleeve to wipe blood from her face. "And I think, neither do you!"

"Funny." Rurik slipped an overhead swing. He slapped a paladin's back with the lance's shaft into Lyue who twisted her sword into an armored chest.

Ally and enemy dwindled. The battle raged as he and Lyue formed a cohesive unit of whirling death. He took the brunt of the blows, deflecting weighted great swords with his near impenetrable suit as Lyue danced in his shadow; agile, the blue tint of the Thalian blade flashing in precise strikes that rent armor asunder. Terrible screams cut short as impossible weapons severed the highest quality arms. Rurik pushed ahead and Lyue came with him, his furred shoulders matted with endless muck. He grabbed a slit visor and pulled a holy warrior close, wrenching the helmet off and bashing an armored forehead into bare flesh and bone. Rurik launched the corpse into another paladin that fell, with Lyue nearby to finish him off.

From the back of the Adirians the breakers spilled over, their ferocity too great. Their split focus widened a gap within the red ranks. Karil gathered the last of his soldiers and spearheaded a blitz into the thinned column of paladins. Together, they cut a thick swath through the mess of conflict.

The last of the paladins fell, swarmed by halberds. With their loss the tide turned. Caught between two armies the morale of the Adirian's faltered. Unable to run, soldiers disarmed. From potential ruin to slim victory, the shouts and calls and clashes of metal diminished. Those who could retreated up the breach, harried by breakers.

Wails of pain rose in the resulting quiet. The wounded cried out. Some broke into fits of laughter while others sobbed, caught with too much adrenaline in the last moments of battle.

Rurik jogged down the road with Lyue close on his heels. Karil, his armor dented and cracked with a pellet lodged into his shoulder, kept pace. They met with Sahira and what remained of Rurik's original crew. Feral, coated in layers of blood and gore, Sweets, Rust, and Jerk, most with cuts and bruises, but none mortally wounded. Katriene found them next. Sarette and Melody wandered from the merchant's offensive.

"By th'Sky Father's balls." Rust slapped his scalp, a dual-headed Thalian axe resting on his shoulder. "We won."

"Shari blesses us! A song for ages to come, hah!"

"We're not done," Rurik said. "The soldiers from the fort are gone."

"They spared us a siege. Must've run," Karil mused.

Lyue pointed at the lowered portcullis. "Gate's closed. Why wouldn't they fight? More guns would've ruined us. Worse yet. Haven't seen the Adirian breakers. What did they do with them?"

"I didn't see Celesti on the field. She's got something planned." Rurik flattened his palm and thrust it at the fort's gate. A loud crack struck the metal bars. Again. They bent inward. A third blast launched the portcullis into the stone courtyard.

From within a black gateway hummed with energy, blue runes alight over its exterior. How? Rurik screamed. The others followed him inside.

"Shit. How'd she get one of those to work here?" Sahira said.

"She has my slate. Loremasters could translate the language and diviners could use the ring to find anything. All she'd need is access to the webway matrix, which she has. Fucking voidshit!" Rurik slammed the haft of the lance into the ground. "She's going after the Avatar."

"We need to go after her," Lyue said, "She cannot—what is that?"

Screams. Howls. Wood splintered in the distance. Something crashed and rumbled as a roar of vicious cries traveled from the eastern camps.

"That's comin' from the Adirian camps. Shit, Rik, do you think they?" Sahira's question caught in her own throat.

"Karil, get your men in here now!" Rurik ran for the wall. He summoned a gravity rune and launched himself onto the palisade. A swarming hive of ghouls broke free from a dozen Adirian camps. Hundreds of them. They carried sledges, smart enough to wield weapons as they fought furiously toward the row.

Karil and the others ushered whoever they could into the fort. Breakers and soldiers and merchants split. Some ran for the breach. Idiots. The ghouls were faster, stronger. Most piled into the safety of the stone walls, filling the yard in their haste to escape the wailing echo of hollow howls. Rurik descended the wall in a single bound, his leap ending in a walk.

"Barricade the gates. Anyone able to fight needs to get to the walls, now." His voice boomed. They listened. "Halberdiers, any of you left." He addressed Kalthier's soldiers. Few Lynesse troops remained, and they kept close watch to the Adirians that didn't make for their freedom. "Form up around the gate. If they break through, you stop them." Tired, but resolved, faces greeted him. They formed up.

"Shari asks, Rurik, how do we fight so many?" Sweets ran over, his loose brigandine jostling with his movement. A gash covered his cheek, still wet with blood, his hair knotted with sweat.

"We do not." Jerk pinched his nose, greasy, wild bangs hanging over his face. "We are, as the Cavari say, fucked on both ends."

Feral grabbed Jerk's face and pushed him to the ground. He issued a few muffled complaints to no avail.

"A'ight, anyone else gonna say something stupid?" Sahira dared them, dried blood splattered amidst her golden tattoos.

"He's right." Rurik approached the arch and depressed a rune. "About not stopping them. I need to go after Celesti." Another rune.

"We cannot abandon these people." Melody said, calm. Always calm. "Soon the dead will rise and bolster their numbers. Your abilities are needed."

"None of this matters. If we can get to the Avatar, we can stop them all."

He lied. He needed to destroy the Avatar, the city. All of it paled to their lives. If Celesti reached it first, if she gained its power, more than just the remnants would die.

Lyue said nothing, though her gaze bled with the truth.

"Assumin' that's true, Rik, there's no way in the void you're goin' alone." Sahira joined him as he depressed a third rune.

"You can't. There'll be sentries at the beacon, stronger than the others we fought."

"Exactly. We."

"Sahira–"

"Ahuh. None'a that. What happens when you get winged? Don't care how fancy this armor is, everyone makes mistakes. Now shut it, we're comin'."

"She's got'a point, Rik." Rust joined her. "'Sides, I'd rather be breakin' rocks than fightin'a hoard'a voidspawn."

"Vari says maybe we get lucky."

"*Je viendrai aussi, même si c'est juste pour tuer cette putaine.*" Katriene flourished her knives.

The black portal filled the archway, looming.

"Karil."

Kalthier barked an order, overseeing the defenses himself. "Go, Rurik. I don't understand what in the void is happening here, but this'll all be worth it to see Adirian's favorite daughter get hers. We'll hold."

"Fine. But no bitching if any of you die."

"Hah. We're breakers, Rik." Sahira crossed her arms. "It's what we do."

Personal Log, 8.21.0268 C.E.

SENTINELS. Lynesse came up with the idea. Embed a battery foci into runecasted stone and layer them with data runes. They work, partially, but the joints are a bitch to get right. She asked me to alter my gravity formula to generate smoother movement. Maybe? I think friction runes are a better way to go. That'll give them more fluid motion and they'll be able to generate more speed while simulating greater strength.

Oh, idea! Bolt weapons onto the arms. They don't need to be pretty.

Chapter 28
Drink From the World

K ALI RAKED her sword down a sentinel's side. A spouting gout of flame erupted on impact and melted stone as she plunged the weapon deep into the construct's torso. She twisted the sword, pivoted, and sliced the top half of the construct into pieces. Kali growled and kicked what remained of it down the stairs with the dry slap of bare feet.

More constructs streamed after her, their black stone carapaces elegant, sculpted as lean humanoids, their torsos thin and hunched over with no neck or head. Their bladed arms dangled at their side, their movements quick, erratic, and deadly.

"What are these?!" Kali parried a strike meant for her chest and Ishta, the paladin, intercepted the other, her magnificent steel blade flashing.

"Guardians. The Magi are aware of Ymatsu's death, they must be sending them after us." Lesandre's voice modulated from the pilfered skull mask. He swiped over his slate, fingers working diligently. "There are alerts and failsafe activations throughout the tower. Outside as well. I think we pissed them off."

"Thanks for the–" Kali ducked a swipe and drew a sentinel's attention as Ishta swiveled, blades careening in defense. Their swords met the stone in a simultaneous strike that rent the creature asunder. ". . .for the speculation. How many more are there?"

"Mm. Hundreds. I think that's what the flashing red dots are, and most of them are concentrated on the ground floor. Honestly, I expected the Magi to come themselves. Perhaps they–"

"Focus, Les." Kali and Ishta jogged down the spiral stairs, their wide construction of white steel a sterile oddity. The rapid click-clack of ascending sentinels greeted them. "We can't keep fighting. We need another route."

"This way!" Luc, the luckiest man alive as Kali saw it, stumbled into the metal wall. He poked at it and a door hissed open, retracting from the center as its six components slid into a hidden frame. He pulled Zevra in after him.

"What is this man? A demon?" Ishta chided, skeptical.

"Who cares? Follow the magic wetlander!" Kali bolted after Luc, her baggy sirwal fluttering. Pants pilfered from Ymatsu. Once a duchess, she resulted now to looting the dead. Wonderful.

They poured into another metal hall and followed the strip of light to the dead end. Another construct clicked after them. Ishta set up in the rear, her weapon held horizontal to the floor, arms back, body pivoted to present a profile to her adversary.

"Here!" Luc flailed at the wall.

"There's nothing there. Oh. No, I stand corrected." Lesandre tapped.

Kali's gaze flickered between the apparent exit and the incoming mass of bladed death. She bounced in place, shifting her weight from one foot and the other. The tight conditions meant two slashing swords did more harm than good.

"Faster!" Luc urged.

"There is no faster!"

A construct barreled into the hall, nearly tripping over itself in its fury. It lashed out and tore through Ishta's side as she countered in the same breath, her sword thrust into its neck column to a sudden lack of movement. Ishta fell to a knee and clutched the fresh wound.

The wall of the dead end separated, and Kali pulled Ishta in behind the desperate bunch. Lesandre issued a command and the door slammed shut as yet another construct rammed the surface with a rapid series of bangs.

"Zev!" Kali called and the sunpriest responded, her amulet aglow. While Zevra knit the paladin back together Kali surveyed their new surroundings. Her countenance grew dark. Rows of glass tanks spanned from one barren wall to the other, each filled with a clear viscous fluid. Shadowed figures drifted inside. Lifeless, half formed bodies, pale with scaly skin; they bore faces with more teeth than flesh, lidless black eyes. She went to them. Kali placed a hand on the glass exterior to little purpose. Were they asleep, or not yet alive?

The thread tugged. It recognized the body, it's shape. It wanted her to reach out and take hold. To break the glass and free the voidspawn.

Beautiful, aren't they? You can feel it, can't you? Listen to it. It yearns to be free. Just as they yearn to wake. Shall I stir them?

"What place is this?" Luc stuttered. He shivered.

"Our Magi appear to be experimenting." Lesandre wandered to Kali and tapped on the glass. "This one looks like the creature below Iskvar. Smaller, less formed. They are. Hm." He tilted his head and consulted his slate. Kali glimpsed the surface. A language she did not recognize ran from top to bottom, left to right in a constant stream of information.

"They are what? Insane?" Luc's voice held a twinge of incredulity.

"They're learning." Lesandre said.

He's wrong. They've learned enough, now they seek to control.

Kali removed her hand from the tank. "We need to get out of here. I've lived enough nightmares, Zev, how's our girl?"

"I am not dead," Ishta groaned.

Zevra ceased her healing chant, the white glow about her palms fading. "We must go. I mended her flesh, but she has lost much blood."

The pounding grew louder and dents appeared on the door. Kali returned to the paladin's side and threw an arm over her shoulder. They rose together and Ishta dragged her blade as they limped as one.

"How do we escape this unholy place?" Zevra followed, heavy bags under her eyes.

"Ask the wetlander. He brought us here," Kali said.

"My name is Luc. And I have no idea."

"There's a gate." Lesandre pointed them to the far side of the room, nose buried in that device of his. He led them deeper, snaking among rows upon rows of voidspawn. Sickening creatures. Kali saw one twitch.

"We need to move. Les, you can work these gate things?"

"I believe so. I was able to connect my data slate to the webway network here in the tower, the coori–"

"So yes?"

"Yes."

The banging grew into a wrenching whine of torn metal. A construct squeezed as others continued to rip at the hole, wicked blades and twisted bodies begging to chase. They followed in a rush and spread out among the glass tanks, searching.

"Les!"

"It's here! Here!" A black archway appeared, inert, its runes gray and idle. Lesandre ran to it and frantically tapped at his slate. The others formed up with Kali at the rear, blade up, eyes wide as the clicking approached. Ishta groaned and joined her. She hunched her shoulders, weapon low. A sentinel reared around a row of tanks. It aligned itself to them and straightened as its joints snapped into place.

It ran.

"Les!"

"They deactivated the webway! Give me a minute!"

"We do not have a minute!" Ishta snarled. Kali's grip tightened on the leather wrapped hilt. They could take one.

A shadow twitched from inside a tank. First a subtle jerk, it became more frantic. Limbs thrashed. Talons, like daggers, clawed at the containers, screeching from within until cracks appeared on the exterior. Not from one, but all of those circling the ragged group. Glass shattered throughout the chamber.

One of the spawn crashed out of its tank and into the sentinel. Together they tumbled to the floor as another beat its way out, greenish, garish liquid spilling out behind it. A gang of monsters overwhelmed the construct, tearing its limbs and stone body apart with a reckless abandon.

Kali stared. None of the creatures came for them. Instead, they scampered off as a unit, squirming and writhing as they went. One stayed. It chittered in a hideous cackle and bowed to her before it scampered after its kin.

"We going to address that?" Luc said, hiding behind the gate.

"Nope. Les?"

"Just a few more–got it!" The runes on the arch lit up. Lesandre dialed an address and a portal sprang to life.

"Go. I will keep the rear," Ishta said. Kali snorted and pulled her along with the others.

•   •   •

A volley of gunfire blasted a group of constructs into rubble. Bolts of electricity followed, arcing currents slamming into stray sentinels and eviscerating stone on contact. Lines of Cavari gunners encircled the Haven Tower accompanied by lamellar clad legionaries wielding oval shields and long bladed spatha. They formed iron walls in front of the arquebus lines with warcasters on the flanks, men and women in layered red and white robes, their faces veiled and hooded.

They advanced to the bellowing commands of plated knights. Adirian retainers, their sabers out, pitched their voices to cut through the roaring gunfire and crackle of summoned lightning. Niati moved into the western yard with Oswin, the duke unarmed. Her braids bounced with her step, a chime of trinkets and beads, and shared a weary gaze with Leinani.

"How many can there be?" She mused as another dozen hunched constructs emerged from a set of golden plated doors. Or what used to be doors. The warcasters initiated the conflict by blowing off a portion of the foundation. Stone came away in chunks, but the metal interior resisted. Was the entire tower steel? Niati mused at the resources required for such a thing.

"Doesn't matter," Oswin observed, his hands clasped behind him, shoulders straight. He wore no jewelry or any sign of his rank. "These are distractions. I expect a magus to intervene, busy the Lindrisi casters. This stalling is interesting."

"Interesting?" Niati shifted her weight onto her back foot. Another volley brought a voluminous puff of smoke wafting by her nose.

"They're not defending themselves. Only allowing us to swat down these gnats."

"You want to get inside, eh?"

A warcaster wove her arms and a section of the garden sunk to trap a pair of sentinels within dirt and rock. The root-like extensions off the tower created isolated corridors, their walls more than ten stories tall, with each approach filled to the brim with lush greenery. Flora now aflame.

"Time is not a commodity one gifts their enemies."

Niati bowed. She unsheathed her rapier and moved to the head of a Lindrisi shield wall. They parted, heeding her temporary command at the will of their consul.

"*Ei*, who wants to stand around all day and watch?" She spoke to the soldiers. "Time we started a proper fight."

A caped legionnaire addressed his compatriots in their native tongue and they lifted their shields in unison, weapons clattering in sync to sign their approval. The warcasters joined them and Leinani fell in with their number. Seven in total, enough to wreak havoc on hundreds.

"On me!"

The scuffle of metal greaves trailed the charge between punctuated bursts of gunfire. More constructs emerged from the tower. Expressionless, their joints clicked with every movement, hunched forms sprinting to meet their attack. The soldiers roared. Niati slid a token from her braids and whispered a Nui incantation as she whipped it at the front line of sentinels.

Ice exploded from the trinket. It expanded, spiraling out and rolling over the stone warriors, encasing them in a deep freeze. The Lindrisi smashed into the constructs, shields first, their bodies shattered into thousands of shards. Legionnaires engaged the remaining sentinels with their blades aflame, an enchantment fed by the warcasters' rigorous chants.

They fought their way inside. The base of the tower rose multiple stories with no floors; the interior a single, open hall with rows of constructs arrayed in a cross, dormant by the entryways. They activated a dozen at once, a row making for their assigned direction. Clinical, silver, without decoration, strips of light adhered to the ceiling with little else except for a spiral staircase in the center of the tower and two black, glowing arches. As many sentinels pathed their way up the stairs as out the doors.

The Lindrisi reformed their wall. More constructs came, stalled by warcasters' lightning that created pockets of explosive force. No form of intelligence guided the defender's actions. They came in the same waves and at the same intervals as if unaware of the invasion's scale. Cavari joined them and reset their firing lines.

A portal filled an archway.

A masked, disheveled man emerged first. Wearing an unbuttoned coat in a fashion similar to Oswin, he carried a black slate and moved aside to make way for a frantic wetlander, a scared, wounded paladin, a haggard sunpriest, and a weary Arkalis. Niati tilted her head. As if inspired by their arrival, every remaining construct activated at once.

"*Ei ei!*" Niati tore another trinket from her braids. "They need us!"

•   •   •

Rampant gunfire and scraping steel greeted her. Constructs piled out of holes blown into the tower's foundation and were torn apart by hot lead and casted force. A line of Lindrisi fought their way into one of the breaches headed by a Nui woman in vibrant blues. Nui? Kali rubbed her eyes. Not crazy. Niati led a column of legionaries and warcasters and met her gaze from across the hall. A friendly face was better than an endless horde of stone destroyers. A horde she stood in the middle of.

Oh, shit.

Dozens of constructs sprung to life at her arrival. They flipped, their faceless torsos locking onto her in recognition. She heard Niati call for a charge. The soldiers broke their formation and sprinted, too far to outpace the freakishly fast sentinels. Ishta lifted her sword in a valiant folly while Zevra weakly clasped her amulet, the light too dim to notice. Luc turned back to the portal only to watch the inky black surface dissipate.

Kali's heart raced. The sentinels came too fast.

The voices returned. They whispered sweetly. They knew. Death came with swirling blades. Too many to fight. Who would die this time? All of them. The thread tugged at the back of her mind. Embrace me, it said. Save them. Power lay in her reach. All this time, all those lives, all lost. For what?

Embrace me.

Kali closed her eyes and pulled the thread.

Time slowed. Heat rose from her veins and coursed through her blood as colors swelled around her. Auras replaced physical form, bodies, connections, all lost to data. Endless streams of information flooded her mind. Dimensions, energy, elemental compositions. The constructs operated from a hidden core at their base, greenish mist encompassing their movements. She swiveled her head from one to the next, the world caught in slow motion while she moved at speed.

She looked at her hands. Fuzzy, out of focus, her skin vibrated in her vision, radiating heat. Sounds came next. Clear, clarion calls, the thud of metal boots, the clicking of arched, stoned feet. Something yelled a name. Arkalis? From afar, from nearby. Arkalis. Her. Of course. She almost forgot. Memories of her life pierced a veil of fog that took her mind. Faces, names. She cared about some of them, used others.

What were they doing? Escaping? Death loomed, man-made sentinels, imbued solarstone mined from a star's focused energy.

How to deal with them?

You remember how, sweet girl. Drink from the world.

The lights flickered. Kali expanded her senses, seeking sustenance. Decadence. The auras directed her. From stray casting, from runic imbuements, from the constructs and lights, Kali drew in the power that surrounded her. It fed an intense hunger, one she discovered only in that moment. From the world she stole energy, internalized it, then shaped it. From her fingers she focused that energy and pushed her arms out.

A ripple shuttered the world. A circular pulse emitted from Kali's body, vibrating across the air, spread impossibly fast, passing harmlessly through flesh yet seeking stone. As it hit the constructs they collapsed. Dozens at first, all that threatened her, they fell in heaps of debris and dust, their energy leaving their cores and drawn to her like gravity. She fed upon it, satiating her hunger. Their power increased hers. A second ripple echoed the first. Farther, faster, it crashed from one wall to the other, tearing the sentinels to shreds.

Another wave of nourishment washed over her. She stretched, invigorated, her mind clear, her focus crisp. Rage subsided to an eerie sort of calm. Time caught back up with itself and the lights stabilized. Not a single construct remained. Kali allowed her vision to resettle. Allowed? That felt right. Physicality returned. Shapes reverted to their normal form, yet alterations persisted. An overlay. Something she could access on a whim, and it told her things, age, power, their degree of sustenance. She shivered. Sustenance?

Kali returned to some semblance of herself.

"We must address that," Luc said, eyes wide. "I mean. What under all the stars was that?!"

From the doors soldiers streamed into the tower. Cavari and Lindrisi; legionaries, gunners, and warcasters. Niati approached with Nihilus and Silsara close on her heels. And Oswin Adirian, the Red

Bastard himself, picked his way carefully among the discarded mess of rubble.

"I let it in," Kali said, softly. Disappointed? Relieved? The voices no longer sat at the edge of her notice. They vanished. Silence ruled, a blissful, lovely silence.

Leinani rushed to the wounded group. Ishta, drained, dropped to her knees and Zevra with her, brought to the care of the Nui priestess.

"Let what in?" Luc came to Kali's side.

"Arkalis!" Nihilus halted. He furrowed his brow, examining her in that knowing, analytical way. "Are you still you?" Niati, close enough to hear, gripped her rapier and waited for an answer, tense and ready to pounce.

"Sort of. What are you doing here?"

"Mounting a rescue. Unnecessarily. Intentions matter, I suppose." Oswin's voice cut clear through the rest. Kali felt the rage swell in her mind. A normal, human anger.

"You." Her tone dripped with venom. "You scum sucking voidspawn. You." Kali's body shook with anger. She raised her blade in his direction.

"Arkalis, you mustn't." Lesandre placed himself between her and his father. He raised his mask to his forehead to the surprised countenance of Oswin. "The Cavari soldiers are all sworn to my house. My father is responsible for this."

Niati bobbed her head. "Aye, Arkalis. He arranged it."

"Not without his own benefit of course." Lesandre added. "Altruism is not a family trait. Father?"

The duke flexed his fingers, closing them into fists. He shot his son an appraising glance. "The general and I hoped to wipe out the Magi with your rescue being a secondary objective, admittedly. I understand your vehemence but for the time being might we focus on what lies before us? The Cabal have yet to show themselves, and I fear the reason."

You are ready, Arkalis.

Kali froze.

"A more pressing matter. Arkalis is in control, but the Void surrounds her," Nihilus said. "This must be dealt with."

"I'm sorry did you say the Void?" Luc shied away from Kali.

They no longer matter, my sweet. It is time. Come to me. You know where I am.

"Yes. She is possessed. Unlike any other I have seen." Nihilus squinted.

"She did us a favor." Oswin waved the sentiment off. "Whatever this power is she controls it. This is a boon."

Lesandre pulled the skull mask back over his face. "I can't trace any of the Magi. They've either left or are hiding."

"They're in the audience chambers," Kali spoke. She fumed at the duke's presence, but that changed little. Somewhere above *she* waited. "I need to go there."

"Nothing's changed." Oswin clasped his hands together. "The warcasters will accompany you. Soatu Kanhe has volunteered her aid along with some of my retainers and the pontifex, of course. The rest of us will secure the tower."

"Don't go up there." Kali nodded at the stairs. "Trust me. Not safe."

"Are you up for this, Arkalis? You are dealing with much and the Magi are no easy foe," Nihilus asked.

"I've run long enough." She glowered at Oswin who only smiled back. "From all of it. I won't run any longer."

"I can reopen the gate from here. Best make it quick or they could lock you out." Lesandre dialed an address into his slate.

Have no fear. Come. It is time we spoke.

Oswin and Silsara gathered a host of knights and casters. Clear cut orders sent them into the black, murky portal. Warcasters gestured, creating swirling blue mists to act as shields as they and the knights ran into the arch. Nihilus and Niati went last.

Oswin hovered over Lesandre's shoulder, watching his son work the slate.

"Ishta, you've bled enough. Stay behind, yeah?" Kali glanced at the paladin.

Ishta made no complaint as Leinani washed a calming, white glow over her wounds. Luc, visibly upset, trailed her. He measured his breathing, close to hyperventilating.

"You can stay, Luc." Kali paused in front of the humming portal.

"Nothing would make me happier. Alas." He took a deep inhale, centering himself. "You still need me."

• • •

Bodies littered the ground. Knights and casters. Those that went before her lay in pieces, limbs separated, blood splattered in fresh pools of red over a barren floor of cold steel. A single magus stood at the center of a runic platform beneath a crystalline ceiling that filtered the light of dawn into a half circle of seven arches and a pair of black oval energy sinks. She recognized the massive chamber from her first encounter with the Magi.

Niati and Nihilus strayed to a corner, the latter with his arms out, a circle of energy protecting the duo from waves of oppressive force. Three other Magi, shriveled into husks, hovered upon obsidian spears, impaled, pierced through their chests and into the floor, their once white robes stained with blood.

"There you are!" The woman's voice reverberated throughout the chamber. *Her* voice. "Did you lure them here? Such a delightful meal." The waves of energy ceased and Kali heard Nihilus gasp. He fell to his knees and Niati went to his side. "My dear Arkalis. I've waited so long for this."

The magus removed her mask. Unlike the decrepit, exsanguinated faces of her peers this creature boasted a divine beauty–perfect, unblemished features, sharp yet full, her skin flushed with natural color. Long locks of jet black fell over purple irises that radiated with raw power, effervescing into a mist.

Kali's legs shook. Her knuckles tightened around her sword, but the pressure did little to alleviate her tremors.

"What are you?" The quiet scuffle of Luc's boots underpinned her words as he dipped around the archway, its portal closed.

The magus pouted. "Come now, my darling. You know me. Are your memories so slow to return? I suppose centuries of death play havoc on the mind."

"Death? What are you talking about?"

"How drab. I hoped we could do this easily, but I've not the patience." The magus flicked her wrist and heat crept into Kali's chest. She fought against it, tugging at the thread of power in her mind. Instead of the exhilaration of energy she felt cold. Chills took her, seizing her muscles and forcing her prostrate.

"This may sting."

All Kali could hear was the terror of her own screams.

Þersoɴɑl Loꙅ, 6.16.0276 C.E.

MY STUDIES on Voidtears have revealed them to be problematic. At best. They're not so much portals as they are rifts in space. Whatever is on the other side generates an infinite degree of energy, but not without risks. It's alien. Foreign? All-together not-from-here. No wonder the Emissaries are so powerful, they're working with a power source we've no access to. It's a simple equation of in and out. What worries me is while I've been able to adapt this dark energy to power Thalian tech it seems to infest it. Corrupt it? There are no signs of negative impact, but there's something in those veins.

Something evil.

Chapter 29
Slay All Intruders

A PUFF OF SMOKE drifted over Rurik's shield. The mist dissipated at his behest and the snarling, wailing form of Feral leapt into a line of halberds to their demise. A sledge sent a man sailing and she headbutted another, his sallet crushed by the strength. The other breakers swarmed in after. Sahira and Lyue split off from Feral's flanks, deadly weapons making quick work of the few soldiers at the gate.

Rust and Katriene rushed the gunners. Caught in the midst of reloading, the viper slid from one soldier to the next, dual daggers flashing, her strikes drawing blood. Rust, axe in hand, split a woman's head then grabbed the barrel of an arquebus as it swung about, his palm emitting a green aura that seared the wooden weapon in two. The gunner frowned and Jerk sapped him in the back of the head with a sledge.

Sweets and Melody trailed Rurik as he approached the beacon's walls. Tall, black stone buildings created a corridor that led to the open gates, six, even seven stories high, shaped as smooth cylinders with pyramidal roofs.

Rurik remembered his last visit. The Solarstone caught the rays of the sun and hummed with life, filling the street with roving streaks of energy that zipped to and fro, arcing around congested traffic. Now, it lay dormant, dark and silent beneath a sky of rock. Their steps echoed across the urban cityscape, the tower looming ahead. It stretched higher than he recalled, higher still if not for the peak embedded into the cavern's ceiling.

Gunfire heightened their pace. Sporadic fighting carried the sounds of steel against stone, a hollow sort of clatter. Voices followed. Some screams, cries, then nothing. Rurik and the others ran. He rushed ahead, his speed augmented by his suit. Blackened scorches from where Celesti blew the metal gates from their frames hugged the walls and road, lacking the time needed for a proper breaking.

Inside the remainder of the Adirian forces lay in disarray. Soldiers intermixed with white robed diviners dotted the scene. Stone sentinels joined the corpses, riddled with holes and chipped by ineffective steel while two roamed among the survivors. They impaled the dying on the edge of their wing-tipped spears.

"If we hurry, we can swarm them." Lyue reached Rurik first. "Split up into even groups and–"

Rurik pointed the lance at one of the sentinels. He cast through it, amplifying the power from his soul. A column of light encircled the guardian. It exploded into dust and debris, showering the field in its death throes.

"Or that."

He repeated the process with the second guardian before it even saw them.

They filtered into the courtyard, breakers going about the gruesome work of corpse mutilation. The rectangular, metal constructs of the past were dormant. Rurik's augmented vision flagged errors with the long disused rune work. He ignored the warnings and searched for any survivors. There, behind a battery his senses picked up a fluttering heartbeat.

"Someone's over there. Melody, see what shape they're in."

Lanatir popped his head up from the conduit. He held the dataslate, his finery ripped and shredded; finally, he looked the part of a breaker.

"Rurik? Is that you?" The baron's voice croaked. He stumbled out from his hiding spot. "And Loo-ah. Oh! It is you. Sunlord be praised!"

"*Regardez, c'est un putain de lâche,*" Katriene snarked.

"You'll never believe it! I went for help and Celesti, well, she took me prisoner. Dragged me here, said I'd be perfect bait. Those things came from the tower after we got inside. Killed the lot of them!" Lanatir spoke erratically, wringing his hands together as he tripped and wobbled his way over to Rurik. "I can't believe you're alive!"

"He's lying." A weak, but sardonic voice came from the stairs of the beacon. It spoke between wet, bloody coughs. Celesti. She sat with her back against an open door, her runecrafted armor pierced through the stomach, saber discarded. She managed to lift the visor of her helmet. "That you, Rik?"

"It is." Rurik's helmet segmented into multiple plates and sunk into the armor. "Can't say I mind seeing you this way. Fits you."

Celesti laughed. Painfully, with fits of wet coughs. The breakers gathered nearby.

"Foreman, I assured you I'm in no–"

"Shut up, Lanatir." Rurik crossed to Celesti. "Don't let him move." Feral snarled and placed her hand on the baron's shoulder. He squirmed.

Rurik ascended the stairs and bent over the dying woman.

"Never thought I'd be killed by rocks." Celesti spat blood.

"I always figured the Void would swallow you whole once it realized you were missing."

She snorted, then winced, holding her stomach. His ring glinted in a flash of light on Celesti's finger.

"I know I don't deserve mercy, Rik. All the pain I caused you. But you mind finishing the job? I'm cold. I hate the cold."

Rurik stared into her eyes, that deep blue glazing over with a gray sheen. He wanted to feel anger. To hate her. No Adirian ever made his life better. In either life. He swiped the ring from her finger then rose and placed the glaive-blade at her neck.

"Lanatir. He ratted everything. Your deal, the gates. Even your girl crush. Thought it'd break you. Coward ran at the first sign of trouble. Get him too."

He wanted to hate her. More than anything. Yet here, he remembered a past love. An earnest betrothal. If he won the field at Ilduan that day would Celesti stand over him now? In two lives hate never solved any of his problems.

He withdrew the lance.

"Melody!" The sunsinger rushed over and he tossed her the ring. "Can you save her?"

"I will try, foreman."

Rurik tore himself away and joined the others who circled Lanatir.

"Now listen Rurik, I don't know what she told you." Rurik's fist interrupted the speech. Lantair twisted and fell and writhed from the strike.

"I won't kill you. But them?" He gestured to his crew. "They deserve some revenge."

Lanatir groaned.

"Rust, Sweets, Jerk, I need you three to take Celesti and head back to Kalthier. If I can get to the seal, I should be able to use the beacon to clear the ghouls." He dialed an address into his wrist plate and deactivated the lockout he placed ten centuries previous. The gate fired up a portal. "I don't expect, or want, the rest of you to follow me. The Avatar is beyond anything you know, but I will end this."

"Certain death or potential death." Lyue shrugged and flurried her sword. "I came here for the weapon. I'm not going anywhere."

Feral stomped her agreement, snarling.

"Cannae say I won't miss ya." Rust rubbed the back of his bald head. He handed his axe over to Feral who handed him back her sledge. "I get what yer doin', Rik. If I get free'a this my grandkids'll know yer name."

"Shari's boon and Vari's blessings, boss. These things I will pray." Sweets said then kicked Jerk's shin.

"This godliness is foolish, no? But I will wish you luck in the face of chaos."

"Sky father, you really are a jerk." Sahira rolled her eyes. "Alright then, get. Take Melody and that evil woman with ya."

"Sahira." Rurik spoke softly.

"Ahuh. I'm comin', how many times we gonna revisit this?"

"Never again." Rurik grinned and embraced Sahira, drawing her in. He pressed his lips against hers in a sweet embrace. She blinked, stiffened, then melted into him, returning the affection. They held onto each other for too long.

"Rik." She spoke sadly, opening her eyes. "Don't."

"How am I supposed to fight if I'm watching you the entire time?"

"Shit." Sahira slapped him. "You can't just do that and send me away. Two years, and now?"

"And now. Please Sahira. Go with them, they'll need you."

"Son of a bitch." Sahira punched Rurik in his armored chest. "You better survive this, lord. I swear I'll come back just to kick your corpse." They separated, to equal dismay, to find the others having turned away except for Katriene and Feral, one watching with a smirk, the other with muted appreciation.

"*Vous avez terminé? Pouvons-nous aller tuer un dieu maintenant?*"

"Yes, we're done. Come on."

Rurik's helmet slid out from the armor's storage. He spared one last look at Sahira then turned away with the remainder of his group in tow. Leylia waved him down, finished with Celesti whose head lulled in blissful sleep. Pink scar tissue replaced the gaping wound.

"She survives. To complaint." The sunsinger cracked a grin. "But she lives."

"Thank you, Melody. Go with the others, there will be more wounded with Kalthier."

"And they will all be dead if you fail. I will do the most good with you." She flashed the ring. "I believe I can help."

• • •

Light shed from the lance and revealed a blackened mesh walkway. He remembered making the same trek only days ago. Days, or centuries? What he learned as history and what he experienced bled together. The same rattle of metal guided his steps, the same anticipation, the doubt. He failed to destroy the city. Would the Avatar stop him again?

They paused at a dead end, the inert lift reading as absent power. No going back now. He stared, the idle hum of the lance buzzing in his ears. People died while he waited. Did he send them to those deaths? Ilduan, Mithirin, Dula'Thalier then, now, again. More to lose yet.

"*Dépêchez-vous déjà.*"

"We are on a crunch, Rurik." Lyue clicked her blade against a leather boot.

Rurik tapped the lance against the mechanism. An ambient, blue aura appeared beneath the platform along with a runic prompt asking for a slate. Lyue and the others shuffled on. Tight, Feral took up a third of the space while the others crammed into what remained. The wastelander flexed her arms and sighed, her lips smacking together. Her boredom brought levity to Rurik's overshadowing anxiety.

He tapped at the projected runes on his wrist. The lift shuddered. A metallic whir spooled up from beneath. Leylia latched to Katriene's arm who snickered at the startled sunpriest. Shakily, the group ascended at a crawl.

"There are defenses." Rurik broke the silence.

"Figures. Like what?"

"Sentries. Like the others, but stronger, better armored."

Feral grunted.

"Could've mentioned that."

"Could've," Rurik said. Lyue stretched, cracking her shoulders. She slid a hand over the runes of her sword, mumbling under her breath as a green glow encompassed the surface. Another Justiciar trick.

"*Pas juste! Donnez-moi ça aussi, non?*"

Rurik gestured with his free hand, circling his palm and twisting his fingers in with the motion. The same green aura emerged from the axe and Katriene's daggers. The Singuli nodded, satisfied. Feral sniffed her weapon. From above a pale illumination broke the darkness. It drew their collective attention, snaking over a ledge and bleeding below. Leylia clutched her amulet and chanted, her words incomprehensive and quick.

"Get ready."

The lift docked. Earthen walls of stone cradled the tower's zenith as if consuming it. Runes clung to the rock, thousands of them, aggressive, and sharp, they lit the chambers in their image, a pale red that bathed the interior in an eerie coating. Shattered glass littered the grounds. The crystalline prisms that once gathered energy now dispersed it, drawing a swirling aura from the golden doors on the far side of the housing. Those foci amplified that energy and projected them onto the rock–the very source of the runes, it spread from the tower over the cavern, creating and shaping the death that plagued the city.

Movement flickered from the shadows. Warnings flashed in Rurik's display, a sudden onset of power spikes. Shrouded, black forms lifted themselves from a state of rest. He recalled destroying three before the others overwhelmed him. He tapped at his wrist, reading Lynesse's last order: slay all intruders.

"Go, go!"

Rurik took the lead. Lyue and Feral fell in behind while Katriene disappeared into the shadows. Leylia's chanting grew louder and gained a harsh melody as his interface indicated rising temperatures.

Nine sentinels shuttered to life where he left them centuries previous. He focused, siphoning energy from his soul into the lance. White columns appeared above a construct, rupturing with force as it tore the body to pieces, limbs falling with a weighted crash.

The others rounded on him. Eight constructs took off at impossible speeds. Rurik set the haft of the lance into the ground and ran a series of projections in his mind. He fed the calculations into the artefact which amplified the directions, a tangible mist expanding in a sphere from the weapon itself. It spread among the chamber and washed over the sentinels, their movements slowing as their joints stiffened.

Feral snarled and closed on a construct. It swung at her and she bashed her axe into the offending weapon, her brute strength sending it careening off course. She reprised by sinking the head into an extended arm. The enchanted edge cut clear through. She roared and spun, the axe following as it took out a chunk of the construct's body. The sentinel launched a second, bladed arm at the wastelander only to find itself buffeted by a solid shield of orange. It appeared from nothing, though Leylia cast her hand toward the brawl, her amulet shimmering. Feral raised her axe and struck, cleaving half the sentinel's torso from top to bottom.

Lyue wove in and out of danger. She dipped under strikes meant for her, following discarded momentum and sliding along the outside, blade flourishing and striking at exposed joints. She worked her way around the construct, slashing, shifting low to score its legs then coming up for another set of strikes. Lyue slid from one form to the next, precise and fluid, until she hacked the construct into disconnected debris.

While the others fought, Rurik wove more spells. Once the mist circled their foes, he reached out and manipulated it further, the surrounding runes dimming as he drew on their presence to preserve his power. He shaped a wave from the aura and directed it at a grouping of the guardians. It held them in place, lifeless.

A sentinel cracked Lyue from behind and sent her sailing. She landed in a heap, gasping in pain. The construct followed and loomed above her. It raised a leg then tottered as Katriene's nimble frame scurried up the constructs back. It flailed, arms reaching and clawing at the Singali. She cackled as she ascended to its shoulders then sunk her blades into its neck. She let her weight fall and rode it down while carving two wicked gashes into its body, avoiding the grasping hands and landing into a silent roll away from the sentry as it collapsed.

Leylia rushed to the lowlander. Her song shifted from an aggressive chant to a calm aria. She placed a hand over Lyue's ribs and bones snapped back into place with insidious cracks. A construct changed course to the healer, slowed, but intent, until Feral intercepted. It tipped at the collision, then paused. It righted itself and thrust a bladed limb into the wasteland's gut and out her back.

"Feral!" Rurik snapped the lance at the woman. He funneled power through the shaft, igniting the engravings and directing the mist to engulf the construct, restricting its movement like the others. Sweat beaded over his forehead. The effort to hold all four guardians locked him in place as they fought against his will. Feral howled. Her muscles tightened as she lifted the axe, panting, spitting up blood, she crashed it into the construct's head. It shivered then bucked under a wild foray of strikes until the weapon split its torso, pieces of stone flying from the sheer force. It collapsed and Feral fell with it.

Katriene juked another construct's blow, following it with a riposte of slashing daggers. They scored an arm. When it reared up for another try, she ducked inside of its reach only to have it step with her, limbs crashing onto her shoulders. Katriene sacrificed one side of herself to break the brunt of the impact. Her arm snapped and dangled. She yelped then struck, single dagger hacking at the same scoring until she removed the limb from the joint. She recoiled in pain, desperately crawling away from the guardian as it persisted.

Rurik formed a gravity rune and projected it to the sentry's side and sent it sailing, colliding with an exposed rock wall.

Runes flickered. Energy expanded into a bristling orb out from the impact then retracted in an instant, a sudden onset of flames lapped over the construct and charred it to a lifeless mass. Katriene leapt away into a roll, screaming as her broken shoulder hit the metallic floor.

Three remained, stuck within his bindings. With the last sentinel's destruction they ceased their struggles. Their bodies lit up. Lines of red appeared in intricate webs as they redirected power from the prisms, beams of light absorbed into their solarstone exteriors.

Rurik groaned. He opened his palm and the mist gathered around the convalescent energy, hardening and shifting, they took shape as dozens of spears. Rurik extended his arm and they flew into the guardians, piercing their shells and ripping deep into their cores. Their energy grew. Crimson lightning arced from one to the other, crackling, it flailed, erratic lashes of power streaming out in flashing eruptions. A bolt struck his armor and seared into it, leaving a trail of smoking vapor. Another followed. It ripped a plate off and exposed the skin beneath.

Warnings flashed in his helmet. Imminent danger. Rurik brought the lance about and channeled through it again, creating a half sphere that intercepted the lightning as it came. Of all the familiar places. Before he ran. Now? He clenched his teeth and slammed a heel into the ground, redoubling his efforts. Someone called his name.

Leylia and Lyue stood next to a prism with their hands pressed against the crystal. The sunsinger's amulet blazed now with a brilliant resplendence as her voice sailed to an aggressive, clarion sting, siphoning the raw essence in her being. Lyue acted as a battery and fueled the priest. Fire exploded around the sentinels. A deluge of white plasma consumed them, melting hardened stone. The torrent of power between them changed in response, forming into a protective shielding and eating the summoned firestorm. They clashed, sparks sent throughout the chamber.

Now. Rurik closed his palm. The spears of blue detonated. One after the other, they ruptured fractures within the sentinels. Their shield dropped and plasma rained over them, destroying all vestiges of resistance.

Rurik gasped and released his spells. Leylia did the same. Lyue fell to her knees, wheezing, while the sunsinger reluctantly released her hold on the prism and stumbled to Feral's side. The wastelander curled into herself, rocking as she clutched her wound. Rurik followed. Weak, but persistent, Leylia chanted, her amulet flickering with the last dregs of her will.

"Will she be okay?" Rurik spoke with a husking exhaustion.

"No worry," Feral grunted. "Chiefman must save others." She winced, her voice gentle. "Finish thing."

"I can help," He said, raising the lance.

"You have to stop the Avatar." Lyue's breathy voice came from labored pants. "You can't weaken yourself more. Listen to her. Go!"

"*Arrêtez d'être un imbécile si dramatique et finissez ceci!*"

"Don't die," Rurik said as he jogged over to the golden door, its circular shape carved with hundreds of sealing runes. Set in the only flat wall of the chamber the door latched itself to the interior with no visible sign of release. He recalled its construction, a prison built for a singular entity in the one place with enough strength to hold it indefinitely.

This was a bad idea. A terrible, necessary, horrible idea. Images of battle flashed through his mind. Power unmade. The others counted on him. Sahira, the breakers. Kalthier. Hundreds of lives teetered on the brink.

Five stone plates circled a depression constructed solely for the weapon he possessed. He plunged the lance in and funneled a stream of his essence into the haft of the artifact. The plates ejected. They thunked out from the door and popped off, falling to the ground with a calamitous clatter. They revealed carved circuits, snaking lines that spanned from the center and out to the door itself. Steam hissed from the outer lining. The door shuddered; it spun, slow at first, gaining speed with every clicking revolution. At each cycle a portion retracted toward the apparatus at its heart until the section stood open, leaving the lance's housing hovering on its own.

A zephyr blew from inside. Salty, ocean air. It lured Rurik in. He retracted his helmet. From shadow he made out the silhouette of a grand throne, shining links of pure light bound to blackened arms and legs. It sat, surrounded on all sides by runes of every shape, color, and purpose. From the floor to the ceiling, they boasted mastery beyond anything he knew. And at the center it waited. Its fingers–shaped like any–tapped against its metal throne, clicking, one after the other.

Behind it all the lightest tear in the fabric of reality lingered, spilling forth a purple mist that infested the runes with sickly, purple veins.

"*At last.*" Its voice pierced his senses. His ears, his mind. It repeated those words a dozen times, echoing in foreign tones. "*We have unfinished business, Iskarion.*"

Excerpt from the
high Loremaster's Journal

SOMETHING I'VE LONG QUESTIONED. The Litanies, the loremasters. Are we to believe that all knowledge of before was wiped out during the Desolation? Surely, some small pieces would survive. A lost tome, an isolated cathedral. Traces remain, always. Unless the purge of information was intentional. That befits a more sensible explanation. Hunted, extinguished. But by who? The Faith? They did not possess the resources for such a massive undertaking, their forces engaged so with the Void.

All my research leads me to believe there is an unaccounted entity in all this. One obfuscated by design. What does it mean for Yaros if we have been manipulated all this time to ignore the very facts before our eyes?

Chapter 30
The Avatar of Chaos

FLASHES OF GRAY flooded his mind. He stood upon a bed of silver liquid, undisturbed by his touch. It reflected his self. All of his selves. Iskarion, Rurik. And others. People of whom he possessed no memory. Yet, he knew them. They stretched into infinity as did the lake of mirrors. No horizon, no sun, only a white sky of absence above. Alone. Bereft armor and weapon, naked, and whole. He raised his arm and the reflections followed him. One after the other, silent shadows that mocked his actions.

"What is this place?"

Your soul.

He did not hear the words so much as know them. They came as thoughts, spoken in his own voice. His soul. The reflections mimicked his confusion, all of them in their unique expressions.

"My what?"

Your soul. Your essence. The chaos that feeds your life. You've been here before. Many times.

Nothing gave way to form. His toes curled into sand as water lapped over his feet. The sun blazed at full light above with the cliffs of Iskvar behind, catching the echo of crashing waves and sending it back to the ocean. This is where Iskarion took him, where she spoke to him with her cryptic messages. Where she urged him on, lured him to all the right places. His own soul?

Yes. We are the truth of what defines you.

Iskarion did not speak to him here. He spoke to himself. Visages helped him process, they guided him, but they came from him.

Find me.

Remember what you did.

Do us all a favor.

All of it was him. A soul recycled, used by generations, stripped and reforged time and again since the beginning. The beginning of what?

"Of it all."

Sahira's voice spun him around. She smiled at him, wearing the fresh version of her black breaker's blouse tucked into tight pants. She skipped into the foam of an ebbing tide, splashing water with her bare feet.

"You're not her."

"Correct." She winked at him. "But this is who you want to see. As you'd prefer it."

The Sunlance appeared in Rurik's hand. He summoned it, or an image of it. The edge bristled as it harnessed energy from a brilliant sun.

"Who are you?"

"What am I." Sahira folded her arms under her chest. She pouted. "You know what I am. What you don't know is why."

His grip loosened. He lowered the weapon, its edge slipping into the sand. He stared into the mimic's eyes. Swirling, gray irises stared back. Not Sahira. An image of a creature bound to a golden throne plagued his mind. Its bored expression matched the endless tap of expectation. The Avatar.

"You're–"

"Yes."

"You won't save yourself with cheap tricks." The lance rose with his will. Its etchings filled with light.

"You don't need that here." The Avatar flicked its wrists. The Sunlance disappeared. "You rule here. You can change me, cast me out."

Sahira's body morphed into the visage of his father. Denrik. He wore his black coat lined with the deep blues of their house, a ruhk sewn into the side. Their scenery changed with him. The vast, open ceilings of Iskvar's audience hall.

"Enough of this. I came here to destroy you, not play games," Rurik said.

"No games. I control none of this." Denrik's voice rolled over him, his deep bass like a grasping dream. "You know you should listen to me. These are those you heed, people whose word carries weight. It is why you hesitate."

"Fine. You want to tell me something. So tell me why."

"Why what?"

"Why you're such an asshole." Rurik threw his hands into the air. Naked, his arms slapped against bare flesh. Right. A garb similar to Denrik's appeared over his body, same coat, leather pants, thick boots.

"It has been seven-hundred and fifty-nine years since I've communed with a sentient creature. I am owed some jests."

"You've been trapped here for a thousand."

"Incorrect."

"The histories–"

"Are wrong. Human memory is spectacular, isn't it? You need only believe a thing and it supplants reality."

"Not making a strong case for why I should listen to you."

"Forgive me. It is in my nature to be distracted. I will attempt to be succinct if you have the patience." Denrik, or the Avatar, flicked his wrist. A ripple shuttered through the world. The hall disappeared, replaced by the original silver lake and a frozen wasteland appeared upon its surface. They stood above it, viewing from the heavens like gods. At the edge of the world snow and ice effervesced into an ether of mist, a nothing, unmade into the Void itself.

"Eight hundred years, or so, ago I came to aid this precious creation." From the end of the tundra a formless, translucent shadow crept from the mists. As it trekked, it gained mass. It absorbed the world around it and changed whatever it touched.

"From the Void," Rurik said, his brow narrowing.

"No. You've always had that wrong. You and I come from the same realm. One of chaos and infinite possibilities. It is the very essence of creation, it is where all life begins and where it returns at the end."

"Our bodies return to the Sunstar. Not even the scholars of Dula'Thalier thought differently."

"They do. Your star feeds upon the matter you leave behind the same as it draws from the realm of chaos. It's all the same. But your souls return to their true home to rest. They mingle and add the experience of one lifetime to dozens of identities, they grow and split, they join others and relish in their freedom. Then, once they are ready, they return to the world of order where the cycle begins anew. This is how you are Rurik and Iskarion, and many others."

Within the pool the Avatar's shadowed body journeyed over the western wastes of Thalas. It drew the attention of wastelanders, tribes of individuals very much like Feral. They worshipped it as it went, studied it; they built structures where it touched the world, visages to its likeness where they made their homes and embraced the change it bestowed upon their very bodies. As it continued, it begged the notice of more advanced civilizations. The five Rune Knights of Dula'Thalier staged their assault to little avail.

"We attacked you. We believed you had no will, but you could have destroyed us."

"Yes."

"It was the first time we witnessed something unmade. Our spells. It terrified us, more than the Emissaries. We believed you were another threat. You said you came to aid us?"

"Against the Emissaries, as you call them. The Void." For the first time Rurik saw anger creep into Denrik's expression. Ripples shuttered and the lake changed. It showed a land of dull gray where mists swirled and shadows, both human and without cohesion, mingled, shifting their surroundings to their wills. A Voidtear ripped itself into the realm and from it tendrils of black energy assaulted the beings.

"They came first against Chaos. Invaders. They sought to feed, to take all for themselves but they were not prepared for the realm itself to fight."

Together, the shadows of the swirling realm fought back. The land itself resisted and the tears closed, their violent hosts sundered and cast out. The inhabitants of the realm wielded powers beyond anything he imagined. They needed no weapons, possessed as they were by a supply of infinite energy.

"Or so I believed. I did not understand their corruption, for it did not exist then. They infested souls and upon their return to Order they opened new means of ingress. Order gave them form and rules. So long as they abided by these confines, they were free to infest, to feed, and drain. They spread their influence and bestowed their power to loyal followers."

Another shift. They stood above the Sunstar, a pulsing sphere of cells, of burning plasma. Rurik knew they looked upon the original splendor of the Sky Father. The source of life and creation, the one that shaped the world and gave birth to order and form. The image shivered and time advanced. Black tendrils breached the corona and the light diminished.

"They fed, but your star did not defend itself. Why? Why would it let these parasites take its splendor? It took me centuries to understand that this did not break the rules. Entropy is natural, for all creatures of Order consume to survive. All life feeds from its light and what results from it, but those of the Void took too much and gave nothing. Order waned. And I did not wish to see it die. I came to rally the children to fight. But I am not a child of Order."

Denrik's expression softened. The golden throne appeared beneath him and he sat, overwhelmed by a profound sadness.

"I broke the rules. I unmade the land in my wake. I challenged Order with my very presence and drew the ire of its disciples. I wanted to save you, to save everything, but I could not bring myself to destroy. I allowed myself to be captured. I was helpless. When you and your knights took me I grew too close to Order and weakened enough to be bound. I could not know you would go too far."

Beneath them lay an ancient city built within a cauldron of greenery, a luscious landscape of gardens and trees mingled with a metropolis of white marble palaces and miles of urban sprawl. Bridges of pure energy spanned over a snaking river where children played. Bustling markets hummed as millions busied about their days in the perfect harmony of nature and technology.

A bright, blue day lost its light. The peace and calm of the city turned to confusion as its inhabitants looked to the phenomenon, only to watch as columns of shimmering light fell from the sky.

"Mithirin," Rurik choked out. He watched as the columns tore the world asunder. Anything they touched became dust. It lasted for minutes. Only minutes. By the time they stopped nothing but bare, brown stone remained. "We used the beacon–you–to destroy it, to destroy the Emissary there."

"Yes. And you succeeded, but in doing so you broke the rules. Your actions then and after, started the Desolation. The Emissaries, knowing that they could be killed, fought back. They goaded what civilizations they could into war. Even after you destroyed Dula'Thalier the remaining knights learned what they needed, and from their experiments others drew that knowledge. No atrocity was too great. One bred another until the cities of the world disappeared as if they never were. Eventually, the armies of Cinderfell left their isolation to purge those that would dare challenge the rule of Order."

"You're saying we destroyed ourselves. That the holy isle purged the world of civilization? The Sunlord has armies?"

"Not as you understand them. Servants, avatars of its power, those like myself. They used implements similar to your Sunlance. And when they reaffirmed the hand of Order they left tenets. Guides. Your faith calls them Litanies. Others have similar instructions. Warnings."

"I suppose that solves the debate of legitimacy. Where does that leave you in all of this? Why preserve the city?"

"I didn't." Denrik raised an arm. The bands of light rose with him then forced him into the throne. "My power is limited. I can watch, send whispers. Otherwise? I sit." He shifted, leaning back into the throne. "Come now. Who benefits from my eternal imprisonment? The Emissaries stoked the fires of war until any power that could challenge them vanished from this world. I am one of those powers. And that, Rurik, is why you must release me."

Rurik reeled. Their setting, his soul, shifted to the beach. Denrik vanished. Rurik settled into the sand, his fingers digging deep. He remembered this day. His last at Iskvar. No one knew of the private inlet, so far away from the town and settled away on the far side of the cliffs. He came here to be alone, to think. To brood. Gentle waves rolled onto the shore that day. They lulled him into a restless sleep, plagued with nightmares of his failures. When he woke the only person he wanted to see sat beside him.

"She is important to you," Arkalis said. She wore her hair tied in a tight braid down her neck and allowed her blouse to open at the top. Her toes wiggled in the sand. Lost her boots again, no doubt. She turned to look at him with a sly grin, her arms propped up on her knees.

"She was. She never blamed me for any of it. Only wanted to make me laugh." He frowned at her visage. More than ever, he needed her snark.

"Was? You speak of her passing." Confusion rippled over her face.

"She died attempting to escape Iskvar, along with my father and those that raised me."

"Your father has passed on, correct. Such is not the case with your sister. She yet lives, though she is in great peril."

"What? She." Celesti. Rurik rolled his eyes and rubbed his temple between his thumb and forefinger. "What peril?"

"Let me show you."

·   ·   ·

Kali heard herself scream. It seemed unreal. That coarse wailing did not belong to her. Yet, the pain that locked her in place radiated in every fiber of her being. Prickling, sharp stabs spread as the magus plunged into her mind. She dug and Kali lay helpless. She doubled over onto her side and curled her limbs in, fighting. Aching cold and coursing magma wracked her insides.

The magus *tsk'd* at her. "Maybe you deserve a break." The pain vanished. Kali gasped for air, her body convulsing. "I know you're in there. It's this world. It forces us to feed slowly, as if I wasn't starving. These idiot Magi were the best meal I've had in seven centuries. Did you know they believed you would teach them to ascend? Hah. As if such primitives could do such a thing."

Kali groaned as her senses flooded in. First sight. Though hazy, she saw Nihilus and Niati sequestered in a corner, unmoving. Neither dared draw attention to themselves. Her enhanced vision told her the pontifex grew weaker by the minute.

"You're not hearing me, hm? Arkalis, dear, please. This will be easier if you let me in."

Kali coughed. She set her shoulders straight, resolved, and dragged the obsidian blade across the floor, grinding it against the cold steel. She pushed herself up to the humored countenance of the magus.

"I heard you," she managed. "I've heard you for too long. And all I want is for you to shut. Up."

"If that's how you want to play it." The magus reached out, binding Kali in tendrils of invisible force that lifted her into the air. She hung, arms to the side, squirming. "You can resist all you want, girl." A sinister edge laced the magus' tone. "But you will not hide from me."

• • •

"What is this?" Rurik stared into the image. He stood beside the visage of his sister while she fought in the real world, suspended in midair, tortured, her screams haunting his ears.

"That is an Emissary of the Void. She seeks the one merged with your sister's soul and is tearing her essence apart to find it."

"It?"

"It. The one your soul chased into the world."

Images raced before his eyes. Iskarion in the realm of chaos and an essence unlike any other, a soul borne of the Void, an alien force caught in the cycle of rebirth. Iskarion found and guarded it. She managed to contain it for centuries. Until it escaped.

"Arkalis is–"

"Unique."

"She's a Void God. Iskarion–or, me. I chased it back into the world. To stop it."

"When that Emissary died it became part of this realm, bound to chaos. It reforged itself into a being like you and me. Her soul is something new, but fragile. Should it take too much stress I fear the Void will shape it into another weapon. Your sister can be saved, Rurik. She must be." The Avatar placed a hand on his shoulder. They shared a long, hard look. "Free me."

•   •   •

Runes surrounded him. Lined with cruel, purple veins, they infested the walls and formed a concentrated halo of illumination around the shaded throne. The blackened body of the Avatar waited placidly, its limbs bound with chains of pure light. Rurik stood only paces away. He did not remember coming closer.

Without the guises the Avatar took no specific features. Smooth of skin, it favored no gender nor boasted muscle of any kind. It bore a thin face with the same swirling gray eyes, expectant, patient. It clicked its fingers.

"*Have you made your decision?*"

Its voice came from everywhere at once, layered in a chorus that sang with a myriad of tones.

"I free you and you save her. You save them. All of them. Anyone trapped in this pit."

For a moment they shared the silence.

"*My power is diminished. I may not be able to stop the Emissary if I help the rest of them.*"

Rurik's eyes watered. "Then I take my chances. This." He lifted the lance toward the Avatar. "This ends you and I do what I can. Or you save all of them."

"Don't be foolish, Iskarion. More lies in the balance than your friends."

"No!" A tear rolled down his cheek. "You said it yourself. You came here to save us, so help them. The Sunlord's armies destroyed all that we were. And for what? For the world to end slower? They are what matters. Without them none of this means anything!"

Rurik held the Avatar's gaze. For what seemed like hours he waited. Until, finally, the clicking stopped. The Avatar sighed. Rurik basked in the surreal state of a literal god's resignation.

"So be it. Time is short."

Rurik bowed his head. He knew the commands to loosen the chains. Commands issued by five, power drawn by five. And worse, the corruption of the runes meant interference from the Void. Even if he did free the Avatar could he escape? He needed to wipe the slate clean. That limited his options. Memories flooded to the forefront of his mind: the cathedral's dais. He recalled kneeling, so he knelt. Rurik failed his people at Ilduan, he failed his crew time and again. He failed himself, as Iskarion and Rurik. He would not fail again.

Power gathered in his chest. No gesture, no command. Heat rose from his body. It consumed him as the raw essence of his soul swelled. Gently, he slid his hands to the glaive-blade and pressed its edge against his ribs, the tip slicing into the already scored armor plating.

"Of all the familiar places," Rurik whispered. He closed his eyes and plunged the lance into his heart.

A sharp ring overwhelmed his senses. Pain exploded in his mind. Rurik railed against it. Focus. He calmed his panic and cast his essence onto the wave of power that pulsed from his soul. He could feel everything. The solarstone of the tower, the runes, the Avatar, his companions within the foci chamber. Feral lay still while Melody worked desperately to save her. Farther, he went beyond the tower. Hundreds of ghouls swarmed a compound as the remains of the living fought against them. Sahira protected the gates, fighting the unyielding horde as gunners used their weapons as clubs, beating back what they recognized as their deaths. And farther. Outside the city he drifted east, to Haven.

Screams guided him inside another tower. Arkalis hovered, suspended against her will. He saw the tendrils of black extend from the magus at the center of the chamber. They dug deep into the woman's flesh, they tore at her soul, looking, seeking. Rurik wrapped her in his essence and for a moment her voice quieted. Her eyes snapped open. He saw pain and desperation. Fear. Then hope.

I love you.

Rurik snapped to the present. No more time to waste. He reached out, his senses flowing over the throne. Its power resisted him. Fueled by the corruption of the Void it washed over him like bile, sickening his soul. No matter. He let the Void sink its claws into him. He pulled it free from the runes, cleansing it from the surface. There. Rurik grasped the chains, his presence expanding to encompass the room. They snapped.

"Save them!" He heard himself yell. Not him, his body. Nothing more than a vessel. Free from its bonds the Avatar vanished into nothing.

Now, to end this. Rurik embraced the runes. All of them. Those in the beacon, the cavern. Every surface of every stone. He envisioned the one rune that plagued him, a simple expression of force and fire. It appeared in his mind, a jagged, aggressive meeting of script. It pulsed red. He ignited them all.

Explosions filled the Beacon. They washed over his body and turned it to dust. Yet he lingered. He followed the blasts through the tower as the foci chamber burnt crimson with fire. It consumed all it touched. Down the lift shaft to the ground floor, it met with more runes as they erupted along the walls. Solarstone burst forth, sending debris out into the city. The runes on the cavernous ceiling detonated out in concentric circles, raining fire and stone onto the city as its structures joined the calamity. Bellowing flames seethed from the ground. They charred all they touched as no building escaped the wrath.

From the tower to the outskirts, ruptures shook the very foundations as buildings collapsed. They scored a path to the encampment. The breaker's compounds went first, collapsed by earth and flame. He looked ahead to the fort where the ghouls continued their assault, unphased by the coming disaster. As the destruction reached them a blackened figure appeared above the garrison and, as if they never existed, the survivors blinked away. The rest of the cavern caved in.

Rurik felt relief. Satisfaction. Peace? Time, at last, to die.

Excerpt from Hardent's Bestiary

NEW SPECIES are not uncommon among the wastes. As it is, I believe most creatures native to Yaros were once "wastespawn," having emerged from the edges of creation and slowly migrated their way inward. As I've seen it the closer a creature's home is to the Isle of Cinderfell the more "rules" it seems to follow. Not so for the noble wastes, infinite stretches of infinite possibility.

I admit not all these discoveries serve the common good. For instance, I recently cataloged a species I've named the Ice Wyrm, a vicious reptilian carnivore near ten times the height of a man. Beautiful to behold. Unique. Yet. Altogether terrifying.

Chapter 31
The First of her Kind

"W E DON'T HAVE much time."

Kali opened her eyes to emptiness. A silver liquid rippled at her touch, its waves cascading out into eternity. Rurik's voice reached her in a whisper as if it came from leagues away. It brought a sense of peace.

"Kali."

Rurik appeared as if from nothing. He bore a clean-shaven chin and closely cropped hair cut to a military fashion, though his bangs stood upright from too much time spent grooming. She smiled. A true, warming expression, it spread from cheek to cheek, her eyes alight. Until he spoke again.

"You're naked."

Kali examined herself. She lost a fair amount of weight in the month previous, slimming her to a more gangly specimen.

"Oh."

"Happened to me too. Project whatever you'd prefer."

She did. A fur robe, gentle against her skin. She nestled into the comfort and tied it off at her waist. Wherever she was, she made a note to find a way back.

"Better. Now, we don't have much time. I need to speak to you."

"You're real?" Kali watched her brother with suspicion. "You're no different from the day you left. I expected some manly scars, at least."

Rurik scowled.

"Hah! Definitely real."

"Kali, I need to tell you–"

"They told me you died, you know. I always expected it. It's why they sent you to that pit. I never thought I'd blame myself for it. But I did. Same for father. And Din. Gariant." Kali rubbed a sleeve over her eyes. "Ah. I'm a mess, Rik. I'm dead though, right? This is the Sky Father's garden. And you're what? A messenger? Come to whisk me off."

"You're not dead."

"The fuck I'm not. Last thing I remember was that magus tearing me apart."

"She is. Or she's trying to. I can hear you screaming."

Kali's eyes widened. She heard it too. A spasm of pain jolted her body. The viscous surface shook with the interruption, threatening to split apart. She willed it away and the bliss returned. She realized the peace for what it was, the simple absence of pain. One never appreciated the status quo until discomfort replaced it.

"I'm not. Then you?"

"Not yet." Rurik grew more serious if that was possible. The fringes of his body turned to dust and disappeared. "You ready to listen?"

"Yeah. Yes."

"The magus. She's more than that. She's a Void God, Kali. And she's not trying to kill you. She's digging."

In the distance a storm darkened the horizon. Fierce lightning roared from black clouds that spread with the intensity of a stampede. A wound in reality spilled mist into the air, festering an ill shadow. Tendrils of black energy pierced its edge.

"For what? I don't understand, Rik, what are they all looking for?"

"You, Kali. You are the first of your kind. Voidborne to the realm of Order. You are the reincarnation of a god, the first to die. You must resist her."

"I tried! She's too strong."

"Help is coming." Rurik did not move, instead he appeared closer. He brought Kali into a tight embrace. More of him flaked off into nothing. "You must hold on." Rurik withdrew and held her arms. He smiled. For once. "Live, Kali. Take care of the others."

"Help? Others? Rik, don't. Don't go. Not again. Don't leave me alone."

"You won't be." His voice faded as did the rest of him. "I love you, sister."

• • •

Kali crashed to the floor on her knees. Her eyes snapped open. Rurik? The Emissary lifted her brow, puzzled. Kali rose and grabbed the obsidian blade on the way up.

"Who was that?" The Emissary spoke, unsure.

Help is coming. The thought echoed in her mind. Her vision wandered to the gates,

"Expecting company, are we? Let him come, dear, I'm quite famished."

A blue flash filled the room as inky black portals sprung to life within all seven arches. The Emissary spun to face them. She summoned a coiling energy from a palm as shadowed tendrils pulsed from the staked bodies of the Magi. The Emissary thrust her palm into the air and the energy lashed out like a snake. It bit into the portals, blasting the solarstone into ruin with a raucous eruption. She straightened and lowered her hand, grinning wolfishly.

The ceiling exploded. Crystal glass shattered and shards rained from above. A shield took form above the Emissary and Kali felt the wall disappear from her mind.

She pulled the thread.

Power coursed through her veins once again. Her vision shifted to the endless process of data and essence. The Emissary appeared as a shadow. A swirling mass of purple veins infesting a black void over a vessel of blood and bone. The glass descended. Kali made no effort to avoid it. She knew its composition. She saw the sum of its parts and disassembled them. The shrapnel turned to sand in a sphere around her.

"How?!" The Emissary snarled.

A being emerged from the light of the exposed ceiling. A tall, humanoid creature, devoid features of gender or individuality. It stood between Kali and the Void God. To her the creature wore an intense haze, the air that circled it vibrating at its mere presence. Pure, fair; to consume it would bring overwhelming power.

Shuffling came from nearby. Niati and Nihilus ran to Kali's side.

"What is that?" Niati whispered, having abandoned her rapier for the favor of her runestones.

"Help."

"You." The Emissary spread her arms out as she drew more power from the Magi. Black, purple flames infused her body. "You will not stop me." Her voice took on an ethereal tonality, deep, lined with authority.

"*This madness ends now.*" The Avatar's voice came from all directions at once. "*I will no longer suffer the Void within the realm of Order.*"

It lifted its hand. Shards of broken crystal mimicked the movement, hovering. It flicked its fingers and the glass cut through the air to converge on the Emissary. She responded in kind. Her flames consumed the shrapnel, an arm shooting up amidst the foray and spilling black smoke into the air. It formed a vertical column, solidified, then sharpened, puncturing nothing to form a scar. A tear. A bed of emptiness that shuttered reality around it.

The sand at Kali's feet rushed to the Avatar's aid as spears of cold, chilling black launched from the Voidtear and impaled themselves into a thin bed of stone formed from the debris. The Avatar cast the rock aside as it was engulfed by unstable energy. Tendrils lashed out from the tear. Purple, sickly flesh thick as tree trunks assailed the Avatar. It brought its palms together as the wind picked up within the chamber. Raw force collided with the hideous limbs in a wave of force.

You must aid me. My power is not yet restored.

The Avatar's voice boomed in Kali's mind. She closed her mouth, her jaw agape at the display.

"We need to help it," Kali said.

"What can we do against that?!" Niati's voice verged on the edge of panic.

"She's feeding from the dead Magi somehow. Destroy them."

"As you say, duchess." Nihilus split, circling away. Niati did the same from the opposite side. Annoyed, the Emissary struck. She raised her arms and gouts of black flame sprung forth to block their paths. Kali felt the energy stream forth from the Voidtear. She saw it take shape. More importantly, she could feed from it.

And she did. From the light of the sun, from the flames themselves, Kali allowed it all to flow to her. It sated a lust deep in her soul as opposing forces collided. The flames dissipated. Nihilus and Niati resumed their run and Kali joined her will to the Avatar. She thrust a palm and it sent a shockwave against the god. The Emissary crossed her arms and weathered the blow, her concentration broken enough for the Avatar to gain control of the alien limbs. It twisted a wrist and the wind ripped the tendrils to shreds, digging deep into the flesh and cutting whatever connected it to the tear.

The Emissary roared in pain. Her eyes turned black. Her power grew as she siphoned anything she could. Light bent around her. Shadows spread in her rage. She screamed with a guttural cry and launched an explosive blackness that bore upon them in a wave. The Avatar placed an arm protectively over Kali and extended an open palm. It connected with the blast and split the wave down the middle, slicing it as it blew out a wall of the chamber in a burst of stone and metal.

The wave continued as a steady stream. Kali saw the first sign of exertion from her godly ally, his body seeming to diminish in stature the longer he resisted. Whereas the Emissary stole her power from the world, the Avatar's came from itself.

Jump.

"What?"

You must reach her. Jump.

Kali flexed her fingers over the hilt of her blade. She jumped in place. The Avatar flicked its wrist. Instead of inches she sailed into the air, reaching the height of the blown-out ceiling. The Emissary continued her assault as Nihilus and Niati ducked their way around another fleshy tendril that curled from the tear. It swept into a wall, breaking apart the stone and collapsing another section. Kali began her descent with a yelp until she felt her weight propelled with the same intensity toward the tear. What did the Emissary do to her before? She envisioned the energy wrapping at her limbs. If it could suspend her, could it guide her also?

The Avatar's push sent her flying, but her influence allowed her to change direction. She angled past the Emissary to the opposite side of the tear then halted her momentum. She sank her sword deep into the base of a tendril, cauterizing as it cut. The limb hit the ground with a shattering thud and Kali landed with it, one knee down, her eyes narrow.

The Emissary turned her head. Remains of the tendril flailed. It condensed, curling into an amorphous blob as it took the shape of a body.

"Destroy them!" Kali shouted to her companions. Nihilus rounded on a staked Magi, issuing a blast of energy that tore the body to pieces. Kali saw its stream dissipate with its dissolution. Niati whipped a trinket at another. It froze on contact then shattered as she landed a kick into its base and despoiled another thread.

The Emissary's clone finished its gestation. It mirrored its creator in every facet–without blemish, unnatural in its perfective beauty.

The clone summoned a spear from the dead magi to its hands. Kali ran to meet it. They clashed, a flare from the obsidian blade depleted by the emptiness of the Void. She reared back, her sword strike deflected by a precise stroke that ended with a solid crack to the side of Kali's head. Her vision blurred, and she lilted to the side, catching herself mid stumble. While she struggled the clone sent a wave of force that slammed into Niati as she made for the last Magi. The Soatu sailed into a wall, grasping at her chest as she sank to the ground, shaking.

Nihilus brought his arms into his chest. He thrust his palms out and pumped them, centering his breathing as a series of red runes appeared beneath the clone's feet. They sparked and unleashed a torrent of electricity that coursed through its body, charring skin, the current cracking in a consuming sphere. Laughter followed. A burst of pressure scattered the runes and with them the spell. Kali straightened, blade brought to bear.

The Emissary released her focus. The wave dimmed, dying out as the last of it washed over the Avatar who knelt, its eyes dim.

Both women laughed. Their scorn rose into the air, hearty arrogance masking their collective tone. When they spoke, they did so together.

"You bleat, tiny insects. You fight with so much *desperation*." Nihilus adjusted his collar to hide the thin weariness in his face. His eyes drooped and his body hung low, defeated, "But enough fun. Let us move on, shall we?"

Kali maneuvered around the clone, her steps matched to precise thrusts that wove into a wide, cutting arcs that glanced harmlessly off the cold steel of the void. The clone moved with an unmatched grace and cunning, meeting blow-for-blow as she led Kali in a dance of frivolous violence. Nihilus ran to meet them. He prepared his assault, arm held back, only to find himself thrown to his knees as an overwhelming pressure interrupted his stride. The Emissary looked on with a wicked grin.

Kali was left to the amused mercy of the void flesh made whole. She paused, withdrawing from the melee to look back at the Avatar who fought against the same aggression as the pontifex. Energy streamed from the last Magi while the tear pulsed, its presence now consuming the light of the sun. It seemed unnatural, a rip in space, a terrible harbinger of the end of all things. Yet, to her, it felt familiar. What did Rurik say? Voidborne. The Emissary fed from the world, it drained life and crafted it to its will. If it could take from hers, then maybe she could do the same.

Kali let her senses expand. She tasted their auras. Nihilus, drained, offered little. The clone revolted her, while the Avatar's essence made her thirst with desire, yet it all paled to the brilliance of the void itself. Decadent, tempting, it called to her, it pulled her into its embrace. Why not indulge? She drank. Deeply.

"What are you doing?!" The Emissary glowered. The clone closed, wearing a scowl, it lifted the spear to strike. Kali redirected her fury. She felt the whole of the chamber, the warm stone of the walls smooth against her fingers despite the distance. She clenched her fist. An avalanche of stone wrenched itself from its foundations as a section of the wall broke to her whim. Drawn to her will she pulled the stone debris toward her. They sailed to their target, a mass of rubble collapsing on the clone, crushing it.

The clone writhed under the weight. It twitched, one exposed arm spasming as if trying to attack her.

An invisible force rammed into Kali's back. She exhaled, the wind wrenched from her chest. Her muscles tensed. The Emissary gripped her, she knew. Her body lifted from the ground, legs going slack, nothing responding to her will. Kali fought, her senses clashing against a will beyond hers.

"I will not be disobeyed!" The Emissary spoke erratically, her voice strained and wild. "Give me what I want!"

Kali's body wrenched to face the Emissary. Pressure tightened around her neck, wringing air from her lungs. The Avatar lay prone and struggled to right itself. Nihilus roared from the same stress, his red garments ripped to shreds as he fought to free himself. And Niati? She struggled to stand. Bone pierced her leg.

"I am ascended. You are nothing. A parasite, a mistake."

A shadow crept from behind the Emissary. Another trick. Even with the aid of their own deific figure they did not stand a chance. What now? Rays of warmth bled from the open ceiling. Did the Sunlord care for their plight? No. They were alone, and they would die alone. The shadow flickered and Kali caught sight of a wide-brimmed hat. What?

The edge of a thin blade burst from the Emissary's chest. Her eyes widened at the rupture. Luc clung to the hilt of Niati's rapier. From the corner of her vision Kali saw beads collide with the remaining Magi and ice encased its corpse. Niati screamed for Nihilus. Free now, he launched a wave of power that broke the Magi to pieces.

The Emissary knocked Luc aside with a burst of power and turned toward Kali, who landed on her feet as the pressure abated. Pieces of her face cracked and flaked. They drifted from her to the Voidtear, revealing a pale, sickly white beneath. Wounded, without support, the Emissary showed her weakness. Kali sent her senses against her foe. Powerful, ancient, familiar. She lapped up the succulence of its aroma, shining and decadent like the Void itself.

Kali fed.

"No! I will not be–no. Please."

The Emissary shrunk as more of her cracked and bled away, consumed by the tear. She railed against Kali's power but to little avail. Kali's presence swelled. It dwarfed the Emissary. The harder she fought the faster she tired until her struggle ceased entirely.

Now is the time. Destroy her.

Kali met the Avatar's gaze. Deep, silver, resolved. She saw a piece of Rurik in that expression.

She dug. Deeper than the bliss of her sustenance, through the vibes of power, deep to the soul itself. A vast emptiness lay there. A hollow, utter loneliness. From a distance Kali saw a projection of warped flesh and bone, structured to look human but cold and distant, wreathed in shadow. Kali inserted herself into the space, her visage appearing within.

•   •   •

Kali towered over the cowering soul of a god. It, a shriveled, alien-thin husk of a corpse, shied away, refusing to look at her. She shed golden light that misted with darkness along the edges. Here, silence prevailed. No howling winds, no desperate forces or vibrant hum of otherworldly powers. Only stillness. Death eclipsed the horizon. Falling stars and a cracked, purple sky wilted to a hollow end.

"All I wanted was my love back," It spoke, its voice weak and distant, absent the echoes of power it once held.

"What are you?" Kali startled at the strength of her words. They bellowed into infinity and cast strands of golden light into the faded soul.

"Me?" It cackled. Its sunken eyes lit up as the jagged, torn corners of its mouth curled into a sadistic grin. "I was forever. Untouched by time, ascended. But it is not me you need fear now. The others will know. One of us you beat before, but never this, never destroyed. They will know. And they are stronger. They will come for you, sweet Arkalis, and they will not show you mercy."

It laughed. Shrill, horrid screeching leapt from its decrypt throat. It wailed and shuttered. Kali watched in horror. She envisioned the obsidian blade and it appeared in her hand. In a single blow she cleaved the creature and severed its life from the Void.

•   •   •

The world returned in quiet gusts of terrestrial winds. Kali lorded over the Emissary as large pieces of it slid free and fluttered away. Slowly, she effervesced in totality. It took seconds. The amorphous, black cloud that stalked the god's physical body scattered along with the rest of her as the Voidtear shuttered. Its edges splintered then thinned, whatever mass it possessed winking out of existence, leaving behind a thin wound in space.

With its departure Kali felt a weight lift. Her shoulders straightened with a series of solid pops. She released the obsidian blade. It clattered against the floor; red, violent runes losing their color.

Fresh air wafted in from the gaping holes in the chamber's exterior. It brought warmth with it that spread to her chest. Luc was the first to stand. He ran to the pile of discarded robes, careful to test the vestments with the toe of his boots. Kali choked up a chuckle.

"She's gone," She spoke with surprising strength. Neither weary nor worn, Kali stretched with a refreshed sigh.

"You're sure?" Luc hesitantly kicked at the pile again.

"I am." Kali smiled at the wetlander. "How many times is that now?"

"Times what?"

"Times I owe you my life."

"Oh." Luc blushed and glanced about the room as if disturbed by her attention. "Three?"

"Arkalis!" Niati's pained voice drew her gaze. The captain limped her way over to Nihilus who lay on his back, still. Kali ran to his side. With her senses alert she felt his life ebb. Weak, but alive. It tasted sweet. No. Kali reached into the recesses of her mind, releasing the thread of her powers. Her vision returned to its mortal gaze, no longer processing the world as a means of sustenance.

Scars and burns marred Nihilus' face and arms. Little was left of his tunic and he bore only half a head of hair with parts of his shawl fused to his skin. Niati fared better, but not well. An arm hung limp at her side while she dragged her broken leg, her hair loose and scattered, absent most its decorative trinkets.

"He's barely alive."

Niati joined her. She lowered herself with a grunt, blue eyes half closed from exhaustion. Luc followed.

"I think there's little for us to do." Luc said.

"*You've done enough.*" The Avatar's layered voice surrounded them. It appeared within the group, diminished, yet still divine. It extended a palm. At its behest winds swirled from it to Nihilus. His body quaked. In a desperate gulp he inhaled then settled, his eyes flickering. The worst of his burns faded to lesser wounds.

"*He will be fine. Give it time.*"

The chill of an empty sky drifted into the tower's open plateau. Kali shivered, the absent power succumbing her body to the standard needs of mortality. She rubbed her arms in an effort to generate warmth–her chest clad in little more than Ymatsu's bandages. Luc, nearby, slid his arms out of his coat and handed it over.

"Here. Was always too big for me."

Kali accepted it wordlessly, donning the warm, surprisingly comfortable patchwork. It fit, as if made for her.

"I know we just fought a voided uh–Void God together and all, but is now a bad time to ask who the fuck you are?" Kali snarked, snuggling into her new attire. She managed to stop shivering.

"What I am," the Avatar said.

"Excuse me?"

"You want to ask what I am."

"Fair point." Kali rolled her eyes. "So what are you?"

"The Avatar of Chaos."

"Of course you are. That clears it all up."

"Not to be rude," Luc added, his head swiveling as he examined what remained of the chamber, "But you wouldn't have a way down, would you, Lord Avatar?"

"I do. First, we chat."

A Letter from Ilya Iskarion

ARKALIS. My sweet, sweet daughter. You will never know me, I fear. The sunpriests tell me I may yet rally, and your father is so very hopeful, but I know I will not see the new year. My only regret is that I will not live to discover the woman you will become. Whether you will mother children or study poetry and art. Denrik will certainly force a sword into your hands. Your potential is limitless. I would hope that you are happy and whatever you choose to do with your life, it brings joy to you and those around you. Care for your people, my darling girl. Care for yourself.

Chapter 32
The Master of Haven

A RMED COMBAT with a god terrified her less than this
assembly. Kali reeled at the assortment of soldiers and
diplomats. To her left stood a full contingent of Cavari
gunners and knights, Lesandre and his father at the head. On her right
a line of Lindrisi legionaries and warcasters flanked the consul. And
across? A new arrival. Caul Supplicants: a gaggle of turbaned, dark-
skinned men and women in vibrant greens and purples, trimmed
sherwani arrayed with bright sashes over their waists and laden with
gems and jewelry of every sort.

No sweat.

Kali inhaled. The scents of gunpowder and foliage tasted bitter on
her tongue–enhanced now, as everything seemed to be. She perceived
every imperfection of the garden. The trampled flower beds from the
Cavari siege, the cracked, shattered mirrors above, the debris that
rained from the altercation at the tower's zenith. A crowd of Haven
locals gathered at the outskirts of the garden. They stretched from one
leg of the tower to another, hundreds of curious bystanders held in the
throes of fear as they wondered at the fate of their overlords.

She wondered that herself. Two mages were unaccounted for.
Either dead or smart enough to hide. She mused at her own lack of
wisdom. Hiding, at this point, seemed a less terrifying course of action.
A warm, quiet fire and a bottle of spiced wine. For the briefest of

moments she indulged her imagination. The toughest decision she wanted to make was whether she preferred a woman or man's touch.

"I think they're waiting for you." Luc nudged Kali's shoulder. Her retinue contained a sad showing of wounded, exhausted allies. Nihilus leaned on Leinani for support, his burns less severe, but a permanent scar scored the right side of his body from his neck to his chest. Niati stood under her own power. The Avatar managed to heal her leg, if just enough to make use of it.

The Avatar. Its words swirled in her mind. Emissaries, souls, stars, and realms. Order and Chaos in perfect, brutal harmony. And Rurik. Kali sniffed, her eyes watering at the thought of him. She cleared her throat, surprised at the weight of its volume.

"What of the Magi?" Oswin spoke with that calm confidence of his. He projected his voice so that the assembly could hear.

"They're dead." Unintentionally loud, her voice carried a raw strength.

"Dead?" Silsara wielded a spatha, unsure of its grip. "Where are my warcasters? They will verify this."

"They're dead too." Kali eyed the consul who visibly struggled to hold the gaze without flinching. Did she command such fear? The others assembled appeared weary, damaged. She did not possess a single scratch. Though hardly a grandiose sight. Luc's patchwork coat and the pilfered Magi's pants bemoaned her status, and after all her adventures she remained barefoot.

"I speak for Aklesia," Nihilus vouched, his voice little more than a whisper, "She speaks truth, you need not doubt her admissions." The consul nodded. Good enough.

"And what is the meaning of all this?!" A frustrated baritone joined the conversation; a Supplicant, one hand on a talwar at his hip. He sported a thick, bushy beard with many creases above his brow. "Why attack the tower? Who are you?"

"Arkalis." A tired boredom filling her tone. "Why attack the tower? For power. Wealth. To fight tyranny?" She snorted. "No clue. You'll have to ask them." She gestured at the grand duke and consul respectively. "What I do know is that your Magi were infested by the Void. That we, this place, everyone is in greater danger than we know."

The Supplicant spat. "The Void? What blasphemy is this?"

"It is no such thing." Oswin folded his hands behind his back as he spoke. "This is a duchess of Ilvicar." He winked at her. She considered consuming his soul for the briefest flickers of temptation. "With her stands Pontifex Nihilus of Lindras, Soatu Niati Kanhe of Nukati, and a Temple Priest of Vari, of Aenia, I believe. A powerful list of titles with varied motivations." A priest? Kali shot a quick look at Luc who flushed a bright shade of red. "I find it difficult to deny a collaboration such as this."

With Oswin's insistence the Supplicant silenced. Silsara sheathed her blade.

"As you were saying, your grace?"

Whatever game Oswin played Kali found herself grateful.

"The Void." She exhaled, gazing over the nobles and knights and their soldiers. Unmatched political power. She recalled the words of the Avatar.

•   •   •

"You must convince them."

The Avatar regained its stature as time passed. Kali worked to keep her senses at bay, recalling the Avatar's presence and how it tasted.

"How? These are people of power, they only believe in furthering their ambitions." Kali folded her arms over the patched coat. "Consuls, dukes. They won't listen."

The Avatar stood in the center of the now open chamber. It basked in the light of the sun, its eyes cast up, staring into the source itself with little ill effect. Niati held Nihilus who gained some kind of consciousness while Luc punted some rubble with his boot.

"What do you need of them? The soul cares not for your title. Their power is perceived. What remains if you strip those that follow? A lone creature in a sandbox of gold. Convince the people. Bring them the truth of their institutions' corruption. We must draw out the emissaries as we did here."

"We?"

"We. You and me, Arkalis. I need allies. This realm teeters on the brink of annihilation and we must stop it."

"How is that my responsibility?" Kali groaned. She rubbed her temple between her thumb and forefinger, her brow furrowed. "What about what I want?"

"While you yet live, it is your responsibility. There is no choice to make, there is simply a thing you must do. If you do not rise to the occasion, then you resign yourself and anything you've ever loved to oblivion."

"Fuck."

"Indeed."

•　•　•

"The Void has returned," Kali said, her voice a clarion call that washed over the gathered masses. "Worse, it never left." A hush took the otherwise cacophonous crowd. With the events of the day and no one to counter her those words took hold. "The Magi, the masters of Haven, were puppets. And there's more of them."

A worried mumble spread throughout the crowd. Some skeptical. Most worried. Alarmed. She listened. A cool wind blew in from the port. It traveled inland, buffeted by the tower until it snaked in, into the section they now inhabited; the breeze brought her a stillness. No whispers. No static. Only her own thoughts.

"More? Void Gods? This cannot be so! The Litanies teach us–"

"Nothing." Oswin's steel tongue silenced the bearded Supplicant. "Written what? Ten centuries ago?" Seven, Kali thought. The Avatar made it a point to fill her in on minor historical details. The duke continued. "I've had tax reports barely survive contact with a second scribe. You're not foolish enough to not believe human error hasn't butchered the details? Are you?"

Grand Duke fucking Adirian. Ally? Kali reeled at the possibility.

"Forgive, Supplicant." Ishta, upright now from Leinani's interference, approached the delegations from the Lindrisi side. "I am Ishta of Caul, paladin of Pontifex Aluntir. We fought a creature such as this. A denizen of the pit. Now is not a time of doubt."

"Need more convincing?" Oswin rolled his eyes. "We're in the presence of heroes." Lesandre's skeptical gaze flicked to his father. He caught Kali's attention, his expression plain: *be careful*, it warned. "What is more pressing is that Haven stands without a ruler. In the face of this horror the world's grandest city needs leadership. Guidance."

"Bah!" Silsara interjected. "Posturing for power so soon, Cavari?" Soldiers on all sides tensed. Kali felt for the thread of power. It waited at her behest.

"Be calm, consul. I'll spare you a war for now. My posturing is not for myself but only to honor the agreement of all conquests. To the victor go the spoils."

Kali's eyes widened. A ray cast itself upon her visage, the sun cresting its zenith at the onset of full light. From the tower she could make out a vague shape, a friend, a god. Crafty bastard.

"Duchess Iskarion no more. Should she renounce her title I will support her ascendance as Master of Haven. Little else would befit such a champion, hm?"

For whatever reason, no one argued. Oswin folded his arms, waiting.

"I can support this. For now," Silsara added.

"The Supplicants will not challenge this."

"The Church of the Sun agrees." Nihilus, the pontifex, approved as the Faiths' ranking official.

"Arkalis?" Lesandre spoke softly, curious. "What do you say?"

Maybe that light hit her in the right way. Maybe the adrenaline dulled her mind. Nothing remained for her in Iskvar. And here? Master of Haven had a nice ring to it.

"Shit," Kali said. Too late to back out now.

THE END

Epilogue

NIHILUS CURSED under his breath. His leg cracked with a tumultuous pop, sending him to his mattress with a groan. Despite the efforts of the sunpriests and the Avatar of Chaos itself his body burned as it did atop the Tower of Magi. The travel south did him no favors. Four days ride ached in his joints. Worth it, at least, to be at his estate within Lindorum.

His chambers welcomed him with soft velvets, red and purple silks, soft blankets on gentle furniture. Of all the discomforts he most regretted the loss of his bed. Large enough for four, he intended to spend the next few weeks on its most luscious surface. Feathered pillows, thick, gentle fur blankets. Nihilus mused at the prospect of comfortable, wonderful sleep as he slid off a boot and tossed it aside with a study thud. Ah. Lindrisi silk rugs. He curled his toes into the material, a jovial smile spreading over his face. Half his face.

Burnt by Void Fire. Truly, he could ascend to the legends of all the great pontifices.

A quiet rasp drew his ire. He spared a glare at the cherry oak door of his chambers. Were his orders complicated? *Do not disturb me unless Yaros teeters on the brink of annihilation.* Clear. Concise.

"Enter." He managed a full volume response. All the more difficult these days. The door jostled open and Nihilus removed his second boot, discarding it by the other. His attendant, an aged priest, a Xyran, black-skinned and wrinkled from years of tending a civilian flock, shuffled inside. Nihilus opened the small cold box beside his bed and fished out a bottle of wine, removing the cork with a thumb.

"Yes, Daku?"

"Faithful, I apologize, I know you wished to be undisturbed."

"That is no longer possible," Nihilus said, pouring two glasses of wine. May as well relish the company. "Come. Tell me of your health."

"Faithful, I would not have disturbed, lest to follow your command." Daku shifted, uncomfortable. A white, stubble beard did little to mask his hesitation.

"Does Yaros face its immediate end?" He grinned despite himself. The old fool took his duties too seriously. It prevented him from taking a mate, from birthing children. Instead, he opted to oversee the well-being of a self-important fool.

"Sorry, Faithful." Daku removed an object from a set of faded white robes. Plain, they held only a single starburst. A simple garb for a simple man. He extended a mask to Nihilus who looked on with humor. A mask? What foolishness? "This appeared here some five days ago."

"Appeared? What is—" Nihilus snatched the mask from Daku's arthritic hands and turned it over. The brand of a dawning sun was etched into the forehead, its edges hazy with a featureless face in the center. Fading Dawn. Aluntir. Ishta informed them of the demon beneath Iskvar, yet she retreated too early to know the fate of her pontifex. He knew now. Dead.

"You said it appeared here? In the estate?"

"Yes, Faithful. On the doorstep."

"Why here? It should go to the Hierophant." A blue flash caught his attention. Around the eyes. Aluntir left a message. "Daku."

"Yes, Faithful?"

"Fetch us more wine, yes?"

Nihilus put on the mask.

About the Author

Gregory's first story was a detective short with only dialog. Despite his mother telling him he should really reconsider his life goals, he summarily ignored her and doubled down to accomplish his dreams of conning people into paying him for those very same words. Now, he works as a professional nerd, writing adventure modules and mechanics for TTRPGs, while obsessing over second worlds that make it into fanciful stories that tend to favor swords. Most of his success is owed to his wife, who outclasses him in just about every way, but still insists he's actually good at this and he may be starting to believe her.

Note From Gregory Wunderlin

Word-of-mouth is crucial for any author to succeed. If you enjoyed *The Soul of Chaos*, please leave a review online—anywhere you are able. Even if it's just a sentence or two. It would make all the difference and would be very much appreciated.

Thanks!
Gregory Wunderlin

We hope you enjoyed reading this title from:

www.blackrosewriting.com

Subscribe to our mailing list – *The Rosevine* – and receive **FREE** books, daily deals, and stay current with news about upcoming releases and our hottest authors.
Scan the QR code below to sign up.

Already a subscriber? Please accept a sincere thank you for being a fan of Black Rose Writing authors.

View other Black Rose Writing titles at
www.blackrosewriting.com/books and use promo code
PRINT to receive a **20% discount** when purchasing.